Books should be returned or renewed by the
last date stamped above

**KENT
ARTS &
LIBRARIES**

CHARTER MARK

Awarded for excellence

OPEN ACCESS

**Kent
County
Council**
ARTS & LIBRARIES

Winston Graham is the author of more than thirty novels, which include the highly successful *Poldark* series. His novels have been translated into seventeen languages and six have been filmed. Three television series have been made of the *Poldark* novels and shown in twenty-two countries.

Winston Graham lives in Sussex. He is a fellow of the Royal Society of Literature and in 1983 was awarded the OBE.

THE UGLY SISTER

The Napoleonic Wars have ended as Emma
Spry tells her fascinating story . . . One side
of her face marred at birth, Emma grows
up without affection, her elegant mother on
the stage, her father killed in a duel before
she was born. Her beautiful sister, Tamsin,
is four years the elder, and her mother's
ambitions lie in Tamsin's future, and in her
own success. A shadow over their childhood
is the ominous butler, Slade. Then there
is predatory Bram Fox, with his dazzling
smile; Charles Lane, a young engineer; and
Canon Robartes, relishing rebellion in the
young Emma, her wit, her vulnerability,
encouraging her natural gift for song.

Books by Winston Graham
Published by The House of Ulverscroft:

WINSTON GRAHAM

THE UGLY SISTER

Complete and Unabridged

CHARNWOOD
Leicester

First published in Great Britain in 1998 by
Macmillan
London

First Charnwood Edition
published 1999
by arrangement with
Macmillan Publishers Limited
London

British Library CIP Data

Graham, Winston, *1909* –
    The ugly sister.—Large print ed.—
Charnwood library series
    1. Birth injuries—England—Cornwall—Fiction
    2. Romantic suspense novels
    3. Large type books
    I. Title
    823.9′12 [F]

    ISBN 0–7089–9065–7

Published by
F. A. Thorpe (Publishing) Ltd.
Anstey, Leicestershire
Set by Words & Graphics Ltd.
Anstey, Leicestershire
Printed and bound in Great Britain by
T. J. International Ltd., Padstow, Cornwall

This book is printed on acid-free paper

FOR
ANN HOFFMANN

This is a novel, but it is based on houses which still exist, and is concerned with one family, the Spry's. I am extremely grateful to Nat and Valentia Spry-Grant-Dalton, of Place House, for helping me with their reminiscences and putting at my disposal diaries which cover the first half of the nineteenth century. They are not, of course, in any way responsible for the outcome.

It would be undesirable to draw lines between the characters who really existed and those who have lived only in the author's imagination; but I hope I have not dealt unfairly with either.

Book One

Book One

1

I

I was born on 6 December 1812, the exact day, my uncle once told me, when the remnants of Napoleon's Grand Army reached Vilna on its retreat from Moscow. I think of myself as Cornish but I was born in Devon, in the village of Clyst Honiton, off a stagecoach a few miles before we reached Exeter.

My mother was not Cornish but, my father having just died in a duel, she was coming to spend Christmas with his relatives at Place House, St Anthony. My name is Emma Spry and I have an elder sister, Thomasine, who was aged four at the time. My mother was heavily pregnant when we took the coach from the Angel Inn in Islington, but she did not expect the pains to start until at least the middle of January. In the event what she called 'the accursed jolting' was too much for her, and on the second day, right at the end of the second day, she found she could go no farther.

So we were put off near Clyst Honiton and taken in at a villainous dirty hostel called the Pig & Goat and a midwife sent for. My mother tells me it was terrible weather: rain and a gale of wind, and few folk were about, though darkness had only just closed on the wild afternoon. With Thomasine holding tight to her sweaty hand, she was led up a corkscrew staircase where the whiskery woman who kept the tavern was scraping flint on tinder to light a tallow candle. A low raftered room came into view with two trestle beds, torn hessian curtains, a pitcher and ewer on a stool, rain pattering on paper in the unlighted fire grate; a rustling in another corner where a brown rat was making his exit. There had been a remission of the pains while she disembarked, but they began again as the coach horses' hooves clopped and slithered on the cobbles outside, partly drowned in the tantrum of the gale.

An hour later I was born. My mother knew there was a woman in the room and assumed it to be the midwife, but no one knows whether it was the innkeeper's wife or this watery eyed scrofulous newcomer who was responsible for the damage done to my face as I came into the world. There is no reason to suppose that there was anything peculiar about the birth, any let or hindrance which would have compelled a human agency to attempt to assist a normal presentation. The so-called midwife left in the middle of the following day and was not seen again, so it is likely it was her fault.

The fact remains that my looks were marred for life.

II

My father's family was a landed and wealthy one. Place House — some say Place is an abbreviation of Palace — was originally a monastery, the

4

residence of a prior and two black canons. At the Dissolution it passed after some vicissitudes into the hands of the Spry family, who had lived there ever since.

They had a naval tradition. In the side chapel of the church adjoining the house were memorials to one Spry after another who had been 'Admiral of the Red' or 'Rear Admiral of the White'. My father had gone against tradition and became a courtier. 'Equerry of the Queen', my mother said, but I have come to take some of her statements with a pinch of salt. Details of the duel in which he died were never given to his daughters, but my uncle Davey, who could be crotchety on occasion, once muttered to me that my father had been 'killed in a drunken brawl'.

Neither my uncle nor my aunt Anna quite approved of my mother, who was an actress. It became clear, though I do not think they ever said so openly, that they thought brother Aubrey had married beneath him in wedding someone 'on the stage'. Claudine Hall, to give her her maiden and stage name, was about thirty at the time of my birth, tall, sharpnosed and elegant. She had a good presence and a good voice; but I do not quite know how we contrived to continue to live at Place House long after the first month had expired, and indeed eventually to consider it our true and only home. Possibly because it was so little inhabited. The house had a separate wing at the back which was not used, and we came to look on this as our own domain.

Admiral Davey Spry and his wife had four

children of their own: their eldest daughter, Anna Maria, who was fifteen or sixteen and was at school in London; Mary, a year or so younger, who was quiet and simple-natured and had a governess in the house; then came a son, Samuel, who was ten and was at school at Dartmouth; and the youngest boy, Desmond, who was seven and would shortly be sent away to school.

Place House is on the Roseland Peninsula. It faces out to the tidal Percuil Creek, on the opposite side from St Mawes; so while St Mawes looks east and south, Place House looks north. It is sheltered from the winter gales, and the water that slides up the creek and laps against its lawns is usually as placid and as reflective as a lake. You could call it a big gentleman's house, three-storeyed — the second floor being attics lit by dormer windows in the roof — with an unusual spire, or more properly a narrow pyramid above the central hall. The public rooms faced the lawns which ran down to the quay and the creek. Behind the public rooms ran a narrow passage, used by the servants, so that they could attend to the needs of the family in any room without passing through the other rooms.

The wing we came to live in and almost count as our own ran backwards from the main hall, had four bedrooms, a parlour, a sewing room and a nursery. It had been unoccupied for some time and was in poor repair: rain dripped into the bedrooms, wallpaper peeled, carpets were threadbare, dry rot was settling in some of the floorboards.

6

But this condition was pristine compared to the condition of the church to which the house was joined. There were no other big houses nearby, and the congregation, such as it was, was made up of farmers and smallholders who lived in cottages and cultivated the fertile fields of that gentle peninsula; some fisherfolk who waited for the pilchards and trawled the shallow seas for lobster and crab — and the Sprys, who had direct access to the church by opening an oak door in the north drawing room and walking right in.

Much of the roof of the church had fallen in, the altar had been wrecked by a fallen beam during a winter gale, some of the bench ends had been looted, and when the parson came, the Reverend Arthur Miller from St Gerrans, who also had the cure of St Anthony and St Just, he read prayers and preached from the belfry, which had so far stood the assault of wind and weather and was reasonably sound.

When I was old enough to sum up the situation I used to wonder that a family of such considerable wealth should so neglect what was virtually a part of their house. Could it be that they were all unbelievers? From their conversation this seemed very unlikely.

In those earliest years there were few Sprys about. Even in the school holidays the children more often than not stayed at Tregolls in Truro, another big house that belonged to the family, from which base communication with their own kind was much easier than from the Roseland peninsula. This was particularly true at

Christmas and Easter, when the Assembly Balls took place. My uncle Davey was the admiral in charge of Plymouth Dock, and his visits home were frequently cut short because he had bought and was rebuilding a third house in the county, just off the main coaching road between Falmouth and Truro. The reason for this did not become apparent until I was ten years of age and deemed old enough to be told.

The one constant was Aunt Anna. She had had her children late, and was 'delicate'. She slept in the bedroom immediately above the north drawing room and therefore one of her walls was common to the church. When she was not well she lived most of her time in this room; when she was well she spent the day in a rocking chair in the south drawing room looking out over the creek. Her great pleasure was cards. When she was alone or with her companion, Elsie Whattle, she would play solitaire, bezique or sometimes backgammon, but when she could find companions she played whist. Hers was not a social snobbery, it was a card-playing snobbery. Only those who played well were invited and only those who could afford to play for the stakes she regularly played for. So whenever she was well some eight or a dozen of her friends were entertained in turn and one came to know them all by sight or by name.

My aunt was a stout woman with wispy hair, short-sighted friendly eyes and a perpetual sniff. There was frequently a hunt for her handkerchief, which she always sat on for luck when playing whist and thereafter lost.

She was intensely superstitious in ways I was not to realize for a long time.

My uncle was a trimly built man — as spruce as his wife was untidy. He had a bright complexion, pink at all times but flushing scarlet in his brief tempers. One sometimes thought he might have a skin less than most people. He and my aunt frequently bickered and argued, and it was always easy to tell when he was in the house. A cause of constant disagreement between them was a shiny, muscular friendly black dog called Parish, whom my aunt adored and my uncle, for some reason, hated. When he was away Parish would romp around the house like a jolly schoolboy — though never far from his mistress. When the Admiral was home he was confined to his kennel, or, in the Admiral's eye, should have been. In fact three-quarters of the time he spent in Aunt Anna's bedroom, and when my uncle went in Parish knew his approaching footstep and cowered under the bed.

As a tiny child I crowed and toddled and fell down and cried and picked myself up again and played with my sister and the two bigger children and took everything for granted. I even took for granted my disfigurement, and when my mother shuddered sometimes when she picked me up I took this as a natural tremor on her part that had nothing to do with me. My sister too took my looks for granted: knowing her in later life, I cannot believe she refrained from mentioning them out of delicacy or compassion; they just did not impinge on her as worthy of comment. Perhaps my cousins — both of gentler natures — had been told not to speak of the matter. At least I do not think they ever spoke of it.

I suppose my mother was a very handsome and attractive woman and my sister was already showing hints of the beauty she was to become. Mary and Desmond were also good-looking. No doubt I would have been more acceptable in a family where everyone was plain.

I remember the first time I saw myself in a looking-glass and observed my face in a detached way.

III

The butler was called Slade. He had been a petty officer on board the last two ships the Admiral had commanded. He was a heavy man, light-footed as big men often are. His hair was jet black and tied in a pigtail. Tamsin got into great trouble when she was nine by stealing into a back scullery and surprising him dyeing it. It was a while before I noticed that he lacked the fingertips of his left hand: the half-length fingers ended in nail-less stubs.

He came from the south-east corner of Cornwall and was very prideful about it. 'There's been Slades in Polperro and Looe for centuries,' he would growl, 'long before ever there was Sprys in Place.'

He represented the Admiral when the Admiral was not there. When he *was* there he was useful after dinner in helping his master up the stairs to bed. Slade's arms were tattooed

10

with serpents; he had a plump dun-grey face
— which hid a lot of malice — and walked
with a stoop.

IV

Uncle Davey came and went by coach and by
sea, depending on his destination or where he
had come from. So did most of the produce of
the house. The roads were little more than cart
ruts, narrow, hilly and winding. There was no
town to the east of us nearer than St Austell. To
reach Place House from Truro by road one had
to follow the River Fal upstream and cross the
ford at Tregony at low tide. King Harry Ferry
was served by steep lanes usually slithering in
mud. No one essayed these laborious ways when
the growing port of Falmouth lay across a two-
mile estuary of deep water — only unnavigable
in times of storm.

We were self-contained for most things,
seldom if ever needed meat or eggs or poultry
or vegetables. And boats would call twice a
week with fish, cooking spices, lobsters, soap,
newspapers and miscellaneous luxuries, such as
chocolate and China teas. Once a month a
coal barge would sidle up at high tide until it
grounded, when the bags would be loaded onto
wheelbarrows and carried up to the house. The
coalmen would usually wait then for the next
tide to take them off.

It was on such an occasion that I had my
disfigurement first pointed out to me. The quay,
which was built at the lawn's edge, had a small

pebbly beach on either side of it. One day when the coal barge was unloading I walked down with Thomasine and a maid called Sally Fetch, and three ragged boys were on the right-hand beach watching and hoping for some spillage of the coal; they whistled at Tamsin, who already had a head of golden curls. Fetch took Tamsin's hand and guided her away, but I stayed watching the unloading, finger in mouth. One of the boys shouted: 'What's wrong wi 'ee, maid? Been in a scuff, 'ave 'ee?' The other urchins jeered us out of earshot, and then splashed away as fast as they could as Slade came ominously down the path.

Next morning — or maybe it was two or three mornings later — I carried a hand looking-glass over to the window in my mother's room. I looked at the dark-haired round-faced fat little girl I knew to be myself. My unique self. Someone belonging to me alone, from whom I could never never escape.

I must have taken after my father, for my eyes were very dark; but the lid of the left eye was drawn down an inch or more and the eye was permanently bloodshot. Further down on the same side my cheek had a deep scar which might have come from a musket ball. And there was a stain on my neck, part hidden by the lace collar of my dress.

That I recognized was Emma Spry, and other children would laugh and point at her. And grown-ups too. I was an outcast.

V

My mother was absent for quite long periods continuing her stage career. She played at the Richmond Theatre, at Drury Lane, at the Haymarket, and sometimes went on tour. Once in a while she took the lead, more often lesser parts.

I remember a conversation when I followed her into Aunt Anna's bedroom and heard my aunt say: 'D'ye have to do that? It is showing your legs to the common people, *and* your name is in small print. Your children are growing up and you hardly see 'em.'

'Thanks to you and Davey we have this lovely home,' said my mother, 'but I'm hard set to make ends meet. I pay Davey what little I can, but I need more just for the girls. And I shall get bonuses for extra performances.'

'Well, yes,' said Aunt Anna, sniffing and sucking her top teeth defensively, 'the Admiral is not without money, and I brought him a fat dowry; but he has many calls on his purse. There's no depth to the soil around here and the farmers can hardly fetch enough out of it to pay their rents. When he retires he will certainly give up the house in Plymouth Dock. I was urging on him the other day the need for retrenchment.'

I looked up at my mother's face and saw a shadow pass across it.

'It means a deal to me,' she said, 'that Thomasine and Emma have a settled home so far away from the city. That I have to thank you for, Anna. Of course there is much warmth and friendship in the world of the theatre, but also much squalor. Aubrey, as you know, died in debt. He spent the allowance Davey sent him on drink and women, and I kept the family. It is no difference with him gone; I still have to work.'

'A pity you have had no time to learn whist,' said Aunt Anna.

'Do you never persuade the Admiral to take a hand?'

'Oh,' with a sniff, 'the Admiral cannot concentrate. Put him in a chair before a card table and he will grunt and wriggle his posterior as if he had the worms, and frown and grunt again and trump his partner's ace. I do not know how he controls men when he cannot even control himself.'

* * *

Place was never exactly quiet: with four children growing up in it and eight indoor servants supervised by the saturnine Slade, there was constant movement and activity, but when Aunt Anna was having one of her illnesses, the noise was muted. Parish, who had clearly been trained as a puppy that barking was forbidden, still snuffled and snorted as he padded up and down corridors or wriggled his way through a door that had been left ajar. Only when Uncle Davey arrived did he make himself scarce.

Sometimes the head of the house would come in in a bad mood; he would shout at the servants, swear at Slade, quarrel with Aunt Anna, saying the house was like a jakes, the walled garden neglected, the lawns a disgrace; and everyone would tremble. But at other times, especially if he brought one of his elder children with him (particularly Anna Maria, the eldest and favourite), he would have half the house laughing. His own laughter, Aunt Anna said, would no doubt be taken as a signal for sending out the pilchard boats from St Mawes.

'Beware of him,' Aunt Anna whispered to me once, 'he's a great practical joker. D'ye know what happened on our honeymoon? He put honey in my evening shoes!'

All the time we were growing up Mama would be here for a week or two, then gone off to London or Scotland or Bath. She would seldom tell me when she was going, but kiss me goodnight and the next morning be gone. As she seldom showed me much affection (she doted on Tamsin) I became accustomed to her absences and transferred most of my affection to Sally Fetch, who seemed to show less aversion than most adults for my battered face. In no time, it often seemed to me, Mama would be back again smelling of new perfumes and fresh clothes — for in spite of her protestations she earned good money and freely spent it. She usually travelled by sea, sailing in a 'tin boat', and left the same way. Possibly her experience of coach travel when she was carrying me had put her off land travel when another choice was available. Aunt Anna constantly warned her of the danger of French or Algerian pirates,

15

showing an unbecoming lack of confidence in her husband's ability to keep them out of the Channel.

Not that this was an unwarranted apprehension. The St Anthony in Roseland promontory was specially vulnerable to a raider, as in fact was all of Falmouth. During the war, which ended while I was still a child, the defence of Pendennis Castle overlooking the great harbour had depended solely on the threat of three field cannon which dated from Blenheim; and St Mawes on the other headland had been commanded by a seventy-year-old captain of artillery, with two crippled soldiers and a range of antique musketry to support him. There had also been a battery mounted near Zone Point; but through the last years of the Napoleonic Wars the Sprys had paid for two marines to keep watch for their own defence, since Place House was the only substantial property on this promontory. In time of war a landing there would have proved a considerable embarrassment — most particularly to the Sprys themselves — and however shortlived the occupation, it was likely to have outlived the inhabitants of the house.

Even in peace it was a succulent morsel for corsairs — a place to sack and steal from before vanishing into the night — and the end of the war proper had not pacified everyone. There were plenty of discarded, out-of-work soldiers and dispossessed sailors from a number of countries for the hazard to exist. But I do not remember the two marines, and the only guard we had when I was growing up was the lookout who manned the signal station at the head of the promontory about half a mile from the house.

Once when I was about ten Mama came home for Christmas and stayed on well into the New Year. There was no doubt that she had for some time looked ambitiously at Cornish society, for she must have seen that it would be much more likely to be open to her than London society would ever be. A beautiful woman who knew her manners and brought with her an air of metropolitan sophistication and with Place House as a springboard, Mrs Aubrey Spry would be quickly welcome almost everywhere. But the fact that she was an actress, which had a raffish not quite respectable implication — quite different had she been just a singer — her frequent and haphazard absences, the peculiar unwelcoming circumstances of the house in which she lived, together with her own chronic shortage of money, put a brake on what she had so far been able to do.

But now, evidently better off than usual, she began to go about. Taking the bit between her teeth, she went uninvited to Tregolls in Truro, to meet some of the rest of the Spry family. On her way home she called at the new house, Killiganoon, and discovered why Uncle Davey had bought and rebuilt it.

She invited herself or contrived to get invited to a number of the great houses flanking the River Fal, and the new houses — not so great but large and substantial — being put up along the coast between Falmouth and the Helford River, mainly by the Foxes, a large Quaker family who had settled in the district in recent decades and were making fortunes from the shipping and ancillary trades of that prosperous town.

Possibly too by this time she was beginning to have thoughts for the future of her daughters — or at least one of them — who were growing up and who in course of time she would want to see launched and favourably married. So whenever she could she took us with her, and we met young Foxes, young Boscawens, young Warleggans, young Carclews. Parties were held in the vicinity of Falmouth and Truro, but for me these largely tailed off. During that winter I overheard two of the Carclew boys discussing a party they were going to hold. One said: 'What about the Sprys? Tammy is excellently beautiful.' The other said: 'Oh yes and jolly too. But do we have to have the fat little one? She's so exceeding disfigured and monumentally dull.' 'I'll see what my mother says. Maybe we could have one of 'em without t'other.'

When the invitation came it was for both of us, but at the last minute I developed a severe toothache and could not go.

A succession of ailments began to plague me when other invitations were about to be accepted. Of course Mama soon saw through the deception, but what was she to do — take a miserable daughter with tears of pain streaming down her cheeks? Perhaps, I thought, when I was thankfully alone with Sally Fetch, that Mama and Tamsin were also thankful — to be rid of me and my ugliness while they went to enjoy their party.

2

I

During my childhood changes occurred in Place House, particularly to Aunt Anna. My early memories are of tottering naughtily into the north drawing room when three tables of whist were being played, and being hauled out by Sally Fetch as if I'd wandered into church in the middle of the service. Whist was sacrosanct; whist was played five days out of seven. Aunt Anna never went out to play: it all happened in the house. Sometimes while playing, apart from sitting on her handkerchief for luck, she would smoke a cheroot. The smell of that smoke will bring back my childhood almost more than anything else.

One splendid Christmas Uncle Davey arrived with both Anna Maria and Samuel and we had a gay and noisy time; but it was soon after then, after they had all left, that Aunt Anna had an unusually bad turn and was confined to her bed for three weeks. Slade said she was convinced her two dead children were alive and were coming to see her next week. Whist appointments had to be cancelled. Mary, the younger daughter, who had still not gone away to school, was in constant attendance: she continued to have a governess, though now nineteen.

From this point on it became known in the house that Aunt Anna had gone 'a bit maggoty' — Cook's phrase. For two or three weeks she would be quite normal, playing whist with all the usual determination; then the fancy would take her, and she would be caught wandering about the house looking for Clive and David. Sally Fetch at length explained to me what Cook had told her: Aunt Anna had been childless for six years after they were married; then she had miscarried at five months with twin boys. Of course they had not been christened, but Aunt Anna had given them names in her own mind, and often now referred to them as if they were midshipmen at sea. It was a sign of an onset of one of her turns when she started looking for them.

A nurse was engaged, and between the three of them, her daughter Mary, Elsie Whattle, her personal maid, and the new nurse, Mrs Avery, she was well cared for in her bad times. As the years passed her periods of full lucidity became less frequent: she sniffed more frequently, smoked more cheroots and played whist ever more eccentrically, so that her partners, who did not like to say this to her face, began to invent reasons of temporary illness not to come, just as I invented them not to go out.

Yet there was much pleasure in growing up in such a home, especially in the summer. Apart from the property itself with its orchards, beehives and willow gardens, there were gorgeous walks all round the promontory. A beach called

Cellars which was only a half mile from the house was a favourite for picnics: it was a sandy cove, at one end of which when the tide was out you could search for and sometimes find cowrie shells. Apart from two fish cellars, a large hut was the only building on it, and this was used to store or repair our boats. We sailed in the estuary and landed wherever the fancy took us. We bathed and swam in the sharp sea, laughing and squealing with delight. We walked often as far as Portscatho and down to Porth Beach, which also belonged to the Sprys. We rode ponies and got sunburnt and climbed the rocks and ran down steep slopes and grew up healthy and full of the joy of life.

Even in the winter we were able to be much out of doors, coming home drenched in spray or rain or making the most of the fitful sunshine.

Sometimes Uncle Davey would have a shooting party, for duck or pheasant, or he would go out on his own, when we could follow and join in the excitement. Or he and two or three of the farmers would course hares, and make bets on the outcome. Or if he was in a very good mood he would take us fishing.

Uncle Davey, I presently learned from Fetch, had a mistress, whom he kept at the new house of Killiganoon he had bought for her. Her name was Betsy Slocombe, and she was a farmer's daughter from Manaccan-in-Meneage. The Admiral did not care ever to upset his wife by bringing his lady to Place, nor did he want to have her among his relatives or children at his Truro house. So she lived in comfortable isolation between the two main houses, with five servants to tend her. Uncle Davey seemed to divide his time more or less equally between Plymouth and Killiganoon, with odd forays to Place to see his wife and two children, and spare weeks at Tregolls.

II

If there was a shadow over our childhood — apart from my personal disfigurement — it was the bulky presence of Slade. Without there being very much substance to the apprehension, his mere presence cast a threat. Nobody knew quite what he did all day. Sometimes he would be absent for hours, and then he would abruptly appear, smelling of rum, having been indoors all the time. At the far end of the house under the kitchen were extensive cellars. Here the wine was kept, the coal stored, the potatoes stacked, the apples shelved. Just by the main cellar steps was the well, from which all water had to be drawn to supply the house. It had been the duty of the scullery maids, or a boots boy with the unusual name of German, to fetch up the water as it was needed, but during our time there a suction pump was fitted so that, suitably primed to begin, it would by working the pump handle in the kitchen bring water up a flight and into buckets and a sink.

This first cellar, and the fruit and vegetable and coal cellars, were accessible to all, but beyond that was a locked door to which only Slade (and presumably Uncle Davey) had the key. Like most children, we were inquisitive and would go down there and poke about the shelves and the sacks and the discarded pieces of furniture. Fetch could not enlighten us as to what happened beyond the locked door, how many more cellars there were and what they contained. No one was allowed in. The cellars were not completely underground, and netted and barred slits at the top of the walls let in a weak light. Outside we tried to trace how far these slits could be found in the foundations of the house. The chute in the coal cellar was easy to identify; but beyond that the house ended and so must any light or ventilation.

Tamsin and I began to make up stories about it.

Then one ugly day in November, when the greyness of the scudding clouds outside reduced the normal twilight of the cellars to a greater dark, Slade caught us down there trying the locked door and peeping through the keyhole. In fact Tamsin had found a bit of wire and was experimenting with it to try to pick the lock.

Because I was the smaller and because Slade knew Tamsin was her mother's favourite, he grabbed me. I yelped, partly from the awful shock of being found out and partly from the pain in my arm, for his grip was not tender.

'Caught you, eh? Prying, eh? Meddling, eh? What business 'ave you down here? You deserve a good leathering for this!'

'S-sorry,' said Tamsin, so much the elder in manner and bearing. 'It was a dark day. We were just looking round. We wondered what was in the next cellar.'

Although only a servant, he was the superior servant in the household and in that slanted twilight he looked a very dangerous man.

'Wine,' he snarled. 'That's what. Just wine. And what business is it of yours? We don't like Nosy Parkers round 'ere.'

'But we've seen in the wine cellar,' said Tamsin. 'There's a door beyond.'

'And if there is, what's it to you?'

She shrugged her slim shoulders. 'Nothing of course. It was just that we were wondering.'

I wriggled to get out of his grasp. 'You're hurting me, Slade.'

'Little girls is meant to be 'urt, when they poke their noses. Yes, there's a door beyond and a door beyond that. And it's none of your business what goes on or don't go on. It's mine only, I tell you.'

'Yours?' said Tamsin haughtily. 'Why yours? It all belongs to Uncle Davey. And I'm his niece. It is not for you to own parts of the house.'

His manner changed. He said: 'Look, little Missy.' (It was a form of address he knew Tamsin hated.) 'What's between the Admiral and his old shipmate is none of your business. See? But if you want to know I'll tell you. I'll tell you both. Then it'll be a secret between the three of us, won't it now.'

He smiled, but in the half dark with his pigtail, his bootblack hair, his thick lips, his bluely shaven chin, he looked no less sinister. I freed myself from his grasp and made a move

25

to escape, but he said:

'*Wait*! You wanted to know, so I'll tell ye. When I came here first I 'ad two pretty little daughters. They lived 'ere but they was noisy, bad behaved — a bit like you two — they used to upset the Admiral. In the end he said to me, 'I can't keep 'em, Mr Slade. They're too much trouble. I'm afraid they must go, Mr Slade, my old shipmate. If you don't get rid of 'em you'll have to go yourself.' So I says to myself: Their mother, God rest 'er, has long since gone to be one of the blest above, and I'm sure they'll be pleased to join 'er . . . So one day I shut 'em up in this cellar, the one just beyond the wine cellar, and there they still are.'

He smiled at us again, showing a few yellow teeth.

'There they still are. They've gone rot long since, of course. Their clothes've fallen off and their flesh's fallen off, but the skeletons are there. One day I'll show you. Sometimes too, when the wind's in the right quarter, you can still hear 'em calling and knocking.'

Tamsin, of course, told my mother, who was very upset, and when Uncle Davey called in the following week she complained angrily at Slade's behaviour. To her great annoyance he roared with laughter. It was the sort of laugh Aunt Anna said would be heard in St Mawes. The episode appealed precisely to the Admiral's perverse sense of humour. If not exactly a practical joke of his own devising it was the next best thing, and Slade did not receive the mildest reprimand. Nevertheless Tamsin and I half believed his story, and several times on windy nights we thought we heard the knocking.

As we grew older we were ashamed of having taken Slade seriously, but even so there was never much accord between us and him. And even though we eventually saw it as just a nasty joke, there was enough of the sinister about him to make us feel he wished it had been the truth. He never put his hands on me again, but I never went near him if I could avoid it. And sometimes he would squint at me as if relishing my disfigurement.

III

Of course I was bitter about my appearance. My face might make people wince, but it did not absolve me from the normal feelings of adolescence. I wanted to be pretty — like Tamsin. I wanted to enjoy high spirits — like Tamsin. I wanted young men to look at me as they were now looking at her. That I was fat as well as ugly added gall to the wound. I had a quick enough brain — Fetch said I was *too* sharp — but in social conversation, because of a feeling of inferiority, my tongue suffered paralysis and I could only mutter monosyllables in reply.

My mother had a good singing voice, which was of great value in her work. Tamsin had no voice but I was coming to possess one just like my mother's, only lighter. I would practise it sometimes in one of the empty bedrooms of our back wing where I knew, or thought I knew, no one would hear.

27

I would have given much to have some instrument to strum on — such as the harp that stood in the library — but by the time I was old enough to ask to use it, Aunt Anna was prescribed absolute quiet, and the house went on tiptoe.

When we first came to Place I do not think my mother was invited, or even allowed, to take any part in the management of the property. Slade was in charge and Aunt Anna was around most of the time. Now, with Slade often mildly drunk and Aunt Anna searching for her lost sons, my mother gradually took over the reins. Uncle Davey's aversion for her had quite vanished, and on his monthly visits he would go over the accounts with his sister-in-law and arrange for money to be put in her name for the payment of the servants and the maintenance of the property.

It was when I was about twelve that Aunt Anna twice escaped onto the front lawns in her nightshift, and was only just caught as she was about to plunge into the estuary. The Admiral was summoned from Plymouth, there was a council of war, and a week later Aunt Anna disappeared in a black cab driven by two roan horses. She was going to a home where irrational behaviour was suitably catered for.

I cried, for I had grown fond of the eccentric old lady; she had never shown me anything but kindness, and Fetch said we would never see her again. Everyone in the house was surprised — except perhaps Uncle Davey — when a month later the same black cab drawn by the same two horses appeared in the June evening sunshine and Aunt Anna stepped out, sniffing and smiling and ready to play whist again. She had been put in her place, reality had been firmly distinguished in her mind from fantasy, and for the moment the firm, indeed rough, treatment had done its work. Parish rolled and grovelled and salivated in ecstasy.

IV

I remember very well the day I saw Abraham Fox. It was another June. I had been fifteen in the December.

I wish I could honestly say that I appreciated my luck in having been allowed to grow up in such a beautiful part of the world. Alas, fifteen is not an age when one counts one's blessings, handicaps notwithstanding. I see it in my mind's eye now: but that is looking back.

The tide was full in, a westerly breeze strongly blowing. Small clouds, like puffs of white vapour, drifted before the sun. The river was mottled with white froth where the wind could get at it. From all over the great amphitheatre of Carrick Roads gentle fields, sectionally green and green-grey and green-brown and dotted with darker trees, ran down to the dancing water. Ships' sails, white and multicoloured, moved against the theatrical backdrop of Falmouth town's grey climbing streets and crowded jetties. Nearer by and sheltered from the breeze St Mawes warmed itself in the intermittent sun.

It was mid-afternoon, and I was on the lawn

pretending to admire the shrubbery but really looking for a ball I had lost the day before, when a small boat with a single sail and a single occupant luffed its way gently towards the quay, the sail rattled down and a man looped a rope over a bollard and jumped ashore.

I had never, I thought, seen anyone so beautiful. Later I was to realize he was not beautiful at all but had the sort of brilliant masculine looks that outdo the Shelleys of this world. Although I didn't then know his name, he at once reminded me of a fox. People have written of foxy good looks, but that was not it at all. It was his expression: deepset glinting dark eyes, immensely alert, predatory, laughter always in them, but laughter with a purpose, expressing not humour but appreciation of life and of his own sense of vigorous intention.

'Day to you, lady,' he said. 'Permit me to come ashore?'

He had already done this, and it was not likely I should object. Anyway his brilliant white smile in a dark face froze my tongue. Dark, he was very dark; could have been a Latin yet clearly was not. Probably deeply Cornish. Wore his hair longish, inclined to fall over his forehead and to be impatiently brushed back. White frilled shirt open at neck, tight drill trousers, sandals over bare feet. He was looking at me.

'Wind's freshening from nor-west. I'll have to take care I'm not embayed.' He looked around. 'Agreeable house. Are you a Spry?'

I couldn't answer.

He said: 'You Miss Tamsin's sister?'

I couldn't answer.

He laughed. 'My name's Abraham Fox. Bram is what people call me. Bram for short. What's your name?'

There was no one else in sight. Not even a servant.

'*Are* you Miss Tamsin's sister?'

'Yes.'

'Guessed as much. She told me she had one.'

(What else had she said?)

'Didn't she say your name was Eunice?'

'Emma — '

'Ah, yes. Well, Emma, I'll not eat you. Nice as you are to look at. It is such a gallant day I thought I'd call. Know you if Miss Tamsin is in?'

'I'm . . . ' I said. 'I'm not sure.' Suddenly I saw a friendly familiar figure in the distance. 'Fetch will know. Fetch!'

I stared across at two barges dredging for sand in St Mawes harbour. In fact I knew where everyone was. Uncle Davey was in Plymouth. Aunt Anna was in bed. My mother was learning a new part. Thomasine was stitching a dress. Mary was with Aunt Anna, Desmond was riding with his tutor. (I should have been reading French.)

Sally came up, and I asked her to acquaint my mother and sister that they had a visitor.

As she walked away, he said: 'Fetch . . . Do you have another maid called Carry?'

His laughter was so infectious that I almost joined in. But his laughter went on too long.

'People make fun of my name too,' he said. 'Did you ever play 'Is Mr Fox at home?' '

'No.'

'One day I'll show you, Miss Emmie. A pretty little game. 'Where a Fox preaches, take care of the geese.' However, I'm sure you're no goose, Emmie.'

'Emma!'

'Ask pardon. I'm sure my foolish jokes annoy you. Can see it by the rise and fall of your blouse. How long have you lived here?'

'All my life.'

'That's not so very long, is it. Seventeen years?'

'A little less.' I knew he was trying to flatter me.

'Indeed. Your other sister has recently married?'

'My cousin.'

'Who?'

'You must mean my cousin Anna Maria.'

'Ah. Well yes. I expect I do. She has married well, hasn't she? A Carlyon of Tregrehan.'

'He has married well too!'

'No doubt, no doubt.' He considered me. 'The Admiral is well found. He seems to have houses everywhere . . . Ah, here comes Fetch and Carry. She looks not neither to the right nor to the left but proceeds apace towards us.'

Sally Fetch came up. 'Beg pardon, sur, but Miss Spry is from home. Mistress regrets that you will not be able to see her today.'

'Mistress being?'

'Please?'

'That is my mother,' I said.

'Ah . . . Mistress Spry is at home. Fetch.'

'Sur?'

'Pray go in again and ask if Mr Fox may have the honour and pleasure of calling on Mistress Claudine Spry.'

V

'How dare you not tell me he had called!' Tamsin hissed at me.

Tamsin was such a charming mild-mannered girl until something crossed her.

'Mama said you were out. I thought you might have gone out.'

'I was in my *room*! As you must have known! All the time I was in my room stitching my ball gown!'

'But I don't think Mama wished you to see him.'

'Of course she did not! Else she would have received him herself. That was outrageous, to refuse him admittance!'

'I do not know what the etiquette is when someone arrives by sea. I suppose one cannot apply the normal rules.'

'And how *dare* you,' she said, beside herself with anger and frustration, 'how dare you go out and *sail* with him!'

'He asked me! We just went out as far as Anthony's Head.'

'I should think Mama was furious with you!'

'She said some unkind things.'

'I expect it has all gone to your head,' Tamsin

said. 'I expect he was trying to revenge himself on the family. Which side of your face did you turn to him?'

It had been an exciting sail. By now, of course, I could handle a boat as well as most but I was surprised and nervously startled when he said to me, 'Care to take the tiller?'

'Oh but . . . '

'No but . . . '

As we changed places perilously in the rocking cutter he grasped my arm above the elbow and laughed, black hair blowing across his face.

'See how speedy you can drive us on the rocks.'

I was not dressed for boating, and my striped skirt and yellow blouse billowed as much as the canvas as I shortened sail, came briefly up into the wind and then heeled over, making again for the mouth of the creek.

'Heigh-ho,' he shouted. 'Could tell you was a seaman's daughter.'

'I'm not!'

'Then what are you?' When I didn't reply: 'Every Spry is a bit of a sea-dog, ain't he? Admirals, captains, commodores. May be there's a cabin boy among 'em, but if so he's the skeleton in the scuppers. Come a point south, would you, my dear, I see breakers ahead.'

So the sea danced and we dipped and eddied with it, the sun lifted its veil and beat hot upon us; the green headland with its black feet lurched past and in a few moments we were back in the calmer waters of the creek.

'Is it true that your mother is an actress?'

He asked more about my family and gradually my tongue freed itself. Even so, as the sun waxed and waned between the clouds, I was both hotter and colder than the day because of the friendly, hungry way he looked at me.

'To tell the truth, Miss Emma, I've met Thomasine twice and we rather experienced a taking for each other. Nothing serious, mind, but I'd like to see her again. Am I to assume from the rebuff I received today that she is bespoke?'

'Bespoke? Not if by bespoke you mean affianced.'

'That I do mean. So . . . ' He watched me quizzically as, unhelped by him, I lowered the sail. 'In what way am I to be considered ineligible — at least as a friend?'

'That I cannot tell you.'

'Is Tamsin to be an actress? Does your mother want you both to follow her on the stage?'

'I don't know . . . Well, I could not. Not unless it was to join a circus.'

He threw a rope to loop over one of the bollards and drew the cutter into the side of the quay. He jumped ashore and offered me a hand — which I forbore to take.

'Must go before the tide turns,' he said. 'This cutter comes from Feock, and I am not sure if the owner knows I've borrowed it.'

'D'you mean — you just took it?'

He laughed at my expression. 'Take — borrow — it is not stealing.' His eyes narrowed in the sun, gleaming. 'Fearsome is as fearsome does, eh? You think I might want to borrow you or your sister? Not a disagreeable thought. But it would be for more than one tide. Tell me . . . '

'What?'

'Was it an accident?'

I glared daggers at him. 'Of a sort. On the part of the midwife.'

'Has a doctor seen it?'

'Many.' Which wasn't true.

'Should think something could be done. Surgeons are clever johnnies with their scissors these days.'

'Thank you. Good day, Mr Fox, and thank you for the sail.'

'Would you,' he said, 'as a token of your deep gratitude, give a message from me to your sister Tamsin?'

'I think my mother would object.'

'Tell Tamsin . . . Tell her next Thursday at three in front of the new Market House.'

I did not speak.

'Emmie,' he said, touching my hand.

'Don't call me that!'

'Emma, then. Nice Emma? Kind Emma? Pretty Emma?'

'You know those are outrageous lies!'

He said obscurely: 'Many a dangerous temptation comes to us in gay fine colours that are but skin deep.'

He left then with a wicked grin. I watched him sail across the estuary. He turned once to wave, but I did not wave back.

VI

The following day Uncle Davey arrived, bringing with him Anna Maria, who had last year been married in great style and this year had a baby son, born in London. With her came her husband, Major Edward Carlyon, a whiskery, medium-sized young man who liked to wear his regimentals even when off duty. At supper Aunt Anna was in bed, but the other adults, four of them, were spaced down the long dining table. Tamsin and Mary and Desmond and I ate separately.

I have described the main house with its long dark passage running along behind the big reception rooms, so that servants could enter each room by a side door leading from this passage and not disturb the gentry in the other rooms. Sometimes the servants' doors were left slightly ajar, and when proceeding along this passage it was possible to overhear conversations that were not meant for one's ears. I have to confess I had done this once or twice in the past, and tonight, after a sparse supper, I stepped out and along this passage to the servants' door of the dining room, and as expected the last maid had not caught the latch.

Supper was almost over there too, and I had just missed bumping into Slade on his way to the kitchen.

Conversation about Aunt Anna. The Admiral indignantly brushed aside a suggestion from Edward Carlyon that there might be similarities

37

between his wife's condition and that of the late George the Third.

The new baby had been left in care of a nurse at Tregrehan, but Anna Maria, fondly exchanging glances with her husband, was already fuller in the face, generally fuller of body than the slip of a girl whose first heliograph stood framed on a sideboard. My mother on the contrary had lost weight, and one of the rare signs of middle age was a sort of freckling under the eyes, and a hint of gauntness about her shoulders. But she was still a very handsome woman.

I turned away for a moment, thinking I heard a footstep in the passage, and by the time I was reassured the conversation had turned to a subject more pertinent to me. I heard the name Abraham Fox.

'Who?' asked Uncle Davey rather irritably, for he was slightly deaf.

'Eh? Eh? Oh, him. I do not think I should touch him with a bargepole.'

'It is not I who is thinking of touching him,' my mother said tartly. 'Or he me, I assure you. But he was at the Polwheles' last Monday and he was making the greatest fuss of Thomasine. And his name counts for something.'

'Aye, name is fair enough — if you wish to be linked with God-fearing Quakers. But I do not think he is of that family. Comes he not from St Austell? What's his father's name? Eh? Paul? Robert? You should know, Edward, he's in your parish.'

'Yes,' said the Major. 'I've met him. Can't

38

say that I know the man. All I can say is I'd be astonished if you found anything God-fearing about Bram Fox. Nor quaking, so far as I know. Father's in china clay, but no position. I'm told Bram is the only son among a quiver of girls, but came in for money from an uncle. Spent it fast cutting a dash in the county. Suspect the Foxes of Falmouth look on him as a black sheep and want no truck with him.'

'He called here yesterday,' my mother said.

'Did he, now! And did you receive him?'

'I did not.'

'Good. What was his excuse for calling?'

'We had met at the Polwheles', as I have said. If his reputation is so dubious I am surprised they entertained him.'

Anna Maria smiled. 'Oh, he is popular, I believe. Fine company. It isn't always worthy men who create most laughter at a party. But girls can usually discriminate.'

My mother finished her tea and took a last sip of wine. She said to Anna Maria: 'I have had an offer from Mr Keating. It is quite a time since he wrote. He is offering me a short tour of Bath and Bristol and Cheltenham. Mainly classical roles. It is a good offer from him, and if I refuse it I suspect it will be the last.'

Mother had been home since Christmas.

'Then I think you should take it.'

'Caring for the house with your mother in bed so much — and so eccentric — is difficult. I would like to accept but I also have my anxieties about Thomasine. She is now, as you observe, very beautiful and much sought after . . . But in spite of her many qualities she can be obstinate, and like many an impressionable girl before her she is susceptible to young men with good manners and good looks. Of course I talk to her at length on the wisdom, indeed the necessity, of making a suitable attachment, but I should not sleep easy of nights if I were away and she were at home and unguarded.'

'Oh, come,' said the Admiral, 'it is hardly as bad as that, surely, eh? We now have Mrs Avery to keep an eye on things. With Desmond shortly going abroad and Mary grown up, she has little to do, eh? And Tamsin has a sister . . . I know Emma is young but she has a strong will. There will be many people to look after your Tamsin.'

'Mrs Avery would not have the character,' said my mother. 'Nor would my daughter accept her authority. As for Emma . . . ' She snorted. 'She could be *given* no authority over an elder sister. Besides, how could she be expected to be a judge of a man when she would be subjected to the same impulses and influences as all young women of her age?'

Presently Anna Maria said: 'Unhappily I cannot see a likelihood of marriage for Emma. Few young men would not be put off.'

'Her only prospect would be if she were an heiress, and since she is not . . . '

There was the clink of a decanter. The Admiral said: 'If it is Bram Fox you are principally apprehensive of, I think you should not be too uneasy of him.'

'Why not?'

'Because Tamsin has no money, has she? Eh? Eh?'

'You know she has not.'

'Well, where marriage is concerned, I suspect that Bram will be looking for money as well as for a pretty face.'

'I don't think it is simply an unsuitable *husband* you have to fear in the case of Bram Fox,' said Carlyon with a laugh. He stroked his moustache. 'However, no doubt the Admiral can take precautions that will keep him away.'

Something pushed past my legs.

'God damn the dog!' shouted the Admiral. 'How did he get in!' His cry of 'Out, you brute!' was met by the familiar snuffle, and I shrank back into the darkness of the corridor.

3

I

I could not get him out of my mind for weeks. There was something dominantly, frighteningly male about him such as I had never encountered before. I could describe it in coarser terms but will not. Suffice that he walked behind me in the garden, sat in a corner of my room and listened to me sing, occupied a part of my bed at night. Everything I said I said as if he were listening. I was on a stage performing before an audience of one. No one took much notice of any change in me except Sally Fetch, and she seemed chiefly concerned because I had gone off my food.

I suppose it was not only because he was so dynamic that I took it so much to heart; it was also because it was the first time ever that I had been treated as if I were a normal girl. Of course he had referred to my disfigurement, tactlessly perhaps but quite casually as if it didn't make *all* that much difference. I was a fat ugly girl with a drawn-down eye and a scar, but he looked at me as I had never been looked at before.

That it was Tamsin he was really interested in hurt like a stab in the stomach, but it did not affect my feelings for him. I never passed on his message to her, but I think she must have got it because on the Thursday she made an excuse to row across to St Mawes, and must have taken the ferry to Falmouth for she was late home and her face was high-coloured. My mother stared at her suspiciously but her answers were innocent and seemed to conceal nothing.

About this time Desmond Spry, who was now twenty-two and had been travelling in Europe, came home again. Unlike Samuel, who was in the Navy, he had no ambitions either military or nautical. His great preoccupation was birds — watching and sometimes drawing them — of every shape and kind. Whether it was a kittiwake, a black-backed gull, a chough, a swift, a house martin, a black scoter or a kestrel, his interest was equal and intense. Sometimes he seemed only to become animated on this subject. A quiet young man, kind-hearted, thoughtful, a little dull, much more like Mary in temperament. Anna Maria and Samuel were the dominant children. But presently, after having been home some weeks, Desmond began to cast an eye on an altogether different and unfeathered bird.

My mother had risked her daughters' virtue and accepted the theatrical engagement; when she returned it was with obvious relief that she found her two girls unmolested; but it was not long before she perceived Desmond's interest in Tamsin.

I read her feelings pretty well. Of course it should not be pressed. Claudine's hopes for Tamsin were far more ambitious than marriage to a younger son. But she had already perceived that Cornish society was not as different from London society as she had hoped, and that where marriage was concerned a beautiful girl who was penniless was not going to be enthusiastically sought after by the mothers of the county, nor even by the more level-headed of sons. Only quite recently she had had hopes of attracting one of the Boscawens, particularly George Henry who was heir to the new earldom and was much the same age as Tamsin. But somehow it had quietly cooled. Perhaps the Countess had had her say.

So Desmond? A suitable age, good-looking, placid-tempered. Unlike Samuel, who when on leave went straight to Tregolls, and rarely visited his mother and sister at Place House, Desmond whenever he was free came straight to Place. He seemed devoted to the house, and began to initiate some repairs and improvements. As a younger son he would not have a lot of money, but no Spry was poor. There were always parcels of land or part interest in some commercial concern that belonged to them. Besides, Aunt Anna had brought money to the family and some of that was likely to devolve upon the younger children. Uncle Davey was now in his seventies, and Aunt Anna subject to attacks of near insanity. When they were gone, what would happen to this beautiful house? Samuel at sea and apparently content to make his home at Tregolls. Desmond in possession, Desmond living here, possibly with the dutiful Mary. Samuel, though only twenty-five, had the look of a bachelor, not specially interested in girls. And the Royal Navy, even in peacetime, had many health hazards . . .

A lot, of course, would depend on Tamsin. But if she got a temperate and good-looking husband with this house and land thrown in, she might look favourably on the match. Always supposing the abominable Fox had not cast his spell.

In the late summer of that year I caught an indolent fever, and in spite of a lowering diet and an excess of leeches, I could not throw it off. Lying in bed on a starvation diet for weeks on end, I not only lost weight but grew. I suppose I grew four inches. And lost perhaps twenty pounds. With Bram Fox still in my mind, however infinitely out of reach, I resolved not to put the weight back on when my appetite returned.

I remember well that the doctor would not let me eat fish while I was convalescent because it could bring on cholera.

In the October Aunt Anna began to laugh and cry and to talk continuously to her two lost boys, so she had to go away again in her black coach. A few weeks later Uncle Davey arrived in Falmouth by the Bristol steamer from Plymouth Dock.

He had always had a prejudice against these 'boiler things', forecasting that a ship propelled by means of a fire in its belly was sooner or later bound to blow up. But he had been persuaded by a friend, a Captain Morris, to take the trip and his scepticism had changed to enthusiasm. He came across to Place by naval pinnace, and after satisfying everyone's enquiries as to Aunt Anna's well-being, announced that he had invited two other guests along with Captain Morris to sup with them that evening. They were, he said, two engineers, a Mr Bruton and a Mr Lane, who were doing a great deal for the maritime and industrial development of the country.

Since even his own arrival had been unheralded, there was a great bustle and toing and froing while suitable food was prepared. One of the footmen was sent across to St Mawes to buy fresh oysters, sugar, cornflour and damsons for a tart — and extra candles. Uncle Davey said that this Bruton, who was the head man, dressed like a foreigner, was maybe half Frenchie or something of the sort. That Uncle Davey should think of entertaining somebody who was even a quarter French suggested that his guest was in some other way notable or had caught his fancy.

Since he was in a very good mood he also commanded that all his family should sup with them.

When the boat arrived with our guests, among the bobbing lanterns I perceived a very tall heavy man and a slight short brisk one. The small man added somewhat to his height by wearing an unusually high stove-pipe hat which had somehow survived the gusts of the crossing. He was wearing a long black frock coat and a fancy waistcoat with a gold chain. As he came across the lawn, walking with noticeable vitality, he threw away a half-smoked cheroot.

Beside him the other man towered. (They were both youngish, probably in their late twenties.) This one had taken off his hat, and his thick brown hair, worn long, blew in the breeze. He seemed to take only one step to the other's two and to bend his head deferentially to hear what the other was saying.

I had put on my best plum-coloured velvet dress, with lace at the throat and wrists. Tamsin had once kindly said that its colour matched my discoloured eye, but I had nothing much else to choose from. It was two years old and had become too tight: now it was slack again and its hem was four inches from the floor.

We drank canary and presently supped in the big dining room, nine of us altogether. I would gladly have been absent. I sat next to the tall Mr Lane, and on my other side was Captain Morris. Mr Lane had rather kind greyish eyes under thick eyebrows. He moved clumsily and ate slowly, yet he did not give the impression of being mentally slow. You had the feeling that he was in harmony with himself, a very different impression from Mr Bruton, who you would think was constantly disciplining himself — when he wasn't disciplining others.

Mr Bruton was very dark, much better looking than Mr Lane, with bright, dynamic dark eyes, full lips, a high forehead — or it could have been a receding hairline. He talked a great deal, full of himself and his ambitions, a voice almost totally English with an occasional word burred in a foreign way. He had recently been seriously injured by a dangerous fall in the tunnel under the Thames which he and his father had designed and were building; and he talked of some competition he had entered to build a bridge across the Avon, near Bristol, and spoke as if he had already won it.

An arrogant conceited young man, I thought at first. But as the supper went on I fell under his influence — could you call it a spell? — as he conveyed to us his passion for engineering progress, the development of England as a manufacturing power, the conquest of distance by the use of steam trains and steam ocean-going vessels, the building of great railroads, expanding on the present developments in the north of the country and creating a nationwide network of communication and commerce.

And what had Mr Lane to do with this? Mr Lane was clearly a subordinate with few, if any, of the brilliant ideas of the other man. (I noticed that his big hands were calloused with hard physical work.) But clearly he was someone on whom Mr Bruton depended. A steady reliable trustworthy assistant. And likeable. For the first time since my meeting with Bram Fox I found another man likeable. When he looked at me and spoke to me his eyes did not immediately wander to my disfigurement. He was like a big friendly bear. For an hour or two it cured my heartache.

II

They left about ten; the two men in the pinnace that had been waiting to take them back. Captain Morris was spending the night with us, and stayed on with the Admiral drinking

48

brandy. By the time we left Uncle Davey was becoming maudlin. Slade hovered in the background as the Admiral, his face flushing with emotion, told Morris about his afflicted wife and what a tragedy her illness was to him in their happy married life. He seemed temporarily to have forgotten Betsy Slocombe living at Killiganoon.

Desmond and Mary went to bed, and Mother and Tamsin and I went back to our own sitting room, where we drank camomile tea and discussed the evening. As I went into the room I saw an opened letter on the tallboy. It was lying face upwards, with a few fragments of sealing wax loosely on the envelope. The letter was addressed to Mistress Claudine Spry, Place House, St Anthony, in a big masculine hand that I instantly recognized, though I had seen it only once, on a note he had left for Tamsin. It was from Bram Fox.

As I sipped my tea I wondered what Bram Fox could possibly be writing to my mother about. It must be something to do with Tamsin. But clearly whatever was said in the letter had not been passed onto Tamsin, otherwise she would not have looked as bored as she did. How could I get hold of it? Certainly there was no opportunity now.

'I think if you will permit me, Mama,' I said, 'I will retire. Mr Bruton was a fascination, but towards the end he became too technical and I could not follow him.'

''Fraid I did not try,' said Tamsin with a yawn.

'His name was not Bruton,' said my mother. 'Your uncle is getting deafer by the month. I can't remember what his name was, but it wasn't Bruton.'

'Brunel,' said Tamsin. 'As he was leaving I saw the name inside his hat.'

III

That December Admiral Davey Spry caught a cold; it settled on his lungs and turned to pleurisy. He stayed at Place over Christmas, and Anna Maria and Edward Carlyon and their baby — with a second on the way — came over for Christmas Day. In January he recovered, and presently Aunt Anna returned, smiling and seemingly recovered too. Parish was allowed out of the kennels and infiltrated the household again. At the first opportunity the Admiral pleaded pressure of work and left, but got only as far as Tregolls, where he took to his bed again. There were stormy scenes in our own wing at Place where my mother and sister quarrelled fiercely over Tamsin's attachment for Mr Abraham Fox.

The next time I saw Mr Fox was when I walked over with Sally Fetch to St Mawes to buy some lace. Our own boat was in use so we walked to Polvarth and took the ferry, whence it was a short distance to St Mawes and the little bow-windowed street climbing up towards the castle and overlooking the quay. Parish came with us on a lead, which he did not like, but I did not trust him when there were lambs frisking. A blustery April day with bags of cloud being hoisted across the sky, like the bags of coal being taken in at Place. So far none of the bags had opened, but we were prepared. Mama had told me that I must call in at Mr Hoskins, the mayor, and he would give me tea. The tiny town was a parliamentary borough returning two members to Parliament with a minimal number of voters, so there had to be a mayor, and since the Admiral was Lord of the Manor anyone with the name of Spry, be she never so insignificant, would be greeted and treated with esteem. But I had not asked Mama what to do about Fetch, and as she had now become almost a personal friend — my only friend — I did not fancy seeing her go off into the servants' quarters. So with Parish tugging and panting and wanting to stop and snuffle where he chose we walked down through the narrow cobbled streets with the smell of fish and tar and damp rope in our nostrils, keeping an eye on the scurrying clouds, and so almost bumped into my secret lover.

I had only seen him four times but always he was well-dressed in a raffish way. Blue denim trousers over darker blue waterproof shoes, and a high collared almost naval jacket with brass buttons, a tasselled hat which he pulled off as soon as he saw me.

'Ministers of Grace! I was just thinking of you, Miss Emma! This very moment I was thinking of you and up you pop like a cork out of a bottle and nearly hole me below the waterline!'

To my annoyance I had flushed and my

tongue would utter nothing at all.

'And Fetch. Good afternoon, Fetch.'

'Good af'noon, sur.'

'I hope your mistress is well?'

'Thank 'ee, yes, sur. I b'lieve so.'

'And mongrel. A well-bred mongrel, I'll be bound. What is his name?'

'Parish.'

'What strange names you have at Place! Well, Parish, boy, good day to you too.' Rather to my annoyance Parish made a great fuss of him, so there was a lot of patting and snuffling and tugging at my lead for the next minute or so.

'Are you returning home?' he asked me eventually, looking me up and down with his mischievous, urchin eyes.

'Yes.'

'And you're walking? May I accompany you?'

'We're crossing at Polvarth.'

'This far and no farther, eh? I'm content.'

He fell in beside us and with an authority which further annoyed me, waved Fetch to take the dog's lead and to fall a few paces behind.

'You've *grown*,' he said. 'And so much fined off. Is that the expression? You're now a beautiful girl with a flawed face.'

I said angrily: 'So what other discourteous remarks do you wish to make?'

'Not discourteous,' he said judicially. 'Personal, yes. But such comments show interest, not disinterest.'

'Do you suppose I care?'

'Well . . . any woman would. Find me a girl of any class, from the highest to the lowest who

52

does not care to be thought beautiful.'

'You did not say that. Nor could you.'

'Oh, could I not! Challenge me if you dare!'

We left the last cottage behind and walked down the dusty country lane. A few wild flowers were colouring the hedges.

He said: 'This is much like the day I first met you.' When I glanced at him, he said: 'Well, cloud and rain and a fresh breeze. It would be agreeable sailing in the Roads today.' He was carrying a stick with a round bone handle, and he flicked at a waving bramble. 'I was impressed.'

'Impressed?'

'By the way you handled my little cutter. Or James Biggs's little cutter, to be precise. You can tell a lady of quality by the way she trims her sails.'

My anger half turned to laughter but I did not show either. My heart was thumping like one of Mr Brunel's steam engines. Here this man was, walking down the lane, pretending to flirt with me.

What was behind it? Did he think that by cultivating Tamsin's sister he would have a friend at court? I had thought that before, when he had asked me to give her a message. But I had not given it to her, and when they met she must have told him this. Or was it just that he was so predatory a male that he could not resist teasing and flirting with any woman, however disfigured?

He laughed, showing the uneven white teeth against the olive skin.

'What is it?'

'The expression on your face, Emma. You can't make head or tail of me, can you?'

'Certainly not head.'

'Witty as usual. Is it a devil's tail or a fox's tail that you see?'

It came into my mind to say 'a monkey's', but I just did not dare.

He glanced behind to see that Fetch and Parish were following at a discreet distance. 'Do not *try* to understand me. That way one's own notions add to the confusion. I am really very easy to understand. My wishes, my hopes, my needs are plain to be seen. As clear as water. As clear as gin.'

We were nearly at the ferry. Tregrundle stood with his new boat ready. It was half tide and one would only need a dozen strokes. I was short of breath. I half turned to wait for Fetch, but he caught my elbow.

'I want you. As clear as clear. Think on it, little Emma. Now I have exceeded all good taste. All the frilly lace curtains of convention are torn to ribbons. Blown quite away. Polite words are not in me. Shall I ever be forgiven? Not, I'm sure, for this utter disgrace.'

'Please leave me alone!' I pulled my elbow free.

As he turned to Sally Fetch his face was quite expressionless. We might have been talking of the next regatta.

'Come along, Fetch, your mistress is waiting.' He bowed slightly. 'Dutiful respects to your sister and your mother, Miss Emma; it has been a privilege.' He turned and left us, and we stood and watched him walking back the way he had come. Parish barked a farewell.

We still stood there.

At length Fetch said: 'I wouldn't trust 'im, miss, no further 'n I could spit!'

IV

When we reached Place a guest had called. He was an old man of about fifty, a clergyman and relative, Canon Francis de Vere Robartes, who had come over from Blisland at the foot of the Cornish moors, where he was the incumbent, to visit the two invalids. A great-great-grandfather Spry, according to Desmond, who made a study of these things, had lived at Blisland and had been an attorney-at-law, practising in Bodmin and Plymouth. Canon Robartes was a distinguished cleric and had made a new translation of the *Apocrypha*. He was not well to do, but had good family connections, and he was disappointed to find only one invalid here and she an active convalescent, anxious only to talk about Clive and David, who had appeared to her in a dream last night.

So he had to make do with Mama and Desmond and Mary and me. Tamsin was out sailing. What she would have given to have been walking with me in St Mawes! (What he had said! — it was a vulgar ribald jest surely — he could not have been even a quarter *serious*? My flesh crept.)

Canon Robartes took tea but refused an

invitation to sup. He would sleep at Tregothnan, he said, and go to see the Admiral in the morning. When he was leaving a name caught my ear as he talked to Desmond. The name of a man who came and mesmerized us six months ago.

Apparently there had been a meeting at Bodmin among the landed gentry last week about the prospect of building a railway between Bodmin and Wadebridge, and a Mr Brunel had spoken at it. The idea was that the railroad should be eight miles long, with a six-mile extension to Winford if the line were a success. It would be chiefly for the transportation of goods and ore, but passengers might be taken on later. The type of propulsion had yet to be decided. Most favoured a form of steam power, probably by means of an engine drawing wagons, as was usual following the success of the Stephensons; but Mr Brunel had proposed having stationary engines at intervals along the line and drawing the trucks by atmospheric suction. It had been a most interesting meeting, Uncle Francis, as he told us all to call him, said. He had only been invited to deputize for young Mr Agar-Robartes of Lanhydrock, his cousin, who was travelling in Europe. He himself, as everyone knew, had to depend on his stipend, and had no spare resources to invest in such hazardous schemes. Mr Brunel, he had to admit, was most impressive for one so young and already had a number of achievements to his credit.

The Canon raised his eyebrows and sighed. 'So young, Desmond, so young. One trembles

56

for a man's judgment at such an age.'

'Was Mr Brunel on his own, sir?' I ventured.

'No, my dear.' Uncle Francis glanced at my disfigured eye and smiled forgivingly, as if someone ought to be forgiven for such a distortion. 'He had an assistant with him. Equally young, I may say, equally young. Long, was it? Or Lane? But it was Mr Brunel who spoke and who made the greatest impression. Do you understand the properties of steam, Desmond?'

'I'm afraid not,' said Desmond, and looked out of the window to see if Tamsin was returning.

'Well well, I must leave you all. Pray present my loving respects to your mother. £25,000 is the capital needed.'

'Needed?'

'To build the railway. It is a very large sum, and of course as in all such ventures the estimate is bound to be exceeded when it is put into practice. There's great interest. Great interest indeed. I wish I had money to invest. I believe I should indulge in a little flutter.'

4

I

The following spring Falmouth was greatly excited by the visit of the Queen of Portugal. She was only tiny — nine years old — and no doubt, Desmond said, a pawn in some political game. Portugal was in chaos, and England and France were involved — for once on the same side — trying to bring a measure of political peace to the warring factions. What purpose there was, if any, in Queen Maria's visit to Britain's westernmost port I was never able to find out. No one, in fact, ever did seem to know.

But she was already acquainted with Mrs Elizabeth Fox — widow of Robert Were Fox, one of the dignitaries of the town — and it was arranged that the Queen should visit her friend at her home in Arwenack Street, where a reception would be held.

The Queen arrived in a black and gold British frigate, accompanied by Lord Clinton, who was a Trefusis; they came ashore at Custom House Quay in a gilt barge rowed by twenty sailors, and were met by rippling rows of dainty white-clad girls, all of about the same age as the Queen, who strewed flowers in the pathway of the procession as it walked up the narrow street until it reached Bank House.

My mother had somehow contrived an invitation for herself and her two daughters and nephew Desmond to the reception, which was crowded.

By this time I was becoming slightly less self-conscious about my disfigurement. It was there for everyone to see, so what point was there in hiding it? (A few of the walls that I had built around myself were beginning to crumble.) All the same I would have shunned such a public occasion and made my usual excuse were it not for a confidence Sally Fetch had bestowed on me. Sally's sister was a maid in the Robert Were Fox household and she had said that although the old man had disapproved of Abraham Fox as thoroughly as the rest of the family, his wife had always had a soft spot for the young man, and when she became a widow had tended to indulge him. Therefore I went, and was not surprised to see the elegant figure of Bram standing beside his aunt at the entrance.

It was a total and disagreeable surprise to my mother, who froze at the sight of him and, once they had bowed, took a firm if theatrical grasp of Tamsin's arm and steered her away from him. She clearly felt that I was in no danger, so could fend for myself. So great was the crush that, except for a circle at the end of the room, with a slightly raised dais and a chair on which the little Queen was seated, it was not difficult to be lost to view.

The Queen was a pretty little thing, thin and dark-skinned but gracious. Already learning the deceitful arts of the court, no doubt. I wondered what her fate would be. (I had just been reading a book on Catherine de Medici, so my mind was full of intrigue.)

The reception lasted about an hour, and I had withdrawn into a slightly quieter corner of the room where I could be less expected to join in, when across the room I saw Bram talking to my mother. Yes, they were *talking*. I could not see Tamsin, so perhaps temporarily they had become separated. Bram was speaking to my mother with that half-cynical, half-admiring expression on his face that I already knew so well. The disillusioned charming smile that was never far away came and went like a fitful sun. She replied to him firmly but not with any special hostility. Being an actress, my mother had great control over her features and perhaps she had decided that a social gathering in royal presence was not the time to show her active dislike of someone.

Then she half smiled at something he said, and her eyes narrowed and glinted as if she were summing him up afresh. He laughed out loud at what she said, and even amid the hubbub of talk it came clearly to me. I knew there would never be anybody else for me. And what chance had I got?

Desmond squeezed between two people and came to me. 'Emma? Can you come to Thomasine? She is not feeling well.'

I followed him, pushing our way among the dignitaries of the town, and found Tamsin sitting on an oak chair with two solicitous friends beside her.

60

'It is nothing,' Tamsin said sharply, pressing a handkerchief to her lips. 'Nothing more than the heat and the crush. Forgive me, it is quite nothing. Where is Mama?'

'Just over here,' I said. 'I will fetch her.'

II

Admiral Davey Spry, Admiral of the Red, dropped in the following month to see his mad wife.

He had lost weight and his face was smaller, but as quick as ever to flush up at the least constraint. His men must find his humours as hard to predict as a wind in the Channel. But today he seemed good-tempered, and he was lucky to find Aunt Anna in one of her lucid moods. They talked together about old times and he was able to tell her that their eldest daughter was pregnant again. This would be number three in three years, so she was clearly going to outdo her mother. Uncle Davey was able to remind his wife of a practical joke he had played on their first nursemaid. It was something to do with apron strings, but that was all I heard amid his shouts of laughter. Aunt Anna laughed too but her laughter had a hollow sound as if she were looking down a well.

No one knew it then, but it was the last time they were to meet. When Uncle Davey got up to leave he stooped to kiss his wife, who was still in bed, and I saw her put an elderly, white-nailed hand round his back as if to hold him longer. When he straightened up he picked at a tooth defensively and half scowled at her.

'Be sure you're up next time I come,' he said. 'This shilly-shallying in bed . . . it don't do you any good at all.'

'They'll be home soon,' said Aunt Anna, staring out of the window with absent blue eyes. 'Clive and David. You told me their frigate would be home soon. Have you heard when?'

'Not yet awhile,' said Uncle Davey, playing the game we now all had to play. 'Maybe at the end of the summer.'

'You should write to the Admiralty. They have been away so long.'

'Oh, I will, my dear. So I will.'

III

He died on 27 November at eight o'clock in the evening, not at Place House but at Tregolls, where all his children had been summoned. Only three arrived in time, Samuel being at sea. Everyone was greatly upset.

The coffin was brought to Place on 3 December and was laid in the church beside the house until the fifth, when the funeral took place. The wide gravelled carriageway and the larger quadrangle before the house, for turning, were crowded with black carriages. Related as he was to a fair number of the gentry of Cornwall, Uncle Davey was also liked and respected by most people with whom he had had dealings. Naval officers from Plymouth came, his peaked admiral's hat was placed on the coffin among the family flowers, and six naval lieutenants carried the bier. Davey's brother was there — I had only seen him once, though he lived in Cornwall — the four children, including Anna Maria's first two toddlers, Thomas Tristram and Edward Augustus. Two cousins I had never set eyes on. Three Carlyons from Tregrehan — including, of course, Major Edward, his son-in-law — the Earl and Countess of Falmouth, young Mr Agar-Robartes from Lanhydrock, his distant cousin Canon Robartes of Blisland — who took the service — two Foxes — though not Abraham — the Polwheles of Polwhele, Sir William and Lady Molesworth from Pencarrow, the St Aubyns from St Michael's Mount, and the Stackhouses from Trehane. Miss Betsy Slocombe was noticeably absent.

Desmond, in spite of his youth and his preoccupation with birds, seemed to know the name of every one of the mourners, and whispered bits of information and gossip as he stood between Tamsin and me in the church. (For instance that Sir John St Aubyn had only recently married his mistress, by whom he had had ten children, who were already all grown up.) Most of his confidences were whispered to Tamsin, but I was able to pick them up, having the hearing, as my mother once kindly said, of a tame ferret.

Aunt Anna had made two escapes from the house in October, so she had had to be taken away again. They had not told her of her husband's death, nor was she considered well enough to be brought back for the funeral.

63

When it was all over, when all had taken refreshment and gone except the immediate family, there was a gathering in the south drawing room. Samuel, who had managed to get home for the interment, was now, at twenty-eight, the head of the family. A heavily built young man with a mop of stiff bristly hair worn shorter than was fashionable. I was a little afraid of him: I knew the other three by now very well, but Samuel had been so much away that he was almost a stranger, and I knew he had fixed ideas and a strong will. I was anxious — and I knew my mother and Tamsin were — lest our position should be changed. Of course we were cousins and were accepted as such, but we had existed and lived here on the goodwill of Uncle Davey. How would his son feel about it all? Would Samuel have the heartlessness to turn us out? He owed us nothing.

He said: 'Mr Lewis will be here in the morning to give details of my father's will. I do not think there will be any exceptional surprises. What we should perhaps give our minds to over the next few days is the general planning of our futures.' No one spoke. He went on:

'For my own part I intend to resign from the Navy at some suitable early opportunity. I have never liked the life, and went on with it solely to please my father. Now that he has gone the reason for my continuing has gone.'

Mary said: 'Shall you come and live here, Samuel?'

'No. I shall make a home for myself in London and intend to go into politics.'

After a pause Desmond said: 'What is to become of our mother?'

'If she recovers she can return here. But the doctors do not hold out a hope of permanent improvement. They say she may live a long time. Our father, as you know, was seventy-five. Mama is only sixty-four, and keeping her in a comfortable home will be a considerable extra drain on the family purse.'

'I would wish to look after her,' said Mary. 'But she *is* very difficult.'

Anna Maria said: 'When I saw her last it was a great distress to me. She was so restless, so argumentative, and so strong, physically strong. It took Mary and me and Mrs Whattle all our time to restrain her. She is better away unless there is a great improvement.'

'If she does not come back,' said Mary, fingering the lace at her throat, 'I should prefer to live at Tregolls. It is so much more convenient.'

'And you, Desmond?' said Samuel.

'Oh . . . ' Desmond shrugged his thin shoulders. 'I am happy here. After all, this is the family house and I should like to spend something on repairs, which it badly needs. Also I know no place better for seabirds, which are my principal study . . . Yes, I am very happy here. That is so long as you do not want it for yourself . . . '

'There should be room enough here for more than one brother,' said Samuel. 'Or more than one family.' He looked at Claudine for the first time. 'You have made your home here,

65

Aunt — and my two cousins with you. Do you have plans to change, to return to London or Bath?'

My mother said: 'As you know, Samuel, your father had entrusted me with much of the running of the house — that is since your mother became incapable of doing so. I shall be happy to continue in that way, at least temporarily. But you must tell me what you shall want to do. If you are not likely to use it as a permanent home . . . and if Desmond wishes to stay, I shall be glad to look after him . . . until, well . . . '

'Until?' Samuel said.

'Until he marries,' said my mother with a sidelong glance.

'I do not think *I* shall ever marry,' said Samuel. 'There is so much to do in the world. Or not at least until I am forty, when perhaps there may be more time for trivialities . . . I'm sorry, Edward,' he said to his brother-in-law. 'This was not intended in any way as a personal reflection.'

Edward Carlyon half smiled as he fingered his short moustache, but his wife said warmly: 'How fortunate that we do not all think the same! The Major, apart from me, has three fascinating trivialities to his name, called Thomas, Edward and George.'

'Already.' Desmond, smiling at his sister.

'Yes, already!'

'And with that I am more than content! I've no doubt, Samuel, when you have a family of your own, you will find just as much time to pursue your profession — and a greater ambition in doing so.'

Samuel grunted and looked across at Claudine.

'If my mother does not come back, and Mary decides to live in Truro, you and your daughters will more or less have the run of the place.'

'Apart from myself,' said Desmond.

'Of course, of course, of course . . . We shall all come here from time to time, meeting at Christmas or some other suitable vacation. But I think it would be only prudent to cut down the permanent staff by half. Extra servants can be engaged from time to time. My mother's comfort in the special home she is in must come first.'

'Do we know what is going to happen to Miss Slocombe?' Mary asked. It was the first time her name had been mentioned all day.

'Perhaps Papa will have made some provision for her,' said Anna Maria. 'We shall know tomorrow.'

I wondered if he had made any 'provision' for my mother.

'Slade ought to leave,' said Anna Maria. 'Perhaps Papa has left him a suitable pension too.'

My mother said: 'Many of the servants have been here as long as I have. I hope we can consider them individually rather than making a blanket decision.'

'Of course, of course, of course.' It was one of Samuel's pet phrases. 'But I have noticed a deal of slackness since I came home. We must see to that.'

IV

The solicitor and his clerk arrived at eleven and read the will. I was not invited in, nor was my mother or sister. The rest of the family emerged at one, but it took time for the details to filter through to us.

Uncle Davey had left almost everything in trust to his wife, but power of attorney was granted to her children, and of them Samuel was to be the main legatee. On him would devolve the ownership of Place House and all land in or near the Roseland Peninsula, together with numerous investments. The house and property of Tregolls near Truro was left jointly to Desmond and Mary. To Anna Maria he had left his London house and property in Devon. The house of Killiganoon was to go to Desmond and Mary, but Miss Betsy Slocombe was to have free occupancy of it for five years and a life income of £250. Slade was left an annuity of £50, and several of the other servants received small gifts. My mother was left £100, and so was Thomasine, and so was I. I was thrilled for it was the very first money I had ever possessed of my own.

My mother was equally satisfied at the outcome — not for her small legacy but for the future dispositions of our lives. So the family party broke up. Samuel returned to his ship in Portsmouth. Anna Maria and her husband and two children left for London. The Admiral's brother — granted a legacy of £500 — returned to his home near Truro; as did the two cousins — who had been entirely ignored (Uncle Davey never liked them). Always depending on the continuing goodwill of Samuel, Claudine might consider she had been left as undisputed mistress. She had unfailingly been tactful with her nephews and nieces, and she knew she could manage Desmond and Mary. Anna Maria, with whom she did not get on so well, was safely busy childbearing and usually in London. The rest were servants.

Before he left she had had a detailed discussion with Samuel and had agreed which servants should leave. Fetch's position was under threat but I had insisted to Mama that she should be one who must stay, even if I had to pay her wages out of my new-found legacy.

Meanwhile Desmond's courtship of Tamsin continued. One night I asked her about it.

'Oh.' She shrugged. 'He is passably nice. I sometimes think he is more interested in ornithology.'

'Oh, Tamsin, you cannot say that! He comes at every crook of your little finger.'

She sighed. 'Mama would like it, I believe. It would suit her in many ways. But I am only just twenty-two. There are plenty of other fish in the sea.'

'Such as Mr Abraham Fox?'

'Why do you say that?'

'Because I know you have such a taking for him.'

'Have? Had? Which is it? I am not sure if Mr Fox is not really a rattlesnake.'

She was sitting on the end of the bed, her

head up, regarding the fading daylight. The frills of her nightdress ringed her face like the cup of a daffodil, the skin of her neck and chin so pure, the profile so perfect.

'You never told me,' I said, 'what happened when we were in Bank House greeting the Queen of Portugal.'

'What happened? What could happen? I felt faint. That was what happened. You know I suffer severely when it is one of my monthlies.'

I waited, but she said no more. 'What has changed you, then? Are you pretending to yourself to dislike him just to please Mama?'

'Emma, you are always very disagreeable with your probing questions. What are my feelings for Bram Fox? What are yours? What are Mama's?'

'Mama's?' I was startled. 'She has made that clear.'

'And yours,' she said, 'you have made yours clear, have you not? You are besotted with him!'

This was a profound shock to me, that I had allowed any such feelings to show.

'He — he has been kind to me,' I stammered. 'That's all. It is rare for a man not to be put off by my disfigurement. Of course he means nothing, but I appreciate such courtesy.'

'Have a care that you do not appreciate it too much.'

V

A few months before Uncle Davey's death he had come back full of a concert he had been to in Plymouth, and of a musician who had made a great impression on him.

'Black man; would you believe it? Black as a spade. But the way he handles that violin! You know I'm not a great one for music — at least not these cats' concerts that they organize in Falmouth. But this was extraordinary. Made my hair stand up.'

'What was his name?' I asked.

'Oh, can't remember that, my dear girl. Never can. Hemway or some such. But his story is still more extraordinary. Don't know whether 'tis generally known, but Admiral Cawthorne told me, and he knows everything. It seems this feller was a slave taken as a boy by Portuguese traders, sold in Brazil and then brought back to Lisbon as a sort of slave servant — they are fashionable in Portugal among the aristocracy, and the blacker the better! Well, this slave-owner found his boy so highly musical that in a couple of years he was playing in the orchestra at the Lisbon opera! Is that that damned dog I hear?'

'You know it's not,' said my mother impatiently. 'Parish is in his kennel as you instructed. So?'

'So? . . . ' Uncle Davey blinked. 'Oh, you mean about this slave feller. Well about this time, according to Cawthorne, the *Indefatigable*, under Edward Pellew — captain as he then was — ran aground when chasing an enemy and had to put in to Lisbon for repairs. He was there far too long for his own satisfaction, and one night he went to the Lisbon opera and spotted the black man, leading the violins by then; so a couple of weeks later, when he was ready to sail, he had this black man impressed as he came out of the opera and taken aboard the *Indefatigable*, and sailed away with him!'

'From one slavery to a worse,' said Mary.

'Well, yes, in a way I suppose so. They kept him aboard for *years* — would not let him go ashore when they were in port or he would have run for it. It wasn't until Pellew was promoted years later to take over a ship of the line and his crew was disbanded that they gave Hemway, or whatever his name is, his freedom and set him ashore in Falmouth.'

'Falmouth?'

'Yes. He has lived in Cornwall ever since.'

'I've heard of him,' said Mary. 'I haven't ever seen him but his name is sometimes in the paper. By the way, his name is Emidy, not Hemway.'

'Well, if he gives a concert round here we must certainly go to see him,' said Uncle Davey. 'You know I was never a great friend of the sonatas, but he almost cured me of my distaste for 'em. You could even hear the *tunes*.'

This was in the May before he died. A year later, the following June I heard about a concert — I think it was first from Mary — which was to be held at the Town Hall, Falmouth on Thursday week. An orchestra was coming from Bath, and would be led by the well-known violinist, Joseph Emidy, who would play various solo pieces and a concerto of his own composition.

Desmond was away and not expected back for at least a month, Mary expressed herself uninterested — she was not fond of musical

72

concerts — but to my great joy and relief my mother said, yes, she would go and take Tamsin and me with her.

During the last few years I had heard little music — except what my mother and I had sometimes made ourselves singing duets in our sitting room. I had never heard a professional orchestra, nor really an orchestra of any sort, save the military and naval bands that played when the Navy was in port. Last year I had persuaded Uncle Davey to have the harp moved to our wing of the house, and this had given me the greatest pleasure, except when Tamsin complained of the noise. (And one could always defy one's sister.)

But a *professional* orchestra. Not a group of part-gifted amateurs whose efforts Uncle Davey had dubbed 'cats' concerts'. And Joseph Emidy, a performer who had even impressed the Admiral. I would count the days.

On the Thursday, a week before the concert, my mother, after reading the weekly paper at breakfast, suddenly announced that she had changed her mind and we should not go after all. She offered no explanation and no apology. I had rarely seen her so emphatic. Perhaps I should have suspected the newspaper but foolishly did not until much later. The suggestion that Tamsin and I should be allowed to go on our own was instantly rejected. Tamsin in fact was not too upset. There was to be a midsummer ball in Truro the next month, and she would greatly prefer to attend that. I was the one so deeply upset. I said, might

I not be allowed to go alone? Fetch could come to chaperone me and need not attend the concert.

A blank wall. The subject was taboo. All through the weekend I sulked and took Parish for long walks and went off my food. No one took the slightest notice. I began to regret the absence of friends of my own age. My mother would certainly not have refused me if I had been going with a Boscawen or Trefusis daughter.

Sunday was Sally Fetch's half day off, and when she came back about nine in the evening she said to me: 'When I was visiting my sister this afternoon, miss, I chanced to meet — er — him — you know who, miss.'

'What? Who?'

'Mr Abraham Fox. He was coming out of Mrs Robert's house and he recognized me and . . . '

As she hesitated I said casually: 'So? Did he speak to you? Why was he there?'

'I dunno, Miss Emma. Yes, he did . . . Oh, Miss Emma, I dunno whether 'tis right and proper to pass on what he give me . . . Because you d'know I think him hardly the gentleman — '

'*What* did he give you? Something for Miss Tamsin?'

'No, miss. For you.'

My heart missed a beat. 'Well, what is it? Pray give it to me.'

'Look, miss, I don't know if I done right, but when he spoke to me he says, how is Miss

74

Emma, and I says very well, sur, and he says, are they coming to the concert next Thursday? And I says, I b'lieve not, sur, though t'was talked about. I b'lieve they aren't going. Ah, he says, I can guess why not. It is because they have found out that I am one of the organizing committee. I am in bad repute with your family, Carry. (He always d'call me Carry, miss, for some little joke of his own.) So I wish you to take this message to your mistress, he says. Hold hard, while I go and get pen and ink, he says, stop just there, he says, don't move a muscle until I come out again.'

Sally Fetch gave a little twitch of the shoulders, which betrayed that she was not immune to Bram's vitality and zest.

'I dunno whether I should've stayed, but I did, and in a few minutes he comes out shaking a letter to dry the ink on the address. Give this to your mistress, Carry, he says, and you shall have a groat. I dunno what he mean but that's what he d'say. But I don't think 'tis proper of me to — to carry letters, like. I dunno what your Mama would think of me, miss . . . '

I held out my hand. 'It is — addressed to me?'

She fumbled in her bag and nervously extended an envelope with its sealing wax unbroken. I broke it and inserted a finger. Then, aware that the finger was unsteady, I said: 'Thank you, Fetch. I'll call you when I want you.'

She said as she left: 'I hope I done right.'

Dear Miss Emma,

This concert is organized by the Society of Friends, and, although I belong to no society, friendly or otherwise, I have been helping in the seating and the organization. Therefore to this end I offer you a seat in the fifth row, surrounded by persons of eminent respectability, not me, not I, not Bram, but many other Foxes of unimpeachable reputation. I understand your family is not coming, but if you can take flight in some way on Thursday evening and flutter down in Arwenack Street, I believe the music will be worth hearing.

Respectfully,
Bram

And enclosed was a printed ticket marked E 7.

Did he know I was fascinated by music? Why did he write in this way to me, an eighteen-year-old, with a permanently drawn-down eye? Why had he not written — if he wrote at all — to Tamsin? Did he really feel something for me? Was it some heartless charade he was indulging in? And if so, in what way did it profit him? I didn't understand, but with a growing wilful maturity I knew I would get to the concert somehow, even if it killed me — which in the event it might well have done.

I developed a light fever on Thursday morning, and after dinner said I would spend the rest of the day in bed and Fetch could look after me. My mother was never assiduous in her

76

care for me, and I knew Tamsin would not come near for fear of catching the infection. Fetch came with me as far as Polvarth. She was very reluctant to be sent back, but I insisted she must go, for her absence would be more noticeable than mine. Fetch had a touch of religion in her, so I assured her she must not lie on my behalf, simply say that when she looked in on me I was sleeping. (I had built a bolster figure on my bed which would pass for a casual glance.)

In St Mawes I hired a small boat, about the size Bram had first appeared in, that is, with oars and a single sail. Young Mr Coode, who owned it, had rented it out to members of the Spry family from time to time when our own boats were in other use, and saw no particular objection to renting it to me. Money spoke, and the blessed Uncle Davey had provided me with some.

It was a pleasant July afternoon; a hot sun which waxed and waned with the stirring of a low drifting cloud. Far away in the west, in the brilliant sky, other great clouds towered away thousands of feet up, white and biscuit-coloured. There was so little surface wind that within the shelter of the St Mawes creek I thought I should have to row all the way; but once in the mouth of the river it breathed gently towards the land and took me at unhurried speed towards the town.

Dressing had been difficult, but I carried shoes and blouse in a bag, trusting to luck where I should change them. My skirt I tucked into baggy canvas breeches, and an old pair of rubber boots made up the ensemble. With my scarred face and haggard eye I must have looked like a French pirate.

There was a fair amount of shipping in the Roads, and I had to luff and tack several times before I gently laid the little cutter alongside the stone jetty of Custom House Quay, shipped the oars and jumped ashore and made her fast.

I remembered the hotel opposite and I carried my little bag in there and ordered a cordial. When it came I asked if there was a bedroom or ladies' withdrawing room where I might change for the concert, and this was willingly provided. The little maid who took me upstairs looked fearfully at my disfigurement but, I thought, seemed to recognize it. At least the name Miss Spry came easily to her lips. Possibly in eighteen years, because of my scarred face, I had become known in the town.

The concert was to start at six, and I arrived at fifteen minutes before the hour and at once saw Bram. He picked his way among the crowd of people assembled on the Town Hall steps and smiled. 'So . . . madame has spread her wings and come! Very pleased I am. Alas I cannot sit next to you, but I hope your company will be agreeable. No doubt you'll spare a few words for me when the concert is over.'

He was very handsome in a purple velvet smoking jacket with tight black braided trousers, and he looked slightly less predatory.

My memory of that evening is in some respects unfortunately vague; (I lost my programme in the confusion of the following day). An attendant led me to a seat in the fifth row, where I sat between strangers. I had an uninterrupted view of the stage, on which the orchestra was already seated — twelve in all — and the sound of the instruments being adjusted to their proper pitch was infinitely exciting. The hall was full.

There was a rustle of applause and a small black man with curly grey hair, in a creased dinner suit, came from the wings carrying a violin. When he too had plucked a string or two, a tall portly man, balding, with a trim grey beard, stood up with an air of authority at the side of the stage and welcomed the Bath Ensemble to Falmouth on their first visit. Tonight they were to be led by Mr Joseph Emidy, to whom Falmouth bade a special welcome on his return to the town.

When the music began, the resonance of the strings, the reedy tenors and baritones, spoke of a world I did not know before. They moved me. I had not heard anything like this. Mozart, Cherubini, Haydn, Marcello. In all these one watched and listened to Joseph Emidy and marvelled at his extra dexterity, the singing tone of his instrument.

Then came his own concerto, in which all this skill was deployed afresh. It was a very popular jolly piece, and seemed to incorporate sea shanties and other well-known tunes. When it was finished the audience rose to him; it was entirely to their liking; and nothing would satisfy them except that he should play two encores.

Two hours passed in a daze. I could not believe it when suddenly it was over, and the tall bald man got up to make a speech of thanks and appreciation. Satisfied, excited, warm and content, I looked out of a window of the hall, and saw that darkness was just falling. People seemed reluctant to disperse, but I knew I must go.

A hand grasped my arm.

'Good?'

It was Bram, eyes narrowed, slightly laughing. His hand was like an electric charge.

'Wonderful,' I said. 'It was — so very good. Thank you for inviting me. Wonderful.'

'Take tea now. Tea and cakes are always served after these events.'

'Oh, I cannot, Bram. I am already later than I ought to be.'

'You would meet Mr Joseph Emidy.'

I hesitated. It was a great temptation. But . . .

'How did you — how did you know I was so fond of music?'

'Thomasine told me.'

'Why did you not invite her, then?'

'You are musical. She is not. How did you come?'

'Today? By sea.'

'In a small boat?'

'Smallish, yes.'

'Who brought you?'

'I came myself.'

He drew in a breath and laughed. 'You mean just on your own?'

'I hired the boat in St Mawes. It was no trouble.'

'But will you find trouble when you return?'

'Maybe. Yes, maybe.'

'For you must not return tonight.'

'Of course I must!'

'Take tea first.'

'Bram, I *cannot*. I shall probably be in the greatest trouble already. More than you can imagine. Though if I am quick now and very lucky . . . '

While talking I had been sidling up the aisle and he following. People were standing talking, not moving to go at all. So we reached the big doors, where more people were standing, looking out at the day.

The thunderous clouds had moved in from the west and were now overhead. It was just light enough to see their edges twisting and curling.

'Our climate is well known for its changes of mood,' he observed in my ear.

'Well, I have to go, I have no choice. It will be all right. I shall be across in half an hour.'

'Have you yet properly observed the weather?'

We had come down the steps. Suddenly we were in the wind, and there was rain falling diagonally, shining in the lamplight. It fell on my face like fine spray, with a suggestion of salt in it.

'You cannot go in this, my dearest Emma. You would surely drown, and even facing your mother's wrath is to be preferred to that!'

I looked about, angrily up at the sky, frowned towards the harbour, which was not yet visible because of the houses.

'Bram, it's not as bad as that, I'm sure!'

'I might come with you, but how should I return? I only have evening clothes . . . But where are yours? You cannot have sailed over in a billowing skirt.'

'I changed — partly changed — at Blundstone's.'

'Then spend the night there. I will ferry you home in the morning.'

'I could not! They will not know where I am!'

I set off down the main street, Bram following. Now you could see in the twilight, through the slits and alleys, the white lips of the little waves and the boats at anchor lurching and tugging at their moorings. The occasional lit lanterns over house doors dipped and danced out of unison.

'Where is your boat?'

'At the main quay.'

'Is it likely to break free?'

'I don't think so. It is in a sheltered corner.'

'I'll go and look. But first you must go to Blundstone's.'

The scarf over my hair was getting sodden and cold drops were trickling down my neck. He held onto my arm with one hand and kept his hat on his head with the other. There were more people than you would have expected about, most of them hurrying for shelter. As we came up to the hotel I said:

'It will not take me more than five minutes to change. But please do not wait. I can look after myself.'

'That is precisely what you are not able to do! I will come with you and then . . . '

We pushed open the door, and light and welcome warmth met us. As it happened Mr

Blundstone himself was crossing the hall, and he came towards us.

'Good evening, Mr Fox. Good evening, miss. What a change in the weather! Can I get you some refreshment?'

'Thank you,' I said before Bram could speak. 'I left a change of clothing in the ladies' room upstairs, and I would be glad to use the room to change back again.'

'Of course, miss. May I get — '

'Blundstone,' Bram interrupted. 'This young lady, Miss Spry of Place House, St Anthony, came over for the concert tonight and has been overtaken by the weather. Have you, if necessary, accommodation for her so that she may spend the night here and return home in the morning?'

'Bram!' I said, forgetting etiquette in the stress of the moment. 'You know very well I could not stay here tonight! My family would be *very* anxious and *very* angry. And — ' I hesitated, not wanting to say too much in front of the innkeeper; 'And if I stayed it would — jeopardize Fetch's position. My maid will be in greater trouble even than I. I do not wish to go into detail, but it is absolutely *necessary* that I should return *tonight*, and very soon!' I pulled my arm away from his and turned to the innkeeper. 'Mr Blundstone, if you would call a maid . . . '

Bram took my arm again. It was not gentle this time and it led me to a window. The curtains were not yet drawn and one could look out at the foam-flecked harbour.

'Observe, Emma. Observe the storm. Mr Blundstone!'

'Sir?'

'Miss Spry is anxious, as you see, to return home. Can you supply her with a suitably manned ferry or schooner or cutter to take her over to St Anthony *at once*?'

'Er — well. I — er . . . ' Blundstone peered out of the window from under shaggy brows. 'I do not think there will be any — er — public or private transport while this storm lasts. Of course, it will abate. Perhaps by midnight the sea will go down — you know how quick these things can change and it is low tide then. But I do not think I could hire a private waterman just at present. I do not suppose even if it were a medical emergency that the apothecary would not consider a few hours' delay . . . '

'Miss Spry,' said Bram, 'came over on her own. She is a good sailor. But now she wishes to return on her own.'

'On her *own*! My dear sir, ma'am. Forgive me, ma'am. That would be madness. A lady like you . . . '

'Oh, I have lived at Place all my life. I am used to boats. One has to use them regularly . . . '

'No, my sweetheart,' said Bram. 'On an evening like this you cannot and you shall not. Do you suppose I could call on your mother tomorrow and say, 'I'm sorry, your daughter has been drowned; it was all because I did not trouble sufficiently to persuade her to wait until the morning. It is too bad, and very sad, but there we are, she was headstrong and I was too

84

weak to prevent her going.' '

'We have one very nice room,' said Mr Blundstone. 'Let for tomorrow but free for tonight. It overlooks the harbour and is warm and dry. If you would care to see it; Miss Spry.'

5

I

It was a very pretty room. Not at all like the one my mother describes which gave us shelter for my birth. It was panelled, hung with pink-painted calico, and it had a bow window looking out over all the humours of the market place. The hotel was built so close to the harbour that a sizeable schooner projected its bowsprit below my window, so that I could look down on the decks and almost into the lighted cabin where figures moved to and fro against the half-drawn curtains.

I was in very serious trouble. I had thought to be home by ten, and with Fetch's connivance might have been about the next morning and innocently protesting that a long night's rest had cured the fever. Of course in the end my mother might have heard from someone who had been at the concert, but the evil day would have been put off for several weeks; and somehow an old misdemeanour is less awful than an immediate one. But now it was impossible that there should be any escape. I earnestly hoped that Fetch would find some way out by protesting ignorance of the deceit and so protect herself from blame. She had done nothing but what she had been told to do and could well have been deceived by the sleeping bolster.

I did not know if my mother cared for me very much, but clearly she would have been full of anxiety, and when she found me returning well and unharmed that anxiety would give way to anger. I would have to lie above all to keep Bram Fox's name out of it. But here was I, only eighteen, flouting my mother's orders, travelling to Falmouth without an escort, and spending a whole night, totally unescorted, in a public hotel. If it were generally known it would damage my reputation, indeed create a new one, of unladylike behaviour, wilfulness, brazenness and indiscipline.

It would surely have been better to have risked my life. Was this storm not exaggerated, by Bram, out of mischief, by Blundstone, to let an empty room? Perhaps even now, now that Bram was out of the way, I could steal down and let myself out and take the boat across. Men had such a patronizing view of a woman's ability to be practical and handle a small boat.

I stared out. The sound of violins and cellos was still in my ears, in my head, possibly in my heart. I felt enlightened, uplifted, capable of anything.

Two gulls tumbled past my window screaming after some scraps that had been thrown. The sky was slightly lighter; a moon was probably rising; but a piece of awning on the schooner below me was flapping and straining as fiercely as ever. And the puddles on the cobbles were still stirred by driving rain. I had not brought a watch with me in case the sea spray got in it, but the time could hardly yet be ten o'clock.

Because of the flapping of the awning I mistook the first tap on the door, but the second was more distinct.

'Yes? What is it?'

No one answered. I went to the door and lifted the latch. A familiar figure stood there, hatless, cloak still damp about the shoulders.

'I thought,' said Bram, 'you would be hungry. You would have nothing at the concert, and I suspect you have not had a bite since dinner.' He carried a tray, on which was some chicken, a miniature loaf of bread, a square of butter, a half carafe of wine, a pot of mustard, a canister of salt, some salad leaves, an apple and a dish of jam.

I stared at it, my breathing tight again. He was smiling a singularly sweet smile.

'I thought you had gone home. I thought . . .'

'I went to look at your cutter,' he said. 'It's safe enough — you secured it well — but there's about three inches of water in it. You can get a man to bale it out in the morning. May I come in?'

Before I assented he was in and placed the tray on a semicircular table near the bed.

'Eat this. It will warm you.' He put his hand on mine. 'But you are not cold. Good. This room is over the kitchen.'

I said, trembling inwardly: 'You should not be in here! You — you realize it is very improper. I never expected you to come back. I am not hungry, though thank you for the thought. Please go!'

'No one knows I am up here,' he said. 'I

88

ordered the food as if it were for myself. Then I took this pretty tray down from the wall. It is just the right size.'

I said: 'Please go!'

'Must I?'

'Yes!'

'Do you not care for me?'

I looked at him through a mist of tears. 'That is not the point.'

He put his hand on mine again and laughed silently. 'The point, little Emma, is that I care for you. I want to look after you. See, this is a lovely capon, take a little bite. Allow me to butter the bread. And a sip of wine . . . I'll taste it first myself. We once shared a boat. No one gossiped. No one complained. So why should it be wrong to share a glass of wine?'

'You are *perverse*, Bram. How can you compare the two? In one case — '

'I do not compare the two. When we first met you were a dumpy child, now you are an attractive, delightful woman — '

'With half a ruined face! You're *lying* to me! You're pretending — just *pretending*! It's unfair! Why do you not leave me alone?'

'Because I cannot bear to. I have a very great taking for you. Tell me you have half a ruined face and I will say look at that whole of you which is not at all ruined but glorious with youth and elegance. I love you, little Emma, and I want you very much. Do not cry, now, do not cry. I have not come to hurt you. I have come to *feed* you, and *wine* you, and perhaps just to help me a little bit to show how much I care.'

Those who would condemn me cannot ever have felt as I felt then. People have different tempers, different temptations. Perhaps I was not born to have the character of a restrained spinster, as no doubt should have been dictated by my disfigurement.

I have never thought of myself as a 'fallen woman', as no doubt the moralists of the day would dub me.

I found myself sitting on the edge of the bed, sipping wine, eating chicken and new-baked bread thickly spread with butter, at first a little tearful but presently drying up and staring at him cold-eyed as at a serpent. But presently we drank canary wine from the same glass, and a newly relaxed warmth came over me that took away some of the electric tension but none of the desire. What am I saying, that at eighteen and a repressed virgin I should have been capable of experiencing such an overwhelming emotion?

He began to unbutton my blouse, and I made a feeble effort to restrain him.

'My little starfish,' he said. 'I am going to turn you into a starfish.'

'I'd rather be a crab,' I said.

He laughed soundlessly. 'That's what I love about you,' he said. 'You have — a ready — wit.'

With each hesitation of his voice he tugged at my blouse and then it was off. He began to kiss the soft part of my upper breasts, then, tiring of such trivialities, he pulled the inner garment down and cupped me in his two hands. It's no good pretending I expected the sensations that came on me.

Presently he stopped and insisted that I should share the last of the wine with him. A piece of chicken and crumbs from the bread were scattered on the rug. The rain was still pattering on the window, though it seemed more lightly.

'I think,' I began, the wine on my lips, warming as it chilled them.

'What do you think, Starfish?'

'I think the storm is — is nearly over.'

'On the contrary,' he said, 'it is just about to begin.'

III

I was home by half an hour after nine. I did not know if I was too old for a beating, but I was prepared to endure anything that was meted out.

My mother said: 'You have demeaned yourself and disgraced yourself. I have always known you as wilful and disobedient, but this is a new chapter in your life. There is some doubt in my mind as to whether I shall continue to accept you as my daughter.'

'I — am very sorry, Mama.'

'Sorry! Do you realize the anxiety we felt? I am only glad that your uncle, who has done so much for us — for you — is no longer alive to witness in what coin you have repaid his kindnesses!'

'I had no idea,' I said. 'I did not

suppose . . . That storm. It came so suddenly. Would you rather I had drowned?'

'You had every idea of disobeying my decision that you should not go. And you embroiled Fetch in your deceit, which only shows she is no fit companion for you. She shall leave at the end of the week, and without a reference.'

This was what I had been fearing most of all. 'Mama,' I said. 'I am to blame. Utterly and without question! Myself only. Fetch was only obeying instructions. She did nothing of her own free will! I pray that you punish me in any way you think fit, but please, please, do not punish someone who is without blame — '

My mother said: 'I am of the opinion that part of your punishment is that you shall be deprived of a lady's maid — for in all but name that is what Fetch has become. Apart from that I shall reserve my judgment — for the time being. For some time I have felt that it was not suitable that you should spend the rest of your life here in idleness and comfort. Why, even when your aunt was in the house and bedridden, I do not remember your helping her or helping Mary or Mrs Whattle to care for her — '

'I did offer! Many, many times! Mary always refused!'

'Well, be that as it may, I have come to the conclusion it is not right that you should spend the rest of your life here in idleness and comfort. Some sort of useful, worthwhile employment would enable you to feel self-sufficient and independent. I do not as yet know what it may be, but this wildcap exploit has convinced me that such a solution is right for you. Then you will be out of my hands, and it will be for you to obey your employer — or lose the employment.'

As I walked up to my room I did not know what to feel for two moments together. I was deeply upset, deeply sorry, deeply ashamed. But behind that as the waves dwarf the little ships sailing the sea — as the waves in the harbour had still been big enough at times almost to swamp my cutter this morning — were all the memories of last night. First there was *music*, the reedy sob of violins, the deeper moans of the cellos; this new music speaking to me and asking me to unfold my heart. But after that came the experience which carried everything before it. In the cold light of a July morning I was already half-disbelieving what memory told me had happened. It was at once a wonderful exotic dream and a terrifying nightmare. I was not so ignorant as not to know the likely outcome. That was the nightmare. And somehow in the middle of all the sensations, one drowning another in the heady experience of pleasure, had come the feeling of pain, of wrongdoing, of excess, of the utterly forbidden.

Perhaps it was just me, brought up in a not very strict Christian family but a family in which right and wrong were clearly defined. Perhaps it was Bram, exquisitely teaching me too much in a single night. I had a leaden ton of apprehension as to the consequences, but a youthful hope that Bram would somehow be able to 'make it all right'. Even if he offered to marry me there would be the objections of my family, all sorts of obstacles to overcome. Perhaps he was just playing with my feelings and would want to continue in some way with secret notes and clandestine meetings.

And at the back of it all was the hideous knowledge that I would never be an attractive wife. Yet he had wanted me. Skilfully he had taken me. Seduced was the word, and like a broken leaf I had crumbled in his hands.

God in Heaven, I thought. What happened to me last night? 'My little starfish' he had called me. I understood now very well what he meant. My knees trembled at the thought of it all. I felt physically sick and bitterly humiliated. I felt half contempt for him and half love. I felt half contempt for myself and half love. Nothing, nothing, nothing could ever be the same again — I was irretrievably damaged, morally and psychologically, as I was irretrievably damaged of feature.

When I got in I sat for a long time in my bedroom, taking nothing to eat or drink. The house was quiet, but that was not unnatural since Uncle Davey had died. I thought: somehow I must go on living — at least for the time being — and somehow I must face my cousins and my sister with the disgrace. But to them my sin was only one of outrageous disobedience — as it was to my mother. She had not mentioned Bram Fox by name, but I had denied meeting anybody special at the concert. My far greater sin was not known — not yet. That I alone had to live with. If Bram came here and claimed me, then more would come out. (But it would not quite so much matter then.) If he did *not*, then more would still only too probably come out, even if that was in the future, weeks, months ahead. For the moment if I could only learn to live with myself and the surging frightening knowledge of what had happened, then I could face them for the time being, be dutifully humble but no more.

Did my mother mean her threat that I should be sent away somewhere to earn a living as a governess or a seamstress at sixpence a day? I was fit for nothing better. There are few occupations for a woman. In other circumstances I might have tried with her influence to get on the stage. That clearly was not a prospect. Perhaps, in view of what had happened at Blundstone's Hotel, I might make a living on the streets of Falmouth. (Bram had praised my body, said it was perfect, adorable, beautiful; but those were love terms expressed in the excesses of the moment and not to be taken seriously or considered in the light of day.) I could certainly earn more on the streets than looking after someone's children. Falmouth had a constantly changing population of seamen who had money in their pockets and would not be too particular about a girl's face.

Somehow the day passed. I supped with the family. In the middle of the meal Desmond appeared suddenly, looking rather subdued, and saying he was glad to be back. After making a fuss of Tamsin, he asked her if she had enjoyed the concert. Tamsin said she did not go but Emma had. I tried to mutter an explanation while everyone else at the table sat stony-faced.

Desmond was not slow to notice 'atmosphere', so he dropped the subject. Then he said:

'Has Slade gone?'

'Oh yes. A couple of weeks ago.'

Slade had left muttering and ungracious, leaving my mother undisputed mistress of the house. He clearly blamed her for his dismissal, but in fact it was chiefly Anna Maria's decision, though all the children disliked him. Anyway, he was Uncle Davey's servant and now the Admiral was gone.

He had left by sea, taking six large bags with him, and no one had dared to ask him to open them. After all, he was leaving after twenty years. I had been specially glad to see him go. He had never laid hands on me since that dark afternoon in the cellar, but he had tried to intimidate me in all sorts of ways.

Just before he went he had said to me: 'Turned away without so much as a 'thank you' after all these years. And a miserable pension. But you look out, Miss Clever Boots, you and your family, you ain't finished with me yet. I'll put you all in a hole afore I've done with you.'

The following day Tamsin had said to me: 'Come on.'

'Where to?'

'Let's have a look in that cellar.'

'Oh, Tamsin, you can't still be interested?'

'Aren't you?'

'Well, yes. Come to think of it. Yes.'

We went down with a candle lamp to give us extra light. The wine cellar door was open, but the big one beyond was firmly locked. We went in search of the key. None of the servants had it. We sneaked into my uncle's old bedroom. It smelt still of him, dangerously so, as if at any moment he would step out of a cupboard. A lot of his clothes had not yet been moved, but most of the drawers were empty. In one drawer there were three keys, but none of them was remotely big enough to fit the cellar door.

In the end we asked my mother. She said she had no idea. 'Perhaps Slade took it with him.'

'That would be a great liberty.'

'He was a law unto himself,' said my mother. 'Or thought he was. Anyway, the place probably hasn't been opened for years.'

'That's what we thought,' said Tamsin.

IV

My relationship with my sister had always been uneasy. The four-year difference had always given her an edge which had allowed her to treat me with semi-affectionate contempt.

And I, for my part, often felt jealousy towards her for being everything that I was not, and never could be. But only since I grew into a woman and, after a long period of solitariness, had begun to show independence and initiative had Tamsin seemed to resent me, as if I were an impediment to her enjoyment, a nuisance, a spoilsport, someone with whom she was happier to be without. Always she was derogatory about my disfigurement, drawing my attention to it when sometimes for a short while I had been able to forget it.

Fetch left the following week. I had tried my hardest to move my mother on this point, but she would not budge. It was a tearful parting. I pressed five sovereigns on Sally before she left; these she adamantly refused and I as adamantly insisted she take.

'I shall be all right, miss. Reely. Thank you. I can stay with my mum till something else d'turn up. Thank you, reely.'

'But with my mother refusing a reference . . . That is outrageous!'

'Well, I got yours, miss. Though I reckon it do make my chances of a good post more harder to come by. But Sister June d'say maybe Mrs Elizabeth might find a vacancy for a scullery maid. Don't you worry, miss. 'Twill all come right in the end.'

The end! I wondered what the upright and very proper Fetch would think if she knew what had happened to me. She would have been as horrified as my mother. And would blame herself most bitterly for having connived at this unimaginable event. *Her* young lady. In the first bloom of her youth and innocence . . .

Ten days had now passed since the night of the concert. I had hardly stirred from the house, scarcely aware of what to expect of my own physical feelings, desperately hoping for some sign from Bram. Perhaps he would not want to write even in an innocent and formal way until he knew how I had fared. Perhaps he did not want to commit himself to a letter at all. Perhaps he thought any letters addressed to Tamsin or me would be opened. Obviously he had offended both my mother and Tamsin at the Queen's reception, even though I could not guess what it had been about.

After Fetch had left, I began to go out more, on the lawns, and I would loiter a few minutes each day on the little stone quay. The storm of last Thursday week had broken the spell of fine weather, and I had stared out from one window or another of the house at scuttling clouds and curtains of hard-driven rain. As the weather at last cleared, we had a couple of days of sea fog which cloaked Falmouth entirely but only just reached our headland and creek. Being right on the edge of the fog, you could watch it coming and going, moving like engine smoke. One minute the sun would be blazing, burning hot, then it would pale and glow like a new penny trying to break through the shifting mists.

It was on the second of these days when I had come from a walk exercising Parish that the second parlourmaid, an elderly woman called Vennor, told me that there was a letter for me.

'Letter? Where? Who brought it? . . . '

'Young Gunnel. Him what brings the papers and the magazines. He's just gone. You just missed 'im.'

I ran into the entrance hall and looked round. On a silver tray, such as one uses for visiting cards, was a small package addressed to Miss Emma Spry. My mother and sister were out, so no one had seen it who would want to know its contents. I tore it open. A small cardboard box. Inside the box was a brooch in the form of a starfish. Pinkish in colour, the stones looked like coral, or imitation coral. Something you might find in an antique shop. With a little gold pin at the back. But the message? I peered into the box and could find nothing. I pulled at the wrapping and the tissue paper in which the brooch had been wrapped. Nothing.

He had sent this without comment, without greeting, without suggesting that we might meet. Of course, it was infinitely certain whom it was from. Certain only to me. Was he being as cautious as that? He did not have the reputation for such caution. So had he sent it as a joke, a promise, a reminder? I could hear his laugh, see the narrowed eyes, full of predatory fun. Laugh, my little starfish, he was saying. Wear the badge because now you belong to me. My flesh crept. I did belong to him. I felt like a chattel, ready to do what I was told. Did he have many women like me, accepting his favours, waiting for his favours? In what way was I unusual? Just another scalp?

Part of me seethed with anger, part of me prickled with something like pride. I thought, I shall destroy myself — otherwise he will destroy me. Why was I born, mutilated, weak as a kitten yet militantly angry?

There was a step in the hall. I crushed the

brooch back into the box and dropped it in a drawer. Tamsin.

'Where's Desmond?' she said.

'I haven't seen him.'

'Where have you been?'

'Walking Parish. Is Mama here?'

'She's been out but has a headache, so has gone to lie down.'

'I see.'

Tamsin looked me up and down curiously.

'What were you up to that night?'

'What night?'

'You know very well. Did you really stay at Blundstone's Hotel?'

'Of course!'

'On your own? You know you've broken all the rules of decent behaviour? Why did you not call on Mrs Elizabeth Fox or the Millets? They would have given you a bed for the night.'

'You've no idea what the storm was like,' I said. 'I went down to the boat: you know I was determined to get home; but that took me right to the wrong end of the town; I was soaked and nearly blown away. What else could I have done? I was sorry to offend the Mrs Grundys of the town, but I didn't expect my sister to be one!'

It was strange how that wonderfully pretty face could close up and become mean. I was quite used to the change, but very few other people were shown it.

'Call me what you like, but I'm right: you've created a lot of talk; this is only a little local community though it may think otherwise. I'm always embarrassed by having a sister who looks

101

so peculiar, but I don't want to be associated with someone who brings a bad *name* on the family.'

'Maybe you won't have to be embarrassed by me much longer!'

'What d'you mean?'

'Never mind.' Suddenly the prospect of going somewhere to earn my living had become not so much a threat as an opportunity.

She waited for me to say more, and then evidently concluded I was just being emotional and self-pitying. 'Well don't ever forget that Mama is an actress, and that suggests to the Mrs Grundys of this world a rather brassy woman with loose morals. If you go off the rails it won't do *my* reputation any good, and I can't afford to have my life ruined by your pranks. I have to *live* here.'

I stared through one of the hall windows at the slanting sunshine outside. I was thinking of the brooch in the drawer and only half attending. Then it soaked in. 'Why should you have to live here?'

She said: 'Desmond has just asked me to marry him.'

6

I

It was a reasonable solution, as I had part foreseen, as far as my mother was concerned; though she had had much higher hopes for her pretty daughter. Tamsin was still very young and becoming no less beautiful, and even though the prospect of a Boscawen had fallen through, there were others to look for. A Molesworth, a Lemon, a Courtney Vyvyan, would do very well; but either no sons of suitable age seemed to be about or there were evidences that an actress's daughter, and penniless at that, did not quite come up to snuff.

Time would tell. A little farther afield in the country were many other families, such as the Prideaux-Brunes and the Pole Carews, as yet virtually unknown and therefore unplumbed. But now a decision was on her.

Desmond as a 'second son' might never inherit Place House, though he seemed to be the only one of the four children who wanted to live here. Nor since his father died had Desmond seemed short of money, and he already had some men repairing the church. They could live a comfortable life in one of the most delightful situations in the county. Apart from our mother, who was often away, and our aunt muttering in the mad house, she would be the only

Mrs Spry. She would certainly be entertained as such. Even if Samuel survived the Navy, Place House was not an ideal position from which to pursue a parliamentary career, and if he suddenly changed his mind and decided to marry and be a country gentleman, there was room aplenty for two families in the house. Samuel had always been fond of his younger brother and would probably be unwilling to displace him.

Of course it all depended on Tamsin. Though much influenced by her mother, she had a decided will of her own and would make her own choice on such an important matter as a husband.

A few weeks passed. My mother was not yet on full speaking terms with me: Tamsin never referred to Desmond's proposal again, so I did not know whether she had accepted him or not; but I thought not. I had my period but concluded that it would stop next time. Desperate for news of Bram, I went over to St Mawes a couple of times, accompanied by a formidable housemaid who had none of Fetch's compliant companionship; but there was no sign of him there, and Falmouth was strictly out of bounds. I didn't even know where he *lived*. He seemed to spend his time in and out of people's houses and have no fixed address. I could, I suppose, write to him care of Mrs Elizabeth Fox, but so far could not summon the courage to do so. I began three times, thanking him formally for the gift of the starfish brooch, but each attempt ended in the kitchen fire.

It was not a time for ordinary fires. The weather had set fair — as often happened after fog; the creek was like a blue plate split once in a while by seine boats leaving or returning. (Pilchards were scarce this year.) Water in the Roads was never wholly still, there being too much traffic plying up and down; but the shallow trembling of its blue depths was broken only by the greater ripples of the shipping. As lack of wind reduced all movement to a crawl, half the town of Falmouth and its farther bank were obscured by the masses of sails raised to catch the slightest breeze.

Desmond came to sit beside me on the edge of the quay. 'Do you know,' he said, 'what a shearwater is?'

'What? Is it a bird?'

'I spotted a pair near the St Anthony lookout. The first I have ever seen. Quite big birds — wings a foot across. It must be the great shearwater.' Desmond plucked at his lip. 'It is a surprise to see them close inland. They usually stay well out to sea.'

'What colour are they?' I asked.

'Palish brown — bit mottled, I should think. I only saw them for a few minutes as they whirled about the rocks.'

'When was this?'

'Just now. Half an hour ago.' He looked at me quizzically. 'You are interested?'

'Of course. Though I know little about the subject.'

'I'll lend you some books.'

'Thank you.'

Silence fell. Then he suddenly said: 'Emma, do you know that I have asked Tamsin to marry me?'

'I had a feeling . . . Has she said yes?'

'Not yet. Not in so many words. But I believe she will.' There was another pause. 'Has she said anything to you?'

'You know I'm rather in disgrace with my family at present.'

'Oh, you're not in disgrace with me,' he said. 'You — er — kicked over the traces a little, but it was in a good cause. I'm as starved of music as you are. When — if — we marry, I shall take her once a year to London to all the concerts.'

I forbore to say that Tamsin might not enjoy this.

'I want you to know,' he said and stopped.

'Yes?'

'I want you to know that if we marry, Tamsin and I, her sister need not feel it necessary to leave and find employment elsewhere. She will always be welcome in the house.'

So he had heard something; they had been talking about it; my mother was still considering her threat.

'Why, *thank* you, Desmond. That is — very generous and kind. I really have not considered my future very much since Uncle Davey died. Clearly I shall never marry.' The last sentence came out abruptly, and I thought: it may not be *true* — it still may not be true! But what has happened? Perhaps Bram is disgusted with me. Perhaps even disgusted with himself. Not a

106

sign, not a note. Only a starfish brooch. 'Has my mother mentioned it to you?'

'Mentioned? . . . Well, not in so many words . . . She did say . . . '

'What?'

'But that was in her moments of worst anger. I am sure that things have cooled down a great deal since then. Don't you feel it?'

'Desmond, what did she say?'

He made a little gesture of impatience. 'She and I have, of course, discussed my proposal of marriage to Tamsin; I mean when Tamsin has not been there. And my aunt did say once that if we did marry it would not be suitable if you stayed on here. She wishes to go back to London herself, and she thinks as a young married couple we should be left alone together. I was simply assuring you that it is not my thinking. There is ample room if you wish to stay.'

'Thank you,' I said, touching his hand. 'Thank you, Desmond.'

'Of course,' he went on, 'it will not be all plain sailing just yet. I'm not sure about Samuel, and Anna Maria does not favour the match.'

'Oh? Why?'

'I think she has taken her opinion from Edward Carlyon who does not approve of the marriage of first cousins.'

'I had not thought of it.'

'Also, to be blunt, Anna Maria thinks I could have done better for myself. Oh,' he hurried on as I was about to speak, 'she has not been as explicit as that. But she appears to feel quite

107

strongly that a younger son should have looked elsewhere.'

'Samuel is the head of the family. That is if your mother does not come round. But shall you take any notice of what they say?'

'I have to take notice,' he said gently, 'we are a close-knit family and care for each other, and I shall not wish to offend. But I believe persuasion may make them think different. If I can only get Samuel on my side . . . '

'And Mary?'

'Mary I think is not well. It is not a complaint of the body. But she looks inward so much and has so few opinions on anything. I have a superstitious fear that she may in a few years go like our mother.'

II

That night I said to my mother: 'Is it true that if Tamsin marries Desmond you will go back to London?'

She still had beautiful eyes, and in the dusk the lines scarcely showed. Over the years her mouth had grown tighter, thinner.

'Not permanently. This is my home. But if they marry they should be left to themselves for a while; it will be better for all concerned. I shall return more often to the stage: there are still plenty of opportunities for the not-so-young, and I have recently had an offer to play the Nurse in *Romeo and Juliet* at Drury Lane in the autumn, and people there remember my name.'

There was a pause. I took the bull by the horns. 'So I can stay here?'

'No,' she said firmly. 'I believe by your escapade you have forfeited that right. But in any event it would be much preferable that you should move away and earn your living.'

'I cannot act,' I said. 'I can sing.'

'They would not have you. You must know that.'

'Do you expect me to become some child's governess? No mother would employ me.'

'They might. It is a disfigurement that makes you quite unsuitable for the stage, but in a house one gets used to it.'

'Thank you, Mama,' I said.

She looked at me suspiciously. 'At one time, Emma, you could not find your tongue. Now you frequently use it to ill effect. Being in employment will guide you to its proper use.'

The maid came in with lighted candles. By the flickering new flame I looked at my mother again and thought: I can never, never tell her. But what when my belly begins to swell for all to see? There will be no concealment possible then.

After the maid had gone she said: 'As a matter of fact, I believe I may have found something for you.' She hesitated in a fashion she had no doubt used to effect in the theatre. 'Your Uncle Francis.'

'D'you mean — who took the service at the funeral?'

'Yes, the Canon.'

'Who lives on the moors?'

'At Blisland. On the edge of the moors. He

109

has recently lost his housekeeper companion and wants someone to take her place. He would normally be looking for someone more mature and with more experience, but in a letter to him I have pressed your case. He has the advantage of having met you and knows about your handicap, and you are distantly related. You have had the advantage of seeing how this house is run, and have been trained in simple cooking and domestic affairs. He is, he tells me, very poor, so he cannot afford to pay more than a nominal sum in wages; but you will have two servants, and the run of the house. I only hope he will accept you.'

I listened almost indifferently for I could not see myself taking employment in a rectory carrying an illegitimate child. I thought I knew enough about the Anglican church to be sure it would not want to give shelter to a fallen woman. Perhaps if I were to strangle the child when it was born, or contrive an abortion . . .

Hope was ebbing. I knew no one to speak to, no one to confide in.

'Mama,' I said.

'Yes?'

'No matter.'

'It will be a different household from this,' she said, 'more devout, more spartan. That sort of discipline will be good for you.'

I stared at the cupid on the wallpaper, which was still peeling, in the state it had been ten years ago.

'Desmond is going to spend more money on the church here. I heard him discussing it with

110

the Canon at the funeral. He could well spend some on this house too.'

She looked at me sourly. 'I wrote to the Canon ten days ago. I heard he was looking for a housekeeper. I am hoping to hear any day.'

III

Celebrations were to take place that summer to mark the Coronation of William IV. A *West Briton* was delivered to us, and I read the details with attention.

King William had now reigned a year, and had expressed the wish that his coronation, which was due to take place in two weeks' time, should be an altogether quieter and less expensive occasion than when his brother had been crowned. Nevertheless this did not deter his loyal subjects from celebrating the occasion, and, as often happened in Cornwall nowadays, Truro had been made the centre of the rejoicing. On the Sunday there was to be a solemn service in St Mary's Church, to which all the distinguished people of the county were invited; but on the day before there was to take place an outdoor fête, a regatta timed for full tide, a banquet in the streets, a ball in the Assembly Rooms, fireworks. Now if there was one man I could name who couldn't fail to be in the swim of such an occasion it was Mr Fox. He was drawn to 'events', celebrations, balls, concerts. In some capacity he would be in Truro a week on Saturday. It was now or never for me. How could I get there? Clearly I would receive no permission from my mother. But if I again took French leave, how could I physically *reach* the town? Falmouth was just across the bay. Truro was ten miles inland at the last important navigable point of the River Fal. The distance from St Anthony might well be fifteen miles. I could walk that.

It would mean crossing creeks like Percuil, and eventually the river at King Harry. But it could be done. Of course the simplest way would be to hire a cutter at St Mawes and take it all the way. But with life ahead of me looking very bleak I was not anxious to go to the added expense. I had a substantial amount of Uncle Davey's legacy still, but who knew what privations I might have to face if Bram continued to ignore me?

It had been the habit of Desmond and Mary when they were in their teens to walk to Truro sometimes and spend a night with the Boscawen children at Tregothnan on the way, but I had never gone with them and I shrank from arriving at the Falmouths' great house as an unannounced guest.

I thought of enlisting Desmond's help on this second adventure, but I could not trust him not to tell Tamsin if some crisis arose. After all, his first loyalty was to her.

Leaving Place House was no problem if one were prepared to be brazen about it — even Aunt Anna had several times got as far as the quay in her nightdress — but it would be too humiliating to be brought back. So a degree of contrivance was worthwhile.

Dawn was breaking late now, but if I left at six in the morning there would be plenty of light in the Cornish sky. Six hours, seven hours it might take. Celebrations were due to begin at eleven with a parade, but the day was to be a full one, ending with fireworks at midnight. That should be time enough. Provided I could find him. What was he most likely to be interested in? The regatta, which began at two?

What would I take? Something to eat and drink. Strong shoes. A cloak against a shower — a light dress so that one did not become too hot walking. A comb; three guineas to be on the safe side. Small change. A silk scarf to hide the disagreeable side of my face. Did I intend to walk back the same day? I would be too late to catch Joey Dixon's market boat back from Falmouth to St Mawes. If I absented myself for another night my mother would be beside herself. But had I anything to lose?

The weather was changing. Clouds were drifting up from the south-west. By the Friday the sun was fitful, and now and then a cloud let drop a few speckles of rain. So be it.

I left the house at five. There should have been a glimmering of light by then, but the clouds were lowering, and I stumbled twice in the black sleeping depths of the house and stood heart in mouth waiting for discovery. The greatest risk was that Parish should bark, but he had been so severely trained not to wake his mistress that he was no guard dog.

Side door, then skirting the church, which raised a pinnacle in the dark, past some

113

scaffolding that the workmen had put up, walking on grass when I could to avoid the crunch of pebbles. A cow's white face peered at me over a hedge and made me jump. Out of earshot of the house I returned to the pebbles, saw the big white farm gate between the granite posts, slid through with a click of the latch, slung light pack on shoulder and the adventure had begun.

Somehow I felt more hopeful than I had done since the night of the concert. I was at least doing something, taking an action which with any sort of luck would enable me to meet him again. Truro was a small town, and though it would be crowded with people from the country around, Bram was one of the gentry. He would be organizing something or taking some prominent part in it all.

I carried with me a map that Aunt Anna had kept in her drawer, marked with crosses where her whist-playing friends lived. It did not extend to Truro but it covered the area as far as Carnon Downs. The problem was negotiating all the little inlets of the River Fal, but I had worked out what seemed to be the easiest route. First obstacle, right at the outset, was the Polvarth Ferry which would enable me to cross to St Mawes. I knew this did not begin until six, but Tregundle lived on this side, and moored his boat for the night at the quay below his cottage.

The steep lane to the quay was much overgrown and full of glow-worms. Their tiny greenish twinkling lights flanked me all the way down. They seemed a good omen. Then an owl screeched overhead and I was not so sure.

By now daylight had almost come, and the creek glimmered through the trees. There were steps from his thatched cottage to the quay. In the distance a cock crowed into the still air. It was half tide and the boat leaned on its elbow in the sandy shingle, the water glimmering a foot from its bows. I stared across. It was no distance to the other bank. I could wade it. But I never had. In the middle it might unexpectedly come up to my waist and I had no wish to get my skirts wet. I walked awkwardly across the pebbles and looked at the creek. The water was perceptibly rising, inch by inch. In an hour the dinghy would be afloat. I could not wait.

Unlatch the rope and push. An inch at a time at first. I was sweating, and a drift of rain in the wind was not unwelcome. Halfway in the water the pressure was suddenly taken off. I gave the boat an extra shove and as it floated jumped in. The ferryman had taken the oars but left a paddle, and with that I propelled myself to the other side.

IV

From St Mawes I took the coast lane to St Just, skirting the inlet, watched the bats flying in the dawn light among the sentinelled trees. Tregorland, Tregellans, Penperth; then the long descent to Tolverne and King Harry Ferry. I waited for the first crossing, ate a piece of cold pasty and bought a cup of milk from a nearby cottage. A dozen bullocks were also waiting for the ferry. Roped together, they snuffled and stamped and snorted until the oarsmen had brought the ferry to the quay. Then, with one farmer to lead them and one to beat them from behind, they were launched into the River Fal and obliged to swim to preserve their lives. The farmer at the back followed me onto the ferry, leaping on perilously as it slid away from the bank, then with his partner took a hand at the oars as we launched into midstream, followed by twelve animals dragged along with stout ropes. At the other side there was much confusion as several of the animals struggling to get ashore nearly upset the ferry. Ignoring this I went quickly on up the hill, past Trelissick, then on to Come-to-Good (it was a Quaker meeting house: would Bram Fox be known there?). Soon after that I joined the coaching road for Truro, and from there it was straightforward, though up hill and down dale.

It was when I came to the outskirts of the town that I realized the enormity of the task. The streets were crowded, the harbour too, and the pool full of small boats. The milling crowds were of all conditions, from beggars in bare feet to fops carrying walking sticks and pomanders against the stink. Stalls had been set up, further narrowing the streets. The Town Crier was ringing his bell and shouting something about coal. Pigs rooted everywhere among the refuse and the horse dung.

I fought my way into the centre of the town to High Cross, near the church, where the parade was forming up to move off. There were trumpeters at the front and four men with drums. A single church bell was ringing, hardly to be heard above the shouts and the loud chatter.

I edged myself towards a tall elderly man in a frock coat and a silk hat who was talking to a group and might, I thought, be organizing things. When he paused for breath and two of the others drifted away, I said:

'I beg your pardon, sir. I wonder if you could help me. I am trying to find Mr Abraham Fox.'

He looked at me, frowned at my face, cupped his ear. I had to repeat the question.

'Mr Abraham Fox? I've no idea. I don't have his acquaintance. What is his position in these celebrations?'

'I don't know, sir,' I said, 'I'm afraid I don't know. Is there somewhere I can enquire?'

He had been hostile, but perhaps my educated voice made him soften or my face convinced him I could not be a prostitute.

'If you were to ask at the Town Hall, in Boscawen Street. This way, then down Church Lane. They might know. Ask for Mr Vage.'

I thanked him and went off in the direction he indicated. By now it was raining steadily, a soft damping rain drifting with the breeze. The narrow slit of lane was almost impossible to get down, but once through one came out into the widest street in Truro. What looked like the Town Hall was almost opposite, and I wended a way among the horses, the carriages, the carts, the donkeys, the street sellers and went into the building, squeezing past a crush of men in the doorway. One or two made crude jests as I slid through.

Inside was a large room, tables, a chair, some men arguing over a banner. A tall man in a frock coat with a sash from shoulder to waist.

'Pardon me, sir, do you know if Mr Vage is here?'

He looked at me with quite a different eye, benevolent, paternal. ' 'Orace Vage, m'dee-ur? He'm down to the Moorfield, nigh to West Bridge. They was proposing a procession of maidens all in white, but he's thinking to hold it back a while on account of this spiery old weather. You'd best wait a while yourself.'

I smiled at him with the sideways look I had grown accustomed to to make the best of my face. 'Thank you, sir. In fact it was Mr Abraham Fox I was seeking. Someone said that Mr Vage might know.'

'Mr Jonathan Fox?'

'No. Abraham.'

'Seems me I've 'eard tell of such a one. But he bain't known to me. Ye don't mean Dr Joseph Fox, him as lives at Restronguet? Now there's a fine man for 'ee . . . '

I excused myself and went to the door, but saw the heavy shower was not yet over, so I slid round the corner of the room and stood against a cupboard, took out the rest of my pasty and ate it there. The water was dripping off my hair and into the pasty. I was tired and dispirited. It seemed a long way to walk home in this downpour.

A man breathed ale over me and said: 'What's amiss with 'ee? Come 'ome along o' me. Tis dry 'tome and we'll 'ave a bite t'eat.'

'Now then, now then,' said the tall man, coming up. 'Be off with 'ee, leave the maid alone.' He peered at me. 'You bain't crying, m'dee-ur?'

'No,' I said, 'no, it is the rain.'

'Well, if so be as you're set 'pon finding this here character called Abraham Fox, why don't 'ee go to Lemon Bridge, where Jonathan Fox be acting as marshal for the regatta? You can always rely 'pon it that one Fox'll know another.'

7

I

At two the regatta began, but Jonathan Fox, if he was the man standing in the anchored boat giving directions, was quite out of reach. (I thought I had seen him before somewhere.) The rain had stopped at last but there was the sort of damp in the air that did not encourage one's clothes to dry. I was wet and chilled. *Must* wait until the regatta was over and then start back: with luck I should be home by midnight. There would be the devil to pay, but that could have been borne if the object had been successfully achieved — or at least with some better equanimity if I had found Bram and faced him out. The utter failure of the day brought me to a low ebb. I understood now why Annie, a maid at Place, had thrown herself over a cliff.

The regatta dragged on, as regattas usually do, and another man, standing beside me, began to make remarks. It was unusual, no doubt, that a young woman of any decent class should be unattended in a crowd and on a day like this, and he wanted to test the water to see if I was as unapproachable as I tried to look.

This was a middle-aged man, not as ragged nor as easy to put off as the man in the Town Hall. I walked away and he followed me, took

120

my arm gently, then when I pulled it away, more firmly.

It was a bad part of Truro, by the Town Quay. At normal times respectable folk would probably not be seen here unless on business. Today it was crowded with all kinds watching the regatta.

'You're tired, mistress,' he said. 'Have a gin. This yon tavern'll do nicely. I'll never harm 'ee.'

'Let me alone!' I said, wrenching my arm free again.

Two old market women laughed out loud at us, gaping gums where their teeth should have been. The Town Crier now was quite near, a big man with a white beard in a battered blue uniform and a tall hat.

'If any man have the mind to buy very fine Neath coals, as good as any as can be burned in forge or hearth, let 'em come to Enys Quay to the ship *Kingfisher*, Cap'n Enoch Beddoes, where they may have the said good Neath coals at 6^d a bushel.'

I shook the man off again, slid past some people and caught the Town Crier's arm.

'I am sorry,' I said. 'But this man is pestering me! Can you please tell him to go away!'

The Town Crier peered down at me, through his bushy beard. He had tiny pin-point eyes which expressed surprise, suspicion, irritation and finally responsibility.

'What man's that, mistress?'

I pointed to where my oppressor was shaking the rain off his hat.

'That man! He will not leave me alone!'

The Town Crier stared. 'Why, Mr Arnold. What be the trouble, eh?'

Arnold put his hat back. 'Pesterin' her?' he said indignantly. 'Nothing of the sort. She've been following me for ten minutes, whispering lewd invitations. Tedn't right, Joseph, for decent folk in broad daylight to be pursued by light women, in a respectable town. When I were a young man women like she was flogged at the cart-tail. I've a good mind to give 'er in charge!'

Joseph hesitated. I'm not sure whether he altogether believed Mr Arnold — they knew each other, it was true — but after some rubbing of his beard he looked at me again. 'I reckon 'tis best if you was going, miss. 'Tis not proper for you to be on your own. Where d'you live? What business do you have in the town?'

'My name is Spry,' I said, knees trembling. 'I came to see the regatta. Now that it is over I will rejoin my party.'

Arnold gave me a venomous look. 'Be off with 'ee! You've no right nor business round 'ere!'

There had been a stirring near the steps of the quay, and a tall portly man with a trim grey beard came up them. I knew now why I recognized him: I had last seen him introducing the orchestra and Mr Joseph Emidy at the Falmouth Town Hall on that fateful night. I made a half relieved step towards him before realizing that he would not know me at all.

He was carrying a book and some tickets. My glance flew to the harbour and I saw that, though sails still abounded, the controlling boat was no longer there.

I was past ordinary manners, nerves only just in control of voice and actions.

'Excuse me. Pray excuse me, but are you Mr Jonathan Fox?'

He stopped at the top of the steps to get his breath. 'I am.'

'Oh . . . ' Now that I had come close to one quarry, my tongue and mind hesitated to put the next question. 'Pray, I wonder, I am . . . I am — was looking for Mr Abraham Fox. I wonder if you know where I could find him?'

He frowned, and took out a handkerchief to dab his lips. 'Mr Abraham Fox? Mr Bram Fox?'

'Yes, sir.'

He looked me over. I must have been a pretty sight, with disfigured face, hair sodden, the sleeve of my dress torn where the man had grasped it, still the distress in my eyes.

'May I ask what business you have with him?'

'No — no business, sir. I — know him, and he — he wrote and asked me to meet him. I understood — I thought — he would be — be here.'

Mr Fox hesitated. 'The rain is coming on again. I think you should take shelter. Penrose, will you take this book, in which I have recorded the results. Keep good care of it. I shall not be long.' He turned and looked at me more sympathetically. 'There is a coffee house down this ope.'

It was the first really friendly voice, and I nearly burst into tears. I choked them back and followed him down an alley and up stairs to a low-raftered room, where men in green aprons were waiting on a few tables. I nodded indistinctly when he suggested hot chocolate and presently I was sipping it and staring out of the rain-mottled window while he looked me over.

'It's good to have a moment's peace myself,' he said. 'When you have rested perhaps you can tell me what you want with Abraham Fox.'

Obviously I could not do that, but I told him my name and where I lived and how I came to meet his cousin when he called at Place, and how I had met him again at the orchestral concert last month, to which he had invited me . . .

Mr Fox interrupted. 'But I remember now. I saw you there. You were in the fourth or fifth row. But you were on your own, weren't you? I think — '

'Yes,' I said. 'Bram was organizing things.'

'I remember. But did you *come* on your own? You're a very self-reliant young woman. Did you come here alone *today*?'

'It was not from choice, sir. I could not find a companion, so I came by myself.'

'To see my cousin?'

'Yes, sir.'

'Or second cousin, to be exact. Well, Miss Spry, I have to tell you that Bram is not here, nor are you likely to see him for some time to come.'

We looked at each other. 'M — may I ask . . .'

'Of course. Bram is in gaol.'

II

Mr Jonathan Fox said: 'Let me get you a drink of water. The chocolate perhaps was too rich. No? I expect it is the damp and the chill — who would think it still summer . . . No, I cannot tell you how long he will be in prison for he has been gaoled for debt, so his term will depend upon how long it takes him to discharge his liabilities. My father and I have often said it is an inequitable sentence for such an offence. Many a good man has failed in a legitimate business and been cast into prison for his sins, where he has no means whatever of recovering himself by hard work or new enterprise, and therefore languishes behind bars while perhaps his wife and family are in want.'

I picked up the cup which still had some chocolate in it, but I could not bring it to my lips.

'And Bram?'

'Ah, that is rather different. He was a great favourite of my aunt, Mrs Elizabeth Fox. Bram has great gifts but makes too little of them — no *commercial* use whatever. He lived too high for his means, which were slender, and relied upon her to help him out of one scrape after another. But it happened just once too often and Elizabeth at length listened to the advice of her family and called a halt. I should

125

not be surprised if Mr Abraham Fox finds his sentence salutary. Although some people will never learn.'

Mr Jonathan Fox had a puffy face and seemed at times to have difficulty with his breathing.

'Where,' I said, 'Where is he? In prison, I mean.'

'The case was heard in Truro, but I think he will have gone to Bodmin. Mind you, once his aunt has vented her wrath, I have no doubt she will grant him enough to discharge his debts. The other night she was mentioning the time of three months as a likely and suitable duration. In the meantime one or other of his family will see that he does not lack all the creature comforts. As indeed I believe there is to be some provision made to ensure that his wife does not fall into want. The Foxes, my dear, are a close family, and we have some regard even for our black sheep.'

'His . . . Did you say? . . . '

'His wife, yes. Meliora. Perhaps you did not know that he was married? He tends not to talk of it in the company of other ladies.'

'I see. Thank you.' I half got up, but he went on talking, and I forced myself to listen. Now that he was launched, Mr Fox seemed to want to go on.

'Abraham is the son of my cousin by his second marriage. His mother was a Trejago. He was the only child of this marriage, though he has two half-sisters. From infancy he seems to have been a nonconformist, using that word in the wrong sense. His father was a devout

126

Christian, and they quarrelled often. Corrective treatment, which normally is necessary in the disobedient young, was repeatedly opposed and prevented by his mother, who thought him the most beautiful of boys — as indeed he was — so he grew up wild, adored by his sisters who thought he could do no wrong. Both his parents died young. His father cut Abraham out of his will, but his mother left him all her money which he went through in about three years. Fortunately there are two small trusts left him by his grandfather, and these he cannot break; but his income from them is small. He first went into the wine business with a friend in Plymouth, but it did not prosper. Then when he came into his mother's money he set himself up as a country gentleman. And so it has gone on.'

I waited for what I had to hear. He had stopped and was staring out at the rain.

'And his wife?' I said at last.

'Ah yes. Meliora Webb, as she was. D'you know . . . '

'What?'

'She was a beauty, but she came from a family in the tanning business and was virtually without money. He got her in the family way, and her brothers — both of them in the militia — insisted — not without intimidation — that he do the right thing by her.'

'They — have a family, then?'

'No. The child died — or was stillborn, I can't remember which — and they have had no more. They live in St Austell — or she does. They have

127

a small place there, near where they were both born. Already she has lost some of her looks.'

'How long — have they been married?'

'I suppose it would be nearly three years.'

I stirred the remnants of the chocolate. 'Has she been ill?'

'No. Not as far as I know. But some women are like that — a quick short flowering. Excuse me, I should not observe this to you.'

I said: 'I have had no flowering. I am just as ugly as I have always been.'

'I should not call it ugly,' he said. 'Your face is — is quite like a rose, but with a flaw in it.'

'The worm in the bud,' I suggested.

He looked at me in some surprise. 'No . . . I wouldn't say that. It is not my wish to enquire into its causes — if you know them — '

'It happened at my birth.'

'I am very sorry. I suppose your parents have consulted surgeons on the matter?'

'My father died before I was born.'

'Ah, Aubrey Spry, Admiral Davey's brother. I do remember him. I met him once in Falmouth when we were both young. Well, I would have thought some treatment, possibly surgery, might help.'

'That is what Bram said.'

'Did he indeed? Was that why you wanted to see him?'

'Not exactly. In fact, no.'

'And you came all the way from St Anthony? On your own? By river?'

'I walked.'

'And you propose to walk back? In this

128

weather? That you cannot do — have you not relatives at Tregolls?'

'Well, yes. But I could hardly trouble them.'

'I think you must. Even that is a long walk in the rain . . . Let me see, there should be chairs for hire in Boscawen Street. Do you know Miss Letitia Spry?'

'No. Mary, I know well.'

'She will be there? Good. Then when this heavy shower relents I will take you. This ope runs behind the Mansion House and will afford some shelter.'

III

Mary said: 'I cannot begin to understand you, Emma. Does it mean you have a taking for this awful man? Don't tell me! I don't want to know. The Foxes as a family are most highly esteemed — one could not wish for better people — but Abraham . . . him you must keep at a distance! I'm sorry if you have an accord with him. I thought at one time Thomasine was his target, but that, all that has evaporated, thanks be. I cannot — forgive me — suppose that he transferred his attentions to you, but perhaps you are unduly susceptible. He is, I will admit, a handsome man. But you, if you marry at all, should look for some sober hard-working man who will appreciate your sterling worth and not look for — well . . . but in any case, Bram is married. Did you know?'

'Yes.'

'Of course you must spend the night here!

Then we must consider what means is the easiest by which you may return home. I think if you are in such trouble with your mother regarding this unpermitted absence, you could say that you had had an arrangement to meet me for this fête and celebration. I do not like to be untruthful or engage in any deceit, but I think it is justified if it enables you to plead a suitable excuse. Your mother will no doubt blame you for not telling her of it, but the fact that it concerns the Sprys will induce her to make more allowances than otherwise. Your mother, forgive me, in spite of her marriage to Uncle Aubrey, has never been quite a Spry in the way you have become. It is very strange but I personally believe it to be so.'

'Thank you, dear Mary. I am desperately — desperately — depressed — exhausted by the day: the walk, the rain, the crowds, you know . . . I am happy and relieved to put myself in your hands.'

Mary said: 'You know, of course, that Desmond has proposed marriage to your sister?'

'Yes.'

'I suppose she will accept. She is a very handsome young woman, and will make him a beautiful wife. I think she could have done better. It is perhaps disloyal of me, but I think she could have done better. There was Geoff St Aubyn looking at her. And John Treffry — though he has no money. And Henry Le Grice. No doubt your mother felt that Desmond, with the virtual occupancy of Place, and a fair amount of money, was a safer investment. I am not so sure, dear Emma.'

'Not so sure about what?'

'I am not sure about Desmond's stability — though I'm certain I should not say so to anyone else. Oh, no doubt he will be a good husband and a loyal one — which is a great deal to be considered these days. *And* he will be an amenable one. That too. But . . . I think he is too inward-looking. Too much like dear Mama. I think it is possible that in a few years he will come to thinking of nothing but his birds.'

8

I

Desmond and Thomasine were married quietly in the church at Place House just a year after Admiral Davey Spry had been laid to rest there. Most of our Spry relatives in Cornwall were present, except for Anna Maria who was in London with her husband and about to be brought to bed of her fourth child. Since she did not quite approve of the marriage, I wondered if hers was a diplomatic absence.

Two weeks after the wedding, while they were still on their honeymoon, my mother took me to my new home at Blisland, and then herself caught the London coach at Launceston.

Of course I was not with child. I should have known earlier but in my inexperience did not. Although a single first seduction is commonly supposed to produce a baby I have learned since that it is not unknown for a virgin to escape from her deflowering.

I heard nothing more of Bram, and made no further attempt to communicate with him. The whole infatuation had gone sour. Instead of being in love with him, nearly all my feelings had turned to hate. The heady experience of that night, which even at the time had been part mind-consuming passion, part revulsion, part a reaching for new unimaginable sensations, part a shrinking away from losing my own identity as until then I knew it, part a wild relish for an overflowing rebellion, part a heartbreaking shame at what was happening to me — all these conflicting emotions had turned ultimately to ash. I felt I never wanted to see a man again, nor ever to be touched by one. Despite what a consoling friend — if I ever had one — might say, that I had been betrayed by a scoundrel and was certainly not the first woman so to suffer, my utter conviction was that I had betrayed myself. My disfigurement made it ten times as bad. No doubt it was conceit that persuaded some innocent unsophisticated girl of eighteen to suppose that a good-looking depraved man of thirty-odd wanted anything more of her than a night in her bed before he passed on. Girls who can look in the mirror and see a pretty face are capable of any sort of silly self-deception. But I had no such excuse. I had been blind, fascinated, like a bird by a snake, and there was no excuse. I had been betrayed and had willingly, sensually but senselessly, connived at my own betrayal. It was a feeling almost impossible to live with.

There was always the possibility that I might not choose to live with it. For some weeks, especially after arriving at Blisland, that loomed as a way out. Had I been carrying Bram's child this step would have been almost certain. But with only burning hatred and humiliation to press this course I hesitated over the means which, short of a rope and a hook in the stables, were not easy to find.

But presently there was a change, though

for a while I was not conscious of it. In the cold monotonous religious routine of this new life there seemed little extra reason to relish being alive, but the Canon may have been responsible by facing me with new challenges which, domestic though they were, allowed me less time to brood.

Blisland is a moorland village on the edges of Bodmin Moor. Though there are pleasant woodlands nearby, its position is essentially bleak. It is on a plateau on the lower slopes of Brown Willy, one of the twin mountains that mark the highest peaks of the moors. It is nine or ten miles from the sea and, except for a belt of trees around the village, totally exposed to all the wild and vigorous winds that Heaven sends. Although the village is only a couple of hundred feet above the sea, all the land west of it is lower, with level fields that do nothing to break the power of the wind.

The hamlet was pretty: thatched and slated cottages clustered round a green sentinelled with tall trees, and the beautiful, ornate church on a corner. It was old — the list of rectors in the porch beginning in 1510, but the Canon said it was much older than that. The rectory was fairly recent, having been put up at the beginning of the century, but in a short time it had come to look nearly as ancient as the church. Much of the moorstone of which it was built had been weathered by the elements before it was put to its present use, and inside it seemed full of big rooms with big furniture, and was echoing and gloomy.

134

The change from the windowed sunny Place House reflected the change in the neighbourhood, and the two locations were as extreme as any Cornwall could achieve. The first had all the gentle lushness of the southern coast, the second the wildness of the deserted moors. A year or two later, when Uncle Francis and I were on good terms, he showed me an ancient document which stated that the parish of Blisland comprised 6,300 acres, of which over 2,000 was arable, 1,000 pasture, forty woodland, thirty meadow and 2,500 common moorland. That speaks for itself.

Yet the distance between the two houses was not more than thirty-five miles. That day in early November when I went, we took the coach from Falmouth to Bodmin and then a gig over the muddy lane for the last few miles. I had asked that I might take Parish with me, but Desmond said he wanted him to stay at Place just in case his mother improved in health and was able to return. So after I parted from my mother I was quite alone.

There were three servants and I had to learn new names: Clarice, Florrie and Tom. It soon became clear that I had been engaged to take over the house. The cook had suddenly died, and Uncle Francis's housekeeper had left for a better post in Devon. So the Canon had been left without his two main servants. It looked as if he was now calculating that one strong, willing, educated girl could be expected to replace the two. He explained all this to me on the first evening. Clarice had helped with the cooking,

Florrie had helped with the housework, Tom had helped in the garden. But they all needed a guiding hand, a strong animating force behind them. Because of the rising cost of living and some misfortunes in his small investments it was necessary to exercise the utmost stringency in all matters.

It seemed to me that a high degree of stringency had been exercised for some time. Outside, the stucco had fallen off the front porch in big patches, and paint was peeling or absent from most of the window frames. The pebble drive was overgrown with grass, and weeds flourished in the garden. Inside, carpets were threadbare, and wallpapers hung loose to a degree far worse than anything to be seen at Place. Upstairs there were no mats on the landings, and the floorboards creaked so that no silent movement could be taken. The paintings, mostly of ancestors of Canon Robartes, were mildewed and faded. Heavy furniture stood about in the living rooms as if not sure of a permanency; the Canon's study was swamped with books, all so far as I could see religious, not only filling the shelves but planted in haphazard pyramids about the floor. A huge desk was scattered with his writings — some, it seemed, the drafts for sermons, some articles by him printed in religious journals; but some were household accounts, from which it appeared Uncle Francis kept an unremitting eye on what he and others spent, down to the last penny.

The kitchen quarters were down three steps and were flagged with great grey Delabole slates which sweated in the wet weather. In spite of the fire the kitchens were damper than the house itself, and every cooking utensil looked as if it had survived from the last century. Heavy saucepans, clome pitchers, wooden baskets, huge iron trivets, and the well was in an outhouse leading to the stables.

November is not the best month to arrive at a new house to occupy a new position. Lamps and candles — only tallow allowed — were not to be lit before full dark had fallen, and then grudgingly, so that it was almost impossible to read, and shadows lurked in every room and passage. In the daytime the candles, one for each of the staff, stood in a rigid row on the hall table, and remark was made if one of the candles came to be burned down more quickly than the others. The house was draughty, leaning, it seemed, into the heavy winds. One wall of my bedroom had a huge patch of damp on it, and the sash window let in both the wind and the rain. Blankets were not lacking but the bed always seemed cold, and when the winds turned north after Christmas, bringing hail and snow flurries, I was usually wakened by the chill of dawn.

My uncle, as he still called himself, though he was far removed from this relationship, was a tall plump man. His hair was thin and grey and curling; his eyes large and a clear blue, his lips thick, his manner gentle. He had never married, was intensely religious, cared for music, even secular music, and in spite of his deep clericalism was interested in things like railway development, bridge construction, the building of steamships. As he had said on his visit to us, were his means more substantial, he would have invested in some of the ongoing projects of Mr Brunel. But even without money, as a senior canon of the church, his influence over his more conservative colleagues was important. I learned that Mr Brunel had been to see him again last year, and Mr Brunel, I imagined, did not waste his time on social visits.

Of course there were still the two ways open to me to react to banishment and disgrace. (In spite of the busy days there were the long cold nights.) To give way to shame and remorse and end my life in some convenient bog, of which I soon gathered there were plenty in the vicinity; or vent a sense of anger, of betrayal, of utter self-contempt, upon the household that I had been invited to run. This is what I did.

After supper at the end of the second day, the Canon had said: 'My dear, I have invited you to look after me and this household in a spirit of Christian reconciliation. Your mother tells me you have been wilful and wayward, but gives the highest references as to your true capabilities. Well, I have no quarrel with any wayward escapades that you gave way to before you came here. Wilfulness and a certain wildness are not unknown among the young — particularly, I have observed, among the more talented young. Well . . . this is an opportunity to express those talents. You are still so very young — too young, many would say, to take over the responsibilities of caring for this rectory. I am frequently absent, often in a physical sense, and not uncommonly in a spiritual sense, and as you will observe, much has been neglected. I do not think Freda, my late housekeeper, was very efficient: that is, in the way in which she supervised the conduct of the house. But she was my companion in many things, and for that I was appreciative and chose to overlook a slackness in the upkeep. This also applied to the cook, and to the servants who have remained with me. From you I do not expect miracles but your youth and — I trust — your enthusiasm will stand you in good stead in this highly responsible task I am setting you. Your mother said you had great potential, but that your religious instruction had been neglected. I hope both these conditions will be influenced by your new environment.'

'Thank you, Uncle,' I said. 'I have never managed a household before and will have to rely on you for a few weeks for some guidance as to what I may and may not do.'

'Look upon it as a sacred task,' he said.

II

I never looked upon it as a sacred task. I went to church twice in the middle of each week, and three times on Sundays when everyone went together. Sometimes that winter he had me into his study for religious instruction, but often he would divert from a study of Joseph of Arimathea to the price of coal or the need to economize on candles. Then, with a little encouragement from me he would come to talk about the revolution in transport and the difficulties that the railroad builders were encountering in laying a track from Exeter to Barnstaple. Or he would go on about the relative merits of the narrow and the broad gauge track.

My relations with the three servants who were under my direction were soon strained. They had been used to a quiet life; I changed that. Wood floors had to be scrubbed, the slate ones washed with damp mops on long handles, curtains came down and were washed and ironed. Even in the howling gales of February sheets and blankets flapped crazily on makeshift lines; all the silver had to be polished, the crockery, of which some was cracked and a good lot missing from breakages, was assembled and properly shelved and the better put away. Fleas were almost got rid of.

The Canon allowed himself two bottles of claret a week, and I soon came to notice that he greatly enjoyed the food that came to his table. So far as he was concerned I had a completely free hand: the staff could walk out if they wanted to, he told me; there were plenty waiting to take their places. I did not cook very well to begin, but he was tactful in his complaints and suggestions, and even discussed the cooking of the food with me. I interviewed individually the tradesmen who attended on the house and persuaded them that we wanted better produce at the same or cheaper rates. I became known, apparently, as 'wall-eye' — which was unfair because I could see perfectly well with both eyes.

The one thing I could not do was prevail upon the Canon to sanction any extra expenditure, however slight and however sorely needed. He gave me the same tiny allowance he had given Freda, but not a penny more. When the expenditure of money was raised his face would undergo a significant change. His bright eyes would mist over like a pane of glass that had been breathed on; then he would look away, his full lips would tighten and he would refer to his wretched stipend and the depressed state of his trivial investments. In the end, the only way I found of spending a little extra on the house or garden was by making small economies that he did not notice and that I did not tell him about. Surprisingly it was possible. Freda had not been as careful with the housekeeping as he supposed.

In March the weather began to clear, primroses yellow-tufted the garden, and there were crocuses and snowdrops around the clumps of damp pampas grass. Looking over the dishevelled quarter acre I saw that there were a surprising number of shrubs and plants, as if at one time the place had been cared for.

In April the Canon said: 'You must join the choir, Emma. I think you have a voice.'

'I'm not sure that I should be welcomed. I am an outsider — almost a foreigner.'

'That doesn't matter. They will take my direction. Let us try a few notes on this spinet.' He sat down and lifted the lid.

It was a dusty old instrument and sounded tinny, but I sang a few notes.

'Oh,' he said. 'You should have told me! I will inform them next choir practice. Your mother should have told me!'

So I joined the choir, and after a few weeks began quite to look forward to it. They were farmers and farmers' daughters, a generally mixed dozen, but apart from one girl who had to give way to me they took my arrival moderately well. The girl spread the rumour that I should not be allowed in church because I had the Evil Eye.

In May the Canon was taken ill with bronchitis. He was in bed some days and I got used to the fusty sandalwood smell of his bedroom. I longed to change the smell to that of furniture cream and floor polish, but he would not allow the new broom to sweep in here.

However, I cooked all his meals and took them up and sat with him while he coughed and wheezed. Although the cough was very loose he never brought anything up, which was a relief to me as I cannot stand the sight of phlegm.

I read to him sometimes from a book called *Imitations of Christ*, and so far as I understood it it was full of beautiful thoughts. Perhaps at another time it would have brought me spiritual enlightenment, but my soul was much too dark.

Then, when he was feeling better and able to get downstairs for a few hours a day, he asked me to sing to him. I did this helping myself with a few tentative chords on the old spinet. At first it began with hymns, but after a while I found he was not averse to a little light secular stuff, and he seemed vastly entertained when I sang him the theatrical ditties that I had learned from my mother.

For more than a month now I had been attacking the garden — Tom put in twice the work if there was someone with him — and all sorts of pretty things were emerging. It was surprising to find more spring flowers here than in the gentler airs of Place. I did not think the Sprys were specially interested in formal gardens; the walled kitchen and fruit garden, living as they did so far from fresh supplies, was their preoccupation. Here, in a more confined space and in apparently more adverse conditions, all sorts of plants and flowers poked up their heads as the air grew warmer. Daffodils grew wild under a pink horse chestnut. Fuschias overspilled from the hedges and grew tall and lanky among the Bourbon roses. Lily of the valley came and went, with primulas and tobacco plants and Solomon's seal.

In the summer I had a letter from my mother telling me that Thomasine was with child. She was expected to be brought to bed in October. Anna Maria had had her fourth, another boy. Following Thomas Tristram Spry, Edward Augustus and George Gwavas, the new baby was named only Richard. Apparently he was a sickly child, unlike the first three. Aunt Anna was reported a little better but was still not well enough to come home. Desmond was spending more money on the church — too much money in the writer's opinion — and was thinking of having the spire rebuilt. Thomasine and he were very happy together. She, Claudine, was staying with them for a few weeks between engagements in London. Her latest appearances at Drury Lane had been the greatest success and she had been invited to return. The coolness between Place House and Tregrehan persisted, but she hoped that in another year the young mothers would find an interest in common and the breach would be healed.

Some gossip of Falmouth and Truro followed, and that ended the letter. She was 'your loving Mother'.

No mention of Bram Fox.

I had had two previous letters from my mother — stiff little formal notes, and had replied to them with stiff little formal notes. This was the first proper letter, with at least a trace of affection in it. When she left I had lost touch with Sally Fetch; I had soon regretted this, not only because I was so fond of her but because, if she had been able to get work with the Fox family, she would probably have some information about Bram. I was fairly sure that Fetch could read and write, and, in spite of my bitter resentment, I wanted to know.

Sometimes in the dark of the night I wondered still if I had partly misjudged him. Even though he could never marry me, perhaps his imprisonment for debt had prevented him from coming to see me, to explain — to confess his weakness and say he was sorry for the way everything had happened. Would I then have forgiven him? Could I still forgive him?

Only in the darkest, coldest part of the night.

When I could find the time I took long walks. Like most Cornish villages, even on the moors, Blisland and its neighbourhood had little valleys with softer climates in which, sheltered from the harsh winds, all kinds of lush vegetation flourished. And also small animals and birds. I thought how Desmond would have liked to see them. In the trickle of a stream a kingfisher would be flaunting its colour, so much brighter than the periwinkle growing under a cluster of nearby alders. Or under a warm stone I would disturb an adder coiled like a spring in a sandy hollow. Small mice flourished and wrens and linnets and a host of insects. In the district too were old mining excavations, mostly derelict, but one or two were still worked for tin or clay or mica or quartz.

One evening the Canon, having returned from a visit to Bodmin and having taken a late supper, said to me:

'I wish you were not so bitter, my child.'

'Bitter?' I was surprised. 'Have I been in any way disagreeable to you, because — '

'No, no, no, no, no. I do not mean it quite that way. You are always willing, lively in your answers to me, companionable in a manner that Freda never was able to be. And you have done wonders in the house and garden. Although I have so much to occupy my mind at present, I am not unaware of the — almost

145

transformation you have wrought. I appreciate that and I appreciate you — '

I lowered my eyes. 'Thank you.'

'But always I am aware of a bitterness in your soul. You must be very lonely here.'

'I have always been lonely,' I said.

'I have prayed for you. I still do. Your disadvantage sets you apart. Do you miss your sister?'

'Well, yes I do . . . though she was not always very kind. Most of all I miss Sally Fetch, who was a maid at Place but who was discharged on my account.'

'I had hoped — I still do — that your frequent attendances at church, the Christian atmosphere of this household, will turn you more to God and to a view of the eternal verities which would enable you to see your disfigurement in its proper proportion. That is to say in its very *small* proportion. Our body, our face, is but the mortal shell in which flourishes our immortal soul. That you are not as other young women, that you have a cross to bear, does not mean you are any less worthy, less to be admired than they. Indeed your personality, your honesty, your sense of purpose, your *soul* can be the greater, the more worthy, the more honourable for the disadvantage that you have to overcome. In the course of time we shall fade and rot away, and what will be left? All that is noblest in your character for suffering and enduring this misfortune will earn its reward in the life to come. It is often the less abled of human beings who develop the sweetest natures in adversity.'

146

I thought about this on the way back to the kitchen. Of course I was bitter, bitter to the depths of my soul — if that thing of which my uncle was so fond of speaking was something I really possessed. But my bitterness was twofold and compounded by what had happened last year. Indeed it was because of what had happened last year that it had become insufferable. Over eighteen years I had slowly adjusted to my disfigurement, the increasing knowledge that I could never be as other women, that no man would ever look at me with admiring eyes, this had to be accepted. But Bram's appearance, his good looks and charm, his apparent lust for me, his seduction and then his betrayal . . .

When I went back into the dining room the Canon had gone, so I followed him up the creaking stairs to his study.

'Uncle.'

'Yes?'

'I please you as a housekeeper and companion, and that is important. But I do not think I have been an apt pupil for your Christian teachings.'

'Possibly not. But there is time. You are young. Water, they say, weareth away stone.'

I looked at him, and he was smiling. He had a finger in his book, a pipe waiting to be lit.

'Do you think I am of stone, then?'

'No. But there are many ways to God. If I can help you, I will.'

'Thank you.'

'In all ways, the most essential guide is humility.'

'That I certainly lack.'

'Do not confuse humility with resentment.'

'No . . . no . . . Thank you, Uncle.'

As I was about to leave he said: 'I have not involved you enough yet in my secular interests. You know of my interest in railways.'

'You have mentioned it.'

'The laying of the rail between Bodmin and Wadebridge has been encountering some problems. I do not doubt they will be overcome, but I am going tomorrow to see the situation for myself, and if you would care to accompany me, it might give you a change of scene.'

9

I

We left at seven in the trap the Canon used for most of his travelling around the county. It was a very light vehicle, drawn by a piebald pony called Joseph. It was a fine warm day, which was just as well for we had little cover.

We drove almost into Bodmin and then forked right down a narrow lane which presently became no more than a track. The land was moorland, with an occasional cottage, usually in a copse. The ground was level — you could see for miles.

After about half an hour we came into a woodland valley and then saw the line. A group of about forty navvies were at work, most of them constructing a rough stone bridge across a stream. The road was being laid by a team of the men on a slightly raised bed about fifteen feet wide, while another team, not far behind, built the rail track. The sleepers were of granite blocks, about two feet square by a foot thick, and it was a big effort to carry them and set them in place. Where the rails joined, a single granite sleeper six feet wide was used. Most of the men wore sleeveless singlets with brown corduroy breeches and heavy boots. I could see their muscles standing out as they strained to edge the blocks into place. Many of the men looked exhausted with the heat. The rails by contrast looked very light as they were bolted into the chairs.

The Canon was talking earnestly to the foreman, and they went to compare notes at a trestle-table on which was pinned a map. I wondered what practical business my uncle really had here. Was he a dark horse? After his visit to Place he had, I remember, been going on to some meeting in Bodmin the following day, representing his wealthy young cousin Mr Agar-Robartes, who was travelling abroad. But Mr Agar-Robartes was home now, had attended the Admiral's funeral.

There was a workmen's hut on the other side of the stream, and a man came out whom I instantly recognized. He was young, tall, heavy, wore his curly hair parted in the middle. He walked with an easy but clumsy gait as if he was not yet quite accustomed to his own size. He went across to my uncle without seeing me — I was standing by the trap — and they shook hands and engaged in conversation which at least on my uncle's side looked argumentative.

Charles Lane, whom I had last seen at dinner at Place House in company with Mr Isambard Kingdom Brunel. I wished now I had not come.

I patted the pony's nose, which was in a bag. He gave a little tossing snort to make it easier for him to reach his refreshment. I slid further behind the trap where I should be less visible. I smelt the leather and the heat of the pony and the iron of the wheel rim and granite dust, and nearby gorse dropping its flowers in the sun and a touch of salt in the breeze. Then I looked up and saw Charles Lane coming towards me.

There was no getting away. He seemed to flush as he came up.

'Your uncle told me you were here, Miss Fry. I had no idea you were living at Blisland.'

'Yes. I have been there nine months, Mr Lane.'

His flush deepened. 'Er — it's Miss Spry, isn't it? I am sorry for the mistake. There's a Mr Treffry intimately concerned with the railways and projecting a great bridge near Luxulyan — and for a moment I confused the names.'

I did not answer.

He said: 'I am not accustomed to the — the company of young ladies. My tongue ties up.'

I said: 'I am not accustomed to the company of young gentlemen.'

'Oh,' he said. 'I do not — I do not know that I am a gentleman. Mr Brunel has raised me up, but I began life as a bricklayer.' He looked at his big hands as if about to show me how rough they were.

'Is Mr Brunel here?'

'No. Oh, no. He is far too busy. He left me here to superintend — to — to see that his instructions were carried out.' Charles Lane hesitated, his eyes going beyond me. 'I do not know how long I shall retain his confidence.'

'Why? Why is that?'

'It is a technical point, Miss Spry. This line will be eight miles long when it is completed — that is without the possible extension. Most

151

railway tracks in Cornwall are still drawn by horses, but there is now such development in the power of steam that the adventurers feel this line should be steam operated.'

'Yes. I follow that.'

'Well, Miss Spry, there is a division of opinion as to how it should be operated. Mr Brunel insists that we should use the atmospheric method. That — roughly . . . ' He stopped. 'Am I taking your time? I can't believe you can be interested in such a dull technical matter . . . '

'Pray believe that I am,' I said.

He looked at me in embarrassment, then moved his gaze to the middle distance again. 'Mr Brunel prefers the use of stationary engines at each end of the line — and at least another one halfway — which will propel the wagons by atmospheric pressure. The adventurers prefer the idea of a locomotive — or even two, one at the front and one at the back of a train — propelling the trucks with their own steam power.'

My uncle had now walked across and was stooping down peering at the structure of the new stone bridge.

'And you — and you,' I said, 'have taken the side of the adventurers?'

He smiled awkwardly. 'How did you guess?'

'I guessed.'

'Yes, that is the crux of the matter. Mr Brunel does not like his subordinates to disagree with him. He thinks I am here to obey his instructions. And so I am.'

My uncle had straightened up and was looking this way. His visit was coming to an end.

'What is there against the — what did you call it? atmospheric — way of working this line?'

'Mr Brunel asserts that it is technically more advanced. He also points to the fact that if this line begins to carry passengers — as it surely will — they would be saved all the noise and smoke and smell of an engine close in front of them: sparks, coal dust, vibration.'

'You are arguing for him. What have you against that?'

'I do not think the pipes would sustain the pressure. Of course it does work — it has worked. But I believe there would be frequent breakdowns, that maintenance would become prohibitive in cost.'

'So what do you suppose will happen?'

'If the investors stand firm they will have their way. It is their money.'

'And you?'

'Mr Brunel pays me.'

'Ah . . . ,' said the Canon, rather breathless as he came up. 'You have been renewing acquaintance? Lane tells me that you met at Place a few years ago, Emma.'

Conversation was general for a moment or two, then as the Canon moved away to pay the farmer for Joseph's fodder, I said:

'What does that mean?'

'What?' Charles Lane turned his absent-minded grey eyes on me with a look that was shy but friendly. 'Do you mean about the line? Mr Brunel does not brook disobedience. Either I shall be moved to some other project or I shall be dismissed. That, I fear, is more likely.'

'If that happened, would not the investors here be happy to employ you?'

'They might. But I'm not anxious to lose contact with Mr Brunel, because he has helped to make me what I have become — little though that may appear in your eyes.'

'Is my uncle an investor?'

'He has been at all the meetings I have attended. Though I have no idea whether his involvement is small or large. Most of it, you know, comes from the landed gentry.'

'Possibly my uncle would be able to influence Mr Brunel.'

Charles Lane smiled wryly. 'If Mr Brunel forms an opinion it takes an — an explosion to move him. Indeed in the six years I have known him I don't remember one occasion when he has changed his mind as a result of outside influence.'

'No doubt, then,' I said, 'he will influence his investors to install the atmospheric system.'

A flicker went across his face. 'He may. Yes, he may.'

I detected a steeliness in Mr Lane's tone which suggested that under the rather shambling exterior he had strong opinions of his own.

On the way home I asked my uncle if he had invested money in the building of the line. He was silent for some moments as if I had been guilty of an indelicacy. Then he said:

'A mite. A widow's mite.'

I thought of the extreme penury in which we lived and hoped he had not ventured too much.

'It seems there is a difference of opinion between Mr Brunel and Mr Lane as to whether the trains are drawn by moving engines or stationary ones.'

'I do not think you can have a difference of opinion between one of the supreme engineers of our time and a subordinate. Mr Lane is here to obey orders.'

'You agree with Mr Brunel, Uncle? I mean on this point?'

'I am not qualified to judge. Nor, I think, is Mr Lane.'

I was rebuked and said no more and we were nearly home before he spoke again. 'These Stephenson engines which are coming into use in the north of England are proving a great success. We will have to see. It will be a year yet before the permanent way is complete. A decision will not be taken until then.'

II

Tamsin gave birth to a daughter, who was christened Celestine. Mother returned from London for what I gather was almost a society christening, but I was not invited. However, a few months later my mother wrote me from London after another successful season and said she would be spending Easter at Place and thought I should perhaps ask the Canon if I might take a week off and visit the newlyweds and see my new niece. I put this to Uncle Francis, who said unfortunately Easter was the busiest time of the year for him, and I could

155

hardly be spared, but if the week following would suffice . . . I said it would suffice: I could travel to Place myself, and my mother could bring me back when she returned to London.

Easter was dull and rainy, but in the week after came brilliant weather with a light northerly breeze: a time to blossom in the sunshine and shiver in the shade. Mixed feelings going home. The weather had changed conveniently so that it seemed as if I were moving to a lighter, brighter scene. Not merely was the contrast in the houses, but in the landscape, the sky, the glimmering water, the softer air.

Aunt Anna was still away and no better, Tamsin looking well but a little strained, my mother older but quite suited by her dyed auburn hair, Desmond seemed happy and occupied his time between watching the baby, superintending the repairs to the church and spotting the arrival of migrating birds. Celestine, with fair wispy hair and blue eyes, slept contentedly most of the time. The staff the same — except that Slade was there.

As black-haired, as sallow-skinned, as sour as ever, he cast a shadow that followed him about the house like a miasma. As soon as I got her alone I asked Tamsin.

'Oh,' she said lightly. 'We felt he had been rather harsh done to by Uncle Davey's will, so, chancing on him one day in Falmouth, Desmond invited him to return. Rather to our surprise he said he would like to, and that was that. In a way it gives a house a better look to it, with a butler.'

156

'I should have thought, after our childhood here, you wouldn't want him back at any price.'

She gave me a slanting look. 'Oh, all that's long forgot. He's very proud to be here, you know. He feels he is still serving the Spry family.'

'In the end did you ever get into those cellars?'

'Cellars? . . . Oh, that. No, I didn't. When Slade came back I somehow couldn't be bothered.'

'You couldn't?'

She gave me another look. 'No.' Then she laughed. 'I have been rather busy, you know. And now that I have Celestine I'm not sure that I care.'

'I understand,' I said, though I didn't quite.

So I said to Desmond one day, 'You probably won't remember that about ten years ago Tamsin and I got into trouble with Slade about the cellars?'

'Afraid I don't. What was it about?'

I told him. He laughed. 'I didn't think Slade had that much sense of humour. Have you never been in? It was a tunnel. At some time in the days when it was a priory the prior and the black canons dug a tunnel from the priory to the edge of the cliff. I think it was some sort of an escape route. Can't think why — it was before the Dissolution of the Monasteries. Anyway it has long since fallen in. Samuel and I explored that way. There are only two cellars beyond the wine cellar, and there aren't any skeletons in them. Not even Slade's.'

I said: 'I'm afraid I never liked him much. I am a little surprised that you chose to re-engage him.'

Desmond looked at me. 'Oh, I did not. It was Tamsin. I always found him too possessive of my father, too ambitious to dominate the house. Tamsin persuaded me.'

'She — persuaded you to take him back?'

'Yes. I was surprised myself, as she had never, as far as I can recall, showed any liking for his ministrations. But when I pointed this out to her she seemed to become rather angry, as if I were attempting to thwart her of her whims.'

III

On the Wednesday of my visit Desmond had planned a visit to St Michael's Mount. The St Aubyns had issued an open invitation and had suggested it should take place while my mother was there. Sir John was fascinated by the theatre and liked to talk to a real live practising actress. The plan was that we should go by sea by steam paddle from Falmouth to Penzance, visit the Mount about midday and have dinner at Clowance, Sir John's country house near Marazion. We were to return to Falmouth in the evening by coach.

It was a fine day, cloudy but with little wind; we left Place at seven and took the steamer at eight. The power of the engines which belched smoke from the single funnel and propelled the great paddle wheels impressed us all, and I thought much of Mr Isambard Brunel and his prophecies, and the tall clumsy person of Charles Lane with his good-humoured kindly face and his modesty and determination. Sir John and Lady St Aubyn met us at Marazion, and we took a large row boat across as the tide was in. There followed the long climb up to the castle, then so much to admire in the medieval church, the Chevy Chase Room, the Armoury, the Blue Drawing Room, and the views across the Channel and Mount's Bay from every window. The sun finally came out and glinted through the tall granite-framed windows on coats of armour and chain mail.

We took refreshments there, and then returned to the mainland, where carriages were waiting to take us to Clowance.

Until now it had just been the St Aubyns with two of their sons, and our own party of four, but at the big house there were another dozen guests invited to dinner. Two of the first to arrive were Mr and Mrs Bram Fox.

Clearly the St Aubyns could have had no idea at all about the maladroitness of the invitation; both my mother and Tamsin stiffened up at the sight of him. What emotion I showed I had no idea but my heart missed a beat, my mouth dried and I could feel the heat of a flush on my stained neck. Fortunately, close on their heels came a group of another half-dozen youngish people, all of whose names I took in and instantly forgot, and then another quartet, so that it was not too difficult to avoid confronting him.

He looked different from what I remembered. His hair was shorter. (Had he had it cut off in prison? But that was too long ago.) In formal clothes he looked as usual killingly handsome. Was it also true that he looked killingly domesticated and in some way cut down to size? He only needed two children holding his hands. Was it the presence of his wife?

I found myself next to her. As tall as I was, but thin. She was beautiful, but it was as if on her face, even when she smiled, there were puckers of disappointment.

'You are Miss Spry? Oh, yes. From St Anthony. I think my husband has mentioned that you have met.'

'So he did,' said Bram, coming up behind her. 'It is what — two years? That was a splendid musical evening. Do you recall it?'

'Well,' I said. He still had the power to move me, to stir me so that my knees shook. But how much of this was rage I cannot tell.

We talked about the musicians and Mr Emidy's progress. He had settled with his family in Truro and, apart from concerts, gave tuition on half a dozen different musical instruments. During this Meliora carefully eyed my disfigurement. Was she speculating as to whether I was one of her husband's conquests, or whether my damaged face had put him off? Then Lady St Aubyn came up and Meliora turned to speak to her.

Bram said in a lowered voice: 'And how is my little Emma? Does she prosper?'

'Thank you,' I said. 'But no thanks to you.'

He laughed. 'Sadly no. It was all a trifle unfortunate, was it not? I made efforts to see you but you were not to be seen. Then my misdeeds — were they such terrible misdeeds? — caught up with me. I had been living beyond my means and was declared a bankrupt. For that I served a term in one of His Majesty's prisons. Five months. I cannot say it was altogether enjoyable, though efforts were made by family and friends to make the conditions bearable. Eventually these same family and friends clubbed together to satisfy my creditors, and out I popped like a weasel out of a hole, blinking in the bright sunshine and starting life all over again! I gather you are no longer at Place House.'

'I took employment at Blisland with an uncle.'

'Blisland? What a hole! I admit it has the only decent village green in Cornwall, but there is not much else there but moorland and wet winds.'

'I find it agreeable.'

'Good. Good. And Tamsin married Desmond, who looks well on it, don't you think? And how well your mother wears! She must be in her mid-fifties. But perhaps it is impolite to speculate on a lady's age.'

'I think so.'

'Very-well-brought-up-Emma. And how do you like my wife?'

'Very pretty.'

'Do not choke, my dear. There is much in life worse than what happened between us. You were so lovely to take. Anyway I have forgiven you.'

It was fortunate I did not hit him across the

face; but Sir John St Aubyn came to speak to us and so defused the moment.

There were sufficient at the dinner table and the convenient arrangement of places that I had hoped for, so I saw him only at a distance during the meal; but afterwards, after tea and port and the remixing of the sexes, we came together at a window. Or, to be more exact, he followed me.

'And Slade is with you still.'

'With my brother-in-law, yes. Do you know him?'

'Slade? Of course. Well. A ruffian.' He laughed. 'I gather he was sacked and then brought back.'

'You should ask Desmond all about it.'

His glance moved to the tall long-necked figure of Tamsin's husband, and then back brilliantly to me. 'What have you done to your eye?'

'What do you mean?'

'It's not any longer so bloodshot. Have you seen an apothecary or someone?'

I said: 'I think it's just the better company I've been keeping.'

He laughed. 'Always quick on the answer. Well, it has improved, hasn't it?'

'Has it?'

'You could do something with make-up too. Your mother's an actress. Does she never advise you?'

'No.'

'Why don't you ask her?'

I stared at him with hatred. 'Why don't

you stay faithful to your wife and keep out of debt?'

'Seriously,' he said. 'Good make-up would hide a lot. It should be worth trying. You're otherwise such a pretty woman.'

I muttered something under my breath.

'You question me,' he said. 'I'll tell you something. Why am I not faithful to my wife? Because she will no longer let me touch her. That is why. Strange, isn't it? And me such an attentive man! . . . As for the rest . . . I am no longer in debt. An attempt has been made to keep me in solvency. To save me from myself, you might say. Well-wishers, some friends in high places, but mainly family, have sought around to help me to a fresh start. Last year the Commissioner for Customs and Excise for West Cornwall, Captain Tremain, was killed in the hunting field. I have been appointed in his place . . .'

A movement was now being made to leave. We had the prospect of a long jolting journey home.

Bram said: 'I inspect, I supervise the gaugers, I keep an eye on attempts to evade the excise duties. Which of course is impossible in Cornwall, since almost everyone here condones the running and sale of contraband goods. But it's not altogether a sinecure. We live in Ponsanooth now, but I travel all over the west: St Ives, Portreath, Newquay, Penzance, Helston and the Helford river. Sometimes I stop 'em, sometimes I don't. It's a game of hide and seek, which suits me, and I feel better

163

for it. Of course — goodbye Miss Pearce, it has been a great pleasure to meet you today — '. When she had gone: 'Of course those who have appointed me to this position have done so with my best interests in mind. Nevertheless it may have stirred somewhere in their grey matter to recall an old proverb, with which I am sure everyone is familiar. 'Set a thief to catch a thief.' '

'Are you a thief?' I said after a moment.

He smiled at me. 'Dear Emma, you should know.'

IV

My mother travelled home in the coach with me as far as Bodmin, where I would change to a waggonette which would take me right into Blisland. On the Sunday there had been tremendous rain all day, but Monday was bright and the air light and invigorating.

She had been warmer towards me than I remember before. Apparently the Canon had sent her several favourable reports. Tamsin was safely and agreeably settled with her cousin, and at present in complete control of Place House. And a little daughter of the marriage already! She, Claudine, had continued to find work on the stage and to be popular with audiences. Life was pleasanter for her, probably, than it had ever been.

She said: 'It was a good move to send you to help Uncle Francis. It has brought out your best qualities.'

I muttered something ungracious.

She went on: 'He pays you a mere pittance.'

'He is very poor.'

'But not I think that poor. He has his stipend. I will write to him and suggest you should be paid £10 a year. Good man though he is, it is not right he should trade on a distant relationship.'

Presently I said, 'Do you think my eye has improved?'

'What? Your bad eye? Yes.' She looked at it judiciously. 'It's not so bloodshot. Unfortunate about the lid. But the eye itself has improved.'

'Do you think make-up would improve it more?'

'Um. I'll send you some. But don't forget theatrical makeup is meant to be observed from a distance.'

We jogged along for a while.

I said: 'I have little use for money at Blisland. But I need a new dress.'

'You assuredly do. You need two. You are still not good with your fingers?'

'Not close needlework. I've done much repairing of curtains.'

'I will send you some material. Occasionally a piece is left over from a stage costume. There is someone in the village?'

'Oh yes.'

Just before the coach reached Bodmin the road dipped sharply downhill to Lanivet before the long steep climb. The surface of the road, such as it was, had been almost washed away in yesterday's rains, and one of the horses lost its footing among the rubble and fell. The coach lurched like a ship in a sudden cross current, the brakes squealed on the rims as it swung sideways and slowly toppled over against the overgrown hedge. The whinnying of the horses was almost drowned by the cries of passengers as those outside were spilled off and the four inside were tumbled together in a heap against the jammed door.

Luckily we were close by St Bennet's Abbey, which was a private house of some importance, and although the owner, a clergyman, was away, several of his servants came out to help. No one was seriously injured but two women riding outside were sufficiently shaken and bruised to need rest and treatment and decided not to go on when the coach was righted. The horse which had been injured in its fall was tethered to the back of the coach, and the remaining three would have all the collar work pulling us up to the town.

My mother and I were fortunate because we were on the side farthest from the hasp, so that we were thrown against the plump elderly women who shared the interior, and it was their misfortune to bear the shock of our weight and the jolt of being crushed against the woodwork of the coach. All the same I had a bruised shoulder which troubled me for a week or more after. My mother's travelling handbag spilled out on the floor of the coach and the contents had to be regathered and replaced.

We were an hour late reaching Bodmin and I missed my waggonette, so stayed on the main coach as far as the crossroads near Whitecross. From here it was less than a three-mile walk, and I had only a piece of hand luggage.

As I made my way along the country lane to Trewint, my mouth was very dry and I felt faint. It was nothing to do with the accident. It was nothing to do with the exertion. I was not hungry or tired or ill. I was just faint and sick.

My mother's travelling bag was larger than an ordinary woman's handbag, being of leather fastened at the top with a thong. In theory this should have been quite secure, but if the bag was tipped up the contents, or certainly the smaller contents, found their way out through gaps and spilled on the floor. This was what had happened in the coach and I had knelt on the floor as soon as it was level, untied the thong and scooped everything back again. She crouched beside me helping.

She was rather addicted to medicines of one sort and another and so I was not surprised to pick up a phial of Solomon's drops, tolu lozenges, and a box of Dr Lamb's pills. There were also things like kohl sticks, roseate powder, and tiny lace handkerchiefs. All these were put back, and among them was a little brooch, which I glanced at just once before slipping it in. I had seen a similar one before. This one was not very new because the gold pin at the back was tarnished. But there was no mistaking that the brooch was a coral starfish.

Book Two

1

I

Shortly after my twenty-first birthday Canon Francis Herbert de Vere Robartes asked me to marry him. It was still January, with the darkest evenings just past and a chill wind blowing from the north-east. It was the one wind that made the Canon's study untenable, that is if there was a fire to smoke, so he had moved temporarily into the drawing room, where the spinet was. I had brought him tea, Tom had brought three candles in from the hall and I had poured the first cup. It would soon be time for me to read to him — which I did for half an hour each afternoon before leaving him to his meditations.

As soon as Tom left he said: 'Put two of the candles out. We finished Paschal yesterday and I feel in the mood to talk. We shall not need the extra light.'

I sipped my tea, which Francis had persuaded me to take without milk or sugar, saying it was better for my health.

He then put his proposition to me. By then I had finished my cup but was frozen into a position where I did not like to move to get myself or him another.

'I am sure, my dear child, that this will come as a big surprise to you. But you have been with me here over these years and you have made

171

yourself lovingly indispensable. You I know are still a girl; I an old man, but I fancy we could get along in a way not very different from the way we do now. Please understand,' he hastened on, as if afraid I might interrupt. 'Please understand I am not proposing any change in our — er — physical relationship. If — if we became man and wife, though I hope we should grow spiritually more together, you would continue to occupy your room, and I mine. It would be a loving partnership, just as if you were my daughter. After all, when I was laid up with bronchitis, you sat up with me two nights.' His full eyes twinkled suddenly behind their spectacles. 'Many a wife I know would not do that.'

'You had such trouble breathing — '

The slight moment of humour had helped to relax me, and I got up and poured tea again, then went to the fire, which was sulky.

'This coal is bad,' I said. 'I must talk to Robins when he comes.'

He said: 'The idea that I have put to you may not please you at all, but I ask you not to reply at once. Sleep on it. And, if you will, pray on it. Keep it by you for a few days — or weeks, if need be — and try to think the proposition through . . . The coal is slow but it is economical. I don't think one needs to have the bright coal that burns away like dry wood.'

I gave the fire an experimental poke, and a blue flame began to lick at the slack.

'If you consented to become my wife, I

would still pay you your housekeeper's salary; but you would be altogether in a stronger position than you are now. You would be Mrs de Vere Robartes. You would come with me to convocations and ordinations and social gatherings — which I cannot take you to now. In the village you would immediately be elevated to a new status. All that would give me great pleasure.'

'Is that why you have asked me?'

'No,' he said. 'No. But I was attempting to point out the advantages which would come to you.'

I looked at him and smiled. 'Then what is your reason?'

'Because I am afraid to lose you.'

'Why should you fear it?'

'You're very young. I know you are handicapped. Oh, without that handicap I am sure I would not have brought myself to this — this proposal. A pretty young woman of twenty-one is soon in demand. Some young man would come round, and you would be off and away. It might still happen, but now, as you are, as misfortune has made you, such a man may not come. But even so you are young and vigorous and may feel the outside world offers you more than I can.'

I straightened up from the fire and put the poker beside the brass tongs.

He said: 'Freda went off quite suddenly. We had no quarrel. I did not know she was discontented. I was — very upset. But not upset in the way I should be if you left. I have not before had such company and service as yours. Your mind is so bright — if often wayward — I have talked to you and you have talked to me. I need you, Emma, I need you while I am alive. I need you to be beside me when I die.'

'Why should you think of dying?'

'A Christian should always think of dying. He should accustom himself to it, he should have beliefs that convince him he need not fear it.'

'Well . . .'

'Given that full and enduring faith, which of course I have, there should be no fear at all in the soul. Nor is there! But one cannot always maintain a clear division between the spiritual and the corporeal. It would take a long time to explain, my dear Emma. Suffice that I need you now, here on this physical earth, and I don't want to fear losing you. And whatever the depths of my religious conviction I want to have someone — and someone who cares a little — to be beside me at the end.'

I looked at him sidelong. 'It is not quite the customary reason for a proposal.'

'Indeed no. But it can be just as heartfelt. Also . . . ' I waited, and he smiled. 'Though you are I am sure still far too young to think of your future in material terms, I believe . . . When I die of course my stipend will cease, as will the possession of the rectory. But the small investments that I have, if managed carefully, would enable you to face a youth and middle age of small independence.'

I did not answer.

174

'Think it over,' he said. 'There is absolutely no hurry at all.'

II

Nothing more was said between us for a couple of days, then he was in Bodmin for two nights, and returned with a bronchial chill; and so a week passed.

The week lengthened into a month, and that into two, with nothing more said on the subject. I knew he was waiting for me to respond, but as yet I could not.

I had not written to my mother to tell her of the Canon's proposal. Twenty-odd months had passed since the coach accident, and our letters since then had been sparse and unyielding. At least they had been so on my side — clearly she had not been aware that I had seen something in her bag which should not have been there, so the lack of warmth and detail must have come just from me. My mind still reeled from the shock that the sight of the brooch had been; I had tossed and turned through many horrible nights. What its presence meant I could not be sure, but it seemed it could only mean one of two things — each more hideous than the other. Self-preservation had made me shut the thoughts away, otherwise I should drown.

As the days lengthened and the winds warmed, came a letter from Charles Lane to my uncle. Did the Canon know, the letter said, the Bodmin-Wadebridge Railway, which had been incorporated last year, was now in once-weekly experimental operation. Last year there had been a formal opening of the line when a first train, with distinguished passengers on board, had run from Wadebridge to Bodmin. Now, to mark the first anniversary and an increase from one train a week to six, it was hoped to re-enact the celebration, this time starting from Bodmin, for the benefit of shareholders who lived in or nearer Bodmin or who had been unable to participate in the rejoicings of last year. It would give the company great satisfaction if the Canon would join this party, dinner being served at the Molesworth Arms and carriages being supplied for those travellers who wished to return to Bodmin. A footnote added that if the Canon would care to bring his niece, she would be more than welcome.

We had missed the formal opening last year because the Canon had been afraid of catching a chill; but a few weeks later we had met Charles Lane by chance in Bodmin, in the company of a Mr Dunstan, who was Chief Superintendent of the new railway, and Charles had pressed us to go at once and inspect the line. This we did, although the one engine was at Wadebridge at the time so we could not see that. Charles, who was much more at ease than I had seen him, explained that originally it had been thought the carriages and trucks would have to be brought up the gradient to Bodmin by a team of horses, but it had been found that the engine had sufficient power of its own. He also told us of his recent marriage to a young Devonshire girl called Effie Farrow. He came down to Cornwall only about once a month now, the daily working of the line being left to Mr Dunstan. I asked after Mr Brunel.

A shadow crossed Charles's craggy face, but it was not an unfriendly one.

'Goes from strength to strength. He is so busy, I see little of him nowadays. But we were able to persuade him against the atmospheric propulsion for this line.'

'And also to convince him of the virtues of the narrow gauge,' said Dunstan.

'I don't think you will ever convince him of that,' said Charles. 'He accepted it here from the beginning because the survey and estimates were already in existence, it being designed in the first place for a horse-drawn tramway.'

I waited for a day or two to learn of my uncle's decision on this second invitation, but the weather was mild and sunny, no cold winds blew, so eventually he accepted it.

Then the weather changed; he was caught in a fearful shower and retired to his room with a chill. So a letter went countermanding his acceptance, and I resigned myself to disappointment.

By horse and trap from Bodmin came a letter from Charles regretting the Canon's ill fortune and hoping for his quick recovery. But in the meantime might the Canon's niece be permitted to come on her own? Transport would be provided, it said, and there would be a number of ladies of quality travelling, including Lady Molesworth, Mrs Joseph Austen and Mrs Thurston Collins.

The Canon was reluctant to say yes, but seeing my expectant face he relented.

It was after all a fine day when the same trap came for me, but my uncle would not change his mind at the last moment. When I got to where the Bodmin train stopped (as yet there was no station at this end, the line finishing with buffers and a big mound of sand) Charles was waiting for me; he took both my hands, grasping them warmly and led me up three steps to the wooden platform on which a number of notables were gathering, down the other side and into a big shed in which stood the engine. It was a not very large, shiny, polished machine with a barrel body, a very tall chimney and a cab at the end. It had six wheels, attached to each other by strong steel rods, which themselves were part of a complex structure of iron and steel running in and out of the belly of the engine. Behind it was another truck which carried coal and water, Charles explained — a ton of coal, 370 gallons of water — and was called the tender. Behind that was a long string of wagons roofed and unroofed.

The first-class carriages, Charles pointed out, were furnished in blue cloth stuffed with hay. The lower panels of each passenger coach were painted ultramarine blue, the upper panels white, with a bright red underframe. It all looked shiny and smart. Two men were busy shovelling coal into the back of the engine, and there was steam beginning to issue from various parts of the machine, most particularly from one of the two domes along the top.

'Is this,' I asked, 'going to pull all this?'

'Yes. That's not an unusual load. We shall be off in ten minutes, all being well.'

'How did you get the engine onto the rails in the first place?' I asked. 'Was it built in Cornwall?'

'No. Neath Abbey. Shipped by sea to Wadebridge and assembled there. It weighs ten tons and cost us £275.'

'Is that its name?' I asked.

'*Camel*, yes. It seems appropriate, don't you think?'

'And how is this line going to make money? Not on the number of passengers on a normal day?'

'No, we take passengers at present for only two days of the week. Sea sand for the farmers, carried at a much cheaper rate than horse-drawn carts. Coal for Bodmin, and other smaller items. Back to Wadebridge we shall take granite, and timber and ore from the mines . . . Emma.'

I looked at him. 'Yes?'

'All those elegantly dressed folk will occupy the three first-class carriages in the centre of the train. The rest, the open ones, are for the second class. Do you wish to join the elegant people?'

'What? Now? Is there some other choice?'

'I shall be on the footplate. Would you care to join me?'

I stared at the engine. 'D'you mean — up there?'

'Yes. It will be quite safe if you hold to a rail. But it will not be as comfortable.'

'I should like that,' I said.

He smiled. He had lost much of his shyness.

'I have permission for you to travel on the footplate. But before you do I must offer you a cloak, to keep the coal dust off your dress, and a pair of plain glass spectacles to keep any sparks out of your eyes.'

The engine let out two noisy blasts on its whistle. 'That means we shall be off in five minutes. Do come this way.'

He led me into a small ante-room, where a long black cloak was hanging, and in a drawer was a pair of spectacles. It seemed that he had prepared for my acceptance in advance.

III

A while ago I had enjoyed the strange and exhilarating experience of being propelled at sea by means of paddle wheels activated by a steam engine within the bowels of the ship. But this was more exciting, more dangerous-seeming.

After any amount of hissing and puffing we had backed onto the platform, while about 200 people climbed aboard. Then, with this huge extra load the engine had jerked itself into life and with much shuddering and shaking we had begun to move. Even going down the descent to the valley and moving at, Charles said, about six miles an hour, cautious of getting too much momentum, I was deafened by the noise, blown by the wind and occasionally invisible for the steam. I clung to the rail, watching the engine driver with his levers, the stoker with his shovel, two other engineers travelling in case of breakdown. On the very front of the engine stood a young man clinging to a bar, to open gates and clear off any straying cattle. Charles towered over them all in a railway cap and long overalls.

At Dunmere Bridge we stopped for water. After that we ran through a very narrow leafy valley, across and alongside the winding River Camel. Many trees had had to be felled, but others overhung the line, and as the engine gathered speed, puffing heartily, broken leaves fluttered down upon the train which rattled and rumbled behind us like a snake with seventeen vertebrae. Sparks and smoke and steam flew past as we reached fifteen miles an hour, and the fresh green of the trees and the glint of the wild flowers and the fluttering of startled birds disappeared as quickly as they came.

Twice more we crossed the river on newly built bridges. We stopped again to take in water at Tresarrett, but moved along easily then until the tall masts in Wadebridge Harbour came in sight. So the trip was completed, and completed, what was more, with a woman on the footplate!

'Well done, Miss Spry!' Charles said, as he helped me down. 'I *am* proud of you.'

My exhilaration was as yet only slightly coloured by the knowledge that the *West Briton* next week was likely to report my adventure and that the Canon would therefore be sure to come to hear of it.

IV

When I returned the Canon was already peevish. His dinner had been badly overcooked and Florrie had taken to her bed with a headache, we were almost out of cider and his cold was no better. It was unusual to be scolded by my usually benign uncle, and I wondered if that would be a more customary occurrence if we ever married. Or was it possible that he resented my never having answered his proposal and looked on my silence as a contemptuous refusal?

I did not tell him of the journey on the footplate, feeling that a week hence it would not seem so bad.

At Wadebridge I had found myself very dirty in spite of the protecting cloak and spectacles and had done everything possible to clean up for the dinner at the Molesworth Arms, but was a little surprised to find that the rest of the gentry, male and female, had not travelled spotlessly and were constantly apologizing to their neighbours for smuts on their faces or hands or dresses.

I told my uncle about the dinner and how good-tempered and happy everyone had been on the trip, and how well one was looked after, and how I had shared a coach home with Major and Mrs Thurston Collins, Mr Joseph Austen and his mother, and how they had expressed their warmest wishes for his quick recovery. I spoke too with regret for the wild flowers, asphodels, pimpernels, water mint and the rest which had been crushed by the building of the line but were already pushing up again and flowering between the sleepers.

The Canon grunted at all this and sniffed a few times and said he much regretted not being able to go himself. It occurred to me that some of his irritability came from missing such a trip on his beloved railway.

As a result of sharing that coach trip back from Wadebridge, I came to know Mrs Joseph Austen and her son who lived in that other Place House, a castellated Tudor mansion on the very edge of the town of Fowey. It had been the ancient home of the Treffrys for more than 400 years. At one time much more important than the Sprys had ever been, the family had fallen on hard times, but recently had been revitalized by Mrs Austen's son, Mr Joseph Austen, who was now a successful shipowner and mine owner and was spreading his interests county wide. Mrs Austen — herself a Treffry — was in her seventies and rather a severe-looking woman, but we talked on the coach, and two weeks later I was surprised to receive an invitation to spend a few days with her. I had to refuse, for the Canon could not spare me, but her friendship was to be of great value to me later on.

Sure enough my adventure did reach the newspapers, though not by way of a headline. 'One lady, greatly daring, contrived to travel on the footplate of the engine, and, the journey completed, seemed none the worse for her experiences. The young lady in question is Miss Emma Spry, the niece of Canon Francis de Vere Robartes; she is distantly related to the Agar-Robartes of Lanhydrock. Questioned by our reporter, she said that she would be happy to travel on the footplate again.'

I had said no such thing, as Charles had made sure that no reporter approached me. But I awaited the Canon's response with some apprehension, knowing that he would read the report from end to end.

The afternoon that the newspaper arrived tea was taken in to him as usual — only now there was no need of lamps — and he looked up at me as I came in, and smiled a little acidly as he pointed to the paper.

'Your mother warned me you were a rebel! Isn't it fortunate that you haven't married me! 'Canon's wife on footplate', that would have caused quite a stir!'

I said: 'I should not have dared to do it.'

'Wouldn't you? That is a comfort. 'Canon's wife dances down church aisle!' Would there have been no danger of that?'

'No, sir.'

'For I could not then have discharged you, could I?'

'Do you intend to now?'

'Come here, Emma,' he said.

I put the tray down and went slowly up to his chair. He took my hand.

'Dear girl, human beings are animals, aren't they? And young human beings have animal spirits. I had almost forgot. You are here to remind me.'

I smiled at him. 'Thank you.'

'Husband and wife, uncle and niece, canon

184

and house-keeper — whatever the roles we choose to play, I hope we shall continue in companionable friendship and live a Christian life together.'

'I think so,' I said, feeling warm and singularly pleased.

2

I

After long and persuasive pressure from the Canon I agreed to take part in a concert in Bodmin in aid of church repairs. I sang two songs. Mixing with strangers was still a strain and an embarrassment, and there was no hiding my ugliness from my fellow performers. But when I went on the platform I wore my hair in such a way that most of the disfigurement was hidden by curls which fell across the side of my face. Then, by singing with my head turned slightly to the left, I felt it likely that there would be little or no notice taken. My hair is not naturally curly and it was Mrs Thurston Collins, who played the piano accompaniments, who suggested both the hairstyle and the curling tongs.

The Collinses lived in the big Tudor house not far from the village; Caroline Collins, though quite a lot older than I, seemed to have taken a fancy to me, and to this I responded gratefully. I have a mezzo-soprano ('the commonest of all women's voices', my sister had read out to me once when I was trying it out); the Canon said he preferred to call it a 'lyric soprano'; in the event two years' singing in the choir had helped. It was still lighter than my mother's, but now just as clear and unwavering. In the

186

first half I sang a sacred song, but in the second, at the Canon's insistence, I sang one of the comic songs I had learned from my mother; and whereas the first song had been met with agreeable applause, the second was rather a triumph. Fortunately the concert was not being held in the church, and the audience applauded so long that Caroline dragged me in again and I sang another — less comic — song that I had learned from my mother.

We spent the night in ecclesiastical lodgings in Bodmin, and I went to sleep wrapped in the sort of satisfaction I thought only ordinary people had the right to feel.

Thereafter came a succession of requests that I should repeat the songs at this or that village concert, for this charity or that. I went to some, but then my uncle went down with bronchitis again and I felt unwilling to take on commitments without him.

A letter from my mother.

My dear Emma,

Thank you for yours of last month. I am very glad that the concert was such a success. I do so wish something professional could be made of this, but we both know the insuperable difficulty. Should you ever wish to leave Blisland — or if anything happened to your uncle — there might be a living to be made in teaching. Should this occur pray let me know and I will sound out my friends for the best opportunity.

Have you heard from Tamsin of late? She

is in a little trouble. Desmond went to see his mother last month and found her still much out of her mind but greatly distressed by the treatment she has been receiving at Greenlands. So he has brought her home. This has transformed Place House, for Desmond has had to engage two nurses to make sure that Aunt Anna does no mischief to herself or anyone else in the house. Tamsin is very upset and fearful, she says, for Celestine's safety. I do not know whether she exaggerates — Aunt Anna was never violent or menacing in the old days — but Tamsin was always a highly-strung person, and it is a situation not to be welcomed.

Now I have some news for you, which will perhaps surprise you but I hope it will not offend. I am to be married again. His name is Captain Gerald Frensham. He is fifty years of age — five years younger than I — a retired naval officer who fought at Trafalgar, and he has been pursuing me for two years, and I am very fond of him. He has a sufficiency of a private income to live in comfort, and, apart from the fondness I have for him, it will be pleasant to contemplate increasing years without financial apprehension. My acting career is petering out and I have accumulated a number of debts.

Once or twice in the past I have thought of marriage but have considered among other things the future of my two girls. Now that you are both settled I can feel freer to remarry.

Captain Frensham has a house on Richmond Green, and I believe I shall be very happy there, though — as always with people who have lived there — I shall long for Cornwall, and hope to return from time to time. Gerald was widowed ten years ago, and has no children, only a niece who at present looks after him. Sybil and I are already firm friends.

I am in fact to be married next week. I would have wanted my children to be at the wedding, but distances are so great, and it will all take place with a minimum of ceremony. I shall hope to bring him down before long, so that you can both meet him.

Your loving
Mother

Now that you are both settled. In what way was I settled, unless I decided to become the Canon's wife which was a possibility my mother would not have dreamed of?

I began to feel the need to talk to my sister. We had not been close since we were children, and our separation had widened the gap; our letters were sparse and brief. But in one way absence makes the heart grow fonder; causes for discord, irritations, minor or major, tend to be forgotten. I wanted to have a full, frank, friendly interchange about all that had happened to us in the last three years. I wanted to see Celestine again and see how she had grown. I wanted also to see Desmond, for whom I had always had a soft spot. But most particularly it was Tamsin.

189

She was after all, apart from my mother, my closest kin.

I took the letter to show the Canon, but he had heard by the same post. He offered no comment on my mother's decision to remarry. He saw the point of wanting to see my sister again. He suggested that she should come to stay at Blisland for a few days, but on my assuring him that she would never do that he gave way. The question was how long, and how could he manage without me? In the church I had met an earnest old woman called Mrs Tremewan who adored the Canon, and I suggested, rather than depend on Clarice for her cooking — sure disaster for she would not learn — we should invite Mrs Tremewan to come as cook for the week I was away. In order to sugar the pill I offered to pay her wages out of my own pocket.

While feebly protesting that it was not necessary, he allowed me to do this. On the way to St Anthony I consoled myself with the thought that Mrs T made good cakes and pasties for church meetings, so she should be able to satisfy one absent-minded but epicurean cleric.

It was October and the journey was tedious, not of course by its distance but by the constant change of vehicle. I could have walked it in the time. How good if in a few years we could have one of Charles's railways to run from Bodmin to Falmouth! By the time I was crossing Carrick Road the sun had sunk behind an ominous black cloud which reached to the horizon, and a cold breeze stirred. Each time I came back something pulled at my heartstrings; possibly it was just coming home, remembering childhood and teens, possibly it was the thought of all that had happened to me here.

Some smaller purply-pink clouds high in the paling sky reflected light onto the battlemented tower of St Mawes Castle as I stepped ashore on the quay. Then down through the town to the Polvarth Ferry. The tide was in, but Tregundle saw me and recognized me from the other side, and got into his boat and rowed across.

'Evenin', miss. 'Tis time 'nough since ye've been 'ere. I 'ope you're well.'

'Thank you, I am. Yes it is quite a time.' I did not suppose he had ever guessed who borrowed his ferry when she was a naive girl, betrayed, and going to Truro in search of her lost and faithless lover. Although I was only three years older I felt ten. Nothing special had happened to me since, no great formative character shock (except what was happening at that time). Living a solitary life in a rectory on the moors should in no way have helped me to a greater sophistication. But I had grown up.

'How is Mrs Tregundle?'

'Nicely, thank 'ee. We got a grandson since you left. To Millie. Jonathan, they d'call him.'

I murmured polite congratulations and resisted a temptation to trail my hand in the water.

'Goin' up to Place, I s'pose. Like me to carry your bag?'

'Oh, thank you, no. It has no weight. How is my sister?'

He lifted his oar and pulled on the other.

191

Water scintillated. A moorhen fluttered out of his path.

He said: 'She's from 'ome, miss.'

'From — home? D'you mean she's away?'

'Yes, miss. She and Mr Desmond and the baby, they all left this morning.'

'Where have they gone? D'you know? Is it just for a day or — '

'Dunno, miss. They never telled me. They left by coach for St Austell, I b'lave.'

We reached the other side and he helped me step ashore.

'I wrote a week ago,' I said. 'Perhaps the letter has gone astray.'

'Yes, mebbe that's so. Sure you wouldn't like for me to come up to the 'ouse with you? Should be happy to do so. It's quite a climb wi' that bag.'

I hesitated. 'Thank you, Mr Tregundle. But no. My aunt will be there and maybe she will be well enough to see me.'

'Mebbe,' he said and pocketed the coin I gave him. 'Thank 'ee, miss. And good eve to 'ee.'

II

The long twilight was more than half gone before I came in sight of the house. Nothing, it seemed, had changed. The long facade glimmered white in the encroaching dusk. Then I saw the church spire. It had been rebuilt, the broken stained-glass window had been repaired, though with plain glass. There were two lights in the house, one in the west bedroom, one at the door.

I changed hands with my bag, took a deep breath of the familiar air, looked across the creek to St Mawes, where a sprinkling of lights tinselled the quiet water. A solitary fishing boat with a chocolate-coloured sail was creeping into harbour. In the wider bay which I had just crossed from Falmouth a half-dozen larger vessels were showing lights. I turned and pulled at the bell.

No answer. Night birds swooped in the sky.

I tried the door and it opened. I went in. Slade was standing there.

'Miss Emma.'

'Good evening, Slade.'

I walked past him and put down the bag. 'You were expecting me?'

'No, miss. I was just coming to see who was a pulling of the bell.'

'I wrote to my sister saying I was coming.'

'Yes, miss. She wrote back, she says, telling you not to come.'

'Why?'

'She was just going away.'

'Where to?'

'Miss Anna Maria's 'usband's place, Tregrehan . . . '

The house was very quiet. I wondered how many servants were left.

'Her letter did not reach me. How is my aunt?'

He had been looking me over.

'Adrift. Needs taking into dry dock and refitting.'

I realized that if everything else had changed

in nearly two decades, he had not. A bigger belly, and a heavier jowl. But the hair, aided by its dye, was as unnaturally black as ever. Even across the hall I smelt brandy.

'Well, I am here,' I said, 'and do not propose to leave tonight. Perhaps you could arrange for me to have my old bedroom.'

'That isn't rightly possible, miss.' A malicious glint.

'Why not?'

'That wing have been left to go since your mother went. There's slates missin'. Water have got in.'

As I hesitated he rubbed his dark chin. 'If I might make a suggestion, Miss Emma, you could be found a room with the Pardoes for the night. I could send Ted over to make sure, and then he could carry your bag across to save ye the trouble.'

The Pardoes rented a farm from us just over the hill behind Place. I carefully swallowed my anger.

'Is Miss Mary here?'

'She went back to Tregolls yester eve.'

'Then I will borrow her room for tonight.'

Slade shifted his stance. Overtly he was more polite to me than when we last met but his eyes showed their enmity.

'We're short-staffed 'ere, miss. Not like it was when you used to live here. Maids was two a penny then. Miss Mary took her own maid back wi 'er. I don't suppose the rooms have been cleaned since.'

'Then I shall see to the room myself. I know

the house. I know where the linen is kept.'

Veins in his neck showed as I walked past him with my bag and made for the stairs.

Whatever authority was exercised over him by Desmond and Tamsin, it no longer ran when they were away. He was 'in charge' of Place House, with a few perhaps of his toadies as servants, and an old madwoman ranting in her bedroom. My arrival had disturbed the even tenor of his command. Unimportant as I might be, I was still a Spry and could not quite be defied.

Yet it was touch and go. As I went up the stairs my neck prickled as if fearful of being grasped from behind. In the big windowed landing there was just sufficient light to see the way. At least the candles were there as usual, but none lighted. Where were the servants?

Scrape a light and go part way down the passage. Mary's room had always been next but one to her mother's. As I opened the door I heard a low moaning coming from the room at the end.

Except for the cellars, Place had always been light and airy. I had never thought of it as sinister. It had become sinister.

Mary's room smelt of Mary. She never used perfume, except some sort of powdered talc, which lingered. Also at times Mary neglected her hygiene, and this too was noticeable in her room. The bed was made, the curtains hung as they should do, towels on the rail, pitcher and ewer clean and full. Someone had attended to it since she left, and in all likelihood Slade had well known this. He had been trying to put me off. Out of sheer malice one assumed.

I dumped the bag, picked up the candle again and negotiated the rest of the passage with its single step, knocked on my aunt's door and tried to go in. It was locked.

I knocked again. After a while the key grated in the lock and the door opened a couple of inches.

'Yes?' A thin dark man with a heavy nose. Soiled white overall.

'I am Miss Emma Spry. I have come to see my aunt.'

The man hesitated, but again the name was too important in his job for him to refuse. Grudgingly he opened the door just wide enough to go in.

My aunt was sitting up in her bed, hands to her ears. The wispy grey hair was white and so thin that the pink scalp showed through. The face was ashen and greatly lined, and her eyes, once so clear blue and benevolent, were bloodshot and full of despair.

She said: 'Who's that? Who's that coming in? Shut the door, Parker, the wind is terrible. And the noise those sailors are making . . . '

I went up to the bed and tried to touch her arm. She shrank away as if she had been burned.

'I'm Emma,' I said. 'You remember? Claudine's daughter.'

'Don't touch me!' she whispered. 'You make all the noises worse. Where is Parish? He'd

196

drive 'em away.' She stared at me. 'Are you Claudine?'

'No, Aunt. I'm Claudine's daughter, Emma.'

'You're not that chit of a girl who pretends to be married to that man who pretends to be my son? You're an impostor, girl. Leave me alone! No one will ever leave me alone!'

'Ye see, miss, it don't do no good,' said Parker, who had come up behind me. 'You ask Mrs Tizard. She'll tell ye the same.'

'Who is Mrs Tizard?'

'She's in charge. I keep watch along of she. We got to watch the old lady or she'd be up and away. Ye might think she's old and feeble, but give 'er half a chance and she'd be out of this room afore you could blink twice.'

My aunt began to groan again. She would mutter a few indistinct words and follow them with a moan. I stayed for ten minutes more, for twice she went quiet and I had hopes that she was going to become lucid. Once, distinctly, she said 'Emma', but though I waited nothing more came.

Before supper I met Mrs Tizard, a tall woman with a thin grey moustache and the smell of an apothecary. I did not take to her and wondered where the kind and attentive Elsie Whattle had got to. Presumably after my aunt's years in hospital she had become unavailable. I asked Mrs Tizard about my cousin Mary and she said she had been feeling unwell and had gone back to Truro for a few days. Did she know, I asked, how long my sister intended to be away, and she said she thought a week.

197

There were at least two of the old servants left, and I asked them if they had heard of Sally Fetch. They said not for sure but they thought she was married and living in Penryn. I also spoke to Slade once, to ask him what had happened to Parish.

He replied with satisfaction: 'He got a furuncle deep in his ear, so he had to be put down.'

I ate alone in the big dining room, waited on by a man called Williams whom I had not seen before. I wondered if he had been engaged by Tamsin or if he was a Slade recruit.

It was a sparse meal, but I did not mind. I had never allowed myself to be a big eater since the loss of weight in my teens. I felt very much alone in the house and unwelcome. Perhaps it was just Slade's influence and the rest of the staff took their attitude from him. And I was a little afraid.

How could one fail to feel unwelcome with one's sister and cousin gone, and almost everyone new, except for a mad old woman and the ominous Slade?

Although I had permission to be away a week I had no real reason or excuse to stay here beyond tomorrow. To return at once to Blisland would be self-defeating. I could follow Desmond and Tamsin to Tregrehan, if that was where they had gone. I had never been to Tregrehan but I knew it was somewhere near St Austell, so it could hardly be more than twenty-five miles. Or I could call and see Mary at Tregolls which was half the distance.

But had I taken the week off to see Mary,

nice though she was? As a human being probably much to be preferred to Tamsin. But it was my *sister* I wanted to see, and if any sympathy could be established between us, there were questions I wanted to ask her. Perhaps some of the questions would themselves create more ill-feeling. If so, so be it.

After the solitary meal I took up the little lantern in the hall and went to explore the wing of the house that had once been our home.

It *was* dilapidated; on that Slade had been speaking only the truth. The rest of the house seemed well cared for; the back wing smelt only of damp and decay. I was rooting among some old familiar bits and pieces of furniture and opening a drawer or two when I heard a movement in the dark of the door. The lantern shook in my hand as I turned towards a shadow in a white apron.

'Oh, beg pardon, miss, you reely give me a fright! I was comin' up the stairs and I 'eard movements. I thought 'twas rats, and then I knew 'twas more'n that!'

A girl of eighteen or nineteen, eyes narrowed staring into the wavering yellow light, and then at my face.

'I am Miss Emma Spry,' I said. 'What is your name?'

'Lucy, miss. Lucy Ball. Beg pardon. I was just goin' to bed when I heard this noise. I don't belong to come in here, but the footsteps . . . I'm a kitchen maid, miss. I was just going to mount the stairs when — '

'This was my old room when I lived here,' I said.

'I sleep upstairs, miss. The upper floor, over the kitchen. I share with Annie Arthur, who's the other kitchen maid.'

The sudden encounter, in the hollow silence of the house . . .

'How long have you been here, Lucy?'

'Oh, nigh on two years. I mind when you come before with your mother, miss. But you won't remember me.'

'Was Miss Celestine born when you came?'

'No, miss. I come just before that.'

'Where d'you come from? I mean, where is your home?'

'Falmouth, miss.'

'Do you happen to know a girl called Sally Fetch?'

'No, miss.'

I put the lantern down on the table where I had done most of my childish sums. Could I ask her if she had heard of Mr Abraham Fox? Of course I could not.

'Does a Mr Fox ever call here? A Mr Abraham Fox?'

The lantern showed her eyebrows come together. 'I'm not sure, miss. I think mebbe he did. But there was lots of folk here for a — well for two winters and one summer, like; it was all entertaining, entertaining. Dances and tennis parties and the like.'

'This was after Miss Celestine was born?'

'Oh, yes, right up till, well, till about last Easter. This last Easter. It all stopped when

Mr Spry brought his mother home. Then they sacked four servants — I feared for my place — and they brought in that Mr Parker and Mrs Tizard to look after the old lady. It's been a big change.'

'D'you mean much quieter?'

'Oh . . . oh yes, miss. All sorts of things.'

'What sort of things?'

She looked sidelong again at my face. 'Tedn my place to say, miss.'

'It — affected the servants. The sudden change must have affected the servants.'

'Oh, for sure. You know Cook left?'

'I hadn't seen her. She was discharged?'

'Well, she never got along with Mr Slade, y'know, all these years.'

'And he discharged her?'

'Oh, I don't know. I expect that was left to Mr Spry.'

'Are the other older servants happy here?'

Lucy glanced over her shoulder. 'Not the old ones, no, miss. The new ones, mebbe. Mebbe they're friends of Mr Slade's.'

'The man I'm referring to,' I said, 'is known as Mr Bram Fox. About thirty-five, tall and good-looking. Very jolly . . . ' I stopped, aware that I should never have spoken like this to a servant.

'Wi' a terrible temper?'

'What?'

'Beg pardon. There was a Mr Bram once at a Christmas party, miss. 'Tis no business of mine . . . '

'Was that last Christmas?'

'I don't rightly recall . . . I — I think I've said enough, miss. 'Tis not for me to tell tales about my betters. Or next thing I know I shall be sent 'ome without a reference.'

My mind groped for ways of inducing her to go on. But I knew I could not.

'Thank you, Lucy,' I said. 'I shall be seeing my sister later in the week, so no doubt she will tell me all the news then. But be assured, nothing you have said will be repeated. I understand your position and will respect it.'

'Thank you, miss.'

After returning to the main house I considered a walk in the dark, using the stray lights of St Mawes as a guidance, but it had been a long day and a tiring one. I was also depressed, and found the silence of the house morbidly heavy and menacing. So I went to bed.

3

I

Almost instantly to sleep, and then perversely, after about an hour woke and could not settle again. Once or twice I fancied there were little cries from my aunt's room.

There was so much to think of, so much to ponder in what Lucy Ball had told me — much to be inferred, though perhaps wrongly. Perhaps I should see Mary before Tamsin. Mary must know a great deal about what had been going on, though if she had only returned to Place after her mother was brought home her knowledge would be partial.

Tamsin had always had an appetite for parties and entertaining. We had talked about it as girls. Her marriage to Desmond had put her in a position to indulge herself. Here was the house, empty except for them and a small baby, with an adequacy of servants, a notable name, and acquaintanceship — laboriously fostered by my mother — with most of the landed gentry in this part of Cornwall. So it seemed probable that soon after our visit she had persuaded Desmond to give her her head. Extra servants engaged. The house lightly refurbished.

Then, a horrible transformation! Desmond had gone to see his mother and concluded she was not being well looked after and must come home. A transformation of Place from a scene of youthful gaiety to a gloomy nursing home. A shedding of the extra servants who no doubt were young and smart, and the engaging of two grim middle-aged nurses in their place. Had Tamsin acquiesced in this change of lifestyle? That did not match the vivid and intimate memories I had of her. So had there been trouble between husband and wife? Perhaps my mother had hinted at that in her letter, and I had not read between the lines. And did Bram come into this at all?

I turned over and glanced out of the windows, the curtains not being drawn. The sky was not completely black, as it had been when I went to sleep. A vague yellowish flickering; there for an instant or two and then fading. It couldn't surely be a ship on fire: it might be one signalling to another. Yet it seemed too close.

I pulled the curtain of the bed further back, but could see no more. Perversely I was now feeling sleepy. Let it go. Whatever it was was none of my business.

The boards of the bedroom floor were cold to my feet: I groped among the furniture towards the window.

There was a lantern immediately in front of the house. It was shaded, but with eyes accustomed to the dark I could pick out the figures of men, and presently several horses or mules.

Six men and two animals. What time was it? Certainly no time for anyone to be lawfully abroad.

I was wearing only the thin shift I had brought with me but, apart from my own underwear and jacket and skirt of dark broadcloth in which I had come and which lay folded on the chair beside the bed, the wardrobe nearby was full of Mary's clothes, and I had seen a purple cloak which would be easier to slip on. Beside it was one of the newly fashionable long cashmere shawls, which if wrapped round my neck over the top of the cloak would be warm and protective.

First thought was to rouse Slade, for if something wrong was afoot his size and authority would be invaluable; but I did not fancy going upstairs and into his bedroom to wake him. Though he had kept his distance all through, his dislike of me didn't altogether disguise other thoughts he might have.

When I opened the door there was still a light under the door of my aunt's room but the least sensible thing would be to burst in there and raise an alarm.

Go to the head of the main stairs. There was no lamp lit in the hall as there always used to be, but a flicker of light from outside could be seen through one of the windows.

As a child I had hardly ever had to open the front door: it had seemed enormous. I put my hand to the latch and then realized it was bolted and I could not pull back the bolts without making a noise. But I could go through the drawing room into the church and thence to the garden. It was probably not the best of ideas, but somehow I negotiated the furniture and came to the two ancient granite steps which led to the church door. The church struck chill; cold air moved in its high chancel; despite repairs it smelt musty and dank. Just make out the lines of the pews; grope along the slate floor to the door. This was not locked, but as I opened it about three inches the latch clicked.

A man in the dark, silhouetted against the gleam from the lantern. Not more than four yards away. In this silence came the crunch of wheels, the clop of a mule's foot.

'Who's there?'

Slade's voice.

A crisis of nerves. Gently allow the church door to close, the latch to click again, move back on tiptoe among the pews. Some childish wish not to be discovered. Run and hide, you silly fool, you. As I reached the door into the drawing room the church door opened again.

Two doors led out of the big drawing room: one into the smaller drawing room, one into the servants' passage. I chose this one, almost immediately stumbled over a serving trolley which should not have been there. Turn and make for the main hall. I knew the slight collision had given my choice away and that he would be following.

Shoes made a squeak as he moved. Then the breathing. Instead of carrying on down the passage which ran to the servants' quarters I turned into the dining room, stood behind the door perfectly still. The squeak went past, the breathing faded, then silence.

Heart thumped away. What is there to be

afraid of? A servant, a butler, an old man, up to some mischief at part of which you could begin to guess. I was Miss Spry, wasn't I? Twenty-one. A member of this landowning, seafaring family. Confronted by a mere servant.

But tell that to a woman who has grown up disliking and always fearing him, tell it to her in pitch blackness in the middle of the night, with other men, strangers, outside, and no one of your own family within distant call. What if I disappeared? Who was to know what had happened?

It had not been too clever a move to dodge him in this way, because by doubling back I had put him between myself and the staircase and thence the safety of my bedroom. Of course he would no doubt suddenly appear in this room and find me; or, time pressing, he might give up the search and go back to the waiting men outside.

Knees weak, and cold in spite of the cloak and shawl. When a child in some sort of discomfort or pain I would count, hoping this would help time to pass. I began to count now. Then I groped for a chair and sat down.

The light had not quite gone, but there were no footsteps to be heard outside. If it was a sort of procession, it had moved on either towards the gate of the property or the quay.

One advantage of counting is that it gives you some sense of the passing of time. When I got to 500 it was reasonable to suppose about five minutes had passed. My teeth were trying to chatter, not with cold but with nerves. Take a chance.

I slid out of the dining room door into the servants' passage and, careful of any more pitfalls, reached the main hall. It was quite dark. The staircase was in the middle of the hall, and I could just see its white painted pediments. As I moved towards it a hand like an animal's bite grasped my upper arm.

'Got you!' and a fist thumped the side of my head so that the world hummed.

I tried to wrench my arm free. 'Let me go! How dare you! Let me go, I say!'

The grip eased and slowly the hand fell away.

'You, girl! I never thought 'twas you! Well, well!'

'Slade!' I said. 'What are you doing here? How — how dare you!'

'Didn't expect you wandering round the house at this time, neither.' Flint scraped, and presently a candle began to burn. He was wearing a grey jersey and breeches and leggings. The hand with the missing fingertips held the candle.

'I thought 'twas that Lucy, the little bitch. Can't stand young girls interfering and poking their noses into what don't concern 'em.'

I was certain he knew who had been in the church and hidden from him. The Lucy I had met would have been too scared to come down two flights of stairs in the dark.

'I saw lights and heard voices, I thought something was amiss. Do you allow men to tramp across our land in the middle of the night?'

He rasped his chin and looked me up and down as the candle flame burned brighter.

'No, maid. 'Twas just a chance I met some of my old shipmates. They've all gone now. Don't ye think it's time you was off to bed?'

'I'll go when I wish to.'

'Well, there's naught more to see tonight. I reckon I'm for bed soon too — I reckon if you was minded to see me afore you go in the morning, I'll answer what you have to ask.'

II

In the bedroom again. For a while I kept a candle burning. Heart refused to settle to a beat that allowed me to forget it. My upper left arm showed a darkening bruise.

Presently I snuffed the candle, dug into the bed and composed myself for sleep. Difficult to say how long that took, but at last I was gone — and strangely nothing was dreamt, or at least nothing remembered.

Wake as dawn is just breaking. I could see the squares of the windows, the slight sheen on a wardrobe door, the glint of the water jug, a man standing by the bed.

I sat up.

'Good day to you, Miss Emma,' said Slade. 'I did not know what time you was leaving today, but I thought 'twas only right and proper that we should have a little talk.'

'Get out of my room!'

He sat carefully on the foot of the bed.

' 'Twould be best all round, Miss Emma; best for all concerned if you was to listen to what I have to say — even though you may dislike the sound of it. And here in this room there's no prying ears nor eyes as there might be later in the morning.'

It was as if normality had existed only while I was asleep, and this was a return of the nightmare.

He said: 'I been here with the Admiral and now Mr Desmond for nigh on five and twenty years. I served the Admiral because we was old shipmates. But I had other shipmates in and around these parts which as I have kept up with and try to help from time to time. That's what I was doing last night, and but for you arriving when you wasn't invited and wandering down in the middle of the night nobody would've been the wiser. But now you know, don't you?'

Slowly take deep breaths to calm myself.

'Were you running contraband?'

'Well, now, that's a long word, maid. Not one as I'd use meself. See, as I see it, there's God's laws and there's men's laws. Thou shalt not kill, that's what God says. But it is men as builds artificial barriers 'twixt one country and the next. Every pint of rum ye drink, so much has to be paid to the Excise, who then spend most of it paying men to guard the coasts. Don't make sense, do it.'

After a minute, when he didn't go on, I said: 'Do they bring it in at Molunnan Cove?'

'Ah, now, miss, the less you're told the less

you know, eh? 'Tis not a regular trade, like. Nothing like that! Just now and then a barrel or a keg or a roll of something comes to hand, then sometimes 'tis kept here for a little while before it moves on.'

'In the cellar, I suppose.'

'Mebbe yes, mebbe no. It is not for me to go into the detail, like.'

'Then when you have a sufficiency of contraband goods, you arrange a night when all the Sprys are away and half a dozen men and a couple of carts come along and move it off at your leisure.'

The light was growing. I could see the expression on his plump mealy face was not pleasant.

'Did my uncle know about this?'

He laughed. 'The Admiral? Lord bless ye, yes. Of course he did! Wasn't above helping himself to a bit of picking here and there, neither.'

'And Mr Desmond?'

'Ah, well that's best left unsaid, isn't it? Now look, Miss Emma. I've told you all I'm going to tell you. And that's too much. You already know more than it is good for you. It isn't healthy, y'know. We got to think of your safety.'

'My safety?'

'Yes, miss. Folk who know too much are at risk they may run their heads into a bowline.'

'Are you threatening me with breaking God's laws now?'

The first shafts of sun were lighting up a few errant clouds.

'Yes, maid,' he said. 'That's the drift of it.'

I felt my arm where the bruise was. 'It would be difficult to kill me, wouldn't it?'

'I wouldn't lay a hand upon you. Because you're a Spry, see. Even if you're a spying Spry. *I'd* not touch you. But this here is a hobby, like, to me. Not so to all my old shipmates. Some make a living that way. Some has wives and children to keep, to dress and find food for their little mouths. My old shipmates might take it hard if their trade was ruined. See, I can speak for myself, and you've nothing to fear. But it would not be good, would it, if someone tampered with your face so that both sides looked the same.'

III

Tamsin said: 'But why did you come on here? I know I should have left you a note but we were very busy at the end and Celestine was fractious. I hoped my reply would have reached you in time, and at the last minute I forgot to leave a note at home.'

'I thought,' I said, 'when our mother remarries it seems reasonable that her two daughters might exchange a word or two.'

We were sitting in the handsome high-ceilinged drawing room of Tregrehan. The house, which like many others in Cornwall was in considerable need of repair, was a sizeable mansion, much bigger than Place, with a view to the southeast of sand dunes, copses of woodlands, mainly conifers, and the sea.

Tamsin had lost some of her looks after

Celestine was born, but she was as beautiful as ever now. When I arrived Desmond was out walking with Edward, so I had not yet seen either of them. Anna Maria had appeared and disappeared after an absent-minded welcome. She had become almost stout, and I observed that she was carrying her fifth child. William Carlyon, Edward's elder brother by a year, had ushered me in, and for the moment I was alone taking tea with Tamsin. I had taken it for granted that I should stay at least one night here, but had not yet been shown to my room.

'There's nothing we could do about it,' Tamsin said, 'even if we wished to, and I don't wish to. I have been worried about Mama for some time. She still makes a fair living on the stage but it is bound to fall off, and I know she is heavily in debt. Desmond at present is spending all his money on his own mother and we have little to spare for maintaining her. *You* could not help, I know. How much does the Canon pay you?'

'£10 a year.'

'He's as mean as muck, we all know. But I suppose it is near the normal rate.'

'How much do you pay Slade?' I asked.

'Twenty. But he is a man and a butler.'

'Did you know that he is also a smuggler?'

She raised her brows. 'In what way?'

I told her, and ended:

'The mystery of what is in the cellar is quite cleared up. People bring things to Place a keg at a time, and then once in a while it all goes out in a convoy.'

She got up and went to the window, carrying her teacup. 'I hope Maud is not keeping Celestine out too long. The wind today is chilly.'

'By chance I discovered what was happening. Slade threatened me if I told anyone I might be further disfigured by his men.'

'They're not *his* men,' Tamsin snapped in irritation. 'He is only a cog, a link, he commands nothing.'

'So you know all about it?'

'I know little about it. Obviously less than you have discovered in one uninvited visit.'

'Slade says that Uncle Davey was a party to the whole thing.'

She shrugged.

'I don't believe that,' I said.

'Does it matter?'

'I don't know. I think so. Does Desmond?'

'Does Desmond what?'

'Know what Slade is doing.'

'Look,' she said, coming back from the window. 'What I know, what we know, is entirely our business. Since you no longer live at Place, it is no longer yours. Why don't you go back to Blisland and look after your Canon?'

I said: 'Do you see anything of Bram Fox?'

She flushed. 'Not for ages. Not for a year. Are you still besotted?'

'Aren't you?'

A maid came into the room to remove the tea things. It took several minutes before we were alone again.

She said: 'Since you arrived so late you will

214

have to sleep here. I will ask Anna Maria. But I hope you will make arrangements to leave in the morning.'

I said: 'Did you know that our mother had had an intimate relationship with Bram?'

Tamsin flushed again. 'That's an utterly contemptible lie! If you were not my sister you should leave this house at once!'

'I have a very good reason to suppose that she did. I may be wrong.'

'Of course you're wrong! Viciously, wickedly wrong! I'm ashamed to listen to you!'

'I'm sorry.'

'You know how she has always hated him. It's quite beyond *belief*!'

'That's what I felt.'

'I mean it is beyond belief that you could *harbour* such a suspicion! What can you *mean*? What so-called proof can you have?'

I realized rather late that explanations about the starfish would mean telling her of my own experience. I had not intended to say anything at all about it. The words had come unbidden and were already regretted.

But her reaction did not reassure me. I knew her too well.

'Well, I hope she will be happy with her new husband,' I said.

'No, tell me what you mean, what you are insinuating.'

'I cannot, Tamsin. Otherwise I should betray someone else.'

Fortunately for me at this moment Celestine and her nurse came in, and for a time all was chatter and confusion.

Celestine was obviously high strung and excitable. When a few minutes later Desmond and Edward came in she flew into her father's arms. Desmond, as always, was pleased to see me and at once suggested I should stay a few days and then return with them to Place on Saturday. Noticing the continuing glint in Thomasine's eye, I refused as graciously as I knew how and said the Canon would be expecting me tomorrow.

The family talk that ensued was a change from the tension of tea time with Tamsin; but I soon observed that all was not well between her and Desmond, and that tensions of another sort existed. Tamsin's flashing smile which was one of her great assets was plainly absent when she looked at him.

The evening passed quietly enough, and all thorny subjects were avoided. Arrangements were made for me to be taken by pony trap to St Austell, where I could catch a waggonette that left daily for Bodmin.

I had one further sharp exchange with my loving sister before I left. She began it quite amiably by saying she was glad I had not bothered Desmond with my stories of Slade's misdoings. He preferred, she said, not to interfere with him so long as he performed his duties as a butler.

'Does he not fear that if Slade were discovered he would be liable for what is taking place on his property?'

'Desmond is at present learning to play the

harp, and spends much time sketching birds.'

I thought of Mary's apprehensions.

'Why do you not just get rid of Slade? Desmond told me when I was there with Mama that it was your idea that he would be re-engaged.'

'We *both* agreed. We felt Uncle Davey would have been pleased that we should have him back. It's only Anna Maria really who hated him.'

'I don't recall that we were very fond of him when we were young. He still makes me feel as if there were a cold finger on my spine.'

'You were always one with a wild imagination,' she said. 'By the way, your eye has improved. I've been meaning to tell you.'

'Perhaps it's just with growing to be adult. Afraid the other marks are just the same.'

She looked at me, considering. 'Yes, there's no difference in those.'

'When I sang some songs in Bodmin a while ago a lady I know, a Mrs Collins, covered them with powder and it made a difference.'

'It wouldn't make much,' she said. 'You couldn't hide that eyelid.'

'The first person to mention the improvement to me,' I said, 'was Bram Fox when we met him that day at the St Aubyns.'

Tamsin moodily opened her bag and took out a handkerchief.

I said: 'Has Slade got some sort of a hold over you?'

Tamsin unfolded her handkerchief and dabbed her nose. 'I hope I am not taking Celestine's cold. Children's ailments are always more catching . . . D'you know, Emma, you have totally changed over the last few years. You were never very agreeable as a girl, but I used to put your perversity and moroseness down to the knowledge you had of your terrible disfigurement. However, since you went away you have become so much more *aggressive*, as if you want to quarrel with everyone, as if — '

'I never want to quarrel with anybody — '

'As if you resent the good fortune of other people and want to tear it down. I know you always smile and smirk at Desmond, so he thinks well of you, but you reserve for your sister all the festering suspicions and petty spite that your unhappy nature can conceive of. I do not know what your Canon thinks of you. Or do you save all your most unpleasant side for me?'

'Certainly I envy you your looks and your child and your position — and always will,' I said, humbly. 'But I came to see you, and was looking forward to seeing you, in a mood of genuine warmth and affection. I only wanted to talk with my sister and hear about her life and tell her of mine. I didn't want to upset you, Tamsin. I just thought it was time that we met.'

Thomasine dabbed at her eyes. 'Perhaps it was an ill time to meet. There are things in my life that do not please me. Others — forbidden ones — do. I live on a tightrope and fear to fall.'

'Can you not tell me?'

She shook her head. 'I don't trust you, Emma. Already you know too much. Go back to Blisland and forget us. And tell yourself to stop asking questions.'

There was still one more that I wanted to ask her, but now could not.

IV

I left with friendly expressions of feeling all round. Anna Maria and two of her children, William Carlyon and one of his sisters, Eliza, Desmond and Thomasine and Celestine, all to wave goodbye. Their pony cart with a groom was waiting. The weather was fine, with streaky clouds and the Channel quiet.

I had to wait an hour at St Austell, and when it started the waggonette rumbled along only slightly faster than one could walk — indeed, slower up the hills.

Bodmin was busy, and the waggonette arrived at the inn in the centre of the town just as the London coach drawn by its four handsome horses clattered up on the stage from Truro. Instantly I decided that I could get a seat on this coach, drop off at Whitecross and walk the three miles cross-country to Blisland, as I had done when travelling back with my mother that time. If there was no room inside I would sit out. I had no thick coat but the distance was not great.

But there was room inside and when the passengers reassembled in half an hour I found that one of my travelling companions was Mr Jonathan Fox.

He recognized me at once, and was most courteous — as indeed he had been the day we met in Truro. There were three others in the coach so conversation could not be private, but I told him where I had come from and the reason for my visit and what other news I had. He was interested to learn that I was acting as housekeeper to Canon Robartes, and he told me a few casual pieces of information about his family. The coach was making good speed — almost as fast as the *Camel* — and there was not much time to introduce the forbidden subject.

'The last time I saw Mr Abraham Fox,' I eventually got out, 'was a year or so ago when he was at dinner with his wife at the St Aubyns. He told me then that he had taken on a new appointment.'

Mr Jonathan Fox coughed, as if his shortness of breath were a chronic disorder.

'Commissioner for Customs and Excise for West Cornwall. He is still there. I'm afraid his wife has had a nervous collapse and now refuses to go out at all. Very sad. Such a pretty woman and still so young.'

'I'm sorry . . . Does he go out much?'

'Oh, yes. Rather to my surprise, he takes his position seriously, which means he travels about West Cornwall ceaselessly. And, as we know, he is a great party-goer. And of course very good company, which means he is popular with many hostesses.'

With predictable unpredictability the weather was changing and a light drizzle was beginning to fall. A wet three-mile walk lay ahead. Two more corners and it would be time to leave the coach.

'The last time I saw Bram,' his cousin said, 'was about two weeks ago. A reception in Truro. He was with your brother-in-law and his wife. Desmond, that is, and Thomasine. At least he arrived with them. I expect they told you of it. Though I gather they have rather changed their mode of life since poor Mrs Spry returned to Place.'

'They have,' I said. 'They have.'

V

The last time I had walked this way I had been thinking of Bram. (Indeed, did I ever stop?) I asked myself why Thomasine had lied to me when she said she hadn't seen Bram for over a year, and no answer I came up with was anything but disturbing. Bram was a sort of dark angel of my life. In whatever capacity he appeared he produced worry and hostility and dread. Hostility? Well, what else could it be called? Jealousy? Fear?

I had not been surprised at the anger Tamsin had shown when I blurted out my suspicion about our mother; but her vehemence had a little shaken that awful assumption. Had I been making an evil mountain out of a molehill? Or did such vehemence have a sinister spring of its own? Or was Tamsin sure it could never have happened, because of her closer more personal knowledge of Bram?

And if so, how had she gained this closer personal knowledge? Had he been at Place much during their period of parties and entertaining?

A gust of light rain blew like a sneeze in my face as I climbed one of the stiles near Trewint. There was no one about on this grey gusty afternoon. Returning three days before expected, but I did not suppose the Canon would object. Picture the pleasure on his face when I put my head around the door.

My reception at Place, and at Tregrehan had been anything but warmly welcoming, and it was pleasant to feel one was returning to kindly companionship and the familiarity of a known and appreciated home. My feelings for the Canon were warmer by contrast than they had ever been before. Here at least was one unvarying and reliable man. He was old but I enjoyed his company. And he did mine.

It occurred to me, not for the first time, that my failure to respond to his offer of marriage must have hurt him and hurt his self-esteem. However unimportant I might be in the general scheme of things, I had youth, some intelligence, health and strength, and while giving him the general benefit of them I had refused to accept his name and his hand. I thought to myself rather suddenly that perhaps I ought to reconsider. No one else had any use for me. My mother had remarried, and my sister had made her rejection plain. As Mrs Robartes I should, as he said, acquire a different position; and among those people I had come to know in the area of Bodmin — particularly Caroline Collins — this would be a great advantage. Socially, of course, but also in a companionable sense. I should be not just a visiting niece acting as housekeeper; I should become one of them. I would become one of the relatively unchanging gentry peopling the countryside. Mrs Collins had already suggested that we might ride to hounds together. I was not at all certain I could ride well enough: I was more used to boats than horses, but if I were the Canon's wife I would certainly have the confidence to try.

As I came near to Blisland the clouds broke and a weak sun fell on the fields and moors. It was a welcome. A welcome home.

I thought not to mention it this evening, but perhaps tomorrow. When we're having tea together. Apologize for having been so long in making up my mind, saying I wanted to be sure. Now I was sure. We'd be married in early December before the busy rush of Christmas began. Because of my friendship with them I should like Caroline's cousin, the Reverend Frederick Collins, to perform the ceremony.

What a strange occasion it would be! In my childhood before the extent of my disfigurement came home to me, I used to have dreams of a white wedding to a handsome but vaguely anonymous young man in a naval officer's uniform, and after it we would take a honeymoon in Bath and then settle somewhere by the sea in Cornwall and live happily ever after.

This was reality. To an old clergyman, in a windswept granite church, to marry him in order to care for him and to continue to live in this draughty rectory where for the last few years I had already made a home, and hoped to make it now for probably many years to come. Yet it did not depress me. I had grown very attached to the Canon. I enjoyed talking to him, reading to him, singing to him. This might be a million miles from the nerve-stretching, exotic sexuality of that single night with Bram, but I had grown out of that, I no longer wanted — or needed — its return. I loved Francis — as I supposed I should have to start calling him — in quite a different way. If there was no element of passion there was companionship, warmth and understanding. I would be happy to accept that.

A man called Greg Glanville, who worked at the tanners, was standing on the green as I reached it. He gave me a smile and tipped his cap, then slouched off towards his cottage. Two women looked up from tilling their gardens and nodded in a friendly way. Then I had crossed the grass and crunched up the short drive and came to the front door of the rectory. I went in.

It was quiet. Possibly the Canon was out, or he had already got his tea. The three servants usually took half an hour off at this time and had a cup of cocoa and a chat. I did not go into the kitchen, but dumped my bag in the hall and went up the stairs. Halfway up I met Hester Tremewan, who stared at me in surprise.

I had completely forgotten she had come in for the week, and I laughed at her surprise. An anxious expression crossed her face.

'Hush, please: your uncle is gravely ill.'

4

I

She whispered: 'The doctor says it be apoplexy. Wednesday afternoon I took in his tea and he says: 'Mrs Tremewan, I can't hold my cup,' he says. We got 'im to bed before doctor come; he could just manage the stairs; 'tis 'is left side that have been struck. Doctor say complete quiet. Oh we sent for you; first thing Canon d'say when he speaks again is 'Send for Miss Emma.' I was surprised you got 'ere so soon. Did you come back by the trap?'

'I did not get your message. I had moved to St Austell. It just happened that I came home early.'

'Well, God be thanked, I was never one for nursing, and I knew so soon as you come back things would be for the better.'

'Is he conscious?'

'Oh yes. I sat up with him most of last night and he was dozing on and off all the time. Sometimes he would talk to me — 'twasn't that it was nonsense but I couldn't make much head or tail. I'm not book-learned and you have to be book-learned to follow what he was saying.'

Dusk had not yet fallen but his bedroom was shadowy. The pieces of old furniture leaned about making the room dark.

He was half sitting up, propped by four

pillows, his eyes closed, but as soon as he heard movement he opened them. It took several seconds to focus them, then he smiled.

'Why, Emma . . . '

I bent and kissed him — not something I usually did — he had not been shaved today. His black satin nightcap was at an unusually rakish angle, one side of his mouth was drawn down; he smelt of tobacco and wine.

'Good of you to come back so soon . . . '

'I am very distressed to find you like this. Have you had tea?'

He shook his head. 'Not thirsty.'

'I will get Mrs Tremewan to make you some.'

'You — have it with me?'

'Of course. Has the doctor been today?' This was addressed to Mrs Tremewan as she was about to leave.

'Yes, miss. And will come tomorrow. He bled the Canon this morning and he says no solid foods for forty-eight hours, then a very light diet of bread and milk.'

My uncle said with a wry smile: 'This is in accord — with the tenets of my faith. Perhaps it is time — I paid more heed to them.'

When Mrs Tremewan had gone I took his left hand and held it for a moment. 'Can you feel that, Uncle?'

'Very little. But it pleases me to see you doing it.'

Tears welled suddenly into his eyes and dripped down his plump cheeks. They brought a response from me, and I gulped into my free hand.

'My handkerchief,' he said.

I brought him one and removed his glasses. He dabbed at his eyes and I at mine. Sitting on the bed I stared at him feeling sick at heart and lost.

Presently he extended his right hand for his spectacles and carefully put them on again.

He sniffed. 'Enough, my dear little Emma. I shall not do that again. A cardinal sin is being sorry for oneself. You may cry for me if you wish, but I must at all costs avoid self-pity. After all, this is only a small attack. We must carry on as if nothing had happened. Just hold my hand a moment or two longer.'

So we sat silent in the gloomy room until Mrs Tremewan arrived with candles and the tea.

II

The Canon's left leg was paralysed, as partly was his left arm. He had little difficulty in speaking but his words were sometimes slurred.

After about a month he began to move his leg, so I devoted time to massaging it and getting him in and out of bed. Presently he came to walk with a stick; at first he needed a friendly arm but later he learned to get about the house on his own. We ordered a Bath chair, and with this I pushed him around the village to visit his parishioners. On Advent Sunday he took the service at the church. It was not a great success but it marked the peak of his achievement.

Visiting clergy kept the Sunday services going, and after the morning service they came to lunch. The Canon insisted I should be present — indeed for some meals it was essential to be there in order to cut up his food.

So I came to know many more of the local clergymen, who treated me as if I were the Canon's daughter. Meeting them was an interesting experience: most of them were simply concerned with the gossip of the day — you could have found no more trivial conversation at a country fair — but one or two were of a different calibre, and arguing or talking about the *Codex Alexandrinus* or Paul's *Epistle to the Philippians* brought colour to my uncle's cheeks and a sparkle to his eyes.

I could not ever mention marriage to him now, for it would look as if I were suggesting it for the small legacy he would leave me. I knew in any case he would instantly reject the idea. There were conditions he would impose on himself, and this apoplexy put it right out of consideration.

I had a letter from my mother from Scotland. Her husband was half-Scottish and had relatives there. She wrote from Edinburgh, full of praise of the city, which she had, she said, failed to appreciate on her two previous visits. Knowing actors, it occurred to me that perhaps this was because Edinburgh on her previous visits had failed to appreciate her. She said she had not heard from Thomasine for over three months. She had had a letter from Anna Maria saying that Samuel had now resigned from the Navy but was proposing to live in London to be near Westminster. By the time this letter reached me Anna Maria was likely to have been brought to bed with her fifth. So far they were all boys. They both now wanted a girl. Did I see, by the way, in the *West Briton* — which she had regularly sent her — that Abraham Fox had unearthed a big smuggling swindle and several men had gone to prison. 'I would never have believed him capable of such fervour in the cause of law and order.'

It was the first time she had mentioned Bram in a letter to me.

The Canon had a slight backsliding in December, so a relief clergyman took the attenuated services in the church. We had a late supper, Uncle Francis and I, that Christmas evening. He seemed depressed, and after it he said:

'D'you know, Emma, if I do not get better I shall have to resign the living.'

'I do not think you need to at all. Most of the services have been maintained, and you are still able to get around the parish.'

'I have duties in Bodmin. We'll see until Easter. If I am not well by then I think the Bishop will expect it.'

'That would mean leaving the rectory?'

'Oh yes.'

'Where should we go?'

He was a long time answering. He had lost a stone or so in weight, but still kept the colour in his cheeks, and most of the distortion of the mouth had gone. The solitary candle flickered

229

in a wayward draught.

'Thank you,' he said, 'for the 'we'. Where would we go? Probably we could find comfortable lodgings in Bodmin. Of course I should be without my stipend but there would be some accommodation granted me.'

I said: 'Let's face that when it comes.'

He sighed. 'D'you know, Emma, I am glad that you did not agree to marry me, though I took it hard at the time. It would not have been fair to you.'

'I did not refuse you,' I said.

'No, but you should have. In spite of your handicap you are so young and vital. Now that I have had this stroke it points up the tremendous gap between us. Had you been tied to me now I should have felt gravely to blame.'

'I think I am tied to you, whether or not.'

We had opened a bottle of wine for supper, and he reached over and filled my glass.

'That is the kindest thing you have ever said to me. Tell me . . . I have hesitated to ask — is your eye no longer bloodshot? Have you treated it with something?'

'No, it has just happened. Sometimes it comes back for a day or so but mostly it is quite gone. Of course the lid is still so badly drawn down.'

'And you will stay with me even if we have to live in rooms in Bodmin?'

'Yes, I will stay with you.'

'Surgeon Smith,' he said, 'tells me I should not drink wine. I trust he will forgive me on this cold Christmas Day.'

'I'll make up the fire,' I said.

'Emma.' He had used my name three times tonight. 'Even though we are so different in age, in learning, in character, I think I am more deeply fond of you than of any other persons I have known in my life. I would trust you anywhere, at any time. So when you say you will stay with me to the end, I believe you totally.'

I patted his hand as I passed. 'Why talk about ends? Christmas is a time of beginnings.'

'Now you teach me my own faith.' He hesitated, fumbling with his collar.

'Does that fret you?'

'No. Indeed not. But may I be permitted to talk about death for a moment or two more?'

'A moment or two only.'

He waited till I came back from the fire.

'I am, I trust, a fully committed Christian pastor. To believe in God the Father, God the Son and God the Holy Ghost, to believe in the resurrection of the body and life everlasting — these are the central tenets of the Church, and to them I subscribe from the very depths of my soul. I have believed them all my life and have spent my life teaching and promulgating this faith to all who will listen. I have tried in my preaching but much more in my writing to penetrate to the depths of the ultimate meaning of life and death and the great Hereafter. Virtually all my intellectual time has been spent in such study. As you know, I have a more material side which has enabled me also to take an active interest in the development of rail

231

communications in this country, and in all things mechanical and scientific. That has not been in any way a rival to my primary ecclesiastical interest. How could it be? Similarly, you more than anyone, because I have been more often in your company than ever before, must know of my enjoyment of some of the more mundane aspects of life. The food you cook for me, the wine I drink, the jolly songs you sing.' He stopped suddenly. 'Why am I saying all this to you?'

'You have no need to.'

'I think I have. Because as you must now perceive I have an unnatural fear of dying.'

The candle was smoking, and I snuffed it. 'I should not think that so very uncommon.'

'It should be uncommon in a priest, a man of faith. In my own religion there are ample loving reassurances by the Apostles, by our Saviour Himself. Even Lao-tse, the Chinese philosopher and founder of Taoism, said that a man who is afraid of dying is like a person just released from prison and afraid to step into freedom.'

I stroked his forehead. 'Let us leave it now, Uncle. I understand how you feel, and I'm sure many others have felt the same. And surely it is understandable to wish to have someone loving by your side when you go. *That's* not at all unnatural.'

His lips quivered. 'You remember old Sarah Kimmins — she was in the choir before your time. I was at her deathbed in January last. She was perfectly cheerful. She was looking forward to her new life with *real* pleasure.'

'Perhaps,' I said, 'it needs a sort of simplicity of mind to have that sort of faith.'

He half smiled. 'Once again you teach me my own religion.'

'I did not mean to. But seriously is this not a question of how — how complex one's mind is? You have gone deeply into your faith with a brain far more — more questioning than Mrs Kimmins. So you have to pay for it.'

'I think the worst thing,' he said after a minute, 'is that it makes me so ashamed.'

III

Twenty-one years of age became twenty-two and another birthday and Christmas loomed. The Canon had recovered sufficiently to retain his benefice, though he walked with a bad limp and had had to be excused most of his Bodmin duties.

In the June my mother and her new husband, Captain Frensham, had called and spent two nights on their way to visit Thomasine. A fresh-faced very young-looking man in spite of his white hair and portly figure, he had an odd habit of going to sleep for a few minutes while in company if his attention wavered, but this seemed to do no one any harm and he woke refreshed and amiable. It was soon clear that my mother was the dominant partner and this suited her well. Looking back, it occurred to me that she had come to dominate most of the company in which she had found herself. Once or twice I heard Captain Frensham refer to his new wife as 'my figurehead', and one could see that Claudine not only decorated the bows of their ship but helped to steer it.

I did not tell her of my experience at Place House last year. Confidence was still quite dried up between us. No doubt I was foolish, irrational, jealous on small evidence, angry, resentful. Living as I did so much within myself, suspicions festered until they became certainties, certainties grew into enormities. What was to say she had not picked the brooch up on the cliffs?

Twice that year I had had letters from Charles Lane. They were unexpectedly long letters, considering how little he had to say when we met. He seemed to feel that our railway trip together had cemented a friendship between us, and I replied in the same vein. He told me of a trip he and his wife had made to London, and I told him of the Canon's illness and slow recovery. He sent me drawings of the design for a second engine on the Bodmin-Wadebridge line which was to support the *Camel*. The *Camel* had broken down so badly during the spring that it was under repairs for two months and all traffic had been horse-drawn. The *Elephant*, the new engine, was to follow the same general design, but would be more reliable and more powerful.

His second letter told me of an accident in which he had been involved in a train running between Exeter and Crediton. The engine, he said, was reaching its top speed when a horse without its rider, whom it had thrown in the nearby hunt, came at full gallop on the other line in the opposite direction. On seeing the approaching train the horse reared up and turned round and was hit and instantly killed. The train was thrown off the rails. He, Charles, was in the first-class carriage, but when he got out the engine was upright in the ditch up to its gearing in mud, the tender also, and the first two carriages on their sides; the last carriage was on end with its wheels in the air. Yet no one was seriously injured. 'Myself, I escaped with scarcely a bruise.'

His letters made me feel warm, rather content.

Not so comforting was a letter from Mary, from Place.

Dear Emma,

I am sorry to know Uncle Francis is unwell. This will no doubt restrict your activities in the parish as he will need constant attention.

I was disappointed to miss you at Place. I had only left that morning, labouring under an intense pressure to get away, if only for a short break and change of scene. I find my mother's condition infinitely depressing, and, although Dr Culver says she may stay in this state for years, I think she is rapidly losing ground. However much one may love a person, one can hardly sincerely pray that she may continue as she is now.

I remember what a happy house it was when my father and mother were well, and in what a cheerful and agreeable way we all grew up together. Now all is changed. Desmond is morose and depressed, and the servants, such of them as are left, surly and disobedient. Slade continues to enjoy the approbation of Thomasine, and so one is powerless to amend the situation.

Indeed it was only when I spent two weeks at Tregolls that I was aware of rumours and disagreeable gossip circulating about Place. When one is *there* one is in some degree isolated, in the centre of a small group of people with only a passing interest in the outer world. So soon as one moves *out* of that group one hears the whispers, the muttered scandal, the vindictive tittle-tattle which now surrounds the house like a miasma.

Perhaps the ugliest rumour concerns yourself — which is that, because of your disfigurement, you bring ill-fortune to a house, even that it was your presence at Place that first prompted my mother's early derangement. I vehemently stamped on this hideous rumour when I heard it. Indeed, I started to destroy this letter, feeling it would cause you such distress, but then I rewrote it with the belief that you should know even at the risk of shocking and offending you — to understand the depths of the evil scandal which grows around Place.

This calumny — which is so obviously a malicious lie — strengthens my hope that all the other rumours are equally ignorant and dismissible, rumours which cannot perhaps be so easily cast out by the reasonable mind.

The worst of these is that your sister is no longer observing her marriage vows and has been unfaithful to Desmond. Once or twice I have been disturbed at night by whispering voices — as you will know I sleep near to Mama's room and therefore sleep more lightly than if she were not there. Several times I have opened my door at the sound of footsteps, thinking possibly that Mama was taken worse. But the footsteps, were always farther away and in the other direction. Once I heard a strange man's voice raised in anger — indeed shouting — but the next morning everyone denied having heard anything, so perhaps it was a frightful dream. In this house, in which I was born and have lived almost all my life, I now find it disturbing to walk round with a candle in the middle of the night.

Whatever the rights or wrongs of all this, I have to tell you that I cannot feel myself any longer in sympathy or even accord with Thomasine; and this makes the situation very difficult for me. I am bound to Place while my mother lives, and so must try to accept the situation as I find it. Desmond confides nothing in me. He was always reticent. But he is a *good* man, and I grieve to see him so down in the mouth and finding such little pleasure in the gentler, simpler things of life — as he used to do. As I have mentioned to you once before, I have a certain anxiety about him lest he should tend to follow our mother.

Believe me, my dear Emma, I am ashamed to burden you with a letter such as this. But there is no one else I feel I can confide in.
With love
Mary

A couple of days after receiving this letter and having read and reread it many times, I copied it out and sent the original to my mother.

5

I

During most of the summer the Canon achieved a plateau of semi-invalidism. He got about with a stick, but his pronounced limp grew no less. As the stroke had been on the left side it interfered very little with his speech and not at all with his writing — except to make anything he did so much more of an effort. He resumed in full the taking of services in the church, he buried and married and baptized as required, but he relied on me more than ever, so that Mary's supposition that I should have little time for myself was right.

At first his appetite was poor, but gradually it recovered. I bought a couple of cookery books and tried to tempt his palate with new-tasting things. This was successful. He began to eat and put on most of the weight he had lost. Indeed his diet became a constant topic in the household. In the end and after much persuasion I was allowed £1 a week extra to spend on fruit and fish and a few vegetable delicacies. His face always seemed to light up when I saw him in the morning; and almost always he would begin, 'Emma, I have been thinking.' One time in four it would be about something he was going to say in his sermon on Sunday morning. The other three times it would be about food. His clerical collar now no longer seemed sizes too big.

A letter from my mother, four weeks after I had posted mine.

She was again in Scotland, and had been out grouse shooting for the first time. After a longish descriptive passage about the pleasures and perils of the shoot and a further account of the grandeur but coldness of the house in which they were staying she came round to the letter I had sent.

I do not think, my dear girl, to take Mary's epistle too seriously to heart. All she is doing is repeating rumours which may be circulating, or they may not. She does not produce a single fact to bear out her fears, and if her belief in Tamsin's infidelity is as flimsily based as these absurd and superstitious stories about you, I should not worry for them at all.

I said 'or they may not', because of the mental condition of the writer. If her mother's unstable inheritance has passed down to her daughter, and there has always been a suspicion that Mary, while sensible enough in most ways, has a morbid streak in her, then these stories and suspicions *may not be circulating at all*. Mary has always been eccentric, and with the added strain of Aunt Anna's illness, she may feel herself peering over the brink.

I hope Uncle Francis is better.

Love,
Mother

Uncle Francis was not better. As the autumn came on he stayed longer in bed in the mornings, and slept soundly in the afternoons. His interest in life and in the well-being of the church did not falter, but it was as if he were seeing it at a distance from which he was no longer closely involved. He wrote again to the Bishop of Exeter offering his resignation, and His Lordship refused it and said if the Canon's health deteriorated further he would send a curate to assist him. Most of all the Canon seemed to enjoy talking to me.

'I wonder sometimes,' he said, 'whether I have been a bad churchman.'

'Oh, Uncle, that is quite absurd.'

'Possibly yes, possibly no. My principles at all times have been very strict, yet practice has often been imperfect, and then I have punished myself by adopting regimes of thought, regimes of action which smack too much of the puritan. I've lived moderately but often selfishly. Indulging in pleasures of food and wine and giving less pleasure than I should to others. It has been on the whole a *comfortable* life, far too comfortable. This lovely parish with its beautiful variety of scene, its superb church, its separation from much that is cruellest and wickedest in life; I think if I had my time again I would try to find a benefice in one of the great industrial towns of the north, where crime and poverty have to be fought on one's own doorstep. Here, barring the normal effluences of human nature, everything has been so peaceful, so humdrum, an eddy, a backwater of peace.'

241

'If you had been working in an industrial parish, you would not have had time for your writings.'

He lay looking up at the ceiling. His face, with its blue eyes behind their rimmed glinting spectacles, silhouetted against the candle flame, seemed suddenly vulnerable and old.

The following day he said: 'Emma, I think my time is coming soon.'

I said, with assumed indifference: 'I think you will have to postpone such ugly thoughts for a week or two. You have confirmation classes next Tuesday. And a meeting of the railway venturers the following week. What is the matter with you?'

'I feel ill.'

'Is your leg troubling you?'

'No. I have not had another stroke. But I feel different, more composed.'

'Is that anything to complain of?'

'No. I must accept it. It is a sort of composure which portends a new phase in my life. A very late one, I fear.' He coughed. 'Age is an unattractive thing. I wish I had met you ten years earlier.'

'I'm afraid I was not a very agreeable child. You wouldn't have liked me.'

He turned his head to look at me, and a little glint of laughter showed in his eyes. 'Then you might have married me after all, and it would not have been good for you.'

'Why not?'

'A soul dedicated to God — in the way a man's is — does not have quite the lively

242

incentive you have, not quite the savour. That is very irreligious of me, I know, but perhaps I may be forgiven a little apostasy at this late stage.'

'My influence would have been very bad. You were safer remaining a bachelor.'

He smiled slightly. 'I think you must allow me to decide that.'

He died the following day. In the evening he sent for the Rev. Vernon Hext to administer the sacrament. Dr Smith came and went. Mr Hext had gone down to supper; he was a very old friend and he was aware of some change in the Canon which made him offer to stay the night. I would have been glad of his company, but in fact the Canon looked at me quietly soon after Mr Hext had left the room and said:

'Don't have him back.'

'What?'

'Don't have him back. I want to go quietly. If you are here, that is all that is necessary — '

'Can I get you something to drink?'

'Thank you, no. The Sacrament has moistened my dry lips. Walter Ralegh, you know, the night before he was executed, called it his Bottle of Salvation.'

'You have no such sentence,' I said, trying to keep back the tears. 'Tell me what you'll have for breakfast.'

' 'You must sit down,' says Love, 'and taste my meat.' So I did sit and eat.'

'Did you write that?'

'No . . . Let me see, I think it was Herrick . . . I should like to meet him.'

'Is he alive?'

'Centuries gone. You must read him.'

'Tell me where to find him in your library.'

His attention had strayed.

'I feel much worse, Emma, and much better. More reconciled. God is in my head and in my understanding. That strange fear that I have had all my life . . . In spite of it I think Christ will receive me.'

'Could you ever doubt it?'

'Dear Emma, I can doubt anything. Will you — light another candle.'

I got up from the bed and did so. Then I returned to the cane-bottomed chair and took his hand again.

'That's better,' he said, as the light grew.

'Should I not call Mr Hext? He has been your friend much longer than I.'

'I have the fancy not. I have the fancy that I will be more at ease without a member of my cloth being present. With you I am not on show. It does not matter what I say in front of you. I have no secrets from you. Now, let me doze a little while.'

I stayed with him while he slept for perhaps ten minutes. I wondered how long the tall thin clergyman downstairs would take over his supper.

Then the Canon woke with a start. 'It is growing dark again. But I do not think another candle will help. Hold my hand more tightly. Just pull a little. That's the way. Christ receive me. Christ receive my soul. Christ into Thy hands I commend my spirit.'

He looked at me, his sight now failing.

'Emma,' he said quite slowly. 'For breakfast I would like a chicken sandwich.'

Then he lay gently back on the pillows, sighed, and was gone.

II

It was a big funeral, for he was widely known and respected in the county. The big splendid church was full, and people who could not get in stood in the churchyard bareheaded in the rain. I had come to be quite well known myself and was widely thought to be the Canon's niece, so I received much more attention than had I been just the housekeeper. Desmond Spry came, representing the family, but not Thomasine, who it seemed had just had a miscarriage. He looked grey-faced. Was it his child Tamsin had lost?

Unexpectedly Charles Lane turned up. There was little chance of private conversation with him but, although many of the railway venturers had come, his presence specially comforted me. I knew from the way he looked at me that he had taken the trouble of the long journey just as much to see me as to pay tribute to the dead man.

Caroline Collins pressed me to go and stay with them until the funeral was over but I felt that if I left the house the staff would instantly leave also. I had to give them the backbone to sleep in a house with a dead man upstairs.

I was surprised at my own emotions. Can a girl in her early twenties be in love with a corpulent clergyman well on in his sixties? It wasn't the love I had experienced before, but if it certainly was not carnal love it was something much deeper than affection. Possibly I was responding to his appreciation of me. I had never before been in touch with anyone who was so *interested* in me, who sought my opinions, often trying to correct them but so *appreciative* of me as a person. No one, no one, no one, had ever been like that to me before. I wept for the loss of that attention, that kindly smile, that childish meanness, that fine Christian brain, that interest in locomotives, that relish of food. And that fear . . .

Had he now found his fear to be groundless, or was his personality locked up and buried, tasteless, sightless, mindless in a box for ever?

After the funeral but before the thirty-odd special friends had gathered in the rectory for light refreshments I suffered a severe shock. I saw a man detach himself from a group and climb into a pony trap. He did not look round, but flipped the reins and drove away. It was Bram Fox.

III

I wrote to Thomasine.

Dear Tamsin,
    I was very sad to hear from Desmond that you had lost a baby. This must have been very distressful for you; I send you my love and sympathy. Desmond says it was four months.

I do not know about these things, but was the baby stirring then? That must be awful — if you feel it has been *alive* within you, more or less as a separate individual. I grieve for you.

Now that the Canon is dead I am not at all sure what my position is going to be here. The churchwardens and the clerical establishment from Bodmin and Exeter have been around. No new rector has yet been appointed, but the Reverend Mr Hext, who was one of Uncle Francis's oldest friends, has suggested that I might like to stay on here as housekeeper for the new incumbent. First of all, if the new man is married — as seems likely — they will not probably want to afford a housekeeper, even one so poorly paid as I have been. Second, I do not want, if I can help it, to become such a housekeeper, with none of the small — *very* small — privileges that attached to my working for a kinsman.

So the chances of my staying on here are somewhat remote. I have at present all of £36 in the wide world! — the remnant of the £100 Uncle Davey left me. It has been quite impossible to save on what the Canon paid me — indeed from time to time I have had to subsidize from my own legacy the housekeeping he gave me.

I do not think I shall want for work, but should like to take a few breaths before I plunge into something new.

I could ask our mother if she were able to have me for a month or two while I take stock. But with her frequent absences in Scotland she has become increasingly remote. Apart from which, if it were at all possible, I should like to remain in Cornwall.

I wonder if there is some corner of my old home at Place which could be made accessible to me for, say, at the outside, a couple of months, to give me time to look around? I should be so grateful. And if there is any stringency I would be happy to pay something towards my own food.

I only exchanged a few words with Desmond when he was here, but he did say that if I needed a home either temporary or permanent he would be happy to help. It was extremely generous of him to say this, but *you* are my sister and it is *your* invitation, or at least acceptance, I must receive first, before I make any plans.

Tamsin, I know we were not on the best of terms when we met at Tregrehan last year, but it need not follow that we should continue so. In conversation I should be only too willing to avoid any contentious subject, and, if need be, I could take my turn at looking after Aunt Anna or be of any other help I can. I could well take charge of Celestine from time to time if you so wished.

Naturally I would not expect this to be a permanent arrangement. All I want is time to recoup — I *greatly* miss Uncle Francis — and a little while, with a secure base, so to speak, from which to look around.

Love,
Emma

She must have replied instantly for her return letter came within five days.

My dear Emma,

Thank you for your letter — the miscarriage has taken something more than a dead child out of me. I feel desolate and distinctly unwell. I am sorry I could not come to the funeral, but Desmond has told me all about it.

I do not expect Aunt Anna to last very much longer, she is so frail and will not eat — but to everyone's surprise this very week she has quite recovered her senses! We do not of course know how long it will last — but she knew who Uncle Francis was and was sorry to hear of his death and she was delighted when Celestine toddled into her room. She even asked after some of her old whist friends! We carefully have not mentioned Uncle Davey, as we do not wish to upset her.

Emma, we cannot have you here — you really *should* apply for the post of housekeeper to the new incumbent. You told me you had become well known in the district, and you have made your home there. You have your own friends, you say, and Mother told me you had been out singing at charity concerts — I have never been to Blisland, but it is obviously a different life, a different world — and it has become *your* world.

Not since childhood have we ever been really *firm* friends, and now that I am Desmond's wife — and virtually mistress of Place — I do not conceive we should ever make fair weather of it.

If you are in need I can send you £10, but that is as much as I can manage. Desmond has run deep into debt repairing the church and caring for his mother.

There is one other reason why it will not do, Emma — though I hesitate to mention it. I have heard the servants gossiping when I was not meant to — and there is a feeling that your disfigurement brings ill-luck. It is *so silly* that grown people should believe such things, but you cannot knock their heads together. Even Mrs Tizard — she is in charge of Aunt Anna — even Mrs Tizard was of the opinion that your visit to Aunt Anna last year upset her and caused her distress. She would not take kindly to your return, and with Aunt Anna at present so finely balanced it is a risk Desmond and I feel we cannot take.

Love,

Tamsin

P.S. If you cannot find it in yourself to stay on in Blisland, it is Mother's duty to receive you.

IV

Everything in the house would have to go. It would have been foolish to have supposed that the new rector, when he came, would not bring most of his own furniture.

Yet I lacked advice and hesitated, and waited. Mr Hext said he was assured there was no hurry. For a time we could exist in limbo and, since the staff was all here, I could continue to run the house, feed them (after a fashion) and victual the locum clergyman who took prayers on a Sunday.

Eventually Mr Preston Wallis came from Bodmin. He was not merely the Canon's solicitor but also legal clerk to the Bodmin-Wadebridge Railway. I knew Mr Wallis quite well. He was a small middle-aged man with a deeply lined face and a busy manner, as if time were pressing him to make haste.

'Must apologize, Miss Spry: after your father's — beg pardon, uncle's — funeral I was taken with a tertian ague — it is much about in Bodmin this autumn — and have been confined to my bed for more than a week. I could have sent my clerk, but it seemed necessary I should see you myself. So here I am. Better late than never, eh? I wanted to see you and to discuss your future.'

We were in the big drawing room, where the great pieces of furniture looked as if never really settled here, their purpose all along being to be taken to the saleroom. I wondered if I could keep the spinet? Mr Wallis had a large briefcase which he now put on a table with a lot of clicking of latches, and from this he took a sheaf of paper.

'Not sure, Miss Spry, how far your uncle took you into his confidence. But — '

'I was not really his niece, Mr Wallis. It was a distant cousinship.'

'I see. I see. Well, the Canon thought very highly of his distant cousin, as you may know.

251

But what I do not know if you know is that the Canon has made you his sole legatee.'

Outside the big sash windows I could see Mr Wallis's pony and trap. I saw the pony beginning to eat some of my montbretia.

'I knew *nothing* of this!' I said. 'What does it mean that he's left me — left me his money?'

'Just that. Just that. If — '

'But when? Did he make a new will? I know nothing of it at all!'

'He came into my office just before he was taken ill. I believe you were on holiday at St Mawes. He said he would like to have this settled before you returned.'

'Oh,' I said. 'Does he have no — no closer relatives?'

'A cousin in Australia, I believe. But he was in no doubt as to his wish to make you his sole legatee.'

I was a little short of air. 'But his previous will. Did he not leave it to charities?'

'Very little. But I must point out at once, Miss Spry, that the Canon really had very little to leave. What capital he had was invested in schemes like the Bodmin-Wadebridge Railway, the Treffry Viaduct, the Barnstaple to Exeter tramway, and most lately a Bath-Bristol scheme which has not yet got off the ground. All of these, including the Bodmin-Wadebridge Railway, are incurring losses rather than profits. In our local line we have been beset by problems such as no doubt occur in all new mechanical ventures. As your uncle will have told you, the wheels of the engines have been constantly leaving the rails, which has led to repeated breakdowns, and often the trucks have had to be brought home by cattle. Then there was the snow of February and the drought of July, when the engines had to be stopped after twice setting fire to the woods — '

'I know,' I said absently. 'I know. You will remember we had two meetings in this house. And Mr Lane has written to me as well.'

'I was saying this, Miss Spry, only lest you thought of his capital as a readily realizable asset. I think at the moment you would find it quite difficult to find anyone to take these varyingly speculative investments off your hands.' The little man glanced out of the window. 'I fear my pony has broken free of his rein. I hope he is not damaging your garden.'

'Let him be,' I said. 'Then . . . '

'Of course there are a few small investments outside these ventures. Some £300 in Consols. A cottage that he owned in Devonshire which is rented at £20 a year. A deposit in Martyn's Bank in Plymouth of about £100, a quarter share in a tannery business in Exeter which brings in a few guineas a year. A few other minor things which can no doubt be gathered up. But nothing, nothing at all *large*. Then there are of course his personal belongings in this house, his books, the furniture, the horse and trap. Some of these you might wish to sell, others to keep. Obviously you can make these choices when you come to leave the rectory. I am here — shall always be on hand in Bodmin, to advise.'

'Thank you.'

Mr Wallis put some papers back in his briefcase and took out some others. 'There is one other important item I have to bring to your attention . . . '

I looked up at him but did not speak. He glanced away, no doubt not wishing to seem to look at my drooping eyelid.

'Fifteen years ago, just after he came here and just after I met him and became his legal adviser, an uncle of his in Bristol died suddenly. He too was unmarried, and he left a substantial legacy to the Canon. This has remained untouched so now it has obviously become a part of the estate bequeathed to you.'

'What d'you mean, untouched? Do you mean my uncle . . . '

'Would not utilize it in any way. I argued that if he was personally adamant some charity would be only too pleased to make use of it, but he did not seem to want to do anything with it, not even good!'

I sat on a chair. 'I still don't *understand*, Mr Wallis. Could you please tell me exactly what this is about?'

Mr Wallis twitched and put the documents on the table as if they had suddenly become hot.

'Mr Gregory Roberts — he would have no truck with the new family spelling of his name — Mr Gregory Roberts was a shipping merchant in Bristol and it was generally acknowledged that he traded in slaves. I can understand that your uncle with his principles should abhor such a trade, but I ask myself — and indeed asked him — whether money itself can be tainted? Whether such money however ill-earned could not be turned to good offices to purge itself of its evil origins? I have always believed that, but he would never discuss it at any length. I think he felt contaminated by the connection.'

'Does this mean that the legacy . . . '

'Will come to you, yes. Unless you wish to disown it. Though I trust you will not.' I did not speak so he went on: 'I have always found it difficult to believe that the Canon, even with such frail financial resources as he had, should have considered it necessary to live so frugally. His stipend was not negligible. But if he did so find it necessary, then it speaks eloquently of his Christian principles that he should never have dipped into this legacy which was always to hand. As a man who liked good living it must have irked him to live less than well, but I suppose he found moral strength in resisting the temptation.'

'He never said anything to me.'

'No, he would not. After all, it is a surprise to you, is it not, that your uncle should have made you his sole legatee.'

'The greatest surprise. I have no call on him. There was a time when he . . . '

He waited at my hesitation but I found I did not want to tell him of the proposal of marriage.

'We became very close,' I said. 'He said he talked to me more freely than he had done to anyone else. But even so, he never mentioned this. I am overcome.'

He turned and fumbled for more papers from his briefcase.

'I have here computations which you may like to look at at your leisure, Miss Spry. In this envelope I have put an assessment of the few investments and possessions that the Canon has bequeathed to you. In this other envelope is an account of the monies that will come to you — if you will accept them — from the legacy of the late Mr Gregory Roberts. Aside from the Canon's various railway investments, except at a give-away price, I should estimate that his estate, short of what furniture you wish to sell from this house, would amount to upwards of £1,000.'

The pony had disappeared from view. But I would not have been altogether surprised if it had turned into a camel.

'The other money is almost all in the form of bonds. These of their nature pay only minimal interest, so the legacy has not grown substantially in the fourteen years it was in your uncle's keeping. The advantage, of course, of this is that the bonds can be realized at any time and to any degree you may think fit. It will be a week or two before the will is proved, but before then you will no doubt have decided what you will do.'

'And — this is a larger sum?'

'Oh, yes. Oh, dear yes. My latest information suggests that the figure will be a little less than £53,000.'

Book Three

1

I

Professor Dieffenbach said: 'My English, very poor, Fraulein Spry, therefore and so forth the translator necessary.'

'Yes, I understand.'

'And Herr Doktor Hamilton is to speak so between us.'

'Yes, sir,' said Hamilton. 'I was born and brought up in Hanover.'

'Ach, so.' The Professor put a pair of tiny spectacles on his nose. They were dwarfed by his square face as he reread the letter in front of him. Then he looked over his spectacles at me and smiled. The forbidding expression creased into more benevolent lines. 'Ach, so.'

I was in a room in the Charité Hospital in Berlin. It was an untidy room with shelves and files along one wall carrying headings like *Chirurgie* and *Rhinoplastik* and *Prosthesis*. In a corner was a wheelchair with some of the spokes broken; and in another corner Sally Fetch pulled nervously at the fingers of her gloves.

I have seen one painting of Joseph Friedrich Dieffenbach which made him look a very big man. But he was not tall: the breadth of his shoulders gave the impression of size. When I went to see him he was black-bearded, fortyish I suppose though looked older, and was then

259

surgical director and head surgeon of the Charité Hospital near Charlottenburg.

David Hamilton was thirty and had only just qualified at the Royal College of Surgeons in Edinburgh. I had been put in touch with him in London, and he had agreed to accompany me for a maximum of six weeks.

Dieffenbach spoke and Dr Hamilton said to me: 'The Herr Professor is reading, as you can see, Dr Latham's letter and he wishes to know if you know what Dr Latham has said.'

'I expect I know. But I would like to hear it again.'

Dr Edwin Latham had said to me: 'My advice to you, Miss Spry, is to let it alone. I find it difficult to imagine how these injuries were suffered at birth, since you say you have reason to believe instruments were not used to facilitate parturition; but if the midwife was drunk she may have used undue force with her hands. You are, in fact, perhaps fortunate that you are no worse. The palsy has only affected the eye and not involved the mouth as usually happens. The scar is disagreeable, but to open it and then re-suture it would only have a very long-term benefit, and perhaps not even that. It is not possible to improve the neck stain, and I would advise you to follow the fashions of the day with high collars and the like.'

'Thank you, Dr Latham,' I had said. 'So I suppose I must take your advice and return to Cornwall.'

'That would be for the best.' He sighed. 'I'm sorry . . . Mind you, there are a few techniques

260

at present being practised on the Continent, but they are in the experimental stage and you might well end up with a greater disfigurement rather than less.'

'Where on the Continent?'

'Well, largely in Germany. There is a man called Fricke. And there's Von Graefe. And another called Dieffenbach. All have published papers. All are surgeons of great distinction. In France of course there is Baron de Dupuytren, who is at least the equal of any experimental surgeon living today, but his researches have not been so directly concerned with surgery to the face and neck.'

'If I want to see one of these doctors, which one would you recommend me to approach?'

Dr Latham had sighed again. 'If you insist . . .'

'I should prefer not to say insist, doctor. Persist perhaps. At least I'd like to go one step further, just — just to find out a little more. I can afford it.'

'Hmm. If they would see you. One would have to be quite certain that you were not fobbed off onto some deputy or assistant surgeon. These are all enormously busy men.'

'But they treat patients?'

'Of course. The only one I have had some exchange of correspondence with is Dr Dieffenbach — and that was five years ago, before he became a professor. No doubt he will remember me because I wrote when I was in India, with some remarkable details about the replacement of a nose . . .'

'Can I ask you to write to him?'

'If you say so. I will do that tonight.'

Professor Dieffenbach had finished reading the letter and David Hamilton had finished translating. There was a pause.

'So,' said the German. 'If you please. This place, please . . . '

I sat in a chair by the window. The bearded man, in his black heavy suit, stiff collar and black tie, came and bent over me. He smelt strongly of serge and starch and carbolic soap. His fingers loomed large but rested on my cheek and forehead very lightly. He grunted. 'Ah, so.'

He pulled gently at the corners of the eye and said something to Dr Hamilton which the latter did not translate. Then he pressed the scar. Finally plump smooth fingers lightly brushed along the stain on my neck. Again he said something which Hamilton replied to but again did not translate.

'What did he say?'

'He asked if that was the extent of your injuries, and I said yes. That was correct, I imagine?'

'Yes.'

Professor Dieffenbach brought a magnifying glass and peered again at the eye. Then he went back to his desk and began to make some notes.

'He says you may go back to your other chair.'

I went back. The surgeon fixed me with stern eyes, in which in spite of their fierceness I detected a gleam of warmth and goodwill. Then he began to speak to Dr Hamilton.

After he had paused for breath Hamilton took a moment to gather his English and then: 'The Herr Professor says yes he can help you. He agrees with Dr Latham about the stain on your neck, but says that in the matter of the prime disfigurement, that to the ectropion of the eyelid, he can operate with some prospect of success. He proposes . . .'

Professor Dieffenbach began again.

'*Ja, Meinherr Professor. Ja* . . . He proposes to cut a flap of skin from the upper eyelid and bring it down to reconstruct the lower lid. It is difficult to translate medical terms, Miss Spry, as I'm sure you'll understand, but I believe he called it a pedicled flap. This should correct the prolapse of the lower lid, he says, and will allow the lid to function normally. I do not know, Miss Spry, whether this operation has been done before, but he seems quite confident of the outcome.'

Surgeons often were. 'Will you ask him?'

Dr Hamilton asked him. The Herr Professor nodded vigorously and spoke at length.

'He assures me that a similar operation has been done before, twice last year and twice the year before, always with a degree of success though naturally each case is different in some respects.'

The German spoke again.

'He says he can improve the scar and will do so at the same time. He proposes to come to your hotel at noon on Tuesday next. He says

263

you should engage a nurse for a day or two.'

Although I had come all this way, persisting until I reached Berlin, with an attendant doctor and an attendant maid, although I had been driven on by a bitter determination to see this quest through to the end, now that the outcome was suddenly thrust upon me, *at such short notice*, I hesitated. The Professor had taken it for granted that by coming for his advice I had come for his treatment. Well, hadn't I?

'Will you ask the Herr Doktor if this operation is likely to harm my sight?'

'The Herr Doktor says very unlikely.'

I looked at Fetch, who had given up pulling at her gloves and was staring fixedly at me. I had found her in the spring of the year working in a laundry. Since then she had been my devoted maid and friend. But she did not like being in Germany and she did not at all like what was being proposed now.

I said to David Hamilton: 'Does he know how long the operation will take?'

'He says preparations half an hour, surgery half an hour, convalescence three weeks, inspection monthly for three months.'

I thought, cutting skin from my upper eyelid? Was there skin to spare there? Skinned alive, did not some martyrs suffer that? I was no martyr. Go home. I was healthy enough. Count blessings. Wasn't this vanity? Pride? Arrogance?

And if I left and went home after getting so far? What was that? Cowardice? Timidity? Fear of pain? Did I have the money but not the stomach for this?

264

I looked at Herr Professor Doktor Joseph Frederik Dieffenbach and he looked at me. Even though only a few seconds had passed since the last words were spoken, everyone was waiting. Waiting for me.

I said: 'Tuesday at midday, Professor?'

'*Ja. Dienstag. Mittag.*'

'Very well,' I said.

II

I had taken a suite at the Hotel den Linden, which comprised a bedroom and a small sitting room. Dr Hamilton and Sally Fetch had bedrooms further down the corridor. On the Tuesday morning a special chair was delivered, taken up to my bedroom and set down facing the window. There was an adjustable headrest and straps dangling from the chair that I did not like the look of. Dr Hamilton had received instructions to have hot water available, two empty china bowls, four clean towels and an assortment of gauze swabs.

At ten minutes to twelve Professor Dieffenbach in frock coat and silk hat drove up in an open landau. With him were three other men all equally dressed in sober black. One was his assistant, Dr Scherz, and the other two were students brought to watch the professor at work. The thought crossed my mind that I had not seen so many black-clad men since the Canon's funeral. Unfortunately I was not in the mood to see this as an amusing reflection.

The Professor bent over my hand and led me

265

to the chair, while his assistant poured something into a glass and invited me to drink it.

'What is this?' I asked.

Dr Hamilton said: 'Cognac, laced with laudanum.'

'If I drink all this I shall be drunk.'

'I don't think so, Miss Spry. In any case it is — advisable.'

I gulped some of it down. It caught at my throat and made me feel sick.

Professor Dieffenbach sat down on the windowseat opposite me and began to speak.

Dr Hamilton said: 'The Herr Professor Doktor asks me to tell you that in general operations of today speed is of the essence to save unnecessary loss of blood and the suffering of the patient. However in the operation he is about to perform there is another — another factor to be taken into consideration: that this is essentially a cosmetic operation. Though he believes the function of the eye may well benefit from it — in the main the paramount objective is the improvement of the appearance of your face. Therefore a little greater time, a little greater care, is essential. He trusts that you will understand that.'

I nodded. Dieffenbach spoke again.

'Therefore he trusts you will not object if these straps are put in place. He is sure you are a brave woman, but an unexpected movement on your part might jeopardize the success of the operation.'

I gulped the rest of the brandy. 'Very well.'

There were mutterings behind me. I noticed that the two students had positioned themselves each side of the window the better to observe my ordeal. Professor Dieffenbach opened a small black case, such as one would use for special silver cutlery, and took out a knife and a scalpel. In his assistant's hand were a number of threads and a fine needle.

The brandy was making me feel swimmy as the leather straps were pulled into place. The Professor took off his jacket and rolled up his sleeves. He had hairy wrists. Someone from behind me put a hand on my head and pressed a compress of ice against the left side of my face. The cold of that was a shock and I automatically shrank from it.

While these deadening influences worked the Professor gave a brief discourse to the two students, explaining about the disfigurement of the eyelid and what he proposed to do. This much I could almost follow. I also noticed a new grimmer tone in his voice, which came perhaps as the operative moment approached.

Five people in the small room. Fetch had asked to be excused and had retired to her bedroom and shut the door.

Rustling and muttering behind me. It had been a fine clear morning but was clouding for rain. From where I sat, my head back, I could see the building opposite with my right eye. Crows were gathering on the roof, edging each other along in friendly rivalry. What was I doing here? Vanity, vanity, saith the Lord. I tried to think of the Canon.

The Professor took a large gold Hunter from his pocket and consulted it. Then he muttered something and the ice pack was whipped from my face. Thereupon gentle fingers on my forehead and a sharp knife began to cut and peel the skin from my upper eyelid.

In my life, although I had suffered the usual childish illnesses, and the long indolent fever which had beset me in my teens, I had not suffered any real pain before — at least, not pain like this. The laudanum, the brandy may have given extra courage and fortitude, the ice had helped to freeze the upper part of the face, but the chill piercing pain of the knife in a sensitive part of my face penetrated these feeble defences. I cried out and tried to get my head away from that fearful pain but hands and a strap held it firmly and the knife went on. I was being skinned alive. The speed with which the scalpel was being used seemed to add to the agony. I bit my lip and clenched my teeth, and then, mouth out of control, it opened of its own accord and I screamed. I took breath and choked and half vomited and screamed again. Warm blood was running down my face, clogging my eyelid, was blinked into and out of the eye. Someone was dabbing my face, trying to keep it clear of the dripping blood.

I wanted to get my hands free. I mouthed: 'Stop it, let me go! Stop! Don't do any more! Stop! Stop! Stop!' What insanity had got me into this position? I would go now. It was my own *choice*.

'*Bitte*, Fraulein Spry,' whispered the Professor in my ear. '*Bitte beruhigen Sie sich.*'

The knife stopped and an icy compress was

put over the eyelid. Then the knife began again cutting at the puckered skin just alongside the eye. An awful sick feeling in the stomach, a giddiness and faintness in the head. I had never fainted in my life but this was it. Going, going. Light was fleeing from the room; the window shrank in size, darkened until all the room was gone. But the nightmare into which I descended was not free of pain: the knife penetrated to my half-unconscious mind, demanding, probing; I was in some pit of hell where demons stabbed me with needles: yes, it was needles now. I should have wept for self-pity but the tears, the healing tears, did not come. It was needles now, and then it seemed like pincers and then a sort of gauze put to absorb the blood.

The knife began again, on my cheek where the sharp cutting edge was less unbearable . . .

I think, I suppose, I did faint then, for the next thing I was conscious of was being lifted bodily from the chair and put on the bed, with six pillows to prop my shoulders and head. Smelling salts. There were now two more gauze bandages round head and face, and the left eye was blotted out.

The pain had not stopped, but spread to an infinity which included the whole of my head and neck. The knife — even the needle — had been mercifully withdrawn, but the agony was scarcely less. Someone gave me a drink, and I vomited it up. Every retch threatened to split my head far and wide.

Dr Hamilton. 'It is done, Miss Spry. The worst is over. Dr Dieffenbach is very pleased.

In a moment or two the Herr Professor will be leaving, and then it will be for you to rest — or try to rest — until some of the pain has worn off. In a few minutes when your stomach has settled I would advise you to take some more laudanum. This tincture contains a stomach-settling powder as well.'

The two students had gone. The Professor's assistant was folding the bloodstained towels. Someone was emptying blood into a pail. Dr Hamilton had gone to mix his draught.

The Professor. Beaming at me now, as if my struggles and harsh cries had been nothing out of the ordinary.

'*Gut! Gut! Schön*! You 'ave done well.' He went off into German again.

Hamilton came up. 'He wishes you good day, Miss Spry. He will see you on Friday. If any untoward symptom occurs earlier I am to see him. He asks if the pain is now better?'

'No,' I said. 'Scarcely at all.'

'He says that is the ice. As the skin unthaws it will be like frostbite. By tonight, he says, with the help of the tincture you will be feeling somewhat recovered.'

2

I

I lived with a fierce smarting pain for weeks. At the end of the first week the gauze bandages were renewed, and a few days after that the stitches were taken out. This was the next biggest ordeal. I wanted to see what they had done for me, but Professor Dieffenbach instructed Dr Hamilton not to let me use a mirror.

Of course I tried, but the scar on which he had operated was not yet healed, and the much more important matter was that my eye was still swollen and swathed with bandages.

Fetch read to me and cajoled me to take nourishing soups. I dressed and moved about the bedroom and the sitting room. I wrote a few letters, to Charles, to my mother, to Tamsin, but carefully avoided any reference to the operation. They knew I was touring Europe, and I said I liked Berlin so had decided to stay on here for another month or so. If they cared to write back the hotel would forward their letters to any new address.

One infinitely depressing result of the operation was that my left eye had again become bloodshot.

I do not think anyone had warned me — certainly no one in Berlin — of the great hazard which existed that the skin from the upper eyelid might fail to 'take' in its new situation below. Although this skin was in the form of a flap and therefore always attached and drawing life from its connection, there was the risk that it might still refuse to blend into its new position and then mortify. In which case . . . was the operation a complete failure or — horror of horrors — did we try again?

So it was with profound relief that I heard Professor Dieffenbach's grunt of satisfaction when the final gauze bandage was removed. Even if the improvement was not great, even if I had to suffer a bloodshot eye once again — it was *over*; the worst was over. I could go home, at least no worse — or not much worse — for the ordeal.

'*Spiegel*,' he said.

They brought a mirror.

Hamilton said: 'The Herr Professor Doktor says you may look now. But he warns you, that with the scars still raw and the sutures hardly healed this is still a travesty of what you should look like in twelve months' time.'

I stared. The left side of my face seemed to be a mass of scars, mostly red, some still suppurating. The right side was unchanged. Two dark brown eyes, one of them bloodshot. But the bloodshot eye, among the nest of scars, was *not drawn down*. It was level. It was perhaps slightly smaller than the right eye. I could see fairly well out of it. But was my face any *better* for all this? The old scar was still there though slightly different and the marks of what Dr Hamilton called 'sutures' were prominent down its five-inch length. Would I be any better-looking for all this pain? But, if these scars did eventually heal and almost disappear with time, then certainly no one would have quite the reason to stand and stare. Surely people would no longer have to look elsewhere when they were talking to me. I should be unremarkable, one of the ordinary human race. A woman like any other. Not a beauty. But not a freak. Not someone to be laughed at or pitied. What would my mother think? Or Bram? . . . Or Charles? Or Tamsin? I would not dare to go near them yet. Perhaps I would stay away another year. Even then I would still be only twenty-six. Cornwall would not have changed. Only my looks and my circumstances. What would the Canon have thought of the use to which I had put the money he had left me but would not himself deign to touch?

I looked at Herr Professor Doktor Dieffenbach, who was still considering my face as a sculptor will a model he has half created.

'*Danke schön, Herr Professor.*'

'*Bitte, Fraulein.* But pat-ience. *Über alles.* Pat-ience.'

II

In the October I moved to Switzerland, with Sally Fetch in sole attendance. We toured the Alps while the weather was still open, and then settled at a hotel in Zurich on the shores of the lake. I chose Zurich because I liked it as a town and because it was not so fashionable with the English as Lucerne or Lugano.

A reluctance to meet English people. It seemed to me that Europeans were more tolerant of, or at least less interested in, anyone who departed from the physical norm. And at present I was more sensitive about this patched up face than had ever been the case when there was more to hide or remark on. I had taken to using a fashionable veil that made the scars less observable, and in Zurich we took private rooms so that I did not have to mix with others.

Sometimes I looked in the mirror and despaired. The same visage still stared back at me. Fetch kept saying: ' 'Tis much better than 'twas a fortnight since,' but the improvement, after the early gains, was too slow to be worth remarking. The lines of the operation were like the railway lines on one of Uncle Francis's maps.

The hotel ordered a *Morning Post* for me, so at intervals I was able to follow events in England. King William had died and a young Princess Victoria of Kent was proclaimed Queen. Some sort of a war in Afghanistan had broken out, and there were Chartist riots in Manchester. Britain was also becoming involved with another Colonial war, this one with China, which had something to do with the opium that had proved in its tincture form the only useful painkiller of my convalescence.

From Cornwall I received word that Aunt Anna had at last died, aged seventy-one. She was, Mary said, entirely sensible and in her right mind for some weeks before the end. She had been buried beside her husband, mourned by a suitable company of relatives and friends. She, Mary, relieved of her last loving obligation, had left Place for good and come to live in Tregolls. 'In that letter of last year,' Mary wrote, 'you explained that Uncle Francis had left you a legacy. The fact that you have remained away from Cornwall for so long, and now seem to be touring the Continent, gives me to suppose that this legacy was larger than I had first assumed. No one had ever supposed that the Canon was anything but a poor man. Or are you working abroad as a governess or a companion?'

A month later, when it was snowing hard, the flakes drifting over the lake like a mottled curtain, came another letter, scarcely, it seemed, answering mine at all.

Desmond has left Place and joined me here. His marriage to your sister was in rags and tatters when I was there. He says he is not returning; he says he cannot continue his life there. I told him it was your sister who should leave, but he says his first consideration must be Celestine. Somehow, between them, I mean between him and Tamsin, they have spent far too much money, and I was startled and shocked when he told me the size of his debt. I do not know if Samuel will help him to discharge any of it. I think Samuel is very angry at the way things have been shaping . . .

And as a postscript:

Did you know that Meliora Fox had died? She was only thirty-three, but had been in failing health for some time. Like so many of these pretty young women, she was tubercular, and of course her married life cannot have been a happy one.

I sent this letter to my mother. She was so long replying that when the letter came the early daffodils were colouring the lake shores with their half-bent yellow heads.

I have been very unwell this winter, and could have done with a daughter's care. In November some sort of a low fever settled on London, and I was one of its first victims. These things sometimes clear up quite quickly, but at other times the effects, in the form of headaches, neuralgias, migraines and lassitude will continue on for months. And so it has been for me. Also a tendency to rheumatism, which had shown itself before, settled in me, and now sometimes I have had difficulty in getting about.

So in spite of disturbing reports from Cornwall it is only recently that I have been able to visit those parts. Through a friend of Captain Frensham, who is a friend of a Mr Brunel, who it seems is a great engineer, we were persuaded to essay the journey by steamship — from Harwich to Falmouth. The Channel was rough and it was not an easy voyage, but I must admit it was pleasant not to be embayed by a contrary wind and we arrived in Falmouth only six hours late.

You will want to know what I found on my arrival at Place. I was met by Tamsin and Celestine, very smiling and happy looking, and in good health. It is true that Tamsin and Desmond have separated, but I do not know whether it is to be a permanency or no. It was his decision not hers. It is very sad, especially for Celestine, if this is a permanent break, but these things happen in life. A marriage which starts out with all the auguries of a blissful union can fall apart quite rapidly and for no particular or especial reason. You must know that my marriage to your father was not a very happy one. Drinking and gambling were his weaknesses, and, although he had a modest income from the family, I often found myself at the end of the month paying his debts out of my stage earnings.

Neither drink nor gambling are Desmond's weaknesses. Nor, indeed, are they Tamsin's! But she likes a society life and a convivial table. It may be that Desmond is still feeling the effects of his mother's death, to whom he was inordinately attached, and that when he gets over his bereavement he may return to his wife. I sincerely trust so. In the meantime it would be a mistake to see anything sinister in the estrangement, as Mary appears to. They are lucky, Tamsin and Desmond, to have separate family houses that they may continue to use while their separation persists. And the distance between cannot be more than fifteen miles.

Incidentally the five years since your Uncle Davey died has long since expired, and I understand that his inamorata, Miss Betsy Slocombe, having requested and received from Samuel a three-year extension of her free lease of Killiganoon, has now at last vacated it, so the house stands empty, waiting a tenant. It is quite a handsome place standing in grounds of thirty acres, so I imagine it will soon be let — or possibly sold.

Since I began this letter I have had one from Tamsin, telling me that Slade has left. Of late he had come to have an oppressive presence in the house — I expect you will think it was so all the time we lived there! — but since your uncle died he has been more than ever a disagreeable influence. The rest of the servants I am sure will be happier without him and, although Tamsin sounded upset when she wrote, I am convinced she will be also. Twenty-seven years they tell me he lived as a butler in Place; we can testify to nineteen of them!

Tamsin tells me you have not written to her for a long time. I think you should.
Your loving
Mother

III

It was time to go home. In the last month, as the days lightened, I had taken the ferry to

278

the main quay and done some shopping. In the time since the Canon died I had had hardly any time to put aside for enjoying my new prosperity, and now Fetch and I walked the shopping streets of Zurich and pleasurably spent money, on clothes, on shoes, on hats, on watches, on fairly expensive trinkets of jewellery.

It was during this time that I tested out my new face in the more general public places, and only about once in ten times did I notice the shop assistants' eyes turning towards the disfigurement. People passed me by without apparently noticing anything. True each morning I took half an hour to make up my face, but the result was clearly satisfactory. At last I began to accept Fetch's reassurance almost, you might say, at face value.

It was a tedious journey home: long stretches of coach riding to Paris, where we spent a week and considerably more money, then another journey, much burdened with extra luggage, to the coast, a rough crossing to Dover, then suddenly we were in a land where everyone spoke English. A night in Dover, the coach up the Dover-London road; into the city and the traffic and the bustle and the smoke; a hotel on the river.

I had written my mother from Dover — there was talk of a penny post — and gave the letter a couple of days to reach her, then set off for Richmond. We arrived about eleven. It was a pretty house on the Green, bow-windowed and painted white; the front garden was riotous with roses.

I was shocked when I saw my mother; she walked with a stick and seemed to have shrunk in size. There is a time in some people's lives when age suddenly catches up with them and two years might be ten. By comparison Captain Frensham, for all his white hair, might have been her younger brother. Surprisingly, perhaps, it was not until I went down to supper that either of them remarked on any change they might see in me. (Perhaps not so surprising in that personal illness concentrates the mind on oneself, and my mother, who was too vain to wear spectacles, had become very short-sighted.)

'So . . . Well, so Emma, what has someone been doing to your face?'

I offered a brief explanation, playing down the extent of the surgery, the length of the convalescence, and my fears that it had all been only half-successful. She did not speak for a few moments, and stared across the table at me.

Her husband said: 'But if you allowed a surgeon to do that, was it not very painful?'

'Quite painful, yes.'

'I saw men vastly disfigured after Trafalgar. I do not think anything was done for them — *could* be done for them. Do you feel better for the operation? I seem to remember the eye was drawn down.'

'It is quite an improvement,' said my mother at last, but slowly. 'Can you see better with the eye?'

'Not better, but just as well.'

'Is it not more bloodshot again?'

'Yes, but it is improving.'

'And they have done something to your scar. It has not gone.'

'They did not promise it. I think it is better.'

'Of course you are using a cosmetic. Is it cream of Talcum?'

'Something like that. I bought it in Paris.'

'Perhaps in the morning I could look at it more closely. It certainly gives you quite a different appearance.'

We went on with supper.

'How much did Uncle Francis leave you?'

'Oh, more than I expected.'

'And now, I suppose you have spent it all.'

'Not quite all.'

'I'm glad. It is good to have a little nest egg.'

Conversation changed, and it was not until the little maid had cleared away the dessert that my mother returned to the subject.

'I'm glad for you, Emma.'

'What?'

'Glad that your eye has been put right. After all, all the rest can be covered up. I notice your high collar. But this outcome will surely please you, does it not? I think you will be sure to gain in confidence now that there is not this obvious disfigurement. You might well marry.'

'Hmm,' I said. 'Yes, I suppose so.'

IV

In the morning she came to my room, stick supporting her. 'My rheumatism,' she said, 'was even worse in Cornwall. It is the damp, I expect. Shall you go back there?'

'I think so.'

'You would not prefer to make a complete new start in some new part of the country — say Bath — where nobody knows you or remembers you?'

'I think I should be lost there. I have a few friends in Cornwall.'

'Shall you go soon?'

'In a few days. I am going to meet Samuel in London tomorrow.'

'You have his address? Yes, well, he is now head of the family. I hope you won't say anything derogatory of Tamsin.'

'Certainly not.'

'Her situation is an anomalous one, occupying the main family house almost on her own, except for the servants and Celestine. Shall you try to get another position in Cornwall?'

'Not yet. At the moment I have enough to live on.'

'I'm glad to know it. What *was* the amount Uncle Francis left you?'

'I can't exactly remember. There were a few cottages and outlying things which haven't yet been accounted for.'

'It was so kind of him to leave you what he could. There wasn't anything, well, *between* you, was there? I know he was an old man, but — '

'There was nothing between us in the sense you mean. There was a great affection. I still miss him.'

'Strange he should have left *any* money. He was always complaining of his poverty. He saved and begrudged every penny. A miser. And yet in his own way a Christian.'

'Very much a Christian,' I said warmly. 'I've never known a better.'

She screwed her eyes to look at me again in the morning light.

'D'you know, it is quite difficult to appreciate the change in you. This — thing you have had done has certainly made you better looking. But you were a soft gentle-looking girl before, in spite of your poor eye and the rest of it. Now . . . now you might be considered quite good-looking, but in a harder sort of way. I think it has hardened your face.'

3

I

Samuel said: 'Someone has operated on your eye? It looks a deal better. Where was it done?'

'In Germany. In Berlin.'

'Oh. I do not suppose it was very pleasant for you, was it? But it certainly is different from what it used to be. Have you been to Cornwall?'

'Not yet.'

'Well, I'm glad you came to see me before you went.'

He was a bigger man than his father, inclined to stoutness though only thirty-five. In spite of having given up his naval career there was a look of the sailor about him. The almost inevitable roll in his walk, his bluffness and air of disciplined command of himself. His house was in Mount Street where he seemed to live alone, except for the servants. Whether he owned the elegant small house or merely rented it, I had no idea. It would be convenient for the Commons. Like all the senior Sprys he moved around a lot in the course of a year, and I was lucky to find him in London.

His greeting of me, however, had not been warm. Very different from Desmond, though perhaps even Desmond's welcome would not be as friendly as usual.

'I take it you inherited some money from Uncle Francis,' he said. 'You've been away from Cornwall — what is it? — more than a year. Do you intend to return to live there?'

'Yes, I hope to very shortly.'

'Well, I can tell you I am not at all satisfied by the way things are turning out at present.'

'My mother is worried also.'

'So she should be. She would be better in Cornwall to keep her other daughter's behaviour within bounds.'

'My mother is partly crippled with rheumatism: a journey for her now is very difficult.'

'Ah. I see.'

A brief pause. Then the sting worked.

'You speak of my sister's behaviour, as if it were — specially ill. I know of course that she and Desmond have separated, but that is not an unknown occurrence, is it? My mother was hoping that in the course of a year or two they might come together again.'

'Will you take some wine?'

'Thank you, no.'

'It's a very light Canary. I brought it back on my last voyage.'

I took a glass.

'Your sister,' he said, 'is making an exhibition of herself by consorting with that man Abraham Fox. Not only does she go about with him, he frequently visits Place and has been known to spend the night there. Indeed, according to my information he comes and goes at will. It is the scandal of the county.'

285

Did my throat still contract at the mention of his name? Do hate and jealousy and love spring from the same root? I sipped the wine but could scarcely taste it.

I had suspected something of the sort. At the back of my mind had stirred this old suspicion and this old fear. But blunt confirmation blew the qualifying doubts away. The scandal of the county. Exaggerated, but probably everyone in the districts around Truro and Falmouth knew of it. Truly a disgrace. I thought my mother knew and had withheld it from me.

Why was it so shocking? Uncle Davey had kept a mistress and bought a house for her. Eyebrows had been raised, no doubt, but little said. Of course that was years ago, and morals had changed lately. For me the shock — the confirmatory shock — was the identity of Tamsin's lover. Would I have felt the same were it someone else? I might even have tried to defend her.

'When you go to Cornwall you will certainly call and see your sister. Perhaps you can bring her round to a greater sense of propriety.'

'I'm the younger, Samuel, as you know. I have seldom if ever been able to direct my sister as to her way of thinking.'

'Shall you stay in Blisland?'

'With the Collinses for about a week, then I am going to call on the Austens, who have always been very kind.'

'He's changed his name to Treffry, did you know? It was natural enough as his mother is a Treffry and he is doing so much for the town.'

'It is Mrs Austen I shall chiefly see . . . '

He waited on my pause, brown eyes fixed penetratingly on me.

I said: 'I understand Betsy Slocombe has left Killiganoon. Is it now empty?'

'Yes.'

'I have wondered if it would be possible to rent it for a year or two?'

This was not what he had expected.

'You do not wish to live with your sister?'

'No.'

He poured himself another glass of what was in fact a very palatable Canary.

'The financial relationship between me and my brother is already very complicated. He has run deep into debt because of his expenditure on the house and Tamsin's extravagances. He'll now be much relieved — financially — by the will of his mother. While at Place he paid a rental to the estate, and since he left, your sister has taken over the rental — much to my surprise, as I understood she had no money of her own. This rental, of course, was nominal, a family agreement below the market value. I don't know whether I can extend a similar concession to you if you were to live in Killiganoon — I gather you have some money still?'

'Enough to pay the appropriate rental without any concessionary consideration.'

He smiled thinly. 'You surprise me, Emma.'

I said: 'I am surprised to be in this position.'

'Would you intend to live in Killiganoon on your own?'

'Miss Slocombe did.'

287

'Perhaps . . . ' An idea had come to him. 'Perhaps you could persuade your sister to vacate Place and live with you. The house is amply big enough.'

'As I say, I couldn't answer for her. In fact, I should better prefer to be on my own.'

'It would be an advantage to the family as a whole. Had you thought of that?'

'In what way?' I was being deliberately obtuse.

Samuel got up. 'I have written to her telling her that her unseemly conduct is bringing the house and the family into disrepute. She replied, rejecting my complaint and saying that Place is the home where Desmond installed her on their marriage and she sees no reason to leave it.'

'You've written that, and she has replied in that way?'

'Yes. I can of course have her evicted but that would cause a great uproar, and one has to remember that she is a Spry both before and after marriage.'

'If you've asked her to leave and she has refused, how can you suppose she would listen to me?'

'If you took Killiganoon you could then offer her a home.'

'I'm very astonished and upset,' I said, 'that it has gone so far.'

'We are all equally upset.'

'Is that a condition that you make for allowing me to rent Killiganoon?'

'I should be willing to let you have it at a lower rental if you did that.'

'And what then would happen to Place?'

'Possibly Desmond and Mary would return. I would like to keep it as a family home — which it has always been — and use it myself from time to time.'

'And where does . . . ' I half choked over the name ' . . . does Abraham Fox come into all this?'

'Not at all, I hope.'

'What you want me to do is keep open house for him at Killiganoon the way you say my sister keeps Place for him at present.'

'Certainly not. Certainly not.' He paced the quarter deck a couple of times. 'Perhaps if your sister is persuaded to leave Place she will come to her senses. You are now, it seems, a young woman of substance. It would be your home. You could forbid him to set foot in it.'

'I have no doubt,' I said gently, 'that Desmond tried. I could hardly have more influence over Tamsin than her own husband.'

He blinked. 'I appreciate it would not be an easy solution for you. Presupposing that you did take Killiganoon, and that you persuaded Tamsin to join you, you would be in a position to forbid Fox to call. But, I agree, if he defied you, you have no ready sanction. You don't, I suppose — er — contemplate marriage yourself?'

'Not in the immediate future.'

'You have become,' he hesitated, 'so much better-looking as a result of what you've had done — but in a strange way, Emma. I think probably it will seem strange only to those who knew you before. I don't know.' He stared at

289

me. 'It's really very . . . '

'Strange?' I suggested.

He laughed for the first time. 'I never knew you well. While we were young I was much away, and when I came home you always seemed to be in the shadow of your sister or your mother. I'm glad that we've had this meeting now. And I'm glad that you can in all probability look forward to a normal life.'

'Do you think so?' I said. 'I rather have my doubts.'

II

The last letter from Charles Lane had been sent from Bristol. For a year he had been involved in Brunel's great new project, the building of a paddle wheel steamship which could carry sufficient fuel and provisions to steam across the Atlantic to New York. The ship must be large enough to accommodate all this and to carry enough passengers to make the voyage pay, and it must be seaworthy enough to combat the giant waves and gales that sometimes might beset it. Well, last year, according to *The Times*, it had all happened. The *Great Western*, as it had been called, had extended the railroad not merely from London to Bristol but from Bristol to the New World. Regular sailings were promised.

I had not heard since, but as I had the time I decided to make the westward trip via Bristol. The railway lines so far laid and open did not yet join up to make a continuous line, so rather than be constantly changing transport I took

290

the old-fashioned coach which now, pressed by formidable new competition, did the journey in twenty-four hours.

Sally Fetch, who had never really taken to the continental life, visibly brightened as we proceeded west. The air was different and better, she said, the light brighter, the fields greener. She was — eventually — going home! We stayed at Mead's, a new hotel at the time, and once settled in, I took a cab to No 47 Robertsbridge Street in Clifton, which was the address at the head of his last letter. This was in a suburb about a mile from the hotel, and was a newly built street of small Georgian-type houses. I walked up the short pebbly path, and pulled at the bell. After a few moments the door was opened by a medium-sized but stocky girl with bright blue eyes and straight fair hair worn shoulder length.

'Is Mr Charles Lane at home?'

She was taking me in, as I was taking her in. 'Er — no. He's probably at the Docks . . . '

'Oh . . . D'you mean in the centre of the town?'

'Yes.'

'He — lives here?'

'Oh, yes. I'm his wife.'

'Oh, thank you.'

A hesitation, then, as I was about to turn away. 'Shall I tell him who called?'

'Emma Spry,' I said. 'Your husband and I have met once or twice in Cornwall.'

'Oh . . . Oh, yes.' Her startled eyes travelled over my dress. 'He's mentioned you.

291

I — er — don't know quite what the time is, but I *am* expecting him back for dinner. Will you come in and wait?'

'Oh, no thank you. I was in Bristol and thought to look him up. I have no — special business with him. It was just a call.'

She had a West Country accent and a slightly protruding bottom lip that made a slurring of some of her words. She looked very clean, but her hair was untidy and she wore a black apron over a cream dress. Most men, I'd think, would not have called her pretty but she was wholesome-looking.

She said sharply: 'Do come in, Miss Spry.'

'Thank you . . . I . . . ' Hard to escape the challenge in her voice. 'Thank you.' I went in.

A cosy cottage-type of house: as he was moving around so much this was probably rented. I did not know what his tastes were; he said he had begun life as a bricklayer, but since Brunel took him on he must have moved in all sorts of society.

I sat down in the front sitting room, and she went to stand by the window with a finger pulling back the lace curtain to see if he was coming.

I had told the cab to wait at the end of the street.

I glanced at the clock on the mantel shelf. 'It's only just noon,' I said. 'Do you dine so early?'

'It depends on how his work goes. He was away all last week, but today he expects to be home. He said so when he left that I could cook for the both of us.'

'Then I'm interfering with your preparations.'

'No, no, I have Susie who will look to the joint for me. Can I get you some refreshment, Miss Spry?'

'Oh . . . a cordial would be very nice.' I had noticed some on a side table. Wondering how best to make my excuses. Stupid ever to have come.

Charles, she said, was at present working with the chief engineer on the *Great Western*. He had been with the ship on its maiden voyage across the Atlantic to New York. At present it was anchored off Avonmouth, but Charles was at the Town Docks today on some other business. Mr Brunel was now designing a still larger liner built all of metal and driven by screws instead of paddle wheels. It would cost some huge sum, and there were many critics who said Mr Brunel was overreaching himself and that such a huge vessel could only be run at a loss.

'Where did you meet your husband?' I asked.

'At a church fête at Ashburton. I was looking after a biscuit stall; he came to buy a tin of short-breads for his mother.'

'I was born near there.'

'Near Ashburton? I thought you were Cornish.'

'My father was. My family is. So you have known Charles a long time?'

'About seven years. He is from London.'

'He came to dinner at my grandfather's house near St Mawes. Mr Brunel was with him. That was — oh, about eight or nine years ago.'

There was a pause, each waiting for the other.

'You are dressed very smart, Miss Spry. That's something else I didn't expect.'

'Pray forgive me. I was just travelling. I should have given you notice.'

She let the curtain fall. 'You know that I shall never give him up.'

I stared at her. She had gone a brick red. 'Charles? Your husband? Why should you?'

'Not to you,' she said, 'nor to no one else!'

'I — I don't quite understand. You're *married* to him.'

'I know. And marriage is binding, isn't it? There's no way out.'

'I still don't understand.'

She put her hands up to her cheeks, as if aware of their colour. 'I suppose I shouldn't ever have spoken. It just came out — seeing you here.'

'But I am a *friend* of Mr Lane's! You cannot surely begrudge him having *friends!* We mean nothing to each other on any other — other level.'

'Charles isn't that good-looking,' she said. 'But women take to him. He mixes with many sorts and kinds in his work, and I've seen them make a great fuss of him.'

I took a breath. 'Oh, perhaps. Oh yes. But you surely do him a terrible injustice if you feel — suspect . . . I don't know him well, but I should have thought him one of the most steadfast of men. I do not think, having taken his marriage vows to you, he would ever *allow* himself to be attracted elsewhere — at least not in the way you are meaning.'

She said passionately: 'Not to a pretty face,

perhaps, but mebbe to a lady with a damaged face!'

'D'you mean me?'

'Yes, I mean you, Miss Spry, for I see he has been lying to me too about how bad your face was — '

'I had it operated on last year! But what I cannot understand is how you should think he has some attachment to me over and above a normal friendly relationship — '

'Because he told me.'

I took another deep breath, or tried to.

'Oh, come. I'm sure you are — '

'Before we married, before he asked me to marry him, he told me how he felt about you. He thought you was out of his reach. He thought you was too good for him. He told me this, but I loved him and said I didn't mind. No more do I; no more do I, but I cannot let you suddenly turn up in our lives to put a sort of — a sort of dark stain on our marriage, like. It isn't fair!'

My hand was trembling as I put the cordial glass down. 'The *last* thing I want to do, Mrs Lane, is to upset your marriage. The very last. I'm *astonished* at what you've just told me! . . . But that was *before* your marriage; it's unlikely he feels the same now — if he ever did. You mistook him! You know how — '

'I didn't mistake him at all! I couldn't have. Besides, you have written — and he has written. I know when a letter from you has come: he's different after — '

'Have you read any of my letters?'

She flared up. 'How dare you! I don't look

in my husband's pockets — '

'I wish you had! Then you would know they contain no endearments whatsoever. There's nothing in them to suggest there was anything between us in the way you imply! Nor was there ever! Nor is there. Nor will there ever be. I am fond of Charles, and if he thinks he is fond of me in another way he is quite mistaken to suppose I return it. So your fears are quite unfounded. Now I'll go.'

She barred my way, anger ebbing. 'I'm sorry. I've said too much. It has been so much in my mind and in my heart that when you turned up unexpected I — '

'Thank you for inviting me in. Perhaps this will have helped to reassure you.'

'Stay till he — '

'Of course not! And do not tell him I have been. It will be much better that way.'

4

I

Sally Fetch could not know — and could not be told — why I was so upset. Nor did I actually know the extent myself. It meant a complete break with an old friend, that was upsetting enough. But all that went with it left me depressed and tearful. And I am not a tearful woman.

We were leaving by the noon coach on the following day and would spend a night in Exeter. But Thursday dawned so bleak that I would probably have changed our booking for a later date, had it not been for my encounter with Effie Lane. I couldn't be out of the city soon enough.

A high wind blew in from the Bristol Channel, and sheet-curtains of rain fell almost horizontally across the town. Looking from my bedroom window I saw people in the street below being almost blown over by the wind. One tall strongly built young man was holding onto his hat, and his coat tails were flying as he turned in at the door of the hotel. A panic feeling.

I went across to the mirror staring at my still-marked face, hastily brushed hair over from the temple to hide it. Fetch in the doorway.

'If you please, ma'am, a gentleman to see you. Mr Charles Lane.'

297

I stared back at her. 'Is there anyone in the upstairs sitting room?'

'Dunno, miss. Not likely at this time of the morning, I s'pose.'

'Ask him to wait in there.'

Take a little time. Powder over the imperfections. Whatever the outcome of this meeting, one could not but try to look one's best.

He was standing by the window, hands behind back. In the low room he looked very big. There was a wizened old woman in a seat by the fire. Knitting.

He looked at me, face flushing. Some of his hair was wet. He glanced at the old woman.

'Emma,' he said carefully. 'I felt I had to see you, as you called yesterday.'

'I met your wife.'

'She told me.'

'Did she tell you of our conversation?'

'Yes.'

The old lady looked up from her knitting, then the needles began again.

'How is Mr Brunel?'

'Greatly stressed. Working sometimes twenty hours a day. But very successful now, in spite of so many setbacks.'

'Your wife tells me you crossed the Atlantic.'

'In the *Great Western*, yes.'

The wind gusted against the windows, beating the rain before it.

'Her last voyage,' said Charles. 'It was a race. The London and Liverpool merchants did not want the *Great Western* to be the first steamer to cross to New York. They felt

298

it would re-establish Bristol as the major port, as in the old days. So they chartered the *Sirius* which was being built for this crossing and she left the Thames four days ahead of us.'

'So what — how did it turn out?'

'They beat us by a short head. But their voyage had taken nineteen days, ours only just fifteen: and while they were almost out of coal when they reached New York, we arrived with 200 tons to spare. In the end it was a great triumph.'

'Mr Brunel would be pleased.'

'Unfortunately he was injured in an accident aboard the *Great Western* just before we sailed so he was not able to come with us. Emma, is there somewhere where we could talk privately?'

'Is there any need?'

'I feel there is.'

The knitting needles stopped clicking and then began again.

He said: 'Your face. Your eye, Emma. What has happened?'

'I had an operation.'

'It makes you look different.'

'My mother says it makes me look harder.'

'Oh, I don't think so. Not at all — '

'I *am* harder, Charles. I am sure you chose wisely in your wife.'

'I did not know there was another choice open to me.'

'Nor did I.'

'I thought you were out of my reach.'

'So I am — now.'

The knitting needles stopped. The old lady

said: 'I will leave. You wish to talk in private?'

'Not at all,' I said.

'Yes please,' said Charles.

It seemed to take an age for her to gather up her knitting, her jacket, her stick, stand up, balance herself, narrow her old eyes to look at us, then totter towards the door. Charles gratefully opened it for her, and presently we were alone.

After a second: 'My coach goes at noon,' I said.

He stared at me, frowning his concentration. 'Really you're the same, aren't you. The same Emma I — came to — know.'

'We're going to spend the night in Exeter,' I said.

'Did she — did Effie tell you what she told me she had?'

'I asked her to say nothing about my visit. That would have been easiest.'

'She blurted it out as soon as I came in. I'm sorry she . . . '

Now we were alone it seemed even harder to talk.

He said: 'I told her before I ever asked her to marry me — '

'Yes, *what* did you tell her? What *could* you tell her?'

'That I was, well, it's hard to say to your face, but I was hopelessly in love with you — but that hopeless was the word.'

'Was I such a wonderful catch, disfigured and penniless?'

'You would have been to me. That's how I felt. I'm sorry . . . '

'Your wife told me not to disrupt your marriage. I told her there was no possibility of my doing so — '

'But she told you that I loved you.'

'Whatever it was, it's a thing of the past, Charles.'

He put his face in his hands. '*Could* it have meant something?'

'I don't know. I never considered it. I thought that sort of love was out of my reach. But whatever — I *have* changed, Charles my dear. Two years ago I was ugly and with less than fifty pounds to call my own. Now I am — not so ugly, and have some money. As I have grown older I really have grown harder — everyone agrees about that. But I am still quite young. So I am going to live as I please and where I please, in Cornwall, in London, in Bristol.'

'Without a care in the world.'

'No . . . No one can do that. But I don't want to leave unhappiness behind me *here*. It would be better if we did not write again.'

'Why ever not? Am I to be deprived even of that pleasure?'

I hedged the answer. 'You have a wonderful future ahead of you. Mr Brunel will go on to even greater things. You have a worthy and loving wife. Take care of her and forget me.'

'Will you forget me?' he asked.

'No!'

'You who care so little won't forget. Am I likely to who — who care so much?'

I took out my watch. 'I do not know if the coach will go today. How much better it would

301

be on one of your trains!'

'Then stay another day. You can be in no hurry.'

'I *want* to leave. You know I must. Even if we only get to Taunton.'

He took a step forward. 'Look, Emma . . . '

'Yes?'

'I can't bear that we should separate.'

'We have to.'

He put his big hands on my shoulders. 'All right. If that is the way you want it.'

He bent and kissed me. His lips were not big but gentle. It was hasty and ingenuous, but not so ingenuous as I had expected.

When we parted I pulled a face. ' 'Twas disagreeable. That proves a point does it not. It proves that Effie has nothing to fear from me!'

He took a deep breath, slowly let it out. 'I — don't believe that, Emma. I don't and won't believe what you've just said. I know I have made a terrible mistake in my life, and now I must live with it. I suppose it's better that we end now. It's better that we shouldn't write.'

II

A week with Mrs Caroline Collins, seeing old friends, riding, meeting the new (now well established) rector of Blisland; a week with Mrs Susanna Austen. Caroline Collins was some twenty years older than I was but we got along famously together. Mrs Austen was older still, but was someone who greatly appealed to me, as I apparently appealed to her. Her son Joseph, who was rapidly restoring the Treffry fortunes, had recently been appointed High Sheriff of Cornwall, so he was seldom at home during my visit, but I enjoyed my time there and took especial pleasure from the surprise they all showed at my change of appearance.

Most people must know how it is: you plan a trip — a holiday or a pleasurable visit — and it takes place and is everything you could want. But something happens — or something *has* happened before you start off — and your pleasure all the time is soured by this happening that you did not expect or did not seek; it is a sort of nagging tooth, a sadness and a soreness of the spirit, so that you are aware all the time of this incubus of depression.

I eventually arrived at Tregolls in Truro, to be greeted by Mary and her two cousins. Desmond, they said, was in Bath taking a cure. Here I had expected unpleasantness, so I was not disappointed. The three women were greatly disapproving of Tamsin's behaviour, and did not hesitate to tell it all to Tamsin's sister. It took me a little while to discover that Samuel had been as good as his word, and I had been granted a twelve-month lease of Killiganoon. I stayed two days at Tregolls and then thankfully hired a trap to drive to the house previously occupied by Admiral Davey's mistress.

I had never been there before. It was just off to the left of the main coaching road, about halfway between Truro and Falmouth, and was protected in its privacy by a copse of fir trees. It was a big house, not at all the *bijou* cosy love nest I had pictured.

Yet it was quite a pretty house: half-timbered (most unusual in Cornwall, where wood was always at a premium), with big sash windows, mostly green-shuttered, a long portico over the front door with climbing roses. The garden was wanton with neglect, but some palms flourished.

'Will this do for you, Sally?' I asked.

' 'Tis handsome. But what'll we do with it all?'

'We'll spread ourselves. You'll see.'

A Mrs Bluett was acting as cook and caretaker, and she let us in. She had crimped white hair, spectacles and a cross face. She did not look as if the sun had ever shone for her.

The house was furnished in an old-fashioned style with a number of noticeable gaps, as if Miss Betsy Slocombe had taken some things with her when she left. It all smelt of dust and mildew and mice, but a few weeks of spring-cleaning would put that right.

Mrs Bluett was in touch with three of the maids who had worked for Miss Slocombe, and they were all willing and waiting to return.

That evening I went to the front door, stepped out into the porch and wondered at all this good fortune. Not so many years ago I had walked to the celebrations in Truro, almost penniless, possibly pregnant, enslaved by the fascination of one man, had walked through the rain to try to find him. Now I was fancy-free, a rich young woman, no longer totally disfigured, and in possession of a fine house. The house belonged to the Sprys; my name was Spry.

Killiganoon was on high ground, and not far over the horizon, though miles away, lay the sea. I was a person of consequence. All this thanks to Uncle Francis. The sky this evening was illimitable, immensely remote, as if one were catching a glimpse of Heaven. As the sun sank a few ribbed clouds flushed high above and the sky around them blanched to a pellucid green. A gentle breeze carried a smell of honeysuckle.

So I should be thoroughly content. In a sense I *was* content. But although I was rich, was I fancy-free? Behind me in Bristol Charles ate his heart out and Effie hated me because she knew she was second best. And ahead of me was the meeting with Tamsin and beside her the shadowy but ever formidable figure of Bram Fox. Much had to be resolved, much developed; life, if infinitely more agreeable, was not a bit less complex.

And looking at myself in the mirror I was not altogether convinced that the facial surgery had been the success that had been hoped.

I had not yet written to Tamsin. I was shirking it, and all that the meeting entailed. I went into Truro to make arrangements about the transfer of my London funds. Mr Meadows, manager of the Cornish Bank, was welcoming, and indeed obsequious. I had heard that some shares in the Bodmin-Wadebridge railway were for sale at a bargain price. This was true, said Mr Meadows. The value of the shares had fallen because activity in the local mines and quarries was at a low ebb, neither was the transport of sand as profitable as it had previously been.

I had called to see Mr Preston Wallis in Bodmin while I was staying with the Collinses, and he had painted a bleak picture. The line, he said, was showing a working loss of £200 a half year: his own salary had been reduced from £50 a year to £37.18.0, the engineers' from £104 to £94, and so on down the scale. Unless they could extend the railway to tap new sources of revenue, or arrange and plan some linkage with one of the other lines which were now projected, he could not recommend my investment in the enterprise.

Yet in spite of this, and the doubts of Mr Meadows, I bought the shares that were for sale, paying £850 for them, a parcel that made me one of the largest shareholders. Exquisite pleasure. I did not care whether I lost money or made it, I was employing it as I wanted to.

Next I wrote to Mr Joseph Emidy, inviting him to call. A rather ill-written note came from his wife to say that Mr Emidy had passed away last year and was buried in Kenwyn churchyard. Added was a note in another hand to say that a Mr Charles William Hempel, the organist at St Mary's Church, had taken over Mr Emidy's pupils, and it was suggested I should write to him.

I did not write to him, but grieved for the little black man I had once so wanted to meet and now never should. His spirited vivacious music had lived with me for a long time, in spite of what followed it, and I had looked forward to continuing the tuition begun in Zurich. Unlike Professor Elbruz, Mr Emidy had had no academic musical upbringing, but I felt we could have got on so well. Now, as for some church organist . . .

However the church organist took it upon himself to write to me, and presently he came to call: a fat, rosy-cheeked jolly man on an elderly piebald horse. Mr Hempel was not himself young but his manner while very courteous was not obsequious, and I quite took to him. After all, what was there to lose? We talked a while and he produced a tuning fork and asked me to sing a few notes. He raised his eyebrows and nodded approval.

I told him we had no musical instrument in the house but I proposed to buy a pianoforte, if one could be found. His eyes gleamed at this, and he said he thought one *could* be found. We parted with mutual expressions of esteem.

Now there was nothing more to do to delay the hour. I wrote a note on the Saturday. On the Sunday I went twice to church at St Kea, on the Monday I hired a carriage to take me to Place House.

From Killiganoon the long reaches of the River Fal bar the way, but I was determined not to arrive at my old home by ferry and on foot. So it meant a tedious trip via Truro, Tregony and Gerrans. The weather was fine but with summery showers, and we stopped for a picnic at noon at Portscatho, the journey nearly done.

Sally Fetch was almost as reluctant as I to

return to her old home, though I reassured her that the staff had completely changed and that Slade was no longer there.

The big wooden gate at the entrance to the drive was, rather surprisingly, shut. The driver climbed down to open it, and the carriage crunched up the drive and stopped with a squeaking of brakes, a snort from the horse and a rattle of reins.

As I got out my sister appeared on the threshold of the door.

'Emma! I was about to pick some fruit and I heard the carriage.'

She was in a white muslin dress with flat-pleated sleeves. A dainty apple-green pinafore was the only indication that she had been intending to do the most genteel of work.

'I've brought Sally Fetch. She has been my maid for nearly two years. You'll remember her.'

'Of course. Pray come in.'

'If you please, miss,' said Fetch. 'I'll stay with the coach.'

I went in. The house looked brighter again and better kept. Tamsin too looked brighter than when I saw her last. She'd put on weight, but it suited her. We made polite conversation. She examined my face and expressed surprise that it was so much improved. 'You might even marry now!'

'I suppose it's possible.'

'Mother wrote and told me what you'd had done. Quite a change. And how fortunate that Uncle Francis left you money! When you wrote me after his death you were at your wit's end to know what to do.'

'. . . I hadn't heard then.'

'I wasn't able to help you at the time but my marriage was just going wrong and I hardly knew which way to turn myself.'

'And do you now?'

The look in her eyes changed slightly. 'The same blunt Emma. Come help me pick some plums. Cook wants to make jam.'

I followed her through the house, all so full of bitter-sweet reminiscence, out at the back and into the walled garden.

'Have you seen our new lighthouse?' she said brightly, making conversation.

'No, I didn't notice.'

'You would at night. Built just below the old signal station. Somehow I feel safer here for having this little beacon.'

'How is Celestine?'

'In very good health. She is picnicking in Cellars and should be home within the hour.'

The espalier plums were laden. She had brought two baskets and another apron. Trivial talk passed between us as we began to gather the plums. Then she said:

'Desmond is a pleasant young man, but we should never have married. Mother pushed me into it. It never really worked as a marriage should work. We are better separated.'

'And you are living alone here?'

'. . . Most of the time.' She licked her finger where a spot of plum juice had stained it. 'You will I'm sure have heard the rumours that Bram

309

Fox frequently visits me. So there is scandal. Well, it's true. His wife has died. He needs company and companionship and these I give him. And more, of course. And more. He is — a bit of a wild man, but so exciting. I am not the first woman in the world to break her marriage vows.' She put down her basket. 'But you know Bram. You were obsessed with him yourself at one time.'

Still am, did I ask myself? What rubbish! All that belonged to a nightmare adolescence, no longer extant in the world in which I now lived. As I had said to myself the other night on the porch of the new house, I was fancy-free. Long might it last. A companionate marriage such as Uncle Francis had proposed was now the only one I could contemplate. The night, the memory of the night in Blundstone's Hotel confirmed me, perversely, in spinsterhood.

'I am glad that Slade has gone.'

'Yes,' she said. 'Yes.'

'Did you discharge him?'

'No. He just decided to go.'

'So all that — all those things have stopped now?'

'What d'you mean by all those things?'

'What I surprised in the night. The running of contraband.'

'Oh yes,' she said casually. 'The building of the lighthouse has made it more difficult. And anyway, Bram would not allow it.'

'You surprise me.'

'Why?' There was a sharpness in her voice.

'Oh, just I suppose that I can't see him as a

law enforcement officer.'

'He's been that for years. You're behind the times, Emma.'

'I haven't seen him since that meeting at the St Aubyns . . . Where did Slade go to?'

'What? Oh, Slade. I've no idea. I think he went to Falmouth. You must ask Bram. He may know.'

We picked in silence.

'I saw Samuel in London.'

'Did you? . . . Shall we go in? My basket is full.'

I followed her into the house. A new cook came to receive the baskets from us at the kitchen door.

We took tea in the smaller of the drawing rooms. The showers had cleared away, and a bright sun shone. I could see the driver of my cab sitting inside the vehicle. Fetch had disappeared. The house was quiet.

'Do you not feel lonely living here?'

'Very seldom.'

'Do you have a manservant at all, now that Slade has gone?'

'Only a stableman.'

'I am thinking of getting a stableman myself,' I said. 'Mr Meadows has recommended someone called John Cannon.'

'Indeed.'

She passed me a sandwich and then bit into one with delicate relish.

'So what did Samuel say to you?'

' . . . Well, he was not pleased that you and Desmond had separated.'

'So he has told me. It's bad for the family name. He did not explain, I suppose, in what way this was so different from when his father kept a mistress and bought her a house for all to see.'

I was about to speak but she interrupted me. 'Oh, I can tell you the difference. If Desmond had a mistress and set her up in her own home people would accept it because he is a *man*. I am a woman and I am living on my own and entertaining another man! It is the way things have turned out — I have not sought it — but at present the way it has turned out suits me, so I shall go on as I am!'

'Samuel's view — '

'I know very well what Samuel's view is: in two separate letters he has left me in no doubt. He wants me to vacate the house and take Celestine to live with my mother in Richmond. The disgraced wife! Well, I can tell you, Emma, the only way the family is going to get me out of this house is to *turn* me out — by force if necessary! I have as much right to live here as anyone else! I've been here all my life. My grandfather was Samuel's grandfather. No one else wants to live in the house the way I do. Anna Maria has her own home; Samuel is taken up with his politics; Desmond and Mary both prefer Tregolls. All they want it for is a holiday home; and at present they can't use it; otherwise it would give family approval to my wicked ways!'

'Have you had much to do with Anna Maria? You were friendly for a time . . .'

312

I never heard what Anna Maria's opinion was, for at that moment Celestine burst into the room.

'Mama, I've found two cowries! And look who came by sea and brought me home by sea!'

She was a pretty little girl who had grown inches since I saw her last. She had her mother's blonde curly hair and bright blue eyes, and the way she spoke took me back to memories of Tamsin as a child. But I hardly heard anything she said, and only recalled her appearance in my memory later that night. For, following her into the room, carrying Celestine's bucket and spade and smiling a half-humorous, half-wolfish smile, was Abraham Fox.

5

I

He was wearing a cream linen jacket with brass buttons, a navy open-necked shirt with a loosened purple cravat, tight white naval trousers flared at the ends, bright yellow sandals.

He had changed so little since that first day he arrived at Place and took me, a scarred fat fifteen-year-old, sailing in the Roads. His dark hair was combed back and grown rather long again so that it curled on the collar of his jacket. His face was dark, more lined but as sun-bronzed as ever, his sharp teeth gleamed when he smiled.

'Well, well, how's my sweetheart? And Emma! Can it be Emma? *What* a pleasant surprise!' He laughed, and as always his infectious laugh went on too long, as if he had said something witty.

'I didn't expect you so early,' Tamsin said, with an edge on her voice. 'Emma was just going. What — '

'And now must stay a little while longer,' said Bram. 'It is years . . . Let me look at you.' He took my hands, which I reluctantly allowed him to do. 'Yes. Oh, yes. A very great improvement! D'you remember when we first met I told you, something could be done. And at last it has been! Yes. Oh yes. You were always an attractive creature, even with that handicap:

now you're much more so! Isn't she, Tamsin? Isn't the difference tremendous?'

'I have told her so,' said Tamsin stiffly. 'Where is Annie? Is she — '

'She's walking back,' said Celestine. 'Uncle Bram did not think the boat could take another one. It's just a tiny skiff, you know. We had lots of fun on the way! He pretended he had forgotten how to sail it, and I had to tell him!'

I got my hands free. Bram laughed and poured himself tea in Tamsin's cup.

There seemed to be talk all round then. Everyone spoke and no one listened. To my vexation my colour had risen. Tamsin's face had tightened round the mouth and eyes, as always happened to her if she was annoyed.

Was she annoyed at this disclosure of the domestic scene? 'Uncle Bram' indeed! He was at home in the house. The man of affairs arriving home early, cuddling the little girl and making her squeak, talking to both of the sisters equally, friendly, jocular but slightly sly. I nearly put shy. Was he ever shy?

The talk settled down. Bram was telling us of his day at Penzance, then back to Prussia Cove. Then he asked where I was staying and a moment later switched to a series of intelligently reasoned questions about the operation on my face. No one before had been so specific and, at least outwardly, concerned. He had the terrible habit of concentrating on the person to whom he was speaking, as if that person were the only one in the room, in the world. It flattered women. It probably flattered men.

In a brief pause — the very first — I said: 'So Slade has left.'

He looked at me and then at Tamsin. 'I think we got rid of him, didn't we? He was becoming ever more drunken, and we made it clear we did not like it, so one morning we woke up — or rather Tamsin wakes up, for I was not here — and he is gone. Just like that.' He snapped his fingers. 'Extraordinary, really. Clothes and all. Probably got a couple of his old shipmates to come in the night and row him away.'

'Celestine,' Tamsin said, 'take these lovely shells and ask Annie to find a little box for them. Is she back yet? Go and see if she is back yet.'

'So you are going to live in Cornwall?' Bram said to me. 'Fortunate that your uncle was so generous. Lucky young woman. The world is at your feet.'

'Some tiny part of it only.'

'Which I'm sure includes Place House, don't you think?'

'You were always the tease,' I said. 'Wasn't he, Tamsin?'

'Tammy,' he said. 'I always call her Tammy. But I do not tease. Your inheritance and your operation have made you into a very different person. We are all influenced by our physiognomy. Tammy has the knowledge of her own beauty: that has influenced the way she thinks. You had no such knowledge, but now you find yourself with a new, or partly new, face, which you present to the world and which in itself will alter your character.'

'Not necessarily for the better.'

'Who can say? It is for you to discover for yourself.'

'I think Fetch has just gone out to your coach,' Tamsin said.

'I am leaving too,' said Bram, 'and would cadge a lift, but alas my little skiff has to be returned before my cousin misses it. Now you are in Cornwall, Emma, we must meet frequently. You will be anxious to see more of your niece; she is a charming child.'

'Is Slade now in Falmouth?' I said. 'That's where he lived after my uncle Davey died and the family did not feel they needed him.'

'I hope *you* don't need him,' Bram said. 'You cannot need the luxury of a butler at Killiganoon. Anyway he would not be available for I hear he is dead.'

A maid came in to clear away the tea things. Some conversations continue in front of the servants, but this did not seem appropriate.

'Dead?' said Tamsin eventually, tight-faced again. 'You never told me.'

'I thought to spare you this sorrow,' Bram said, and laughed in high amusement. 'In fact I only heard myself last week. He had an old aunt who lived near Feock, and I believe he died there. A stroke or something of the sort. I do not imagine he will be much regretted.'

II

It would not be true to say I burst into Cornish society. I wrote to a few old friends, or those whom my mother had chosen to call her friends, and so received invitations to visit them. The Boscawens, the St Aubyns, the Bullers. I was busy with the redecoration of my new home, the re-planning of the garden.

A piano was delivered, courtesy of Mr Charles William Hempel, bought from the Polwheles, who had one to spare. Weekly I took singing lessons, courtesy of Mr Charles William Hempel, and realized I had still much to learn and that it was very agreeable — though difficult to learn it.

From Professor Elbruz I had been told about Bel Canto and long phrasing, and true harmony. 'Your voice must be like a flute,' he had said. 'Until your technique is so natural to you as to be almost subconscious, you cannot really forget it and begin to interpret. Of course you do not *need* this as a profession, but the nearer professional you can become in your approach, the greater will be your happiness.'

My happiness; was that what I was still seeking? The meeting with Bram had profoundly shaken me. I had grown, matured, hardened, lived years of my life without a sight of him, but when he came suddenly on me — and when had he not done so? — I became emotionally vulnerable again, pent up, afraid.

Even that visit to see Tamsin had not produced definite results. She looked quite happy. Clearly the ménage with Bram suited her, and to Hell with the gossips. I did not mind this — or would not have minded it had her lover been a stranger. Was I jealous, or only anxious for her future welfare? Bram had only to look at a woman and she was halfway to surrender. How wonderful, how wonderful it would be if one could be, or become, immune! How insufferably conceited the man must be. With what contempt he must view this branch of the Spry family: me, Tamsin, probably my mother. How lovely it would be to hate him! And how impossible!

What was his charm? The charm of a dominant male? Perhaps. But also the charm of the perceptive, sympathetic man; one who cared and needed caring for.

The following week I went to dinner at Tregothnan and there met a young man called the Hon Jonathan Eliot, whose courteous attention seemed to go beyond the degree of politeness expected of a dinner partner. He was tallish and thin, thin-haired though scarcely more than thirty, smiling eyes and with something of Bram's talent for concentrating his whole personal interest on the person he was talking to. Before the evening was out he had invited me to meet his sister. He would get her to write to ask me to stay a few days. He lived at St Germans, which I only vaguely knew as near Plymouth, and therefore a considerable journey. I replied as politely as I knew how, appreciating his attentions and being flattered by them. I had had little enough admiration in life, and it was new and heady to feel a quality of power, of influence, of control.

At the next meeting with Mr Hempel he told me of a benefit concert which was being organized in Truro on behalf of Mr Emidy's widow, who was in poor circumstances. This was to take place in a month's time. Mr Hempel's own son, who was a talented organist and violinist, was to play several pieces. He, Hempel senior, had composed a special *Te Deum* for the occasion; two distinguished singers were coming from Falmouth, another from Plymouth: did I think I might contribute two or so of the songs I had been singing for him last Tuesday?

I remembered Professor Elbruz's comments. 'The production of your voice must be instinctive before you can interpret. You have of course no need to meet professional standards, but the nearer you get to them the more pleasure you will give and the more pleasure you will find.'

I did not want to sing. It would not have mattered so much in some other part of the country. It had not mattered in North Cornwall where I had appeared among amateurs. Here I was among my own people. No doubt there was some talk already of Emma Spry who had been so disfigured and now was no longer so disfigured, and had come into money and was living on her own at Killiganoon. People would come to see me, not so much to be critical or appreciative of the music, but to see *me*, to see what my face looked like now. I did *not* want to be set up like an Aunt Sally to be stared at. Another year.

Yet this concert was for Joseph Emidy's widow. Would it not be better to give £20 to the concert and sit in the audience?

'I don't think, Mr Hempel, that I am quite ready for a public performance. I have really hardly practised enough, let alone anything else.'

'We have a month, Miss Spry. I feel your voice is quite exceptionally good. We can practise as much as you like. After all, this is not London. And I believe it will give quite a fillip to music in Truro, and to some of my more backward pupils, if you were to sing. If only, say, two songs.'

That week came a letter from Charles:

Dear Emma,

I am indeed deeply sorry and sad that our meeting went so badly wrong. Effie should never have spoken to you in the way she did, and I should not have called on you on the following morning to try to explain about what you should never have known. We are all to blame, but you only in the smallest degree because you did not warn me of your coming. I did not even know you were in England!

What can I say that will in any small way undo the damage done? If this really means the end of my letters to you and your letters to me I shall feel I have lost an invaluable part of my life. To whom else can I write with such frankness and confidentiality? From whom else can I expect such thoughtful and sympathetic understanding? If we are nothing

321

more than friends of the pen and the post, yet that is of such value to me that I do not know how I may go on without it.

What has been said between us in the hotel cannot be forgotten. Nor, though I so much regret that it happened, do I *want* it to be forgotten. I only want it to be forgiven. Is it unforgivable to love a woman to distraction and then to marry elsewhere because the first woman seems far out of one's reach? Perhaps you always were out of my reach if it is true that you care little or nothing for me. I do not know and probably shall never know now.

If it is possible to forgive this then, to prove it so, I hope and pray in due course you will write to me again. Will you?

Charles

III

I sang three songs, one as an encore. It was an ordeal. When singing in Bodmin and various villages I had not felt more than ordinarily nervous, but this time I was convinced I would crack on a high note or otherwise break down. Added to the apprehension of being in superior musical company was the knowledge of who was going to be there. Bram Fox (he really did seem to like music); Jonathan Eliot, who was staying again with the Boscawens, and was to bring Lord Falmouth with him; cousin Desmond, back from London, and cousin Mary. The Mayor of Truro, and a fair sprinkling of clergymen. They had all turned up to honour the little black man who had spent his last years, and all his best years, in Cornwall.

Mr Hempel had persuaded me to sing two very simple songs; there would be no need to strain for the high notes. He said I had a sweet middle register; make the most of that until I gained in experience and confidence.

Even so, I nearly broke down. Hands were trembling so much that voice tried to do the same. The first bars were awful but then instead of gulping and stopping short and running for the wings, a desperate pride surged up from somewhere and I went on. Thereafter it was all right. The second song was better than the first. Mr Hempel rushed at me and I sang my encore. More applause — a lot of applause, and I had to return to the stage and bow — and then it was over. My eye and my face were stinging as if they had been hurt all over again.

At the end of the concert — tea and cakes. It was what I had missed at that first Emidy concert; now I was participating in it as an *artiste*. Lord Falmouth congratulated me and asked about my father whom he had known as a young man. Jonathan Eliot was very kind; his face glowed and one could come to believe that he really meant it. Others were complimentary. But I did not see Bram.

'My sister has been unwell, otherwise she would have written you before this,' said Jonathan Eliot; 'and my father is in London. But in the course of the next two weeks I hope you will come and spend a few days with us. It would give me the greatest pleasure, Miss Spry.'

'Thank you,' I said. 'That would be delightful.'

'You could come by sea to Plymouth, that would perhaps be the simplest course; are you a good sailor?'

'Thank you,' I said again. 'Yes, I am not seasick; but if it were agreeable to you, I have been invited to the Treffrys next month, and perhaps I could break the journey by coach.'

He looked disappointed. 'Of course. Please come before Christmas. Promise that.'

I smiled at him. 'I willingly promise that.'

Desmond and Mary took their leave shortly after. It had not struck me before how much they were alike, not perhaps in feature but in character. Desmond asked politely about Killiganoon and how long I had leased it for. I invited them to come to sup and spend the night, and they accepted. This time in front of Desmond, there was no mention of Tamsin.

Just as I was myself about to leave Bram sidled up to me.

'At last,' he said. 'The blow flies have departed. I like that dress. Is it Parisian?'

'Yes.'

'It shows your figure.'

'It is just the fashion.'

'I'm sure.'

He looked round. The hall was almost empty. Fetch had gone to call my hired coach.

He said: 'You can sing better than that.'

'How do you know?'

'I heard you practising at Place when you were a girl.'

'I expect I am getting a little past it.'

'Actually you have a fine voice when you think no one is listening.'

'Thank you.'

'I would like to call and see you, Emma.'

'What for?'

'To renew old acquaintanceship. We have much to say to each other.'

'Have we?'

'I think so. You might even think I have some explaining to do.'

'It's a little late in the day for that.'

'I'm not sure. You have come back to this district when you might have settled up country somewhere.'

'My family is Cornish, you know.'

'Yes. But who in your family brings you back? Do you care much for your sister? She does not seem to care much for you.'

I saw Fetch in the doorway.

'I must go. Good night, Bram.'

He considered me; his eyes humorous, admiring.

'I'll call next week. Would Wednesday be convenient?'

'I'm sorry. I am engaged that day.'

He said: 'I'll come on Wednesday.'

6

I had no appointments on the Wednesday but decided to walk across and visit the Vicar of St Kea, to discuss the repairs to the chancel roof which I had offered to finance. It rained all day, but though the walk was not specially agreeable — it could well have been put off until Thursday — the weather could hardly have been more helpful in demonstrating how badly the roof was in need of repair. Compared to the elegance and magnificence of Blisland, this was a dull uninspired rectangular little building with not much to commend it except its lovely site and the woods around it.

The vicar was tiny, to match his church, and highly obsequious, which was embarrassing. Would one ever slip easily into the persona of a figure of consequence when at heart one was still insignificant?

This attempt to avoid Mr Fox was abortive; he did not call until after dinner; so I kept him waiting half an hour. When I eventually went down he was standing looking out of the window, riding crop behind his back held by both hands.

He turned. 'Ah, Miss Emmie. The elusive Miss Emmie.' He laughed, as usual, as if he had made some joke. The ends of his hair had been wet and were curling up as they dried. His riding boots were muddy but had been clean when he set out.

He moved to kiss me but I turned my face away.

'No longer friends?'

'Is that not also a little out of date?' I said.

He had not stood back, was only a foot from me.

'*Squisito*!' he said.

'What does that mean?'

'It's Italian for something or other. You must guess.'

'Thanks. I don't want to. If you — '

'I am glad you are wearing a dress with short sleeves. D'you know I believe I first fell in love with your elbow — '

'Bram, if you are going to talk absurdities — '

'What better when they are true? When I picked you up that first day and took you sailing it was purely an impulse to be pleasant to a plump unhappy little girl, as one would pick up and stroke a stray cat. But this unhappy little girl, I soon recognized, was one of the younger Sprys and sister to the lady I was interested in. It was not until you got in the boat and we sailed away and I saw your bare arm on the tiller, that I saw it in all its perfection. Shape, form, colour. All right, you may laugh: I am not even an artist. Many women have beautiful arms. But something about yours — '

'Have you told Tamsin?'

'What?'

'How beautiful you think my arms are.'

327

He moved away, brushing damp from the frilled sleeves of his shirt where they showed beneath his velvet jacket. 'Tammy is beautiful in other ways. I am not claiming that all these years I have been exclusively interested in you, but — '

'What a confession! How you do succeed in sweeping girls off their feet!'

'Emma, you will have your sarcasm. Tamsin is a sweet woman. But sweetness is not all. You are not a sweet woman; you are bitter still. It is not I you hate so much as the accident of your disfigurement. Even now, although you are largely cured, you have an incubus on your shoulder, and you cannot forget it.'

'I cannot forget all that happened to me when I was eighteen. And I don't intend to forget it or forgive it.'

He laughed, but this time sobered suddenly. 'I tell you it's life you can't forgive. I was just an incident in that life; still am — '

'No longer. No longer, believe me.'

'Well, if I am no longer important in your life, why do you still care what happened? Forget it. It is long past. I was only the first. There must have been others since then — '

'At least a dozen.'

'And it has done you no harm! You have become more beautiful as a consequence. It is not just the operation.'

'I underwent that chiefly for the amusement.'

'D'you know,' he said, 'you really have the most lovely underarms. D'you remember that night how I repeatedly kissed them?'

'What? Oh, *that* night. I think you were drunk, were you not?'

'Drunk with a special desire that it seems only you can raise in me.'

'This conversation is childish,' I said. 'Can you not grow up, Bram?'

Neither of us came well out of this interchange, and we were both getting angry. He because he could not get his own way, I because I was frightened of myself. His temper was widely known but I had never witnessed it and certainly it had never been directed towards me.

'Get out!' I said, and then in a much gentler tone, 'Please.'

I think it was this last word that stopped him in mid-stream. He swallowed. The muscles seemed to ripple around his throat.

'I'll go then. I'll go now. But don't think this is the end of it, Emma. I feel — I have the strongest feeling — that you belong to me.'

'And my sister? And my mother?'

He smiled. 'I'm not prepared to talk about that — about them. I can only tell you that you are the only person I have ever really loved.'

II

Summer became autumn and autumn winter, and I was twenty-six. The young queen became engaged to be married to Prince Albert of Saxe-Coburg-Gotha. I had not written to Charles. I visited the home of the Eliots in St Germans. Jonathan was very charming, as was his sister.

The house was big and beautiful and my stay a pleasant one. I broke my journey on the way there at the Treffrys, and on the way home stayed a couple of days with the Collinses.

While in Blisland I had a wreath made and took it to Uncle Francis's grave, and knelt there for a while trying to thank him for all he had done for me. Now and then I fancied I could hear his voice, but perhaps it was only the light breeze murmuring among the bare trees.

The following day I went into Bodmin to attend a meeting of the railway adventurers. Naturally Charles was not there, but I had had a sneaking anticipation that he might be, and I tried to come to terms with an equally sneaking sensation of disappointment. Under consideration at the meeting was a letter from Mr Brunel, recommending that they should set aside the *Camel* and the *Elephant* for casual and relief work, and purchase a new engine designed by the brilliant engineer, Mr Gooch, exactly to the design of the *Bacchus* and the *Vulcan* which were now rendering sterling and trouble-free service on the Wootton Bassett line.

Sir John Molesworth and myself and the Chief Superintendent, Mr Dunstan, were for taking up the idea, but there were too many doubts and objections from the others, so our answer was postponed until the next meeting and a resolution passed to explore new outlets for the line. With the mines in the district closed or on the verge of closing, the trucks often ran empty down line. Buying a faster and more reliable engine was not much use if the freight traffic was not there.

Somehow the atmosphere, the feeling in East Cornwall was lighter. One could be oneself, the new Emma Spry, monied, young, with more laughter in her than there had ever been before, less touched by the events of childhood, and with no special regard for what would happen next. Perhaps it would be better to live there. Coming west, to Truro, to Killiganoon, the picture closed in. I was not just returning to my home and all the old memories. I was returning to an indeterminate future, a series of ominous problems that would not go away. I had to face a resolution of these problems, which might be out of my hands. Then, if not resolved, I might have to live with them. That was the direst prospect of all.

III

We had not been living in the house long when Sally Fetch discovered a stray kitten starving to death in the long grass behind the stables. When she brought it in it was too feeble to stand and flopped over on its weak legs, its mouth opening and shutting in inaudible miaows. One of its hind legs had an open wound, and the fur was matted with dried blood. Either it had been caught in a gin or it had been attacked by one of the farm dogs.

We carried it into the kitchen, put a blanket in a basket and tried to feed it with milk. The kitten's startling green eyes glazed over now and

331

then, but presently by squirting drops of milk into its mouth with a tube designed for ear drops, we began to bring it round.

During the next two days life centred round the kitten's basket. The leg did not seem to be broken, so I bathed it with melrose water and hoped for the best. The best was that the kitten was soon able to walk on three legs, to lap its milk from a saucer and presently chewed delicately at a few morsels of fish.

'You'd think there was *bones* in it,' said Fetch indignantly, 'and me at such pain to see there was not!'

'Cats are like that,' I said, not really knowing. 'She's on the mend now for sure.'

I had intended as soon as I settled in to get a dog. At Place in my childhood Parish had been around, but I had found Uncle Francis preferred not to have animals in the house. For the moment this scrap of mewing skin and bone with its brilliant eyes and pointed top-heavy tail fascinated me. We called her Mousie because Fetch had thought it was a mouse when she first found it stirring in the grass.

Bram called twice in the week following my return from Blisland. He was on his best behaviour — something he had never been before with me — and I was able to endure his visits with a greater degree of calm than usual. It was virtually the first conversations we had ever had which were not spiked by sexual challenge. I wondered, after his second visit, whether I had ever really known him at all.

He had an alert mind, but one which seemed

to slip from subject to subject without warning. (Was he even in this not unlike a fox?) His perceptions were acute, but he seemed to have made up his mind on everything before he spoke. He still laughed too much and without proper cause. But his knowledge of so many aspects of life — particularly Cornish life — were unexpected and startling. Superficially at least he knew as much about railways as any man I had ever met, saving only Charles and Mr Brunel. He knew of the progress and of the latest plans to complete the railway to run without break from London to Bristol next year. He knew of plans within the county to extend the line into Cornwall, of an ambitious idea to run along the spine of Cornwall feeding Bodmin and Truro, and of a rival plan to take in Liskeard and the coastal towns.

He knew all about the controversy and rivalry between the advocates of the broad and narrow gauge railways and had made up his mind that Brunel, advocate of the former, was fighting a losing battle against the weight of the midlands and the manufacturing north. He knew everyone I knew and was confident of the way in which each would lean, where expansionist decisions had to be made — and why. Land, property, commercial and political interests, he understood them all and who deferred to whom in the hierarchy of the county. However he used it, he had an exceptional brain and an exceptional memory.

He seemed to enjoy talking to me but usually dismissed my ideas as lacking in a simple

333

appreciation of the facts. I accepted this without demur but frequently wondered, sometimes audibly, if his own information was impeccable. He laughed at this, showing his teeth, and simply became more overbearing, in a jocular way.

Once as he left he said: 'You're the best fun of any woman around here, Emma. Cannot say that is why I so much took to you in the first place all those years ago! Must have been foresight.'

'I congratulate you on your judgment,' I murmured, as I showed him out.

What must it be like to be married to him, I thought, as my new stableman, John Cannon, came round the corner to help him mount.

Substance was added to those eccentric thoughts three weeks later, when he came in half a blizzard and stayed nearly two hours waiting for the snow to stop.

I said: 'You should not go back this afternoon. I can't offer you accommodation here, but Mrs Eames, who is only a hundred yards down the road to Come-to-Good would have a comfortable room.'

He laughed. 'The snow is melting as it falls. I shall slither my way home safely enough. But I'll hold on a while longer for the wind to abate.'

'As you please.'

'But on that point, is there any valid reason why I should not stay here the night? We do not have to take account of the Mrs Grundys of this world.'

'I do not know what your reputation is, Bram, but mine, I believe, is still good.'

'And would be tarnished by my presence for one night under the same roof?'

'I think so.'

'Dear, dear. If they but knew!'

'That was long ago.'

'Yes, yes. Oh, yes, yes. My little starfish. But seriously, Emma.'

'Seriously?'

'You and I belong to ourselves alone. You are unmarried, I am unmarried. There is no one else to consider.'

'Tamsin naturally is not worth a second thought?'

'She is worth many thoughts. She is a pretty wayward creature, but I am not tied to her apron strings.'

'No doubt she accepts that?'

'I think so.'

'And would she accept that you were free to make a close acquaintance with her sister?'

'She need never know.'

'Nothing is private in Cornwall. You should be aware of that.'

'Our meeting at Blundstone's Hotel has gone unrecorded.'

I bit my lip. 'I think this time I am looking for a more settled relationship.'

'Which this could well be. I am not again likely to be imprisoned for debt.'

'Why not?'

'Do you wonder how Tamsin continues to thrive at Place and pay the rent? It is a result of the provision I make for her. I can indulge my friends.'

'You'd like me as a kept woman?'

His eyes glinted. 'I would.'

'How much would you pay me?'

'As much as you needed to continue to live here.'

I stared out at the falling snow.

He said: 'Emma, I suppose you must often have thought of marriage.'

'Not often,' I said. 'Sometimes.'

'So you must — it must have crossed your mind that you could now marry me.'

His voice was actually hesitant as I had not heard it before. Could this joke really mean something to him?

'I don't think it had ever occurred to me as a possibility.'

'Why not? You are careful of your reputation. And you said you were looking for a settled relationship.'

'And do you suppose marriage to you would add to my reputation?'

'It would do it no harm, I assure you. What is amiss with me?'

I said: 'Look, the snow is stopping. You will be able to leave soon.'

He said: 'Marriage to you would be an adventure.'

'It could be looked on as an atonement.'

'No one else could think so — you could regard it as that if you wished.'

There was a brief silence.

I said: 'Thank you, but I would not consider it.'

'May I ask why not?'

'We should drive each other to destruction.'

'I am not of destructible material, Emma. And I suspect that under your elegant appearance there is a rock-hard centre that could sustain any number of shocks.'

'Which you would administer?'

'In course of time, perhaps.'

'And you suggest I should go into such an attachment knowing all the hazards?'

'You'd be twenty times more alive married to me than with most of those weak, conceited, wishy-washy men you might otherwise join yourself to.'

'Have you someone in mind?'

He put his hand lightly on my arm (which was safely covered today).

'Don't you realize what excitement we should have together? Loving, quarrelling, adventuring — not a life for the mealy-mouthed or the faint-hearted. Bram and Emma fighting for a common cause?'

His face was close to me, the eyes glinting.

'Cause?' I said.

'Yes. The cause of our own advancement. I have money as well as you. We can — '

'How do you know what money I have?'

'A sweet question, sweetly put. How else could you maintain the style you do here?'

'I might be spending it all to attract a title.'

'Jonty Eliot? He's no good for you. I am.'

'Bram,' I said smiling. 'You know too much. You're forgetting that I know something about *your* life too.'

'That is to the good. Neither of us would enter

337

into it with our eyes closed.' He kissed me.

'Don't think,' I said, pushing him gently away, 'that I am agreeing to anything at all. Thank you just the same.'

'Please do not hurry,' he said. 'Think it over, little Emma. It would be a great adventure.'

IV

The coaching road ran immediately outside my gates, and the mail coach stopped there as a matter of course. Taking this coach to Falmouth was a pleasant trip, if the weather was fine, and we had a very fine and mild spell following the snows of January.

For a day's shopping one did not have to be in a hurry. The horses were winded after their long climb out of the Kea Valley and had to be eased down the long descent to Carnon Bridge. Then, after winding beside a tributary of Restronguet Creek for a couple of miles, one began the slow ascent of the next hill before another downward slope to Penryn.

Fetch came with me, and we shopped in Arwenack Street (where the young Queen of Portugal had paraded on her way to Bank House). We had nearly done when Fetch touched my arm. 'There's Mrs Foster. You mind her: she was cook when you was a baby.'

A little old woman in the inevitable black. I knew her at once. As a child I remembered her as fierce, fretful but generous. Just seeing her brought back memories of her giving me a slice

338

of squab pie as we came in on a winter's day hungry long before time for supper; or a tasty piece of roast swan that was going to be served to the adults but not to the children. While I was ill with the recurrent fever she had regularly sent up a bowl of cow heel soup to tempt my appetite.

She did not at first recognize me but when she did she showed red gums in a grin of welcome.

'Mistress Emma!' I was just able to detect. ' 'Ow you've grown. My dear life an' body. Well, Mistress Emma . . . '

I was as gracious as I knew how, for I was genuinely pleased to see 'Cook' as she would always be thought of. (Why had she left? Something to do with Slade? Had she disliked him intensely or liked him too much?)

We carried on a brief conversation, Fetch acting as interpreter because of Cook's lack of teeth. I thought of her recipe for saffron cake, which she had taught me and which I still knew by heart. So I quoted it to her:

'Half a dram of saffron, two pounds of plain flour, one pound of butter, four ounces of sugar, two ounces of candied peel, one pound of currants, one ounce of yeast, pinch of salt, warm milk.'

She was delighted with this recital, and I could just see one blackened tooth at the back of her mouth. I always hate the act of giving money personally but got Fetch to take her address so that something could be sent to cheer her up.

A coach would be leaving at five, and we

had yet to walk to the quay where it would be waiting.

'Sorry to hear about Mr Slade,' I said experimentally. 'He was not very old, I suppose?'

Cook's face changed. Her expression was in any case more attuned to disaster than to pleasure.

'Aw, my dear. No one d'know 'ow it 'appened.' She went on chuntering but I could not make it out.

'Did you go to the funeral?' I asked, still uncertain what her private feelings were for the butler.

'Funeral?' She stared. 'Funeral, mistress? No, mistress. Not yet. 'E bain't dead . . .'

'What?' Was she getting deaf? '*Slade*, I said. Slade the butler who was at Place in your time.'

'Slade. That be the one, mistress, and no mistake. Oliver Slade. He bain't dead yet, mistress.'

'I — I was told he had a stroke and died at his aunt's cottage near Feock.'

Cook blinked. 'No, mistress. He were in some sort of a fight wi' some of his friends, and he got both his legs broke. Just above the knee, they d'say. 'E's livin', sure 'nough. I seen 'im last Tuesday. Old devil, 'e be. Takes some killen, I reckon.' She showed her gums again in a pink grin.

340

7

I

During the wintry days of February and March I saw little of Desmond and Mary. Samuel had been down at Christmas and had called on me. He was polite enough but colder than in London, and it occurred to me that it might have become known that Bram was visiting me as well as Tamsin. I could well understand some resentment in the family that two of their Cornish houses were occupied by the two daughters of a younger brother, and that, because of Samuel's weakness or lack of conviction in not turning at least one of them out, they were debarred by their own prejudices from using either of them.

Meanwhile Mousie grew and grew and became an inseparable friend. Fetch was a little put out that the kitten so obviously preferred me. When I was in the house she followed me everywhere, and after a while came to sleep at the foot of my bed. Then I got used to having a soft paw touch my cheek in the middle of the night and allowing her to settle beside me.

Bram's courtship of me progressed slowly. He came and talked and exercised his coercive charm. We argued and occasionally quarrelled; he laughed a lot and I a little, still keeping a guard up. He held his explosive temper under strict control.

I did not mention Slade to him but took out a map to see how far his cottage was from Killiganoon. It was no way — well within walking distance. I asked Sally to make a few enquiries. She said it was his sister he was living with, not his aunt. So I went to see him.

This was close by the village of Feock, a cob-built, slate-hung cottage of four rooms, overlooking the estuary. A large central rectangular chimney rising by decreasing tiers formed the centre of the cottage, and to reach it one took flat stepping stones over a clear-water rill of a sauntering stream with dark cresses growing. The place was in a bad state of repair; the front gate hung on one hinge, the painted front door was down to bare wood; the tall old woman who opened it was overdressed, with earrings — in the morning! — and pendants and brass bracelets, but her dress was stained, had a hole in the armpit and a tear in the skirt. Her hair was dyed an improbably pale yellow. She was not at all like Slade.

When I went in he was in a wheelchair, staring balefully out of the window. Presently he transferred his stare to me. He had lost a lot of weight and looked much older, and this was made grotesque because at last he was allowing his own hair to grow out undyed, so that he had a grey-white head and a black pigtail.

'What do you want?' he demanded in his old aggressive voice.

I told him.

II

In March I supped at the Falmouths and slept there. A big party, and among the guests was Jonathan Eliot, who by accident or request was put next to me at the table. He made a great fuss, and I was flattered. It seemed that the operation had worked well enough, the scars slowly disappearing or hidden by make-up, so that young men like him were not put off. He was the third son of the Earl of St Germans and, though he could have no notion of my fortune, plainly considered me of marriageable quality. I wished I cared more for him.

There seemed to be one man who stood between me and all others.

My correspondence had resumed with Charles. At Christmas I had written thanking him for his affectionate letter and saying that although there could never be anything between us but a warm friendship, his letters to me would too be greatly missed. Therefore I was happy if we could continue to correspond, but in his letters please would he always include news of his wife and her health and well-being.

I had deliberately seen nothing more of Tamsin, but just before Easter Bram was called to Plymouth on excise business, so it seemed the opportunity for the confrontation I was planning and dreading. It was essential when I went to see Tamsin that Bram should not be there, not capable of turning up halfway through as he had done last time.

This was an occasion when even Sally Fetch

might be an embarrassment, so I set out alone with her protestations in my ears. I had written of my intention to call at Place and spend one night there, so that Tamsin should not be caught unprepared. Falmouth and St Mawes, then a walk to the ferry and a further walk.

A different day from that first summer visit. Now the clouds were being driven across the sky by a stiff north-westerly wind. It had been a rough crossing even in the Roads. In a field near the house gulls were clustering like white paper rags behind Farmer Pardoe who was ploughing, two oxen in the plough with a lead horse in front. The whole district looked tired and windswept, winter still scarcely past, the bare alders, hawthorns and nut trees wizened and bent. Even St Mawes huddled.

Over the front door of the house was the family coat of arms. The English translation of the crest was 'Be wise and without harm'. Could I be that?

Once again Tamsin herself opened the door.

'Well, Emma, you have not deigned to call for a long time.' Voice as cheerless as the day.

'Yes, I know, I have much to say, but I have hesitated to say it.'

'Pray come in. Celestine is at her lessons. If you have anything special to say to me, we shall be quite private.'

In the main drawing room I pulled off hat and cloak. There was no one to take them so I draped them over a blue plush chair which Uncle Davey had once occupied. Tamsin waited by the window, taut as a bow.

'How have you been?' I asked.

'Well enough. And you?'

'Yes, thanks. Have you heard from Mother lately?'

'Last month. She's taking some new drops.'

'Yes, she told me. They make her sleep a bit. I expect . . . '

'What?'

'I was going to say they probably have laudanum in them. A tincture of that was the only help when my face was so painful.'

She looked at me. 'Has it been worth it?'

'What, my face? Oh, I think so.'

'It hasn't been a complete success, has it?'

'No . . . I make the best of it.'

'I'm sure.'

There was a brief silence.

'Bram,' I said, 'as you will know, is in Plymouth.'

'Good of you to tell me. I hear you have been meeting him from time to time.'

So she knew.

'He comes to see me, I do not invite him.'

'I suppose you no longer regard him as an enemy, as you used to.'

'Did I? I don't know. He has always been a challenge.'

'Are we going to talk about him or about us?'

'All three.'

'I do not think I am willing to do that.'

'There's not much choice, Tamsin. I'm sorry but . . . '

She turned from the window. 'This is my

house — mine and Bram's. You are my sister, so I give you leave to come here. But you come on my terms. If what you have to say is against Bram or against my association with him, then you can take it elsewhere.'

I had never heard her voice so hard, and the battle not yet even joined.

'I came today because I knew Bram was not here and could not interrupt us. As you say, I'm your sister — and though we have not perhaps liked each other so well since we grew up, the blood tie is there and we owe each other a little frankness, a little honesty . . .'

'Go on.'

'I don't know quite where to begin. I . . . have no option but to . . . Did you know that Slade is still alive?'

She looked up, eyes startled. 'What d'you mean? Bram told you. He's dead!'

'Bram was — mistaken. I have spoken to him.'

'To Slade? When? Where? I don't believe you!'

'He is with his sister at Feock. It is quite close to Killiganoon. I walked there.'

'You — saw him? I don't believe you!'

'He did not die of a stroke. He was attacked by four men, taken from Place with a tarpaulin flung over his head, kept in a shed without food or water; then both his legs were broken and he was dropped in the tidal mud of the Fal and left to die.'

Tamsin took out a handkerchief and wiped her lips. 'Bram must have been told wrongly . . .'

346

'Yes . . . yes. I would like you to reassure me of that.'

'Slade was mixed up in all sorts of shady things. You know that yourself. You took great pleasure in coming over to Tregrehan and telling me what you had found out about him.' She sat down.

I sat on the opposite side of the table. 'Slade had a lot to say when I went to see him. He said that Bram was not only head of the Excise but deeply involved in the trade — in contraband. With his tacit permission certain routes to the continent are — are left open; others, which do not pay him a percentage of the goods run, are closed and the smugglers caught. Slade says — I did not know — that while running contraband is illegal, the sale of contraband, once it has been landed undetected, is not forbidden in law. Bram, he says, draws a profit in this way, also.'

'What complete nonsense,' Tamsin said with conviction. 'Utter rubbish! You know how this county is rife with slander and scare stories. You remember how it was said that your deformed face cast a spell on this house and helped to derange Aunt Anna? Well, if you can believe this you can believe that!'

I put my hand up to my face.

'If what Slade said is true, if, just supposing it *were* true, Bram would have little reason to fear exposure from him. Slade is terrified of what would happen if he spoke out. He says it was Bram's doing, on Bram's orders that he was attacked and beaten. He says he quarrelled with Bram because he took all the risks and should have had a greater share of the profits. They had worked in Place, he says, together ever since the Admiral died. He says there's no one in the trade who would dare stand up in court and testify against Abraham Fox. He even has some of the gentry behind him.'

Tamsin laughed harshly. 'Don't be so utterly silly. You ought to know that nothing Slade says is worth a moment's belief. You remember the story he told us about burying his children in the cellar? Well, *we* were children then! We're not now. *You're* not. You're old enough to know better!'

'Yet,' thoughtfully, still rubbing my face. 'You've just said, Bram told me Slade was dead. You heard him.'

'May be he heard *wrong*! There's no excuse *at all* to suppose that whatever happened to Slade happened on Bram's orders!'

'Did you know anything about this, Tamsin?'

'About *what*, for God's sake?'

'About all I've just said. You say Slade disappeared from this house one day? How did it happen?'

'Oh . . . ' She made an angry gesture. 'It just happened. When — when the house wakened one morning he was gone! It was Lucy who came to tell me. When he did not come down at his usual time they sent her up to his bedroom. The room was empty, the bed had not been slept in, some of his clothes were gone. I simply shrugged my shoulders and continued

348

with my life as normal. Slade had become very eccentric, very strange. I think he had a softening of the brain. It is quite possible that he got drunk and fell down some steps and has invented the rest of the story. He is quite capable of making up any wild tale. No doubt he found you a willing listener. You of all people! That you believed anything that Slade said! You ought to be ashamed of yourself!'

I said: 'If I have made a mistake I must ask your pardon. I shall be very, very, very glad if it is all a mistake — for a reason I'll explain in a moment. But first tell me . . . Tell me — if Bram is keeping strictly within the law, how does he live as well as he does? He never had money when we knew him first. He went to prison for debt. Well, his salary as Commissioner for Customs and Excise can hardly be that generous. Yet he tells me he pays the rental on your behalf for Place House. And although he works hard he lives a gentleman's existence in the meantime. You too are prosperous-looking and as far as I know you have no money of your own.'

She turned suddenly in her chair and shouted: 'What *business* is it of yours! How dare you come here questioning me as if you were a judge! What *right* have you!'

'Only the partial right of being your sister . . . And for another reason . . .'

'*What* other reason?'

'Bram has asked me to marry him.'

349

III

There are times when I forget that Tamsin and I
are daughters of an actress. I find I can simulate
moods that are not quite my own, and usually I
can detect them in her. As young girls we would
challenge each other, instinctively rather than
deliberately, what my mother coldly condemned
as 'striking attitudes'. Tamsin, by reason of her
beauty and the favouritism bestowed on her, was
more prone than I.

But when she laughed at my last utterance I
could not tell how deeply she was moved by
it, precisely because it was histrionic, hysterical,
contemptuous all at the same time.

'You can't be serious!' she said.

'I think he is. I think I may be.'

'You've lost your senses!'

'It's why I came to ask you these questions
about Bram. It is a relief to hear you say that
these stories are not true.'

'You couldn't keep him a month,' she snapped
contemptuously. 'And I don't mean in a money
sense!'

'Nor do I. But he *has* offered to keep me.'

Her eyes glinted. 'Do you love him?'

'I think I always have.'

'And what about me? Have you forgotten
about me?'

'No. I certainly haven't! I've thought of little
else. But I suppose I did not feel that you were
bound together in a — in a — ' I tailed off.

'Why have you *come* to say this to me? Are
you really, really — in your right mind? Do

you suppose that my — my relationship with Bram can be parcelled up and put away in a convenient cupboard? My God, your — your impertinence is beyond belief!'

I took a deep rather shaky breath. 'The truth may be that we are both a trifle besotted with him. We always have been, haven't we? Perhaps I'm wrong, but I felt I could do no more behind your back, so I came to see you, to have it out — as they say. The truth is you cannot marry him, and I can. It will be a stormy marriage, but I am prepared for that. I am willing to risk it. I thought — Tamsin knows him far, far better than I do. In crude words, he keeps her. He uses her house. Her daughter calls him uncle. She must know a *great deal* about what goes on in his life *outside* Place House. So she will know whether these — these lies, these stories spread about him, are true or have some element of truth in them. Now you say there is no truth in them I feel happier, no longer quite so anxious, quite so concerned . . . '

Silence fell while the clock in the next room struck three. I could hear her breathing. Then a dog barked down by the river.

'D'you remember Parish?' I said. 'I never knew why Uncle Davey so disliked Parish.'

She shouted: 'And I suppose if I had said your lies about Bram were true you would have pulled your skirts away in disdain and had nothing more to do with him!'

'I'm not sure, Tammy — '

'Don't call me that!'

'I'm not sure, Tamsin. When you commit

351

yourself to the idea of marrying someone you come to accept what he does, what he is doing, what his view of life is, even if you personally dislike it.'

'I don't believe Bram will ever marry you! Why *should* he? You've been a spinster so long that you have these hot fancies! You don't know anything about it! Coming here — coming here — it makes me choke to see you. Cool and collected, just as if you were here to engage a footman and wanted my references! 'If he's respectable I'll have him.' Well, he's respectable enough for me, and he's not for sale!'

I got up. 'I came to spend the night, Tamsin. I knew this would be a difficult meeting. Perhaps it would be better if I left after supper. I cannot think we should be sweet companions this evening.'

'Go when you like,' she said. 'You'll never get a welcome again in this house.'

I shook my head. 'I didn't want it to be at all like this.'

'The remedy was in your own hands.'

'Was it? Somehow Bram has always been between us, hasn't he? There's been a sort of fatal progression. You've always wanted him, and you got him, even though it broke your marriage in the process. Now I want him, and can offer him what you cannot.'

She too stood up. Her face was paper white. 'And in this cosy domestic arrangement that you have come to — are you supposing that he will give me up?'

'I have supposed that.'

352

'He won't, you know. He won't. He can't!'

'We haven't discussed you because I felt it was up to him. I want no part in it.'

'Part in it! You're trying to ruin my life and you say you want no part in it! Well, you shan't!'

I stared at her, still trying so hard not to break into a matching anger.

'Shan't what?'

'Take him away from me.' She laughed again. 'You don't know what you're talking about. He couldn't go on without me, without the use of this house, without the help I give him.'

'Help?'

She raised her head. 'Yes, help. That was why we got rid of Slade.'

'You mean why he was kidnapped?'

'Nothing of the sort! We made it uncomfortable for him here, so he left.'

'So why particularly was it helpful to get rid of him?'

'You ought to know that! You surprised him on one of his little enterprises years ago!'

'And he threatened me then, you know. If I spoke too openly I might have been beaten. So in the end he was paid in his own medicine.'

'Yes, but not by Bram! By one of his own seedy kind.'

'Bram's seedy kind?'

'Emma, please take your bag and go to the Pardoes for the night. I shall of course tell Bram of your visit when he comes back.'

'So shall I.'

She was waiting for me to go. I wondered if

she felt as badly shaken as I did.

'I'm very sorry, Tamsin.'

She said in whisper. 'You've always hated me, always envied me. Now you're trying deliberately to destroy me. Well, you shan't! Nor shall you destroy my life with Bram. He couldn't leave me. He can't leave me. He wouldn't dare!'

8

I

Spring is so often spoiled by great winds, heavy rains, sudden cold spells under unrelenting cloud, and summer comes late and reluctant with half the blossom lost. But this year we had gentle airs, days of fitful but warming sunshine, showers that seemed to occur by accident to make the birds sing; even the trees, so late in Cornwall, began to unfurl their leaves.

Fetch, now nearing forty and expanding — in all ways — under the undemanding regime of being a lady's maid, revealed important depths of knowledge about birds, and hedgerows and wild flowers, from her early youth on a farm in Madron. She knew, to my shame, far more than I did when as a child I'd had infinite freedom to explore the woods and lanes of Roseland. Often she only had the country names, so I bought a book which helped us on what became a daily tour of inspection of garden and field and hedgerow.

Early wild daffodils, sedum (which she called orpine) scarcely yet above ground, golden saxifrage just showing yellow on the edge of a wet valley in Kea, beside it the Cornish moneywort struggling for space; on the scrubland of Carnon, with its abounding rabbits and whitethroat badgers, redwings, curlews and jackdaws, were many other small flowers and mosses to be stooped over, a little sample of each put into Sally's basket to examine and identify when we got home.

Spring flowers were of course plentiful in the garden, and I compared it to the rectory garden of a few years ago. This was more lush but scarcely more varied. The difference lay in me.

Bram turned up when Fetch and I were pulling up some rank grass in a corner to make way for the bluebells. His shadow fell across us before I knew he had come over the mossy grass.

'Bram! You startled me.'

'Is there something then that can still startle you? Good afternoon, Carry.'

'Af'noon, sur.'

'I trust you are well? Your mistress also?'

'Oh yes, thank 'ee, sur. I — er — and the mistress, I believe.'

'Thank you, Sally,' I said. 'We shall have to put off our gardening for a while.'

We watched her go towards the house, carrying her basket and trowel.

'Carry is putting on weight. Her buttocks are spreading.'

'I think she is happy.'

'Her mistress puts on no weight. It is strange to think what a fat little girl you were when I first met you.'

'Shall we go in?'

'I'm well enough here, if you are. Can the difference between you and your maid be that you are not entirely happy and not yet fulfilled?'

'I hope if I ever am I shall not broaden as a result.'

He looked me up and down. I peeled off my gardening gloves and faced him. His face was dark, determined, the derisive laughter not lurking at the back of his eyes.

'I came last week,' he said. 'You were away.'

'I was visiting the Treffrys.'

'What did you want with them, if I may ask?'

'I've known them for years.'

'You did not go on to see Jonathan Eliot?'

'No, I did not.'

He tapped his boot. 'So, having broken the news of your intention to your sister you decided to go away until the air had cleared?'

'I did not suppose the air would clear at all.'

'Nor has it. Tamsin, as I am sure you know, was greatly upset by your accusations against me.'

'I do not think that was so much the cause of her distress.'

He laughed softly. 'Is it true what you say, that Slade is still alive?'

'He survived his ordeal. He is only a mile or so away if you need proof.'

'So he is spreading these vindictive rumours about me, is he?'

'He told me them when I pressed him to speak. He's too afraid of what will happen to him if he talks openly.'

'And to whom have you passed on his lies?'

'To Tamsin — that is all.'

He swished idly at a rhododendron branch, breaking off the bud. 'Is Slade crippled?'

'He is hobbling with a stick. A doctor would perhaps have amputated his legs, but they have not seen a doctor and he seems to be slowly mending . . . And vowing vengeance . . . '

'So if pressed he will talk . . . '

'I don't think you need worry. Everyone is afraid of you.'

'Do you believe those stories of me, Emma?'

'You're spoiling that bush. Use your crop on something else.'

'Such as you?'

'Does it matter what I believe?'

'You are willing to marry me.'

'I said I was. If something can be done to appease Tamsin.'

'Even if you believed Slade's stories to be true?'

'I think I said to Tamsin that when you commit yourself to marry someone you have to accept what he does, what he is doing with his life even though you may not altogether like it.'

He came up and took my shoulders. I half withdrew and glanced around, but he tightened his grip. 'There's no one to see us. That tree screens us from the house.' He kissed me. I half turned away my face so that the still-scarred side showed.

'How can you appease Tamsin?'

'I'll think of a way.'

'That's not good enough. She accuses you of using Place House in some way.'

'So I do. I use it as my headquarters.'

'For what purpose?'

'All sorts of things. In my legitimate pursuits it's good to have a central base from which to operate.'

'And your illegitimate ones?'

He laughed against my face. 'I've broken a few laws in my life, but they are not the laws given us by God.'

'Slade said something like that to me once to justify his smuggling.'

'Did he? Well, well. Look, Emma, I have an idea.'

'You're hurting my shoulders.'

'You have good arm muscles — not prominent, but strong.' He released his grip. 'Emma, I believe that if we got to see Tamsin together and tell her we propose to marry, she will explode a bomb of hysteria upon us. But if we were to marry suddenly, unexpectedly, quietly in some little private chapel and she was presented with a *fait accompli* she would dissolve in tears and eventually make the best of it.'

'What would 'the best of it' amount to, Bram? D'you want us both on different nights?'

'Yes. But I know I could not have that. *You* would not accept that, I'm sure. But I have a great influence over Tamsin. She is not a strong character like you. She adores Place House and wants to live nowhere else. She has lived there all her life. She takes particular pride in being Mrs Spry of Place, with the rest of the family sulking in Truro and London. The chatelaine. She does not entertain a lot, but she has special

359

friends. And being who she is she has the respect of the neighbourhood.'

'People have accepted your friendship with her?'

'Many.'

'And she would lose that respect, that position, if she denounced you?'

His eyes, so close to mine, darkened. He looked a corsair. 'That was not what I was going to say, but, yes, if you put it that way, yes. She's involved with me. She depends on me. She would not throw her present way of life away just for spite, for spiteful revenge.'

'And you would continue to frequent Place, after you had married me?'

'I have to. Most of my arrangements are made there.'

'You know what the marriage service says? Forsaking all others.'

He laughed, very quietly for once. 'I want you, Emma. To get you I'm prepared to marry you. I believe you want me just as much.'

II

He said: 'Years ago I came in for a house from my aunt. It is near Ponsanooth. You have never been there? I'm always in the position of being the visitor, am I not? That shall be corrected. Come tomorrow. It's a small place but well kept. I live alone except for one manservant. Can you come tomorrow?'

'D'you mean ride over?'

'Yes. Bring Fetch if you fear to be alone with

me. The church is St Stithians, about two miles away. I will see someone in the morning and get the banns read for the first time on Sunday.'

'But — '

'If they are read at Kea everyone will know. But I spend little time at Penmartin and your name will not arouse interest there. Cornwall, as we all know, is a hotbed of gossip, but these smaller inland villages are close-knit — farming and mining, you know — and I'm told that St Stithians is very poorly attended. There is no resident vicar, but a curate comes weekly from Gwennap.'

'D'you suppose this can be done in secret?'

'Let us try. It can do no harm. If it succeeds, so much the better.'

'I had always thought of a big wedding, Bram — all in white, with four bridesmaids in ice blue and two page boys . . . '

He laughed. 'Very droll. But isn't it true to say that for the largest part of your life you did not suppose you would have a wedding at all?'

'So even my closest family is not to know?'

'Your mother remarried without informing you. Your sister we have good reasons for concealing it from. Desmond? Mary? Samuel? Do they count at all?'

'Not as much as my sister. I am dealing her an underhand blow.'

He sighed. 'All's fair in love and war, I know. A dreary aphorism. But even so I have to confess I have sometimes been in that predicament.'

'As for instance being unfaithful to your first wife?'

361

He took my hand. 'What one does in one's youth is not necessarily what one does in middle age. I am not looking for endless adventures any more, dear Emma. I am — shall be — content to have the challenge of you as my wife. Do you not believe that we shall be a challenge to each other?'

'Indeed I do.'

I went to his house the following day — with Fetch — and on the Sunday after that the banns were called for the first time. Penmartin was at the end of a lane and looked over a valley of woodland and pastures. In spite of its being close to the mining districts there was not a chimney in sight.

I did not go to the church, but from a distance it looked ready to vie in dilapidation with the St Anthony of twenty years ago, before Desmond restored it. Would there be someone in that sparse congregation who would rise up when the parson asked if anyone here present should know of just cause or impediment? . . .

But what impediment could there be? Bram was a widower, I had never married. Some woman clutching a child by the hand and swearing it was Bram's? Did that invalidate or make impossible a church ceremony?

The house, as he said, was small. It had been built by a mine captain in the last century, square and functional, and it was furnished without much taste. Had Bram any taste — except one for music? I wondered if this was where he had lived with his first wife. He did not volunteer, and I would not ask him. At least now he seemed to be using it only as a base. Place, perhaps, had now become his chief home. If I married Abraham Fox, would Samuel allow me to renew the yearly lease on Killiganoon?

One day I rode down to Feock and passed Slade's cottage. He was walking beside the wall of the garden with the aid of a stick. He raised fierce eyes to me but made no other acknowledgment. I was glad Bram was not with me. It occurred to me that if Bram did come to live at Killiganoon Slade would be uncomfortably close. Not that Bram would be likely to care.

The following week Desmond called. I was having a singing lesson but it was nearly over and Mr Hempel presently took his leave.

Desmond looked pallid and serious in his customary dark suit as I ordered tea.

He said: 'Your voice is improving all the time, Emma.' But he said it in a grave voice as if the last thought in his head was to pay me a compliment.

'Thank you. I used to think a voice was unlikely to improve much after about twenty-five, but Professor Elbruz whom I studied under for a few months in Zurich said it could get better until one was well past forty.'

'I'm sure,' Desmond agreed, and silence fell. We talked about the family while tea was served. I told him how pleased I was to see him after such a long absence. Mary had a chill, but otherwise was well. He told me that he had recently taken up painting — or resumed it after many years. He wanted chiefly to paint birds.

363

We discussed the exact colour of a male bullfinch's breast feathers, the spotted woodpecker's eggs, the battle to survive of the Cornish chough.

Then he said: 'Mary has heard a disturbing rumour this week. As you know, it is not our custom to listen to the tittle-tattle that circulates through a small town, but it so closely concerned you . . . It is that you are planning to marry Abraham Fox.'

I stirred my tea. So Bram's hopes of a secret marriage . . . And this only the second week.

'I have to admit that I have been considering it.'

'More than considering it, according to the gossip. I hear that the banns have been posted at some obscure country church near — '

'St Stithians,' I said.

He pursed his lip. 'So it is true.'

'Well, yes . . . I suppose so.'

'You suppose so. You know of course as well as anybody else that Fox is at present living openly with my wife at Place?'

'When we marry, that should change.'

'You think so? Hmm, well may be. It is a possibility. But you know what an unsavoury reputation Fox has where women are concerned.'

'Yes.'

'And not only in that respect. He casts quite a dark shadow in the county. Although he has this respectable occupation of Inspector of Customs, there are many whispered stories about his activities in other fields. He spends money like water. He lives in society, but society rather fears him. You have always been a gentle creature — if occasionally headstrong. It would be a great personal grief to me if you allied yourself to this dangerous man.'

'Dear Desmond,' I said, moved by the unusual emotion in his voice. 'You know also that I have always cared for you. On occasions when I have been — headstrong, as you call it, and I have been out of favour with my mother and Tamsin and even sometimes the rest of the family, you have always stayed my friend. It would be a personal grief to me also if I went against your will.'

'But you intend to do so in this?'

I did not answer. I poured him more tea. He waved away milk and sugar.

'If you marry this man, what shall be your plans then?'

'Bram's occupation is in Cornwall, so we shall have to stay in the county. He has a house in Ponsanooth . . . Whether we could live here if we wanted to I don't at all know. It will depend on the family — chiefly Samuel.'

His troubled eyes went around the room. 'Have you thought of the effect this — this marriage will have on Tamsin?'

'Of course. That is what I feel most about. I feel a traitor to her . . . But — he tells me — I don't know if it's true or not — that their affection for each other is wearing thin. Of course she'll be upset — is bound to be. And I'm deeply sorry . . . But might it not — not immediately but in time — might it not

365

lead to a reconciliation between you and her?'

In the stillness you could hear a regular tap-tap through the open window as a thrush beat a snail against a stone.

He said: 'I should consider it highly unlikely. Before we separated she said unforgivable things.'

'Much that is better unsaid can be said in the heat of the moment. Perhaps in two or three years . . . There is your daughter to think of.'

He rose, his second cup of tea untasted. 'I must go. It is looking like rain, and if it rains the wind will get up.'

'Can you not stay a little while longer and talk of other things? I see so little of you.'

He smiled thinly. 'In some ways I would like to. But this — this, what you are proposing is so important that everything else at the moment seems a triviality . . . You need not be told how distressed Mary will be when she hears what I have to tell.'

'I'm so sorry.'

'It is not too late to reconsider. Have you seen your lawyer?'

'Oh yes. Three times this week.'

'You have some money, I know. What would Fox bring to this? There are all sorts of aspects to be considered.'

'I have tried to consider them.'

When he had gone I thought to myself 'a gentle creature'. That was what he had called me. I did not think of the word 'gentle' as one that could be used of me nowadays.

9

I

Unlikely that Desmond would have applied that word to me if he had seen me three days later. Though thank God, he never could have.

I went over to Bram's house for a third time. It had been threatening on and off all week, but the heavy clouds, separated by spells of warm sunshine, had held off. I had ridden over alone in the late morning (Fetch, to her own chagrin, was for the moment being more and more dispensed with). Hollick was away, so Bram insisted on cooking me a light dinner himself. Fishing yesterday, he had caught a hake, and he fried this in butter with a caper sauce. We had a Rhenish wine, light but not too sweet. So one saw yet another side of his character.

I told him about Desmond's visit. He shrugged and said: 'That's too bad. If it is not secret it is not secret.'

'So Tamsin will get to know.'

'At the moment she is laid up with a light fever. Quite likely there will be no one to make a point of telling her.'

'You have been there?'

'Briefly.'

'And did not tell her?'

'No. It would have done her fever no good. But I promise you, she will come round.'

After dinner we talked more comfortably than we had ever done before. For the first time there seemed to be no conflict at all between us. It was as if we had shaken off the dust and grit of earlier associations. Simple words, stock phrases, occasional movement of the hands and eyes, were sufficient to convey new depths, new understanding.

It began to rain.

There is something strange about heavy straight drumming rain. It isolates one. Not only were we alone in the house: it was as if no one outside existed.

We sat at the dinner table, drinking the wine and staring out at the steel rods of rain. Silence had fallen between us. But now and then our eyes met over the rim of a glass.

'Little starfish,' he said.

'Something of a crab by now.'

'With claws?'

'With claws.'

After another silence he said: 'I have not shown you my bedroom, have I?'

'No.'

'It is just at the top of the stairs.'

'I should expect it to be there.'

'Hollick will not be back till eight.'

'You are very good to your servants.'

'Not only to them, little starfish. Not only to them. If given the chance.'

'Two weeks to wait.'

'Why wait? I have had you once out of wedlock. You were so sweet, so innocent. And yet . . . not so innocent. In half a night you became a woman.'

'In half a year I became a deserted woman.'

'Not from my *choice*. You were wonderful that night. I've thought of it so often. I've longed for it again.'

'Two weeks to wait.'

'Too long. Isn't the house growing dark.'

'Light a candle.'

'Not here. Upstairs.'

'Upstairs you would need to draw the curtains.'

'They're heavy curtains, velour or some such. Drawn across it would be like night.'

Water began to trickle off an over-full gutter; soon it grew into a thin stream.

'How long do you think this rain will last?'

'An hour. Just give it an hour. Give me an hour.'

'When I was in Blisland, more or less alone except for Uncle Francis, I used to think about you, dream about you, want to feel your presence near me . . . I would have given anything . . . I hated you for deserting me and yet still longed for the smallest sign. There was no sign.'

'I'm sorry. You know my reason.'

'Reasons. You were married.'

'But am no longer. Whistle and I'll come to you . . . '

'My lips are too dry.'

'Let me wet them.'

'Oh, that's too easy, Bram. It came too pat.'

He struck one of the new wax matches, and

put it to the wick of a candle. A warmer light grew in the room, making the grey dripping scene outside look colder and more hostile. It was like tears on the windows.

'Your horse is well stabled and will come to no hurt for an hour or two,' he said.

'I think the stables look in better condition than the house.'

'They are . . . Do you remember how concerned you were about your boat when you stayed at Blundstone's? I went down to see and found it well moored. You have always had that capacity of efficiency.'

'Not where my own life is concerned! That night I went sadly adrift!'

'Joyously adrift. The music, the wine, the loneliness . . . '

'Which you took advantage of.'

'I have no music now. But there's still some wine. A drop more?'

I took it, and we drank a glass together.

II

We clawed at each other in that darkened bedroom while the rain drummed still more heavily on the slates above. I can only describe it so, though it is embarrassing to admit it. He tore at my clothes until I was naked: I dug my nails into his back. If there can be such a contradiction as a willing rape, this was it. He muttered the very same endearments that he had used when he took me before — I had forgotten most of them, but they came vividly

370

back as if it was yesterday: his head against mine, against my ear, against my breast, against my parted thighs. The storm, the tempest in him was fully — and unexpectedly — reflected in this half-timid, half-brazen, almost virginal spinster that I had become. The discovery of what I was capable of was his discovery and mine together.

As the rain began to stop so our passion gradually eased. He turned over on his back and said:

'As God is my judge, you surprise me, and delight me. Ouch — you said you had claws — my back is sore!'

'I will put salve on it,' I said. 'You have bruised me too.'

'Sorry . . . no, I am not sorry. My little starfish, by God. Where have you learned all this?'

'Nowhere. No man has ever had me except you.'

'All these years? Is that really so?'

'Yes, really so.'

'How long is it, eight years? In some ways it seems longer, in others it's like returning.'

'How many women have you had in that time?'

'Forget it.'

'The rain is stopping.'

'There's plenty of time.' He leaned on his elbow and looked at me. 'This makes our marriage all the more important.'

'Why?'

'Because I want you to myself — for always.'

III

I did not return to Penmartin again, though Bram was frequently, usually briefly, at Killiganoon.

On the Sunday when the banns were called for the third time he said: 'So now we can fix a day.'

'Yes.'

'Tuesday week would suit me.'

'Very well.'

'I hope you have not gone cold on the subject.'

'Cold? You could hardly say that, could you? I am still hot — yes, hot and cold, at the memory of last week.'

He squeezed my arm. 'It proved a lot to me.'

'It proved something to me too. That when I am in your hands I am still as weak as I was in Falmouth eight years ago.'

'That is as it should be.'

'You have a terrible ability to dominate women.'

'I don't think I dominated you then. You were a willing partner.'

'I have thought a lot about it. It means, doesn't it, that you can get what you want from me without marriage.'

'What I mostly want, yes. But I want your companionship, your friendship, to be with you much, much more.'

I looked closely into his eyes. 'Do you mean that?'

'Of course!'

'You still want to marry me?'

'Yes! I have said so!'

Mousie was playing with my skirt, lying on her back, front claws in the cloth, kicking playfully with her back legs.

'Stop it!' I said. 'Behave yourself,' and disentangled the skirt.

Bram picked the kitten up by the scruff, put her on the arm of a chair and gave her one of his fingers to bite. 'She's only jealous.'

'Tuesday week,' I said. 'That's the last Tuesday in May. Have you time off?'

'I make time. After it is over, we should go away for a week. I have a friend on Exmoor. There's good riding. We can take our time on the way there and back, spend perhaps three days on the moor.'

'Who is this friend?'

'Name of Adams. I was at Blundell's with him.'

'And then we come home to face the music.'

'What music?'

'The time will not be too pleasant, I imagine.'

'Imagine nothing. Think only of our coming together in this way.'

'And where shall we live?'

'It will all work out, I promise you.'

'And how much have you worked out for the day?'

'Carvoe — the Rev. Mr Carvoe — will ride over from Gwennap shortly before ten. The ceremony will take place at eleven. That is agreed.'

I stroked Mousie, who at once turned her

373

attention to my hand instead of his.

'I think I shall believe it when it happens.'

'It will happen, never fear.'

During the week that had still to be passed I was several times on the point of going to see Tamsin again, to see if she was really ill. But I could not risk what would surely be the bitterest quarrel of all. And if she were really ill, not just in a state of nervous frustration at the turn of events . . . Instead, I called to see Mr Gascoigne again, and spent another hour with him.

I did not write to my mother. I did not write to Caroline Collins, nor to Mrs Treffry, nor to any other of my friends. I did not tell Mr Hempel that I should not be here for my lesson on the following Tuesday. If he had heard any rumours of what might be afoot he made no reference to them.

My only confidante was Sally Fetch. She listened with mounting colour to all I had to say, the arguments I put forward and then decided against, the careful soul-searching, the questions that would never be answered; but her comments were few and ultra cautious. Perhaps she was coming to have doubts about my sanity. After all it was in the family, wasn't it?

The cook, Mrs Bluett, the other two maids and Cannon, the groom, were left in ignorance.

I did not see Bram the day before. We parted on the Sunday evening. He wanted to send a carriage over for me, but I said I would prefer to ride. We would meet at his house at ten-thirty and he could drive me to the church from there.

On Monday morning Mousie disappeared. She had slid out of a kitchen window, a custom she had followed for several weeks now, and we left the window ajar for her to return. But this time she did not return. The bit of rabbit from yesterday was uneaten, the milk in the saucer unlapped.

Fetch and I went out to call her, but there was no response. It was a large property and there were endless places she could hide, if that was her mood, but she had never failed to respond to my voice before. As the morning wore on I began to be convinced that she had been taken by a dog, or possibly a fox.

We went looking for her farther afield. It was a pleasant spring day, and I wondered what tomorrow would bring. Halfway down the hill to Come-to-Good we met Slade limping up. He looked drunkenly askance at me and would have passed again without greeting, but I stopped and asked if he had seen a stray kitten. He glowered at Fetch but avoided my eyes.

'Nay,' he said. 'I seen nothing, misses. I just mind my own business.'

We turned back in time for dinner, but I did not eat much. When Sally chided me I said I was worrying about the kitten. The fact that that was even half true shows the disproportion, the imbalance.

After dinner I went out seeking her again. When I returned about four Sally said: 'You've done scarcely no packing, miss. Shall I come up and help 'ee now?'

'No. Not just yet. I'm taking very little with

me, as you know. But first I have some letters to write.'

In fact I had been drafting a letter most of last night, first in my head as I lay staring at the moulded ceiling, then seated at the escritoire with pen and ink and paper in the window of the room, by a single lighted candle.

About ten, just after supper, Cannon came in to say they had found Mousie down a disused well belonging to Farmer Eames across the road. The kitten was no worse for the escapade. I gave Cannon half a crown and went into the kitchen to inspect a very dirty sticky kitten wolfing her supper and betraying none of the obvious guilt that a dog would have done.

But thereafter, when she was filled and looked a good deal cleaner, I took her up to my bedroom with me and allowed her to sit on my knee at the escritoire while I wrote the final draft of the letter.

Dear Bram,

I am sending this letter by Cannon so that you shall receive it before you need to leave for the church. It is to say that, after much heart searching and the deepest possible reflection, I have decided not to marry you. I'm sorry. In some ways I am very sorry. In this letter I am trying to explain just what my reasons are.

In the first place you have to realize that I have known you almost all my life. It is not as the outcome of a brief courtship that I am making this choice. Since I was fifteen I have felt your charm, have known how it worked on me and have seen it at work on other women. But slowly the realization has come to me that at heart — at the final count — you love no one but yourself.

In spite of that you can make women happy, very happy. Could you make me happy? Of a certainty, at least for a time. But why do you want to *marry* me?

The kitten stirred on my knee, turned round, settled into a more comfortable position and purred gently.

Why do you want to marry me? I had insisted that we should have no physical contact before we married. That was understood and I believe that you — however reluctantly — had agreed to observe that veto. That, of course, was before last Wednesday week.

I was supposed to believe — and indeed tried to believe — that was why you were willing to go through the ceremony. You really loved me and wanted me for yourself. You really wanted to set up a home with me and have children and live an ordinary married life, as other people do — though I could clearly see that such a life with you could never be conventional. I would clearly have wished to believe all that. But did it not go against all my knowledge of you over so many years?

So came the Wednesday. Perhaps it would be better, because of all I have to say, if

I could claim that what happened on the Wednesday was a heartless contrivance on my part. If I said that you would not believe me and you would be right. I know that day I was truly in love with you. But when our lovemaking began, while it was happening and afterwards — especially afterwards — ignoble thoughts and doubts kept echoing through my mind. I have become hard, Bram, and therefore much more difficult to deceive by your passion — or even by my own.

What I wondered would happen now — now that your desire for me and my desire for you had been temporarily sated? Was it not much more in your nature to try to slip out of or postpone the marriage? Now that I had given way to you once, it was likely to happen again and again, and continue without marriage.

So why marriage? Marriage to me would constrain you — not much but a little — you would not be so free for other women. And you must know me well enough to know I would not be an easy woman to betray.

But what did you do? You asked me soon after for an assurance that the marriage should still take place. So aren't you, possibly might you not really be proposing to marry me for my money?

You may feel that I am putting you in a situation in which anything you do, whichever way you act, it can be interpreted to your discredit. If you gradually tried to withdraw from the wedding, it would show you up as a calculating seducer. If you press me to go ahead with the wedding, you are chiefly calculating the financial gain.

But as the background to this — perhaps in defence of myself — since I saw how your intentions were moving, I began to make enquiries about you in Truro and elsewhere. My lawyer, Mr Gascoigne, tells me that you are heavily in debt. A great deal of money comes to you, he says, from time to time, but with this he says you only discharge some debts and incur others. He also tells me that with your many connections you would have no difficulty at all in discovering the amount of money left to me by Uncle Francis. So I suspect, forgive me but I suspect, that that money is what you want most from the marriage. Is it not so? You clearly desire me well enough for myself, but not so much as you desire my fortune.

Another suspicion, even more ignoble than the first, comes from the feeling that Tamsin has been so quiet. Having been a party to your plans for so long she must surely know that you are in desperate straits and, *very much* against her will, she has come to agree with you that a marriage to me — of convenience — will solve *her* problem — of staying on at Place — as well as yours?

The ink was watery. I wished I had had the inkwell refilled before beginning the long letter.

This will be ill reading for you, Bram, as it is very ill writing for me, but I have to tell you that I believe most of Slade's stories. When I went to see Tamsin and told her we were to be married, her manner and incautious remarks convinced me that she knew Slade's accusations to be more or less true. Last month on a visit to the Treffrys of Fowey, the subject came up and Mr Joseph Treffry, who was High Sheriff last year, told me he had recently met Sir Anthony Pryce, who is Collector of Customs for Devon and Cornwall. Sir Anthony told him of a number of cases that had been brought to his notice, of intimidation and violence connected with the running of contraband goods. This was within the last year, and there was a lot of disquiet about it. Several persons were under suspicion, and attempts were being made to track their activities more closely and to muster reliable witnesses who would be prepared to give evidence at a trial. Although no names were ever mentioned, some of the references did point to you. I said nothing whatever about Slade, or about you at all, but it seems clear to me that you are in some danger of being accused of more serious crimes than owing money and you would do well to leave the county while you can. With my money to buy off your creditors the situation might have been different.

Sometimes I feel as if I am letting you down. You need me — but for the wrong reason. Once, eight years ago, I so very badly needed you.

Emma

10

I

A long restless night. Only the kitten slept. At
eight I sent for Cannon, and gave him the
sealed envelope, telling him to deliver it to Mr
Abraham Fox at Penmartin House, Ponsanooth.
He should be there well before ten. He was to
deliver it into Mr Fox's hand, and no other. He
was not to wait for a reply but to come straight
back. Fetch stood squarely in the doorway and
watched him go.

'Well, miss . . . '

'Yes, Fetch?'

'That means? . . . Does that mean? . . . '

'Yes, it does.'

'Glory be to God!' she said.

'I do not believe Glory exists anywhere in
this,' I said sourly. 'Or God either.'

Later in the morning I took Fetch upstairs
with one of the maids to clear out the attic
which had been undisturbed since we took
up residence. The house had been greatly
extended by Uncle Davey when he bought it
for Betsy Slocombe, so presumably she alone
must have been the hoarder. I had never met
her. After leaving the house she had gone back
to Manaccan where she was born. Three faded
heliographs showed a tall bosomy dark-haired
woman with pink cheeks, smiling eyes and

dimples. On the back of one was written in even more faded ink, 'Dearest Betsy, from Davey, Xmas 1820'.

There was only this one attic; and from its dormer window one had the best view of the outer gate and the drive running up to the house. A bright day with a few clouds riding high. A group of reddish cows in the distant field were lying down. Fine weather. Good weather for a wedding. I did not look at my watch but turned back from the window where I had been studying the heliographs. This tedious sorting out of an old attic was intended to provide a diversion, scant enough, but a sort of different focus for the attention when so very much greater a matter was at stake.

The room was full of cardboard boxes, with three chests, a bureau with a broken leg, a commode, a clutter of pots and pans, a naval uniform, two bottles with ships inside, a set of croquet balls and mallets, a target for archery, some fishing tackle. The two women were standing waiting for instructions.

'Well, start somewhere,' I said, and went across to the rickety bureau, fought to get a drawer open and found inside a mass of papers, crammed down, and overflowing. At the top they were all bills, but underneath were piles of letters, tied in bundles with pink ribbon. I opened one and saw it was a letter from Uncle Davey beginning, 'Dearest Betsy, I hope to be with you at Easter. Pray do not worry about the baby, I will look after you.' I re-folded it, feeling it was prying. So Betsy had had a child. What had happened to it? Died, or given to a foster mother? Or raised by Betsy's parents?

Fetch was opening one of the chests. Three naval hats, but midshipman style, two women's bonnets, a short female jacket with fur collar and cuffs, these badly eaten by moths. Dust rose in the room and the maid, Ethel, sneezed. The difficulty lay in deciding how much of all this stuff to throw away. I lacked the initiative today to come to any decision; yet I would not possibly relax downstairs practising singing or working a sampler.

About noon there was a tap on the door, and Cannon stood there.

'I give the letter, ma'am. The servant wanted for to take it but I would not leave it out of my hands.'

'You saw Mr Fox?'

'Yes, ma'am.'

'Did he open the letter when you were there?'

'Yes, ma'am, but he only read the first few lines, then he sort of crumpled it up and looked at me and said, 'Thank you, that will be all.' '

I said: 'I would like you to be around the house for the rest of the day, Cannon. I am not at home to anyone. If — if someone comes who insists on seeing me, tell them I have left for London.'

'Very good, ma'am.'

'Oh, but Mr Hempel will be coming at three! I had forgot. Will you please offer him my sincere apologies and say I am unwell today but shall hope to see him next week.'

383

'Yes, ma'am.'

After dinner, which proceeded without interruption, I took the girls upstairs again. There was so much damp in the attic — inevitable it seemed in Cornwall even in an otherwise dry house. Every metal surface was rusty, whether it was scissors, curling tongs, leather punches or hairpins. We found baby clothes, a child's potty with stains in the bottom.

'Look 'ere, miss,' Fetch said.

They had opened a larger box in a corner by the chimney breast, and she had taken out a child's tartan suit in green and red. The trousers suggested it had been made for a boy of five or six. There was a strong smell of mothballs, and although the suit was well worn it had been carefully packed in pink tissue paper. So . . .

'And then there's this, ma'am,' said Ethel, holding up a child's frock. It had a small white nankeen jacket over a white lace bodice and a short velveteen skirt. Also well worn but neatly packed.

So had there been two children, and if so had they died or merely grown too big to wear these clothes? There was no reason to suspect the worst. Someday in the future I would ride over and make the acquaintance of Miss Betsy Slocombe. I thought I would like her.

That was, if I had a future.

The women were getting tired by now, and I had no real excuse to keep them up there any longer. They were at present poring over some children's sketching books which had come out of the bottom drawer of the bureau. Nothing had yet been thrown away, but things had been dropped to one side of a rough demarcation line implying what ought to go and what might be kept.

'All right,' I said. 'That will do for today. We'll finish off tomorrow.'

They clattered down the uncarpeted stairs behind me and then moved silently on the furnished landing.

I went into the kitchen. Cannon got quickly to his feet. Mousie, who had been excluded from the attic, rose mewing and stretching towards me. I said to Mrs Bluett: 'I'll have supper in the back room tonight. Cannon.'

'Ma'am?'

'I want to give the appearance of having gone away. Will you close the shutters in the front rooms and draw the curtains in the bedrooms. That means that when darkness falls lamps need not be lit.'

'Very good, ma'am.'

'No one has been, I presume?'

'Well one man, yes ma'am, about 'alf an hour gone. What name was it? Street?'

'I saw no one.'

'He come to the back door, which was where he looked as if he belonged.'

'Slade,' said Mrs Bluett. '*Mister* Slade, he called his self.'

'What did he want?'

' 'E asked for you, ma'am. Then he asked if Mr Abraham Fox was 'ere. I said no to both.'

'Did that satisfy him?'

385

'I dunno, ma'am. I think 'e was half drunk. He just went off down the path limping and grumbling. I didn't know you knew 'im, ma'am. Did I do right?'

'Yes, of course.' I went out.

It was hours to darkness yet. Nothing had happened. Why should I feel in my bones that something might yet happen? Bram, if he had any sense, particularly a sense of self-preservation, would surely by now be packing his things and preparing to leave the county. Or had I misjudged him? Surely not. Could he brazen it out? He came of an influential family.

Was he a man ever to run? I did not know. Was he wise enough to know when he was beaten?

I had lentil soup for supper, with a cold capon and damson tart to follow. The food seemed to stick in my mouth and refuse to be swallowed; but I dallied over it, for there was nothing more to do with the day. I felt safer with Cannon's presence in the house. He usually slept over the stables but I must tell him to stay in the house tonight.

Fetch. 'If you please, miss, Mrs Bluett says she has a bad headache and can she be excused?'

'Of course. And tell Ethel she can clear these things.'

'You 'aven't ate much,' said Fetch, peering.

'It's enough.'

Mrs Bluett was someone who ought to have been discharged. She had these headaches at regular intervals and it was rumoured they

386

were caused by drinking. No doubt my porter or my brandy. She wasn't even a very good cook. Under Uncle Francis's promptings I had become very much better than that. But I had lacked the impulse or severity which was needed to make a change. She was the only one who had 'come with the house' and there had always seemed more important decisions to make.

I had not slept for thirty-six hours, and as the tension relaxed my eyes ached and wanted to close. Yet I knew if I once shut them the wires would tauten again, and a rush of thought and nervous emotion would break in and make sleep impossible. I would have given a lot for some of that laudanum syrup which had been so helpful in Berlin.

At eight I told Cannon that I would like him to spend the night in the house. There was a small bedroom overlooking the front door and I asked him to use that. By now the sun was setting. There had been cloud later in the day but this had broken again and shafts of sunlight lanced through the trees. In twenty minutes or so it would be gone and the long twilight would begin. There was no moon tonight, so after about nine-thirty it would be dark.

I went into the back sitting room and began to read. In spite of all Uncle Francis's efforts I have never felt deeply stirred by religion, but tonight I picked up the bible he gave me for my twentieth birthday and turned the pages. Now if ever I needed strength and comfort.

'Oh, my dove, thou art in the clefts of the rock, in the secret places of the stairs, let me see thy countenance, let me hear thy voice, for sweet is thy voice and thy countenance is comely.

'Take us the foxes, the little foxes, that spoil the vines, for our vines have tender grapes.

'By night on my bed I sought him whom my soul loveth; I sought him but I found him not . . .

'I am come into my garden, my sister, my spouse . . . I sleep but my heart waketh: it is the voice of my beloved that knocketh, saying, Open to me, my sister, my love . . . I opened to my beloved and my hands dropped with myrrh . . . My beloved had withdrawn himself and was gone: my soul failed when he spake; I sought him but I could not find him; I called him but he gave me no answer . . . '

A loud banging. I woke with a start. So I had dozed after all. For how long? I got up and parted the curtains and saw it was nearly dusk. Was that banging in my head?

Or was it Fetch at the door?

'Beg pardon, miss, but it's Mr Fox.'

My heart lurched. '*What? Where?*'

'At the front door. Cannon told him you was away, but though he shut the door in his face he came back like this, bangin' and bangin'.'

I had swallowed the remnants of a bad dream and wakened to a worse one. The house was silent now.

I picked up the bible and put it on a side table. 'He will go away.'

As if directly to contradict this the banging on the door began again. And shouting.

I went into the hall. Cannon was standing

by the front door. He was about to speak but I put a finger to my lips. Ethel and one of the other maids were by the green baize door to the kitchen.

I stole to the front door. Something splintered. It was not the door but something he was using on it outside.

'Emma!' he shouted. 'Emma! I know you're there, damn you! Let me in!'

'There's a weak shutter in the dining room,' Cannon whispered. 'I 'ope he don't know of that!'

'Emma!' came his voice. 'I know you're in there! I'll get you out sooner or later, so you might as well come *now*!'

I looked at Cannon. He was of sturdy build, but his face had lost its usual colour. If the thought had ever entered my head that I might some day need a bodyguard I would have chosen someone taller and younger.

Everybody waited, listening to a scraping outside.

'Whatever's to do?' came a complaining voice from the kitchen. Mrs Bluett appeared, night-railed, wrapped in a shawl. 'Oh, beg pardon, ma'am, I didn't see you was 'ere. What's to do?'

'Be quiet!' I said in a low voice.

She turned to Ethel and muttered something about being waked from her first sleep and her head was something chronic. Her looks confirmed the suspicion that she was on a drinking bout.

The voice outside suggested that someone else

had been on a drinking bout. Bram drank above average always, but I had never seen him drunk. Was this the first time? Nor had I ever seen his temper at its worst. He had reason to be angry after receiving the letter. His life was in ruins.

Now the banging began again. It sounded much heavier as if this time instead of wood he had found a rock or a piece of stone. Mrs Bluett put her hands to her ears and retreated unsteadily into the kitchen.

Fetch said in my ear, 'Farmer Eames will hear this! Surely he'll come over to see what is amiss.'

'Bring a lamp,' I said. 'It must be nearly dark outside.'

The door was shaking and rattling with the assault on it. It was of good oak, but would not withstand this for ever.

Then it all suddenly ceased. Fetch brought a light from the kitchen. I wondered if, as Cannon feared, the wild man outside would transfer his assault to one of the shuttered windows.

Then a quiet voice said, 'Emma.'

He must have been speaking through the keyhole, for it sounded so terribly close, so intimate.

'I know you're there because your little kitten has come out to greet me. He's not afraid of me, are you, Mousie? Kiddy, kiddy, kiddy, what a fine little kiddy.'

I looked wildly around. Glances flew between us. No one spoke. Then Ethel whispered: 'She went out about 'alf an hour gone.'

I choked and said nothing.

Then Bram went on: 'I know you're there now, Emma, because you can't bear to part with your little baby, and if you had gone away you would have taken her with you.'

I gripped the back of a chair for support.

He said: 'I don't want to make any more disturbance for I might frighten little Mousie, and that would be too bad, wouldn't it, kiddy?'

Of the three other people in the hall, none would meet my eyes.

Then he said: 'Come out and walk in the garden. We can talk like ordinary human beings. You've made so many false assumptions in your letter that it would be only fair to hear what I have to say in my own defence.'

I hesitated. 'Don't go, miss,' whispered Fetch, her hands to her mouth. 'Don't trust 'im.'

Sickness was coming and going in waves. I sat in the chair and did not speak. Minutes passed in silence.

Then he said: 'You're so contrary, Emma, I could wring your neck. D'you know that? All I'm asking is for a walk in the garden. *Your* garden. Just let us talk it over. Just let us talk it out.'

I held onto the arm of the chair, opened my mouth to reply, then said nothing. A clock was striking nine.

'Or,' he said, 'if I have to do it I'll wring your little kitten's blasted neck instead. Would you like that? If I have to go away I shall leave little Mousie hanging upside down on your door handle. I've got her in my hands now. She's as friendly as you please. Just as friendly as I want you to be.'

391

'He wouldn't *dare!*' said Fetch. 'Not even 'e wouldn't dare!'

'You'll hear the squawk,' he said.

I got up, went to the door. 'Open it,' I said to Cannon and when he hesitated screamed at him:

'*Open it!*'

He began to pull the bolts back. They creaked and grunted.

'Let me come with 'ee,' hissed Fetch.

'No.'

The door swung open. Outside it was nearly dark. The light from the hall showed him standing there holding the kitten. His coat was off and his cravat was loose. He laughed at the sight of me, all the old devil in his eyes, hair falling loosely across his forehead.

'So there you are, my little Emma, eh? Coming for a little walk? Come along then.' He released Mousie, who landed sure-footedly and fled into the house. 'Think I would have hurt your damned cat? Never! I know you could never love me if I did.' He laughed again as at a great joke.

'Bram,' I said, trembling all over, 'I think you had better come in. I don't want to walk anywhere with you.'

'Anything you say, dear heart . . . ' He stopped and turned at the sound of footsteps on the gravel. He stopped laughing and his eyes changed.

There was a tremendous explosion beside my ear, and a great black stain suddenly showed on Bram's shirt. In seconds the black turned to red and he was lying half in and half out of the porch, his eyes open, blinking, gasping, wandering.

I was on my knees beside him. He put up a hand but it fell back.

'Slade,' he said, and choked on blood. 'It was Slade.'

Cannon and Fetch had gone into the garden, staring after a retreating figure.

'Bram,' I said. 'We must — must get a doctor.'

'It was all a trap — wasn't it,' he said. 'You invited him here — knew I would come — '

'Oh, my God!' I screamed. 'That is not true! Do you think I could wish this? A trap! The only one I was trying to escape from was the one you set for me!'

Cannon back. ' 'E's gone. Can't see nothing of 'im. There's a musket lying in the shrubbery. He must 'f thrown it as 'e ran!'

'Help me!' I cried. 'Help me, Fetch, I must get Mr Fox indoors out of the chill. Cannon, run for Dr Harris.'

We dragged him into the hall. I clawed at a cushion to put under his head, flew into the kitchen for a towel to stem the blood.

'Water!' I said to Ethel. 'Get hot water and a basin.'

Back with him, he looked up at me quizzically. 'Can't breathe.' He coughed, and a blister of blood showed on his lips.

With a knife I cut at his shirt, pulled it back. Red hole, oozing, torn at edges; press the linen towel against it. His eyes glazed over again.

Fetch came with a blanket. 'Cannon has taken the 'orse, miss. 'Tis quicker.'

Dr Harris three miles away. Ethel back with water. God knows I had little experience of wounds, scarcely knew what to do for the best. The other maid shut the front door. 'More light!' I snapped — she carried the single lamp nearer and lit two candles.

Bram muttered something as I pressed gently at the wound.

'What?'

'It was not — a trap?'

'God no, Bram, not a trap, I swear! How you could think it.'

He raised his head an inch or two. 'Oh well, . . . There it is.' He coughed to clear the blood from his throat. 'You know, Emma . . . ' He tailed off.

'Yes?'

'You're the only one I ever really . . . ' He did not finish the sentence. His head fell forward on his chest and life left him.

11

Oliver Slade was tried at Bodmin Assizes in October 1840 for the murder of Abraham Fox.

I did not have to give evidence at the trial, but Mr Gascoigne went. He said it lasted a bare fifteen minutes. Slade confessed to the killing and offered no defence. He refused legal help or advice. With no case to argue the jury brought in a verdict of guilty and the judge put on the black silk cap.

'I found it difficult to believe it was all over,' Mr Gascoigne said. 'The judge's homily was of the briefest, and the condemned man was led away. He had no expression on his face — seemed almost to be unconscious of what was happening. Before I left the court they were preparing for the next case.'

Slade was hanged on 30 November.

In the previous August I had had a miscarriage. No one knew except Dr Harris, Sally Fetch and Ethel. I had done nothing to rid myself of his child. If it had been born I should have brought it up as my own at Killiganoon. Betsy Slocombe had borne and brought up one or more — probably two — illegitimate children here, so why should not I?

A month after Bram's death Tamsin left Place House with Celestine and went to live with her

395

mother — our mother — in Richmond. She left a pile of debts which I discreetly discharged during the following months.

She never wrote to me again, but I heard from my mother that she held me responsible for Bram's death and the collapse of her life at Place House. Perhaps, if you looked at it from her point of view, I was.

Desmond and Mary did not go back to Place, preferring to remain at Tregolls. As the years passed they became it seemed almost as much husband and wife as brother and sister. They were very much alike and grew more alike: decent, kindly, narrow, good-living people, withdrawn, a little ingrown, and completely different from their vigorous, thrusting elder brother and sister. I sometimes thought the shadow of their mother's mental derangement weighed too heavily on them. They watched each other for tell-tale symptoms.

Samuel came to inhabit Place at intervals and Anna Maria and Edward would drive over with their ever-increasing brood in the summer, but for quite long periods Place was empty except for a quartet of servants. Samuel became MP for Bodmin and was knighted shortly afterwards. He was High Sheriff for Cornwall in 1849. He remained unmarried throughout his active life but like his father kept a mistress — called Harriet Hill — but not at Killiganoon and much more discreetly. The year before he died he married her and so legitimized his eleven-year-old son, much to the scandal of the county.

I remember going to his funeral at Place, with my husband and our two sons, who happened to be on leave at the time. I recalled Uncle Davey's funeral almost exactly forty years before and the many members of the Cornish aristocracy and gentry who attended in their black coaches. This time, united in disapproval, most of the gentry sent their coaches empty, and these filled the wide drive before the house in a most melancholy way. It was a wake within a wake.

The moral change in the country since the young Queen and her Consort had come to the throne had been steady and here was dramatically pointed. However the young John Samuel — now Spry — was bright-eyed if tearful, and seemed likely to survive the disapproval. So did Harriet, my new cousin.

II

But I am anticipating.

Killiganoon passed out of the ownership of the Spry family shortly after I left. It was sold to a Mr Thomas Simmons.

In 1841, almost thirty years ago now, I replied to a letter recently received from the Hon Jonathan Eliot. I have it before me.

Dear Jonathan,

Thank you for your long and very kind letter of the seventh. I do greatly appreciate it, and have given much thought and sentimental feeling to your proposal of marriage.

I want to be completely honest with you, for as yet we know each other so little. I am twenty-eight, and for the first twenty-six years of my life I suffered a severe disfigurement. Now it has been partly put right but I sometimes wonder whether I still carry the scars of that injury in my character, in my nature. (Someone once told me that I do.) The feeling of being set apart from others, the feeling of being unwanted, of being an outcast, is still strong at times.

In my life I have been much in thrall to two men, one who softened me by his saintliness, the other who was the opposite of a saint. They are both dead.

I believe I do want companionship and a settled life. I believe I do want the settled life that marriage brings — should bring. But I do not know if I truly love you. You have told me that you love me, and I do believe you, and that feeling is already a warmth in my heart. But marriage is for life. Shall we in a long life find the best in each other or discover the worst?

You cannot answer me, except at another meeting. That perhaps will come soon. But even then there is the risk. Perhaps you will be able to convince me, Jonathan, that the risk is worth taking. Even as I sit here writing this I am *greedy* for a normal life. Can you help me to find it? If so I will marry you.

Your affectionate friend
Emma

I remember after finishing it I spilled the young cat from my lap as I sanded the ink and reread what I had written. Then I sat for a long time head in hands, struggling with my thoughts and emotions — half tearful. There was so much more to say, and yet nothing more to say.

Then I took out another sheet of paper and put the date on it. 15 March 1841. In some ways it was an even more difficult letter to write. I began it.

'Dearest Charles . . .

Other titles in the Charnwood Library Series:

LEGACIES
Janet Dailey

The sequel to THE PROUD AND THE FREE. It is twenty years since the feud within his family began, but Lije Stuart, son of the Cherokee chief The Blade, had never forgotten the killing of his grandfather. Now, a promising legal career beckons, and also the love of his childhood sweetheart, Diane Parmalee, the daughter of a US Army officer. Yet as it reawakens, their love is beset by the beginning of civil war.

'L' IS FOR LAWLESS
Sue Grafton

World War II fighter pilot Johnny Lee had died and his grandson was trying to claim military funeral benefits, but none of the authorities have any record of Fighter J. Lee. Was the old man once a US spy? When PI Kinsey Millhone is asked to straighten things out, she finds herself pursued by a psychopath bearing a forty-year-old grudge . . .

BLOOD LINES
Ruth Rendell

This is a collection of long and short stories by Ruth Rendell that will linger in the mind.

THE SUN IN GLORY
Harriet Hudson

When industrialist William Potts sets himself to build a flying machine, his adopted daughter, Rosie, works through the years as his mechanic. In 1906 Pegasus is almost ready, and onto the scene comes Jake Smith, a man who has as deep a love of the air as Rosie herself. But Jake sparks off a deadly rivalry, and the triumph of flight twists into tragedy.

A WOMAN SCORNED
M. R. O'Donnell

Five years after the tragedy that ruined her fifteenth birthday, Judith Carty returns to Castle Moore and resumes her flirtation with its heir, Rick Bellingham. The tragic events of the past forge a special bond between the young couple, but there are those who have a vested interest in the failure of the romance.

PLAINER STILL
Catherine Cookson

Following the success of her previous collection of essays and poems, LET ME MAKE MYSELF PLAIN, Catherine Cookson has compiled a further selection of thoughts, recollections, and observations on life — and death — together with another collection of the poems she prefers to describe as 'prose on short lines'.

THE LOST WORLD
Michael Crichton

The successor to JURASSIC PARK.

It is now six years since the secret disaster of Jurassic Park, when that extraordinary dream of science and imagination came to a crashing end — the dinosaurs destroyed, and the park dismantled. There are rumours that something has survived . . .

MORNING, NOON & NIGHT
Sidney Sheldon

When Harry Stanford, one of the wealthiest men in the world, mysteriously drowns, it sets off a chain of events that reverberates around the globe. At the family gathering following the funeral, a beautiful young woman appears, claiming to be Harry's daughter. Is she genuine, or is she an impostor?

FACING THE MUSIC
Jayne Torvill and Christopher Dean

The world's most successful and popular skating couple tell their own story, from their working-class childhoods in Nottingham to world stardom. Finally, they describe how they created their own show, FACE THE MUSIC, with a superb corps of international ice dancers.

ORANGES AND LEMONS
Jeanne Whitmee

When Shirley Rayner is evacuated from London's East End, she finds herself billeted with the theatre's most romantic couple, Tony and Leonie Darrent. She becomes firm friends with their daughter, Imogen, and the two girls dream of making their names on the stage. But they have forgotten the very different backgrounds from which they come.

HALF HIDDEN
Emma Blair

Holly Morgan, a nurse in a hospital on Nazi-occupied Jersey, falls in love with a young German doctor, Peter Schmidt, and is racked by guilt. Can their love survive the future together or will the war destroy all their hopes and dreams?

THE GREAT TRAIN ROBBERY
Michael Crichton

In Victorian London, where lavish wealth and appalling poverty exist side by side, one man navigates both worlds with ease. Rich, handsome and ingenious, Edward Pierce preys on the most prominent of the well-to-do as he cunningly orchestrates the crime of his century.

THIS CHILD IS MINE
Henry Denker

Lori Adams, a young, unmarried actress, gives up her baby boy for adoption with great reluctance. She feels that she and the baby's father, Brett, are not in a position to provide their child with all he deserves. But when, two years later, life has improved dramatically for Lori and Brett, they want their child returned . . .

THE LOST DAUGHTERS
Jeanne Whitmee

At school, Cathy and Rosalind have one thing in common: each is the child of a single parent. For them both, the transition to adulthood is far from easy — until their unexpected reunion. Working together, the two friends take a bold step that will help them to become independent women.

THE DEVIL YOU KNOW
Josephine Cox

When Sonny Fareham overhears a private conversation between her lover and his wife, she realises she is in great danger. Shocked and afraid, she flees to the north of England to make a new life — but never far away is the one person who wants to destroy everything that she now holds dear.

A LETHAL INVOLVEMENT
Clive Egleton

When Captain Simon Oakham of the Royal Army pay Corps goes A.W.O.L. immediately after a suspicious interview with the security service, Peter Ashton is asked to track him down. The key to it all is an embittered woman whose unsuspecting knowledge of a lethal involvement makes her especially vulnerable.

THE WAY WE WERE
Marie Joseph

This is a collection of some of Marie Joseph's most outstanding short stories, and is the companion volume to WHEN LOVE WAS LIKE THAT. With compassion, insight and humour, these stories explore the themes of love — its hopes, joys, disappointments and reconciliations.

EXTREME DENIAL
David Morrell

When CIA agent Stephen Decker is sent on a sensitive mission to Italy, his partner is Brian McKittrick, the incompetent and embittered son of the former chairman of the National Security Council. Disobeying orders throughout the mission, McKittrick makes one final mistake: sleeping with the enemy.

THE WOOD BEYOND
Reginald Hill
Seeing the wood for the trees is a problem shared by Andy Dalziel and Edgar Wield, the latter in his investigations into bones found at a pharmaceutical research centre, and the former in his dangerous involvement with animal rights activist Amanda Marvell.

RAGE OF THE INNOCENT
Frederick E. Smith
The first of a trilogy.
Young Harry Miles clashes with Michael Chadwick, son of a wealthy landowner, and sows the seeds of a lifetime's conflict. When the 1914 – 18 war breaks out, Harry is driven into volunteering and finds himself under Chadwick's command. Taking his revenge, Chadwick makes Harry a machine gunner . . .

MOTHER OF GOD
David Ambrose
Tessa Lambert has just created the first viable artificial intelligence programme — a discovery so controversial that she must keep it a secret even from her colleagues at Oxford University. But soon there is to be a hacker stalking her on the Internet: a serial killer who is about to give her invention its own terrifying and completely malevolent life . . .